The Spirit Power

~ Volume I ~

Grace Dola Balogun

"The fruit of the Spirit is

LOVE

JOY

PEACE

LONGSUFFERING

GENTLENESS

GOODNESS

FAITH

MEEKNESS

TEMPERANCE

Against such there is no law."

Galatians 5:22-23

The Spirit Power

~Volume I~

Grace Dola Balogun

Grace Religious Books
New York, NY

The Spirit Power — Volume I
By Grace Dola Balogun
Copyright © 2012 Grace Dola Balogun
Cover design by Lionsgate Book Design, Lisa Hainline
www.lionsgatebookdesign.com
Interior Design by White Cottage Publishing Company
www.whitecottagepublishing.com

Scripture quotations are from the King James Version of the Holy Bible.

Grace Religious Books Publishing & Distributors books may be ordered through booksellers or by contacting the publisher:

Grace Religious Books Publishing & Distributors, Inc.
213 Bennett Avenue
New York, NY 10040
www.Gracereligiousbookspublishers.com

To contact the author: 1-646-559-2533
info@gracereligiousbookspublishers.com

ISBN: 978-0-9851960-7-8 (epub)
ISBN: 978-0-9851960-8-5 (pdf)
ISBN: 978-0-9851960-6-1 (sc)

Library of Congress Control Number: 2012933498

Printed in the United States of America

I dedicate this book to the glory of my Lord and Savior Jesus Christ who emptied Himself, came to this earth to save me, a sinner, and blessed me with the salvation of eternal life in Him. May He receive glory, honor, blessings, and power from this book. May He let this book fill the hearts of everyone who reads it with the Spirit Power, now and forever. May Christ indwell, baptize, and fill the hearts of all who read this book with His Spirit. "But ye are not in the flesh, but in the Spirit, if so be that the Spirit of God dwell in you. Now if any man has not the Spirit of Christ, he is none of his." Rom 8:9. This book is from Him to make the power of the Holy Spirit manifest in the lives of all the children of God called by His name: Christians.

Contents

Preface

This Book, *The Spirit Power*, will let you know the power of the Spirit of God as you have never known it before: From the beginning of creation. It will clear away any confusion about the mighty power of the Holy Spirit, the saving Power of the Holy Spirit, and the Power of the fruit of the Holy Spirit that changes the believer's life.

This book will let you know that you need to be filled with the Holy Spirit; you need to be baptized with the Holy Spirit. This book will let you know the power of the indwelling of the Holy Spirit in the lives of believers immediately after conversion.

There is a difference between the indwelling of the Holy Spirit and the baptism of the Holy Spirit. The activities of the Holy Spirit on earth began on the day of the creation of the universe and have continued until the present.

The Holy Spirit is a living being, one of the three members of Godhead. He was active in creation and in sustaining the universe. He conceived Jesus in Mary's womb. He revealed God's will to men and gave the message of salvation. The Spirit also empowered the believers to perform miracles in order to confirm that their message was from God.

The Spirit dwells in the people of God today from the moment of conversion. When they are baptized by immersion, they claim open identification with Christ. If the Spirit of God does not indwell us, we are not a child of God. The Spirit will continue His work until the end of the world.

The Spirit's presence is the fullness of God's presence on earth in the lives of His people, the children of God. The Apostles received Holy Spirit baptism and they were speaking in different languages. It is the same today when we receive the baptism of the Holy spirit and we speaks in tongues and pray with supernatural power.

This book will renew, energize, and awaken your spirit to accept the Spirit's power that will help you to live a holy, healthy, and godly life as a child of God. You will be able to do impossible things that you cannot imagine through the power of the Holy Spirit's supernatural power.

This Book will help you to know that God continues to pour out His Spirit, just as on the day of Pentecost, to those who abide and believe in His Son Jesus Christ our Savior Lord, with obedience to the Word of God in order to receive the gift of eternal life through the power of the Holy Spirit.

The Spirit Power is a book that will help you to begin a new life in Christ. Salvation is the gift of Grace with abundant life that the Spirit Power offers. May our Lord and Savior continue to pour out His Spirit on all those who believe in Him.

Prayer: May He let this book bring unbelievers to Christ's feet on the throne of grace. All other religions of the earth will know and worship the true God, the King of kings, the Lord of lords and the God of gods. May every soul of human beings worship, praise, and glorify Him where He sits at the right hand of God the Father.

The Spirit Power is an inspirational book and the right book for you. It will lift up your spirit to be in tune with the Spirit of the Almighty God—Father, Son, and Holy Spirit forever one God.

Amen, amen, and amen.

1

The Spirit Power from the Beginning of Creation

The Holy Spirit is the third person of the Trinity. Old Testament believers, such as Moses and all the prophets were saved and sanctified by the Spirit, but not in the same way as New Testament believers the Apostles, people in the early Christianity and up until today because New Testament believers were indwelled with the Holy Spirit.

The Spirit came and went from Old Testament believers like the prophets. He spoke to them and sent them to deliver messages. Old Testament prophets got close to God so that the Spirit of God could use them according to His Will. The signs and symbols of the Holy Spirit in the Old Testament were wind, fire, water, breath, and light.

The role of the Holy Spirit in creation was that God spoke, and the earth was created. The Father spoke, and the earth was created; the Son is the powerful Word through which God created all things. The word became flesh and dwells among us we behold its glory, the glory of the one and only begotten Son of the Father full of Grace and Truth.

"In the beginning was the word, and the word was with God, and the word was God." John 1:1. The scripture plainly tells us why, John calls Christ the Word; the Word is in two folds: Word conceived, and Word uttered. The conceived Word is the thought, which is the first product and conception of the Soul.

Therefore, the second person of the trinity is call the Word; for he is the first begotten of the Father. There is nothing we are surer of then than what we think, nothing we are surer in the dark about than how we think.

So that the generation and births of our eternal mind may well be allowed to be in great mysteries of godliness, the bottom of which we cannot fathom, or comprehend. There is the Word uttered, and this is speech, the chief and most natural indication of the mind.

Christ is the Word, for by him God has in these last days spoken to us. Christ has made known God's mind to us, as a man's word or speech makes known his thoughts. Christ was revealed as the eternal Word of

God. "All things were made by him; and without him was not anything made that was made." John 1:3.

"For by him were all things created, that are in heaven, and that in earth, visible and invisible, whether they be throne, or dominions, or principalities, or powers: all things were created by him, and for him." Col. 1:16.

"God, who at sundry times and in divers manners spake in time past unto the fathers by the prophets, Hath in these last days spoken unto us by His Son, whom he hath appointed heir of all things, by whom also he made the worlds." Heb. 1:1–2.

The Holy Spirit was present and active in the creation of the universe. The Bible states that the Spirit flew over the earth in order to preserve and prepare for God's creative process or activity. The Holy Spirit is the sustainer of the creation; the Spirit of God is the one who has been holding up the earth until today.

If the Spirit of God should leave the earth today, the earth would perish. God created the earth for His glory and honor and He expects glory and honor from all His created beings. God created the universe in order to provide a place for His purpose and plan for humanity to be fulfilled.

God created Adam and Eve in His own image and made them a spirit being so that they could worship, enjoy fellowship, and communicate with

Him in the beauty of His holiness. "God is a Spirit: they that worship Him must worship Him in Spirit and in Truth." John 4:24.

Believers must maintain a personal relationship from this earth to heaven with the Lord. The book of Revelation stated, "And I heard a great voice from heaven saying, Behold, the tabernacle of God is with men, and he will dwell with them, and they shall be his people, and God himself shall be with them, and be their God." Rev. 21:3.

This verse is refers to the New Jerusalem, which is already in existence in heaven and will soon come down to earth as the city of God for which Abraham and all God's faith are waiting, for which God Himself is the architect and builder. The new earth will become God's dwelling place, and He will remain with His people forever.

"The Spirit of God hath made me, and the breath of the Almighty hath given me life." Job 33:4.

"And the earth was without form, and void. And darkness was upon the face of the deep. And the spirit of God moved upon the face of the waters." Gen. 1:2. "If he set his heart upon man if he gathers unto himself his Spirit and his breath." Job 34:14.

"And the Lord said, my spirit shall not always strive with man, for that he also is flesh: yet his days shall be an hundred and twenty years." Gen. 6:3.

The Holy Spirit is the messenger of revelation to humankind, "And Pharaoh said unto his servants, can we find such a one as this is, and a man in whom the Spirit of God is?" Gen. 41:38.

"And I will come down and talk with thee there: and I will take of the Spirit which is upon thee, and will put it upon them; and they shall bear the burden of the people with thee, that thou bear it not thyself alone." Num. 11:17.

The Spirit of God came upon the people in the Old Testament for the purpose of revelation, not for endorsement as a prophet. God will not use those who are not in a proper relationship with him to accomplish His purpose.

The Holy Spirit empowers and enables the people in the Old Testament to build the tabernacle, "And Joshua the son of Nun was full of the Spirit of wisdom; for Moses had laid his hands upon him: and the children of Israel hearkened unto him, and did as the Lord commanded Moses." Deut. 34:9. The Spirit of God selected the leaders of God's people and empowered them to do the work He assigned to them.

The important and valuable desire of all Christians is to know God and experience a close relationship and fellowship with Him. As the children of God, we have the privilege of going to Him through the power of His Spirit that He gave to us. "And I have filled him with the Spirit of God, in wisdom, and in all manner of workmanship." Exo. 31:3.

The spirit of God filled the people of Israel with spiritual equipment and enabled them to carry out a special service to God and to be able to teach others. Believers should pray that the Spirit will bless them with wisdom and know-ledge for the physical skills, medical technological advance-ment, research, and knowledge that will help peo-ple find the cure for all of the deadly diseases that plague the people in the world—a spiritual gift to fulfill God's will for their lives.

The Israelites were able to build the taberna-cle and houses and to find medicine to cure sick-ness. "And he hath filled him with the spirit of God, in wisdom, in understanding, and in knowl-edge, and in all manner of workmanship." Exo. 35:31.

The Spirit of God comes upon individuals with energizing power, temporarily equipping leaders for physical and military service.

The Holy Spirit supernatural power is com-bined with inspirational knowledge of proph-ecy. The Spirit inspires and empowers prophets, sending them to deliver messages to the people of

Israel, guiding them where and how to proclaim the message of God's salvation and judgment.

The Spirit was active in the writing of all the Psalms in the Bible. The writing of Psalms, such as those written by the prophet Isaiah, disclosed the coming of the Messiah as the Spirit revealed it to him. Isaiah develops this in many of his writings: that a new Spirit of judgment and fire will appear.

"When the Lord shall have washed away the filth of the daughters of Zion, and shall have purged the blood of Jerusalem from the midst thereof by the Spirit of judgment, and by the spirit of burning." Isa. 4:4.

Believers will be separated from the sinful universe, cleansed from all defilement by Christ's blood and regenerated by the Holy Spirit over them, which will fly with the glory of God like a canopy.

Isaiah's prophecy is that the Spirit of God will empower the Messiah with wisdom, power, knowledge, and holiness. He will be poured out corporately on all of God's people to bring about justice, righteousness, and peace for all of the people of the earth forever.

We have to consider Prophet Ezekiel's prophecy through the power of the Holy Spirit. He experienced the Spirit power when the Spirit sometimes lifted him up from prostration and often transported him to a new location. God promised to give him a new Spirit, a new heart, and a new name.

He said, "And I will put my Spirit within you, and cause you to walk in my statues, and ye shall keep my judgments, and do them. A new heart also will I give you, and a new Spirit will I put within you: and I will take away the stony heart out of your flesh, and I will give you an heart of flesh." Eze. 36:26–27.

God promised to renew the children of Israel physically and spiritually, which required giving them a new heart that was gentle, so that they would be able to respond to God's Word. God's will imparted His Spirit on them, which continued with New Testament believers.

Without the indwelling Spirit, it is impossible to live a true Christian life and to be obedient to God's commandments and God's will. It is very important for all believers to maintain a close relationship with the Lord so that the Holy Spirit may continue to guide, control, and direct the believer according to the will of God. God sent His new Spirit to the Israelites to move them to obey the law and receive the fulfillment of His promises.

Prophet Joel's prophecy was "And it shall come to pass afterwards that I will pour out my

Spirit upon all flesh, and your sons and daughter shall prophecy, your old men shall dream dreams, your young men hall see visions, And also upon the servants, and upon the handmaids in those days will I pour out my spirit." Joel 2:28–32. Apostle Peter quoted this verse on the day of Pentecost when the prophecy was fulfilled.

Prophet Joel's prophecy was that, through the Spirit of God, God would pour out His Spirit on everyone who calls on His Holy Name. This outpouring results in the flowing of the Spirit's manifestation among the people of God. Peter explained the outpouring of the Spirit on those who believe in Jesus Christ and become baptized.

These promises to all those who accept Christ as Lord allow believers to be filled with the Holy Spirit's Power. God spoke through the prophet Joel many years before it would happen. Joel envisions that, one day, the outpouring of the Spirit will be the impartation of the Spirit of God as a gift from God.

The manifestation of the Spirit through His gifts makes visible God's presence among His people. God pours out His Spirit, on the day of Pentecost, on individuals regardless of whether they are a man or woman, whether they are old or young, and regardless of their social status or ethnicity, according to His good pleasure.

Also, other prophets, like Micah, Haggai, and Zachariah, all confirm the Spirit's Power in their lives; they all connect the activities of its presence with their empowerment for building and rebuilding the temple the Spirit of God gives orders, commands, and directions and the people of God follow.

The same Spirit of God that became active in the creation during Old Testament times is still active in the New Testament and will continue until Christ returns. Our Lord's earthly ministry was Spirit-led; there are many significant manifestations of this, including the fulfillment of prophecy.

"The Spirit of the Lord God is upon me; because the Lord hath anointed me to preach good tidings unto the meek; he hath sent me to bind up the brokenhearted, to proclaim liberty to the captives, and the opening of the prison to them that are bound." Isa. 61:1.

The miracles of our Lord were the activities of the Holy Spirit. Jesus Christ's signs and wonders directly revealed God's Spirit at work upon or on Him. As the Spirit empowered Jesus, Jesus promises believers the Holy Spirit that the Spirit will, in the same way, empower His believers to do the work of God.

The Spirit is the helper who will remain in us forever. The Spirit will equip and enable believers to be able to serve the Lord, boldly do the work of the Gospel, and confidently proclaim the Word of God. Believers will be constantly filled with the Spirit so that they will be able to courageously speak and preach for Christ.

The Spirit is God's agent for bringing people to himself and helping them to mature spiritually; only through His power will individuals first receive God's Word as the divine Word.

The Spirit makes unique spiritual insights available to all believers through the use of the Word of God, which makes believers obedient to God and stand on the truth of the Word of God, which many unbelievers cannot do.

The Spirit of God helps believers in prayers, helping them to maintain an intimate relationship with God. God had a plan from the beginning of Creation and He is the only one who can carry it out, at His own time.

Christ will come back to earth, according to God's plan. When that time comes, God will speak and Christ will return to earth. God is a trinity called the Holy Trinity Father,

Son, and Holy Spirit. The Word of God means Elohim this name is used whenever the power of God is revealed, the Bible tells us that Godhead was involved in the creation and also tell us what each of Godhead's activities during the creation were. God created the earth. The Spirit of God is moving and vibrating with supernatural energy; the Holy Spirit brought energy into the formless, void, and dark earth.

The Holy Spirit poured out energy into the universe, God called light into existence, and this light was the result of the outpouring of energy that the Holy Spirit had pumped into the earth. The Spirit power illuminated the universe and dissolved the dark and void earth.

God the Father spoke and everything was created and He pronounced them good. Sin filled the earth, the Spirit of God spoke again, and His word became flesh and dwelled among us. When God spoke, the Son acted; Jesus, the Son of God, is the creator.

"Who is the image of the invisible God, first born of every creature: For by Him were all things created, that are in heaven, and that are in earth, visible, invisible, whether they be thrones, or dominions, or principalities, or powers: all things were created by him, and for him." Col. 1:15-16.

Our Lord said, "But the hour cometh and now is, when true worshipers shall worship the Father in Spirit and in Truth: for the Father seeketh such to worship Him. God is a Spirit: and they that worship Him must worship Him in Spirit and in truth." John 4:23-24.

Jesus Christ is the creator and the sustainer of all things. The Father spoke, the Son carried out the order, and the Spirit enabled believers to respond to the command of God. "God, who at sundry times and in divers manners spake in time past unto the fathers by the prophets hath in these last days spoken unto us by his son, whom he hath appointed heir of all things, by whom also he made the world." Heb. 1:1-2.

God the Father made the world through the operation of Jesus Christ His son, which brings us back to the beginning of creation, which shows that Jesus is the Word of God. God spoke and Christ came into being; the Holy Spirit put Christ in Mary's womb and sustained Him with Hid power until His birth, throughout His ministry and work, and until the day of His resurrection and ascension when the Spirit took Christ back to heaven.

Our Lord said to Philip: "If ye had known me, ye should have known my Father also: and from henceforth ye know him, and have seen Him. Philip said unto Him, Lord shew us the Father, and it sufficeth us. Jesus said unto him, have I been so long time with you, and yet hast thou not known me, Philip? He that hath seen me hath seen the Father, and how sayest thou then, show us the Father? Believest thou not that I am in the Father, and the Father in me? The words that I speak unto you I speak not of myself: but the Father that dwelleth in me, he doeth the works." John 14:7-9.

Jesus Christ is the Spirit of God; He is the Word of God and the Word of God is God. Our Lord said, "I am the true vine, and my Father is the husbandman, every branch that beareth fruit, He purgeth it, that it may bring forth more fruits." John 15:1-2.

These verses of Scripture indicate that the Holy Trinity, the Godhead, is one that it worked together in the creation and continues to sustain the earth. Jesus is the source of life and the Holy Spirit produces fruit.

God the Father, through the power of the Spirit, washes us clean so that we can bear more fruits. The Father also separates the branches if they are withered and dry. We must realize that each member of the Godhead operates together in unity in bringing about and sustaining the creation.

Elohim means more than one name, it means that God is great and that His greatness is in His power, in His strength, and in His might; God's greatness is clearly seen in all that He has created, especially in his actions towards His people, the children of God. God was the Son on earth doing everything through Him.

He exhibited His greatness by forgiving our sins through our Lord Jesus Christ and showing us His infinite love, loving kindness, mercy, and goodness through His Son. God's greatness is unsearchable, unattainable, incomparable, and indescribable.

After the Spirit of God energized the earth, God said let there be light and light came upon the earth. God placed the light permanently in heaven; God is the light-bearer and the light of the world. The primary purpose of the light activity of the Holy Spirit was to create signs for marking the seasons, days, nights, and years.

The light of God in the universe is one of the most powerful activities of the Spirit of God. All Christians experience the light of the Holy Spirit in their heart. If the Spirit illuminates the heart, that heart will never be the same.

When God said, "Let us make a man in our image." God was referring to the Holy Trinity. The Spirit power is dynamic and powerful; through Him, God brings creation into existence and reaches the goal of the new creation in Jesus Christ.

If the Father functions as the source of being and the Son bears witness of God into the world, the Spirit's function has been to complete the task of creation so that the community of the triune

God may come into the fullness. The Spirit of God continues to renew the face of the earth and He will continue until the end. God's Spirit breathed into Adam and he became a living soul,

"And the Lord God formed man of the dust of the ground, and breathed into his nostrils the breath of life, and man became a living soul." Gen. 2:7. "Thou sendest forth thy Spirit, they are created: and thou renewest the face of the earth." Psl. 104:30.

"The Spirit of God hath made me, and the breath of the Almighty had given me life." Job 33:4. The psalmist is saying, Lord God of creation you created all things and you care for all thy creations. You, O Lord, sustained the earth with thy Spirit because you dwell in the world with your providence and sustain the universe. Your involvement and your work of redemption reflect thy glory.

The Spirit is a life-giver, giving life to those who are spiritually dead and making them alive in Him. The Spirit is the source of life in the universe; the Spirit awakens human life; in beauty and truth, the Spirit of God is present.

The Holy Spirit leads us to experience God in life and the Spirit sheds light on all mysteries when we see the Spirit as the Lord and giver of life, making what we thought was impossible,

possible, and helping us to focus on the divine mystery of the gift of grace and renewed life. The Spirit of God's presence in the world helps us to get closer to the only God, in whom we move, live, and exist, who is not far from us, and who is present with us in all of our earthly problems.

We are able to approach God in times of sadness, joy, hope, suffering, and struggle, and when faced with all other adversities in the world. The Spirit not only formed and shaped our habitable space, but it has also grieved the violence committed against what has been created.

The Spirit is the source of transient life and also of the eternal life of all believers. The Spirit is the Spirit of preservation, preserving and sustaining the universe, as well as preparing the universe for new creation.

The Holy Spirit is active in all corners of creation, moment by moment, in the history of the world. The Spirit of God is present and active in the entire history of salvation. The purpose and goal of creation is for the Spirit of God to unite all things through Christ and for Christ. "Hear, O Israel: The Lord our God is one Lord." Deut. 6:4.

The Bible refers to God as the Father, the Son, and the Holy Spirit. One of the greatest mysteries of God is that He is a triune God; yet, He is one. We have knowledge that the three parts of the Godhead are one; but God works in different ways.

In order to understand the fruit of the Spirit, we must, first of all, understand who the Spirit is, what the Spirit does to help us in our lives, and how He helps us to live a life that will glorify the Lord. The Holy Spirit is the third person of the Godhead, the triune God.

God lives and dwells in our heart in the form of the Holy Spirit; He comes to live inside believers. The Holy Spirit's other names are the Helper, *Paraclete*, and the Invisible Power of God. "In whom ye also trusted, after that ye heard the word of truth, the Gospel of your salvation: in whom also after that ye believed, ye were sealed with that Holy Spirit of promise, which is the earnest of our inheritance until the redemption of the purchased possession, unto the praise of His glory." Eph. 1:13-14.

The Holy Spirit is a deposit, like a first installment of a down payment, guaranteeing our inheritance and given to all believers as a down payment for what we are going to have in full in the future. The Holy Spirit's presence and work in the lives of all Christians pledges our future inheritance.

The Scriptures clarify where the Holy Spirit comes from and what the Spirit's responsibilities in the lives of believers are. "And I will pray the

Father, and He shall give you another Comforter, that he may abide with you forever." John 14:16.

Jesus said that He would ask the Father to give comfort to only those who are serious about their love for Him and their devotion to His Word. Jesus made this statement to let us know how important our continuing love and obedience to God's Word is. "But the Comforter, the Holy Ghost, whom the Father will send in my name, he shall teach you all things, and bring all things to your remembrance, whatsoever I have said unto you." John 14:26.

The most important thing about the Holy Spirit is that He is Holy, and He wants all Christians to acquire His holy character in their lives. The Holy Spirit, according to the Scriptures, was sent by God the Father, to teach believers all things and to bring all of the things that God has said into the believers' remembrance. "And when he is come, he will reprove the world of sin, and of righteousness, and of judgment." John 16:8.

The Holy Spirit will convince believers of Christ of what is right and what is wrong, He will guide believers into the truth of the Gospel, and He will speak only the words that he hears from God. He will disclose to the believer what is going to come in the future and, most important, He will glorify the Lord Jesus Christ. The Holy Spirit prays for us the prayer that cannot be uttered, "The Spirit itself beareth witness with our Spirit that we are children of God." Rom. 8:16. All Christians must know that the Holy Spirit imparts the confidence to us that, through Christ and with Christ, we are the children of God.

The Spirit of God made the truth of Jesus Christ clear to us, that Christ loved us and will continue to love us in heaven as our Mediator of a new Covenant. The Holy Spirit created and imparted the love of God in believers' hearts so that we confidently cry out to Him Abba, Father.

Believers have the knowledge that each person has a spirit and that the Holy Spirit speaks to our spirits to remind us that we are the children of God through Jesus Christ's complete work of redemption. "Now he that hath wrought us for the selfsame thing is God, who also hath given unto us the earnest of the Spirit." 2 Cor. 5:5.

God has a purpose for our life. God's Holy Spirit knows what that purpose is and He will guide believers towards that purpose. The Holy Spirit is given as a deposit to every believer who has accepted Jesus Christ as their personal Lord and Savior.

This means that God wants believers to know that they are the children of God and the family of God as joint heirs with Jesus Christ. God the

Father, who is the Godhead, sends the Holy Spirit; His Spirit lives in believers at the time of conversion and salvation. "In whom ye also trusted, after that ye heard the word of truth, the gospel of your salvation: in whom also after that ye believed, ye were sealed with that Holy Spirit of promise. Which is the earnest of our inheritance until the redemption of the purchased possession, unto the praise of his glory." Eph. 1:13-14.

This verse is telling us that: Heaven is our inheritance. All the blessings that we have in hand are but small if compared with the inheritance. We are sealed with that Holy Spirit of promise. He makes us holy. He is the promised Spirit.

By him believers are sealed and set apart for God. His comforts are earnests of everlasting joys. "If any of you lack wisdom, let him ask of God, that giveth to all men liberally, and upbraideth not; and it shall be given." Jas. 1:5.

We must ask God for wisdom in coping with our trials, not just for deliverance from our troubles; we must ask for wisdom in any decision-making, wisdom about our circumstances, and wisdom and understanding of God's Word and God's will for our lives.

We must ask for wisdom to be able to see this in a spiritual way and to evaluate with our life experience as well as to make the right choices and do the right thing in accordance with God's will revealed in us and with His word and the leadership of the Holy Spirit.

As believers read, study, and meditate on the Word of God, the Holy Spirit helps believers to remember what they have read; in times of need the Spirit will take the word out to comfort the believer and to clear some of the difficulties that the believer might be going through at that particular time.

Believers must read the Word of God daily as food for their soul. "Thy word have I hid in mine heart, that I might not sin against thee." Ps. 119:11. The Holy Spirit convicts believers of sins; the Holy Spirit is the innermost voice that believers hear inside of them, telling them right from wrong.

Believers must be sure that they are listening to the Spirit of God. The way to know the difference is to know God's Word. The way to know God's Word is by reading and studying the Word of God (the Bible) daily.

Reading the Bible will allow believers to grow in their faith and be strengthened this will help them to be able to recognize the voice of the Holy Spirit when He speaks to their hearts, or through Scripture. He guides us into the truth. The truth of the Word of God in the Bible teaches believers the way of God, which is different than the way of the world. "For my thoughts are not your thoughts, neither are your ways my ways, said the Lord. For as the heavens are higher than the earth, so are my ways higher than your ways and my thoughts than your thoughts." Isa. 55:8-9.

The Holy Spirit speaks only the Word of God, which means that believers can be sure that whatever they hear from the Spirit will be consistent with the Word of God. In the Gospel of John, "Howbeit when he, the Spirit of truth, is comes, he will guide you into all truth: for he shall not speak of himself; but whatsoever he shall hear, that shall he speak: and he will shew you things to come." John 16:13.

Human beings shouldn't judge God by their thoughts and by their own ways. God's activities transcend anything human beings could ever imagine. It is in the truth of God that we live move, and exist.

The Spirit of truth will continue the work of God. This means that all truth was given to the apostles by following Christ for three years of His ministry; they passed this truth to us through their writing and preaching and we still have the truth of the Scripture today.

The Holy Spirit discloses what is to come. He discloses the truth about you and concerning God's will and plan for your life. As believers understand more and more the Word of God and His ways, they will see and find out the meaning of their life and the direction in which God wants them to go for His glory. "For I know the thoughts that I think towards you, said the Lord, thoughts of peace, and not evil, to give you an expected end." Jer. 29:11.

The Holy Spirit glorifies Jesus Christ. As believers understand the Word of God and obey the Holy Spirit's voice, they glorify and bring honor to our Lord Jesus Christ and to God the Father. This is the believers' ultimate goal in life; their purpose in life is to live a life that will continuously glorify God's Holy Name.

The Apostle Paul said, "Whether therefore ye eat, or drink, or whatsoever ye do, do all to the glory of God." 1 Cor. 10:31. The main purpose of a believer's life is to please God and promote His glory. We have to do everything in honor of Him as our Lord, creator, and Redeemer King through our obedience, thankfulness, prayer, and loyalty. We have to live our life for the glory of our Lord and Savior.

"Likewise the Spirit also helpeth our infirmities: for we know not what we should pray for as we ought: but the Spirit itself maketh intercession for us with groanings which cannot be uttered." Rom. 8:26.

The Holy Spirit prays for us. Many believers face a time in their lives when they go through disappointment, difficulties, grief, or any number of uncertain circumstances when they don't feel like praying or don't know how to pray about their particular situation, which is very overwhelming, and they lack the words for prayer.

The Holy Spirit helps all believers in their prayers through important observations; as the children of God we have two divine intercessors. Christ intercedes for believers in heaven at the right hand of God where He is seated.

The Holy Spirit, who dwells in our hearts, intercedes for us on earth. Our spiritual desires and yearnings as believers are found in the Holy Spirit, who dwells within them. The Spirit pleads our case to the Father on behalf of our needs, in accordance with the will of God.

Our heavenly Father knows all of our needs and He has given us His Spirit to help us in all areas of our lives. The Holy Spirit bears witness with our spirit that we are the children of God. Sometimes, believers find themselves doubting, feeling that God is far away from them, or feeling that God does not care for them.

The spirit bears witness by reminding them of what God has said in His word. He brings some Bible verses into their remembrance. "We love Him, because He first loved us." 1 John 4:19. "Have I not commanded thee? Be strong and of a good courageous; be not afraid, neither be thou dismayed: for the Lord thy God is with thee whithersoever thou go." Jos. 1:9.

The Lord God Almighty was instructing His newly appointed servant that those who know and obey Him and His word and who follow the Law will have great success and that they will be prosperous and possess the wisdom to live righteously according to God's will for their lives.

The tool for great, successful living is achieved when the believer is very strong in the Lord and courageous and when the Word of God is the compass for their lives. "Casting all your care upon Him; for He careth for you." 1 Pet. 5:7.

Our God cares about the suffering and pain that every one of His children is going through; this truth is also emphasized through the Word of God. God knows all of our troubles, our sickness and pain, and our fears of enemies, especially those who are enemies of God.

Believers must hand it all over to Our Lord and Savior Jesus Christ. The Holy Spirit is there to testify or confirm that believers belong to God; they are the children of God and heirs to all that which belongs to Jesus Christ and God the Father Almighty. "The Spirit itself beareth witness with our spirit, that we are the sons of God. And if children, then heirs; and joint heirs with Christ; if so be that we suffer with him, that we may be also glorified together." Rom. 8:16-17.

The Holy Spirit is given as a pledge, as a promise. God promised all believers eternal life if they confess their sins and ask for the Savior Jesus Christ to come into their hearts. Their sins have been forgiven and they have been offered the promise to be with God for all eternity.

God offered this salvation to both Jews and Gentiles. Then, remember what the Lord said: "Wait for the promise of the Father, which ye have heard of me. For John truly baptized with water; but ye shall be baptized with the Holy Ghost not many days hence."

Forasmuch then, God gave them the same gift as he did to us, who believed in the Lord Jesus Christ, "What was I, that I could withstand God?" Acts 11:16-17. Peter told the leader of the early Church that God gave the same gift to the Gentiles as he gave to the apostles.

The disciples believed in Jesus Christ and they were regenerated by the Holy Spirit. The Gentiles were also included in Christ when they heard the word of truth, the Gospel of salvation. Once they believed, they were marked in Him with a seal, the promised Holy Spirit, who is the deposit guaranteeing their inheritance until the redemption of those who are in God's possession and praise His glory.

2

Breath of the Son of God

"Receive Ye the Spirit." John 20:22. Christ elevated the apostles when He breathed on them, and said, receive ye the Holy Ghost. This sign not only show them, by this breath of life, that he himself was really alive, but to signify to them the spiritual life and power which they should receive from him.

As the breath of the Almighty God gave life to man and began the old world, same the breath of Christ signifies the power of his grace; the Spirit is the gift of Christ that Christ gave to the apostles, he conferred the Holy Spirit by the breathing for He is the author of the gift of the Holy Spirit.

He gave them the Holy Spirit then and the Spirit began working on them before the day of Pentecost. The breath of the Lord, at that time, was how He gave the apostles the power of the Holy Spirit, just as how

Moses had laid his hands on Joshua in the wilderness to continue leading the Israelites to the promised land. The breath transfers the power of the Holy Spirit to the apostles so that they may be able to obey and stay in Jerusalem before the day of Pentecost.

The breath also symbolizes how Elijah transferred power to Elisha before the Chariot of fire and horses of fire took him to heaven. "And it came to pass, when they were gone over, that Elijah said unto Elisha, ask what I shall do for thee, before I be taken away from thee. And Elisha said, I pray thee, let a double portion of thy spirit be upon me.

And he said, "Thou hast asked a hard thing: nevertheless, if thou see me when I am taken from thee, it shall be so unto thee; but if not, it shall not be so. And it came to pass, as they still went on, and talked, that, behold, there appeared a chariot of fire, and horses of fire, and parted them both asunder; and Elijah went up by a whirlwind into heaven. And he took the mantel of Elijah that fell from him, and smote the waters, and said, where is the Lord God of Elijah? And when he also had smitten the waters, they parted hither and thither: and Elisha went over." 2 Kings 2:9-10, 14.

We can easily see the power of the Holy Spirit in transporting Elijah to heaven by the whirlwind wind is one of the signs of the Holy Spirit. Just as the Spirit of God was hovering in the beginning of creation, all the apostles witnessed a rushing wind on the day of Pentecost when the power of the Holy Spirit descended upon them. The breath foreshadows the promise that would be fulfilled on the day of Pentecost. The breath empowers the great commission of Our Lord: "Go ye into all the nations." Luke 24:49.

The breath of our Lord causes the Spirit to be born in their hearts. The Holy Spirit hovered in the hearts of the apostles to bring them to life before the day of Pentecost; without the Spirit power we cannot obey the commandments of God.

Jesus connected the Holy Spirit to the forgiveness and repentance of sins, teaching the apostles of the preaching of repentance and forgiveness of sins. "And that repentance and the remission of sins should be preached in His name among all nations, beginning at Jerusalem." Luke 24:47.

When Jesus breathed on the apostles, they received the Holy Spirit but were not empowered until the day of Pentecost. As God breathed on Adam and Eve, "and the Lord God formed man of the dust of the ground, and breathed into his nostrils the breath of life; and man became a living soul." Gen. 2:7.

They became living beings; Jesus refers to the creation of the first man when he breathed His breath into the Apostles. He made them new creations, born of the Spirit of God. He repeated what He did in the Garden of Eden. God the Father spoke, God the Son created new life and God the Holy Spirit helped to sustain the new life by producing all the fruit of the Spirit that is needed for living a new life.

The breath of God the Father gave life to Adam and Eve and made them living beings; in the same way, Christ the Savior of the universe breathed on the apostles for the creation of a new world, which also indicated the Son's power on earth, as well as the gift of grace to all mankind.

The apostles became a new Spirit-filled, created being; Christ made them alive in Him. This was also applied to everyone who was present on that day, not only to the apostles. It has been shown from then on that in order to be a true Christian or believer of Jesus, one must receive the Holy Spirit regenerated, made alive, which we call born again.

Throughout the three years they spent following the Lord, they did not have the indwelling of the Spirit of God. The Spirit of God worked within them, producing the fruit of patience, strengthening them, increasing their faith, and making them true and strong in the Lord so that they could live a spiritual life.

The Spirit of God made the Gospel alive in their heart. The Spirit opened their understanding of the Gospel Scriptures and enabled them to teach others or explain them to other people around them.

Otherwise, on the day of Pentecost, they would not have been able to preach to people to the extent that three thousand people were converted on that day.

For example, Thomas was not with the Apostles when the Lord breathed on them. Thomas, one of the twelve, called Didymus, was not with them when Jesus came. But he said unto them, "Unless I shall see in his hands the print of nails, and put my finger into the print of the nails, and thrust my hand into his side, I will not believe." John 20:24-25b.

"After eight days the disciples were gather together and Thomas was with them: then came, Jesus, the doors being shut, and stood in the midst, and said, Peace be unto you." John 20:26.

While Jesus was talking to Thomas, He opened his understanding and the Spirit of God was upon him Jesus made him alive in Him. This continues to happen even until today; many people are struggling to live a Christian life. Because they did not have the indwelling of the Holy Spirit, they are always confused, with guilt and doubts.

Some of them will say they believe in God but not in Jesus, and they usually remain like that until someone prays for them and opens the Scripture to them. Then, the Holy Spirit will be able to manifest His power to them as He did to the sinners.

This makes it clear what the Bible says, "Jesus answered and said unto him, Verily, verily, I say unto thee, except a man be born again, and he cannot see the kingdom of God." John 3:3. The first blessing of our Lord after His resurrection and before His ascension was the blessing of new birth, or, the regeneration of the apostles. Christ breathes on them and they become new creations, Spirit-filled beings.

The Spirit of God brought back the apostles to spiritual life from their spiritual death; they received forgiveness of all their sins and began Holy lives. God's breath made the first creation. Likewise, Jesus' breath made the new creation and God's breath to Adam gave him life.

In the new creation, Christ breathed into the apostles and gave them eternal life, life everlasting, which is different from the case of Adam and Eve. A brand-new creation, "Therefore if any man be in Christ, he is a new creature: old things are passed away; behold, all things are become new." 2 Cor. 5:17.

He becomes a new creature in Christ, through the creative command of God. Those who accept Jesus Christ through faith are made into a new creation that belongs to God's total new earth in which the Spirit of God rules.

Christ also blessed them with the Spirit of peace. The Holy Spirit worked and produced the fruit of peace in the disciples before the day of Pentecost. "Peace be unto you." John 20:26.

Christ, through the Holy Spirit, always blesses the believer with the gift of the Holy Spirit and with the fruit of the Holy Spirit, which is peace. The Peace of God rules in the hearts and minds of those who have been persecuted, afflicted, and hurt, and of those who are in trouble due to many different circumstances.

He blesses believers with peace to be strong, to be strengthened, to not be afraid, to be strong and immovable, to have unshakable faith, to be courageous, and to stand firm in the Lord. He blesses the apostles with peace so that they may wait for His promise. The third blessing of our Lord occurred when He breathed on them and He said, "receive the Holy Spirit's joy."

"And ye now therefore have sorrow: but I will see you again, and your heart shall rejoice, and your joy no man taketh from you." John 16:22.

Our Lord wants the apostles to rejoice in what has happened and what is still going to happen the result is that they rejoice in the joy He is giving them, which is a joy that cannot be taken away from them. All believers share the same joy today, which is the joy of resurrection and eternal life.

The apostles were overjoyed to see the Lord after he was crucified, dead, and buried; they never knew that they could see Him again. He was alive, eating, and speaking with them. Jesus compared the pain of the apostles to a woman who was in pain of childbirth and rejoiced, full of joy, after the child was born.

"A woman when she is in travail hath sorrow, because her hour is come: but as soon as she is delivered of the child, she remembereth no more the anguish, for joy that a man is born into the world." John 16:21.

Breathing on the apostles brought great joy to them and showed that the Spirit would produce the fruit of joy and peace on the apostles. The fourth blessing of Jesus' breath on the apostles was the blessing of the power of the Holy Spirit to bear witness.

The Spirit produced in them, before the day of Pentecost, power to proclaim the gospel to unbelievers for forgiveness of their sins. "Then said Jesus to them again, Peace be unto you: as my Father hath sent me, even so send I you." John 20:21.

The Father sends Jesus, His only begotten Son, to save the world. Jesus Christ sent the apostles and all of the body of Christ on earth to continue this great commission. The peace that the Spirit of God produces takes away fear, confusion, and sadness, and calms down believers' fear and confusion. The Spirit gave and produced courage and brought peace of God to the believers' spirit, soul, and body.

The Holy Spirit shed His light and produced strength, ability, and power for the apostles, before the day of Pentecost, to witness and boldly proclaim the gospel of God to all people on the day of Pentecost.

On that day, the apostles were filled with great power, to such an extent that three thousand sinners were converted. Everyone that has the Spirit of God in him or her has a burden for missionary work, for saving sinners and calling the lost unto Christ. This is the automatic work of the Holy Spirit, to make believers strive for the work of the Gospel and to take the Gospel of God to the ends of the earth.

Believers become God's workmanship through the Holy Spirit; they are new creations in Christ Jesus. They are very unique and placed into the body of Christ, regardless of whether they are Jews or Gentiles, black or white.

Regardless of their ethnicity or nationality, believers share one Spirit of Jesus Christ and they are one body of Christ. Believers are created in Christ Jesus to do the good work that Spirit of God has assigned to them before the beginning of creation.

Believers belong to a glorious new creation, which God, through the power of the Holy Spirit, has brought into his existing plan of redemption and salvation through Jesus Christ His Son.

3

Holy Spirit Power in the New Testament

One important aspect of the Holy Spirit in the New Testament is that God is available to every believer through baptism with the Holy Spirit. Every believer must be filled with the power of the Holy Spirit.

The Spirit has given us the power to witness the Gospel to people who have never heard the Gospel before. We do our witnessing as commanded and the Holy Spirit carries out the transformation.

The Spirit of God will transform the non-believing sinner into a child of God. The Holy Spirit empowers believers against the enemy: "Ye are of God, little children, and have overcome them: because greater is he that is in you, than he that is in the world." 1 John 4:4. This verse is telling us that: the Spirit of God dwells in us and that Spirit is more mighty than men or devils. The Spirit of God has framed our mind for God and heaven.

The world will love its own, and its own will love it. The Holy Spirit indwelling is more powerful than Satan and the Devil. The Holy Spirit will convict us of sin, "Nevertheless I tell you the truth; it is expedient for you that I go away: for if I go not away, the Comforter will not come unto you; but if I depart, I will send him unto you. And when he is come, he will reprove the world of sin, and of righteousness, and of judgment." John 16:7-8.

The outpouring of the Holy Spirit occurred after Christ went to heaven. The Holy Spirit's principal work with respect to proclaiming the Gospel will be that of convicting sin. The Holy Spirit will expose sin and unbelief in order to awaken a consciousness of guilt and need for forgiveness.

The Spirit will let us know when we are doing bad things or about to do bad things either to ourselves or to other people around us. The Holy Spirit is our director and controller. He convicts us of sin or warns us of sin before we commit it.

In this, the Spirit helps us to maintain a close relationship with our Lord. After the conviction of sin, true repentance always happens and turning to Christ as Lord and Savior prevails. In order to access the Spirit power, we must be baptized with the Holy Spirit. Each believer needs to be filled with the Holy Spirit every day by following the words of God. The role of the ministry of the Holy Spirit in our lives is to keep us away from the work of the flesh.

The most important thing is that the Holy Spirit has the power to control our lives. One of the powers of the Holy Spirit with regard to believers is the ability to bear witness and to provide strength for performing an activity related to the work of the Gospel.

An example is the day of Pentecost: "And there appeared unto them cloven tongues like as of fire, and it sat upon each of them and they were all filled with the Holy Ghost, and began to speak with other tongues, as the Spirit gave them utterance." Acts 2:3-4.

First, on the day of Pentecost, there was a sound like the flowing of a violent wind as a sign that the Holy Spirit came with power. Second, there was a sign that appeared visibly: the tongues of fire that rested on each of the disciples, indicating the prophetic symbol that the Holy Spirit was coming to empower them.

Third, they began to speak in foreign languages to the people that came from different countries in their own native languages. The disciples knew clearly that Jesus Christ fulfilled His word of promise from His ascended position as exalted Lord and Christ at the Father's right hand of authority.

It assured them of the beginning of the Church. The disciples were clothed with the power of God from above which enabled them to boldly bear witness for Christ to the people of different nations in their own languages. The disciples became ministers of the Spirit. They not only preached about Jesus' crucifixion and resurrection, leading to humankind's repentance and faith in Christ, but they also influenced converts to receive the gift of the Holy Spirit.

Leading people to baptism in the Holy Spirit is the key to the apostolic work described in the New Testament. Through this baptism in the Spirit, Christ's followers became the successors to his earthly ministry.

All Christians continued to act and teach, through the power of the Holy Spirit, the same things that Jesus had begun to do and to teach. The Holy Spirit is God's agent for purifying and illuminating believers.

The main work of the Holy Spirit is to continuously pour power upon the believer. Baptism is an act of obedience in the life of every believer in Jesus Christ, which also leads to the power to commit and proclaim the Gospel of God.

It is also a means of public identification of believers to Jesus Christ following His death, burial, and resurrection "Know ye not, that so many of us as were baptized into Jesus Christ were baptized into his death?

Therefore we are buried with him by baptism into death: that like as Christ was raised up from the dead by the glory of the Father, even so we also should walk in newness of life." Rom. 6:3-4. "Then Peter said unto them, Repent, and be baptized every one of you in the name of Jesus Christ for the remission of sins, and ye shall receive the gift of the Holy Ghost." Acts 2:38.

"Not by works of righteousness which we have done, but according to his mercy he saved us, by the washing of regeneration, and renewing of the Holy Ghost." Titus 3:5.

The spiritual renewal of Christ's believers refers to the new birth of believers, symbolically pictured in all Christians' baptisms. Renewal by the Holy Spirit points to the constant imparting of His life to believers as they surrender their lives to God through Jesus Christ.

The Holy Spirit's appearance in the Gospel of John is the power by which Christians are brought by faith and it is the Spirit that helps believers to understand their walk with God.

The Holy Spirit leads people to a new birth in Christ. "That which is born of the flesh is flesh; and that which is born of the Spirit is spirit." John 3:6. It is the Spirit who gave life to the converted sinners and made them Christians.

"It is the Spirit that quickeneth; the flesh profiteth nothing: the words that I speak unto you, they are Spirit, and they are life." John 6:63. The early Church confirmed the Holy Spirit's work as baptisms occurred within the outpouring of the Spirit's power in the missionary and evangelical work.

The Holy Spirit reveals to believers the profound nature of God and the mystery of Christ. Being baptized by the Holy Spirit means being led by the Spirit, following the Word of God, and thinking with the mind of God. Our Lord made a promise to the disciples of the Holy Spirit, and his promise was fulfilled ten days after His ascension into heaven on the day of Pentecost.

Then, the Holy Spirit was sent from God the Father by Jesus Christ, and all of the apostles were filled with the Holy Spirit. This was also the day when the Church of Christ was born on earth. The apostles were filled with supernatural power, to the extent that they were speaking in foreign languages.

Many people heard them speaking in their own languages and were amazed. The same Spirit of God that indwelled Jesus throughout His earthly ministry, also indwelled all of the apostles, who were able to powerfully continue the Gospel ministry through the power of the Spirit, just as our Lord had done when He was with them.

The disciples already believed. They knew that Christ was the Son of God, the Messiah who was to come; but they needed power from above in order to carry out the work of the ministry.

Even today, all of Christ's believers need the working power of the Spirit of God for the miracle of converting sinners and the lost. Jesus Christ wants all believers to abide in Him so that they can live and walk within the supernatural power of the Holy Spirit. Believers must be born of the Spirit of God, before they can be baptized with the Spirit. Many believers have been saved but were not baptized with the Holy Spirit.

For example, this was the case of the believers in Samaria during the apostles' era. They were saved but not baptized with the Holy Spirit until Apostle Peter laid hands on them. "Now when the apostles which were at Jerusalem heard that Samaria had received the Word of God, they sent unto them Peter and John: When they came down, they prayed for them, that they might receive the Holy Ghost." Acts 8:14-15.

"He that believeth and is baptized shall be saved; but he that believeth not shall be damned." Mark 16:16. "And Ananias went his way, and entered into the house; and putting his hands on him said, Brother Saul, the Lord even Jesus, that appeared unto thee on the way as thou camest, hath sent me, that thou mightiest receive thy sight, and be filled with the Holy Ghost." Acts 9:17.

These two examples make it very clear that the conversion of believers is different from baptism, or the infilling of the Holy Spirit. There are times that people will be converted and at the same time receive the baptism of the Holy Spirit the Spirit of God work differently in the lives of individual believers of Christ.

An example of when people received the baptism of the Holy Spirit was revealed in Cornelius, "While Peter yet spake these words, the Holy Ghost fell on all them which heard the word." Acts 10:44. Cornelius and his entire household were Gentiles. As they listened and received the word with saving faith and acceptance of Christ, God at once poured out the Holy Spirit on them, bearing witness that they believed and had received the regenerating life of Christ.

The outpouring of the Holy Spirit on Cornelius and his household has the same purpose as the gift of the Spirit had for the disciples on the day of Pentecost. The outpouring of the Holy Spirit came upon them also with power from above, just as it did on the day of Pentecost.

As Peter was preaching, the Spirit power fell on the entire household. The regenerative work of the Holy Spirit and the baptismal work of the Holy Spirit are two different distinct works of the Spirit of God.

Each of these works of the Spirit results in the manifestation of the presence of God in the life of the believer. We must know very well that those manifestations are not the same and that our Lord made this clear in the Gospel of John, who was one of the apostles who witnessed and experienced this distinction of the Spirit Power.

"But whosoever drinketh of the water that I shall give him shall never thirst; but the water that I shall give him shall, be in him a well of water springing up into everlasting life." John 4:14.

Jesus was at the well speaking to the Samaritan woman. He was referring to the indwelling of the Holy Spirit in the lives of believer when they were born again and converted, because water is one of the signs of the power of the Holy Spirit.

Drinking the water of life requires regular communion with the source of the living water: Jesus Christ Himself. No one can continue to drink the water of life if he or she becomes severed from its source. The act of drinking is not a momentary act or single occurrence, but rather a progressive or repeated, continuous act of drinking.

The Spirit indwelling is like water bubbling up for eternal life. When believers have the indwelling of the Spirit, it is like a well of water, full of the spiritual power of God that sustains and holds believers to God in the face of any earthly obstacles.

Regarding the river of the living waters, God said, "He that believeth on me, as the scripture hath said, out of his belly shall flow rivers of living water." John 7:38.

Christ was referring to the Scripture because it was the very Word of God and, therefore, the supreme authority for His life and teaching. The Scripture is also the supreme authority for Christians, for God alone has the right to determine our standards of conduct.

He has chosen to exercise this authority by making his truth known in Scripture. The Bible is God's revelation; it carries the same authority as if God Himself were speaking to us directly. The inspired scriptures are the believer's ultimate authority.

The Ecclesiastical traditions, prophecies, doctrines, and human ideas must be tested against the Scripture and should never be elevated to a place of equal authority with the Bible. Therefore, all those who are unwilling to submit their beliefs to the lordship of Jesus Christ by submitting them to the authority of the New Testament, place themselves outside of Biblical revelation and salvation in Christ alone.

When the gift of the Spirit power is given to believers, they will experience His overflowing life. The living water will also miraculously overflow within them to other people around them with the healing message of Jesus Christ.

The difference between the well and the river is that the well is the Spirit power inside the believer that provides him or her with strength in order to be obedient to the Lord and control and to help him or her to live a Christian life.

The river of the living water is the power of the Holy Spirit that strengthens the believer so that God's Spirit may flow like a river inside of him, which also flows within him so that he may carry out many ministry works.

In the Old Testament, baptism in the spirit occurred when the Israelites crossed the Jordan River into the Promised Land and passed through the Red Sea, symbolizing baptism and deliverance from the other nations.

"And the children of Israel went into the midst of the sea upon the dry ground: and the waters were a wall unto them on their right hand, and on their left." Exo. 14:22.

"And as they that bare the ark were come unto Jordan, and the feet of the priests that bare the ark were dipped in the brim of the water, for Jordan over floweth all his banks all the time of harvest, that the waters which came down from above stood and rose up upon an heap very far from that city Adam.

"That is beside Zaretan: and those that came down toward the sea of the plain, even the salt came sea, failed, and were cut off: and the people passed over right against Jericho." Jos. 3:15-16.

God divided the flood water in Jordan, just as he had divided the Red Sea. This miracle was visible evidence that God was with Joshua, just as he had been with Moses. The Jordan River was parted so that the Israelites could go through; God exercised His miraculous power again by parting the Jordan River for the Israelites to pass through.

This also symbolizes baptism in the Holy Spirit in the lives of the people of God in the present day. All Jesus Christ's believers were indwelled with the power of the Holy Spirit. God's Spirit is upon all children of God and those who believe in Him. The Spirit of God helps, controls, directs, and guides them. By this experiential demonstration of the Spirit of God's power, people's faith is strengthened. They were able to face the challenges of possessing the Promised Land.

Without such miraculous power of the Holy Spirit of God, they could not have taken the walled cities and advanced forward, in spite of the numerous oppositions that they faced when they arrived at their new land.

Today, God's Spirit continues to fight His believers' battles in all areas of our lives, when we are not even aware of his actions; the Spirit of God also testifies, "For ye have not received the spirit of bondage again fear; but ye have received the Spirit of adoption, whereby we cry, Abba, Father.

The Spirit itself beareth witness with our spirit, that we are the children of God." Rom. 8:15-16. The Holy Spirit imparts to us the confidence that through Christ and with Christ, we are now God's children. He makes real the truth that Christ loves us and that He lives for us in heaven as our mediator.

The Spirit also shows us that the Father loves us as His adopted children, no less than He loves His one and only Son. The Spirit creates in us the love and confidence by which we cry to Him as our Father with all of our problems.

The born again Christians are like water in the well, while those who are baptized in the Spirit receive the Spirit empowerment which is the Spirit water as a river. Baptism in the Spirit operates in believers' lives as a great manifestation of the presence of God, which empowers believers with the fullness of the power of God.

"But ye shall receive power, after that the Holy Ghost is come upon you: and ye shall be witnesses unto me both in Jerusalem, and in all Judea, and in Samaria, and unto the uttermost part of the earth." Acts 1:8.

Our Lord told the apostles on the day of His ascension, before He ascended into heaven, that they would receive power from above. The primary purpose of baptism in the spirit is to receive power in order to bear witness for Christ so that the lost will be won over to Him and taught to obey all that Christ has commanded.

It is most important for Jesus Christ to be known, love, praised, and made the Lord of God's chosen people. Power means more than strength or ability; it especially implies power in operation, in action, to do the Gospel's work. It also includes the authority to drive out evil spirits. Witnessing and anointing to heal the sick are the two essential signs accompanying the proclamation of God's kingdom.

It means the power to testify, to perform miracles in so many ways that unbelievers will know that Christ is the true Son of God. Baptism in the Holy Spirit is for the work of the ministry, the work of the gospel, witnessing, preaching, teaching, healing, and praying. It is given to those who believe and this power of the Holy Spirit is still available today to all believers who meet all of the requirements for receiving it. It was poured out on the day of Pentecost and it is still available to all believers today.

It is available to those who ask for it after they have been born again, abide in Christ, follow His commandments, and are obedient to the Spirit's control. Our Lord said, "If ye then, being evil, know how to give good gifts unto your children: how much more shall your heavenly Father give the Holy Spirit to them that ask him?" Luke 11:13.

Our Lord was not referring to the impartation of the Spirit, whose indwelling presence was given automatically to believers upon their conversion; rather, He was referring to the baptism in the Holy Spirit that He promised to all believers to whom he promised power from above.

The baptism in the Holy Spirit is a gift from God the Father through God the Son. "And, being assembled together with them, commanded them that they should not depart from Jerusalem, but wait for the promise of the Father, which, said he, ye have heard of me." Acts 1:4.

Christ reminded the disciples of the gift from the Father, which is the baptism in the Holy Spirit. The fulfillment of the promise was described as being filled with the Holy Spirit; therefore, being baptized in the Spirit and filled with the Spirit are, at times, used interchangeably.

This baptism in the Holy Spirit should not be identified with receiving the Holy Spirit upon regeneration. These are two distinct works of the Spirit, often separated by a period of time after the conversion of Jesus Christ's believers.

It is the grace of God not that we deserve it or are worthy of it. It is a blessing from the Lord for the work of the gospel. It has nothing to do with age, or with being a pastor, minister, or priest. It is the outpouring gift of God to believers, after they have been born again and are fully part of the body of Christ.

There is no other way to earn baptism in the Holy Spirit; God gives it when believers ask for it. Our Lord Jesus Christ sent the Holy Spirit to empower the entire body of Christ, in order for them to be able to carry out the work of the kingdom with the power of the Spirit and to proclaim the gospel of God boldly, clearly, confidently, and with great power.

The Church must not wait; they must carry out the work that Christ as assigned to them with the power of the Holy Spirit. The early Church concentrated on the power of the Spirit of God to complete this work we believers today must do the same.

We must do everything in accordance with the Spirit Power that God is sends to us for His glory and take the Gospel of God to the ends of the earth for Christ. The work of the ministry must be done with the Spirit Power of miracles, signs, and wonders. Our Lord said, "greater work than this shall you do. Stay in Jerusalem until you receive the power from on high." Baptism in the Holy Spirit is for all of Jesus Christ's believers. All Christians have the Spirit indwelling power active in their lives, as a well of water bubbling up for eternal life.

God the Father's will is for all believers to have the Spirit power flowing within them as river of water, the river of the living water, so that the Spirit of God will be able to exercise His power, exhibit His power, extend His grace in every detail, exhibit His infinite love, and manifest His power to flow through believers like a river to sinners, the lost, unbelievers, and all other people of different religions.

When the power of the Holy Spirit begins to flow with supernatural power, things will begin to happen in the world. The conversion of souls will begin to happen; every minute, everywhere, Christians will witness, the souls of unbelievers will be converted, the Gospel of God will be preached, and believers will be able to work as tent-makers or boldly witness to the lost and to sinners.

Believers will be able to serve the Lord with joy because they have the supernatural power of the Holy Spirit flowing within them, energizing them. All of Jesus Christ's believers must be baptized in the Holy Spirit in order to serve the Lord from this earth to heaven. "What are we waiting for?" He said, "Ask and you shall be given." Though all Christians are indwelled with the Holy Spirit, not all Christians are filled, directed, and empowered by the Holy Spirit.

The Holy Spirit is the source of overflowing life. "In the last day, that great day of the feast, Jesus stood and cried, saying, if any man thirst, let him come unto me, and drink. He that believeth on me, as the scripture hath said, out of his belly shall flow rivers of living water." John 7:37-38.

This means that when the gift of the Spirit is given to believers, they will experience Christ's overflowing life. The living water will flow out from deep, within the believer to others, with the healing message of Jesus Christ. If any man desires Spiritual blessings, Spiritual happiness, let him come to Christ. He will fill the thirsty souls that come to Him with the water of life.

4

The Spirit Power
at Pentecost

On the day of Pentecost, the power and the filling of the Holy Spirit became available to all who accepted Christ, which means all who had been born in the Spirit.

"Jesus answered and said unto him, Verily, verily I say unto thee, Except a man be born again, he cannot see the kingdom of God. Nicodemus said unto him, how can a man be born when he is old?

"Can he enter the second time into his mother's womb, and be born? Jesus answered, Verily, verily, I say unto thee, except a man be born of water and of the Spirit, he cannot enter into the kingdom of God. That which is born of the flesh is flesh, and that which is born of the Spirit is Spirit.

"Marvel not that I said unto thee, Ye must be born again. The wind bloweth where it listed, and thou hearest the sound thereof, but canst not tell whence it cometh, and whither it goeth: so is every one that is born of the Spirit." John 3:3-8.

Only believers can experience this power. Being filled by the Spirit is conditional, a believer may decide to be filled or not to be filled it depends and is based only on the believer's relationship with our Lord and Savior Christ.

Not all believers are filled with the Spirit. Our closeness to the Lord is measured by our filling with the Spirit, in order to see which one of the Holy Spirit's fruits we use every day, which one do we need to use more, and which one will change us completely to what God wants us to be in this world.

If there is any area in the believer's life where the fruit of the Spirit is not exercised, the believer must do all he or she can to make sure that the particular fruit is utilized: either by reading the Word of God or by consciously putting it into action.

Most believers want to know how can they be more filled with the Holy Spirit, but God has given them the fullness of his Spirit all they need to do is to use it and the only way that they will be able to use it is to stay in the Word of God, pray more and more, and put everything into his Holy hands.

When believers maintain an intimate, close, and pure relationship with the Lord they will automatically be empowered by the Holy Spirit. Everything they do through the power of the Holy Spirit will be manifest and they will see the glory of our Lord and Savior shining upon them in a way that has never occurred before in their lives as believers of Jesus Christ.

Believers must strengthen their relationship with the Lord in order to be empowered by the Spirit of God. Believers must ask for the presence of the Holy Spirit whenever they kneel down to pray; they must also ask for the Spirit of discernment in order to know the difference between the spirit of error and the spirit of truth.

They must ask for the full presence of the Holy Spirit. Once the Spirit fill us up, or, once we are filled by the Spirit and anointed, all we need to do is to ask and it shall be given, in accordance with our heavenly Father's Will.

Most of the time, the Holy Spirit speaks to us through the Word of God, through our heart, and through so many other means that we can only know or be aware of them through the Spirit of discernment.

By remaining within the Word of God and studying the Word of God, through worship, singing praises, and dancing, we will receive the Spirit's enablement, which will empower us and help us to resist temptation and any other obstacles that might try to overcome us.

Believers need to be conscious of the Holy Spirit at all times in order to grow in the Lord. "And we, who with unveiled faces all reflect the Lord's glory, are being transformed into his likeness with ever increasing glory, which comes from the Lord, who is the Spirit." 2 Cor. 3:18.

All believers, all Christians, as we experience Christ's closeness, love, righteousness, and power through prayer and the Holy Spirit, we are transformed into his likeness. "For God, who commanded, the light shine out of darkness, hath shined in our hearts, to give the light of the knowledge of the glory of God in the face of Jesus Christ." 2 Cor. 4:6.

The Scripture tells us that we are changed into the likeness or image of what we behold, look at, and think about. Right now, at the present time, the transformation is progressive and not yet complete. When Christ returns, we will see him face-to-face and our transformation will be complete.

Believers are the body of Christ, which means that we are His Church on this earth. The Holy Spirit equips and enables us to bear witness to the people of the world, through the gifts of the Spirit; when we are filled with the Spirit we produce the fruit of the Spirit.

The Spirit manifests itself in our life to benefit individual believers as one Church, one body, one baptism, and one Lord. In this way, every believer will receive the gift of the Holy Spirit and the entire body of Christ will be complete in him and be able to benefit from the blessing that comes every day to the entire body of Christ—His Church on earth.

When we come to Christ, we receive power because God's Holy Spirit indwells us. God empowers us to take the Gospel of Jesus Christ to the ends of the earth. The entire body of Christ is commissioned we must fulfill Christ's great commission.

The closer we get to the image of Christ through the transforming power of the Holy Spirit, the more we will be able to carry out this great commission. "And he that searcheth the hearts knoweth what is the mind of the Spirit, because he maketh intercession for us with groanings which cannot be uttered." Rom. 8:27.

The Spirit of Jesus Christ searches our hearts and intercedes according to the will of God; the will of God is to bear witness to sinners, the lost, and unbelievers. Not all believers allow the Holy Spirit to indwell them or affect their lives in order to live within God's moral directives through the indwelling of the Holy Spirit.

For example, one of God's moral directives says, "do not commit adultery." Because of their immoral lifestyle, they do not want to be indwelled by the Holy Spirit. Some believers continue to live in sin, struggling to overcome temptation on their own.

Their lives are not, and will not, be fulfilled without the Holy Spirit; they will not experience the joy of the living heart that the Holy Spirit produced and provided to believers.

The main reason believers must be filled with the spirit is to be able to engage in all spiritual activities, all of the Holy Spirit's activities in the world. The second reason for believers be filled with the Holy Spirit is to be able to live in heaven from earth by setting their minds on heavenly things.

When believers are filled with the Holy Spirit, they will have a sense of the love, joy, and peace that the Holy Spirit produces in the lives of the believer. A spirit-filled Christian who possesses all the fruits of the Spirit will be different from other Christians who are not possessed with the fruits of the Holy Spirit.

When Christians are filled with the Spirit, or when the Holy Spirit lives inside or indwells Christians, the Spirit will guide the actions and desires of the believer, or Christians.

The Spirit empowers believers to step outside of their comfort zone to do supernatural and extraordinary things through their faith in God, which will make everyone, or the world, be completely surprised or amazed.

Believers will have the mind of Christ and a sense of partnership with Christ in His work of redemption and in the work of the kingdom, as well as in many of God's plans concerning His creations and His created beings.

The inner power of the Holy Spirit has power over the hearts of men and women. No minister or pastor can win the hearts of men and women by himself. A pastor can win the ears of people and make them listen;

he can win their eyes and cause them to look at him; and, he can win their attention.

Yet, their hearts are very slippery, like a fish that all Gospel fishermen find difficult to hold on to—sometimes almost pulling it out of the water, but it slips between their fingers, and evades capture. Many ministers and pastors have been disappointed in this endeavor.

They wonder why that particular person did not come forward and give their life to Christ after preaching. They have been terribly disappointed. They do not know whether to study more or go through the scripture more. They've wondered where they went wrong, what they should have said and did not say, and approach they have missed in their preaching.

Then they will come to the realization and remember that the Word of God says, "Not by might nor by power, but by my Spirit says the Lord Almighty." Zec. 4:6. The Holy Spirit is the only one who has the power to change the heart or power over the hearts of men and women, young or old.

A minister cannot convert the soul. A minister cannot touch the heart or break through to the hearts of men, for it is difficult. A minister cannot reach the soul of a human being. Yet, the Holy Spirit can change the heart of human being in a minute, turning the heart of stone into a heart of flesh. The Holy Spirit will wash a sinner with the precious blood of Jesus and the person will become new. The Holy Spirit can touch the hearts of men and women and make them perform the impossible in their lives.

He can turn the heart of an atheist non-believer who says there is no God to a preacher of the Word of God. The Holy Spirit can turn the heart of the pagan idol-worshiper to begin teaching and proclaiming the Gospel of God all over the earth.

There is no limit to what the Spirit of God can do in the lives of men and women on this earth. The Holy Spirit has power over the heart, soul, and body. Another inner spiritual power of the Holy Spirit is the will of men and women, which has been called the freewill.

Freewill made Adam and Eve fall in the Garden of Eden. Freewill also made a third of the angels in heaven fall into Hell or the abyss. Freewill can be used to do evil or to do good, to sin or not to sin.

"One man can bring a horse to the water, but hundred men cannot make him to drink." Proverb of John Haywood 1546. No man has power over his brother or fellow creature's will, but the Spirit of God does.

The Holy Spirit will make an unwilling sinner willing to take the Gospel or to learn more and more about the Gospel and make him run to the cross at the feet of Jesus Christ.

The Holy Spirit will make people who have laughed at Jesus and Christians to ask Christ for mercy. The unbeliever will be willing to believe through the power of the Holy Spirit. The unbeliever will gladly rejoice at the sound of the name of Jesus, through the powers of the Holy Spirit.

He is very delighted to obey God's commandments to do God's Word in every area of his life. The Holy Spirit of God is the only one that has the power to change the will of men and women, in order to turn them from hatred to love, from evil to good.

Another inner spiritual war is thought, which we have called imagination, which is difficult to control. The imagination sometimes goes through a power struggle with God. It is very hard to manage.

It can raise people up and it can bring them down. The Holy Spirit is the one who has power over our thought and everything we could imagine. The Holy Spirit's power clears all unnecessary thoughts, all of our imagination that come to us unawares, which we cannot control sometimes.

We always cry out to God to help us. The Holy Spirit of God is the only one who can conquer our imagination, and He will continue to do so throughout eternity. The Holy Spirit works on the imagination here on earth to control and suppress all of the thoughts that plague every human being.

The future work of the Holy Spirit is to perfect us to holiness. There are two kinds of perfection in the lives of Christians. Christians need perfection of justification through faith in the person of Jesus Christ, and, additionally, perfection of sanctification, which is the work of the Holy Spirit in the lives of believers.

Many people are still full of sin and their lives are of a sinful nature. Many Christians are not complete in Christ—their heart is particularly impure, they lust in all kinds of sexual immoralities, and they have greed and evil thoughts.

We have to rejoice because Christ is our hope of the glory of the day, that will come after not very long, when God will complete what He started in the lives of men and women. He will present believers as a perfect bride to the bridegroom Jesus, perfect in the Spirit with no blemishes or spots, presented at the feet of God without impurities or contamination.

Believers will be able to say on that great day that the glorious day is our God. We have been cleansed through the blood of Jesus; through the work of the Holy Spirit we are clean. Believers must praise the power of the Holy Spirit for making us fit to stand before the throne of grace, before our Father in heaven through the love and mercy of God.

The power of the Holy Spirit will continue to pour out to unbelievers and sinners. The Holy Spirit will continue to be poured out in a wonderful way; it will go everywhere to increase knowledge and understanding of the Lord on earth, just as water fills the sea.

Another future work of the Holy Spirit that will become manifest is the resurrection of all Christians.

The resurrection of the dead, using the same power that raised Jesus Christ from the dead, will cause mortal bodies to come to life. The power of the resurrection is the greatest work of the Holy Spirit. The Bible says, "Yes, in a moment at the twinkling of an eye, at the last trumpet the dead will be raised." 2 Thes. 4:16-17.

They are alive—see them scattered. Bones comes to their bones see their bare skeletons. Flesh comes onto them see them still and lifeless, coming from the four corners of the earth when the wind of the Holy Spirit comes. They live, and they stand up on their feet, a very great army of saints.

The Holy Spirit is very powerful. Believers must ask for the power of the Holy Spirit for protection he is omnipotent and all powerful. God's kingdom will come on earth, as it is written in heaven. His will, will be done on earth as it is set up in heaven.

People will see miraculous holiness, extraordinary power of prayer, real communion with God, free religion, and the spreading of the doctrines of the cross. Everyone will see that, truly, the Holy Spirit is poured out like water, just as rain descends from heaven.

The Holy Spirit of God will do all these things and more with his power. Believers need the power of the Holy Spirit to overcome our enemies, and to conquer the power of darkness and evil in our life. The power of the Holy Spirit is our power; the power of the Holy Spirit is our strength. Believers must not doubt the power of the Holy Spirit in their lives. The answers to our prayers might be delayed, yet we must wait for Him.

There is power in the Holy Spirit that conquers violence and all spiritual wickedness. The power of the Holy Spirit will make you strong enough to do the impossible; it will take care of all of the flocks, the lost, and the needy.

The Holy Spirit will continue to be poured out from above until the thirsty water is covered with springs of water and the desert blossom becomes like roses. The power of the Holy Spirit is able to do so many things that we cannot even imagine.

See the power of the Holy Spirit in the missions' field. See it in the tracts given on the side of the street, bringing sinners to Christ in a simple way, by reading the two lines of the tracts. The power of the Holy Spirit bears witness to Christian outreaching.

The power of the Holy Spirit is a great help to us in all the areas of our lives. Through the power of the Holy Spirit, there is hope for the chief of sinners; the power of the Holy Spirit can save you and your entire household.

The power of the Holy Spirit is able to break your rock hard heart—your eyes will run with tears even though they were rocks before. The power of the Holy Spirit changes the hearts of sinners and immediately makes you born again, blesses you with a new spirit, a new heart, and a new name and, moreover, makes you a child of God.

"Behold, what manner of love the father has bestowed upon us that we should be called the sons of God there the world knows us not, because it knew him not." 1 John 3:1.

To save a sinner in Christ, there is more than enough power. There is unlimited power in the Holy Spirit. Bring those who are weak and strong to Christ—the power of the Holy Spirit will overpower your free-will to make you yearn and be thirsty for Jesus and His righteousness.

All believers in Christ must put their trust in the power of the Holy Spirit and rest and rejoice in the blood of Jesus who can make their souls safe, now and for eternity. The Holy Spirit united us with Christ at the moment of our conversion.

Through his power, he causes us to believe in the gospel. All of us are able to experience the life-changing power of the Holy Spirit because the changing power of the Holy Spirit has the ability to be present everywhere, in every place, at the same time.

"Where can I go from your spirit? Where can I flee from your presence." Psl. 139:7. When Jesus ascended to heaven, He promised that He would always be with us. And so He is, through the power of the Holy Spirit. Jesus and the Father dwell in us, as does the Holy Spirit.

The Holy Spirit will change our lives if we so permit Him. But remember, apart from Jesus we will never experience the fullness of life that God promises.

If you have the Spirit without the Word, you will blow up; if you have the Word without the Spirit, you will dry up; but, if you have both the Word and the Spirit, you will grow up. You will be refreshed and continue to grow.

5

Inner Spiritual Power
of the Holy Spirit

Another inner spiritual power of the Holy Spirit is the will of men and women, which has been called the Freewill. Freewill made Adam and Eve fall in the Garden of Eden.

Freewill also made a third of the angels in heaven fall into Hell or the Abyss. Freewill can be used to do evil or to do good, to sin or not to sin. No man has power over his brother or fellow creature's will, but the Spirit of God does.

The Holy Spirit will make an unwilling sinner willing to take the Gospel or to learn more and more about the Gospel and make him run to the cross at the feet of Christ. The Holy Spirit will make people who have laughed at Jesus and Christians to ask Christ for mercy.

The unbeliever will be willing to believe through the power of the Holy Spirit. The unbeliever will gladly rejoice at the sound of the name of Jesus through the power of the Holy Spirit. He is very, very delighted to obey God's commandments and read God's Word.

He is ready to be the doer of God's Word in every area of his life. The Holy Spirit of God is the only one who has the power to change the will of men and women.

Many Christian are not complete in Christ their hearts are partially impure, they lust in all kinds of sexual immoralities, they exercise greed and evil thoughts. We have to rejoice because Christ is our hope of the glory.

A day will come it will not be long, that God will complete what He started in the lives of men and women. He will present believers as a perfect bride to the bridegroom Jesus, perfect in the Spirit with no blemishes or spots, presented at the feet of God without impurities or contamination.

Believers will be able to say on that great day that glory is our God. We have been cleansed through the blood of Jesus; through the work of the Holy Spirit we are clean.

Believers must praise the power of the Holy Spirit for making us fit to stand before the throne of Grace, before our Father in heaven through the love and mercy of God. The power of the Holy Spirit will continue to pour out to unbelievers and sinners. The Holy Spirit will continue to pour out again in a wonderful way that will go everywhere to increase knowledge and understanding of the Lord on earth, just as water fills the sea.

6

The Introduction of the Fruit of the Spirit

The Fruit of the Spirit is: love, joy, peace, patience, kindness, goodness, faithfulness, gentleness, self- control, obedience, meekness, humbleness, truth, righteousness, forgiveness, longsuffering, forbearance, temperance, and self-esteem.

Of all of the fruits of the Spirit, Apostle Paul made nine of them the visible attributes of true Christian life, according to Gal. 5:22. These fruits of the Spirit characterize all who are truly walking in the power of the Holy Spirit.

These are the fruits that all Christians should be producing in a new life with Jesus Christ our Lord and Savior. They are a physical manifestation of a Christian's transformed life. "Being filled with all unrighteousness, fornication, wickedness, covetousness, maliciousness; full of envy, murder, debate, deceit, malignity; whisperers. Backbiters, haters of God, spiteful, proud, boasters, inventors of evil things disobedient to parents. Without understanding, covenant breakers, without natural affection implacable, unmerciful." Rom. 1:29-31.

"Let us walk honestly, as in the day; not in rioting and drunkenness, not in chambering and wantonness, not in strife and envying." Rom. 13:13.

"But brother goeth to law with brother and that before the unbelievers. Now therefore there is utterly a fault among you, because ye go to law one with another. Why do ye not rather take wrong?

Why do ye not rather suffer yourselves to be defrauded? and that your brethren. Know ye not that the unrighteous shall not inherit the kingdom of God? Be not deceived: neither fornicators, nor idolaters, nor adulterers, nor effeminate, nor abusers of themselves with mankind.

Nor thieves, nor covetous, nor drunkards, nor revilers, nor extortioners, shall inherit the kingdom of God." 1 Cor. 6:6-10.

"For I fear, lest when I come, I shall not find you such as I would, and that I shall be found unto you such as you would not: lest there be debates, envying, wraths, strifes, back-biting, whisperings, swellings, tumults."

2 Cor. 12:20. Wicked people will not inherit the kingdom of God. For example, some Corinthians, during the time of Apostle Paul, believed that they could

end their relationship and fellowship with Christ, live immoral and unjust lives, and that their salvation and inheritance in God's kingdom would still be secured.

Paul made clear to them that spiritual death is the consequence of continuously sinning against God. The same applies to all Believers in Christ today nothing has changed. This direct warning applies to the entire Christian community, wherever they may be all over the world. Believers must live a clean pure life.

"Now the works of the flesh are manifest, which are these; Adultery, fornication, uncleanness, lasciviousness. Idolatry, witchcraft, hated, variance, emulations, wrath, strife seditions, heresies, envying, murders, drunkenness. I tell you before as I have also told you in time past, that they which do such things shall not inherit the kingdom of God." Gal. 5:19-21.

Paul made these traits clear and maintained that it is impossible to inherit the kingdom of God by observing the law, as well as that it is impossible to close the door to the kingdom of heaven because one engages in the immoral and evil practices that are going on in the world. "But the fruit of the spirit is love, joy peace, longsuffering, gentleness, goodness, faith. Meekness, temperance, against such there is no law." Gal. 5:22-23.

A true believer of Jesus Christ must produce fruit for righteousness and be obedient to the word and the commandment of God through the Power of the Holy Spirit that indwells us.

"Finally, brethren, whatsoever things are true, whatsoever things are honest, whatsoever things are just, whatsoever things are pure, whatsoever things are lovely, whatsoever things are good report, if there be any virtue, and if there be any praise, think on these things." Php. 4:8.

7

The Fruit of the Spirit: LOVE

"Though I speak with the tongues of men and of angels, and have not charity, I am become as sounding brass, or a tinkling cymbal. And now abideth faith, hope, and charity, these three; but the greatest of these is charity." 1 Cor. 13:1, 13.

These two verses reveal the biblical meaning of Love's supreme importance to life. Apostle Paul, in his letter to the Corinthian Church, concluded that love will never end; love will always be of use.

The gift we receive from God is bestowed with the love of God. God's gifts of the fruit of the Holy Spirit are given with power to enhance believers' ability to serve God in various areas of the Church. The need for love is never-ending; it never becomes absolute.

God wants us to use love on every occasion, everywhere. Love is something we grow in. It must be perfected. God gave us love; He showers His love upon us, as we need it every day. We must see ourselves as mature believers of Jesus Christ. A time is coming when love will be perfected; we will have abundant love for one another as children of God. Believers must pursue love as long as we are still in the flesh. The love of

God comes through the actions of God through His Spirit, something supernatural. "And hope maketh not ashamed; because the love of God is shed abroad in our hearts by the Holy Ghost which is given unto us." Rom. 5:5.

Christians experience the love of God. God's love for believers is in their hearts through the Holy Spirit, especially in times of trouble. The Spirit of God continues to flood our hearts with the love of God and the full presence of God in order to sustain us through any problems and circumstances.

God is the source of love; His love abides in us forever. Apostle John said, "Beloved, let us love one another: for love is of God; and every one that loveth is born of God, and knoweth God. He that loveth not knoweth not God; for God is love.

"In this was manifested the love of God toward us, and sent His Son to be the propitiation for our sins. Beloved, if God so loved us, we ought also to love one another. No man hath seen God at any time. If we love one another, God dwell in us, and His love perfected in us." 1 John 4:7-12.

Love is an aspect of the fruit of the Holy Spirit and the evidence of new birth. It is also something that we are responsible for developing as believers in Jesus Christ. Apostle John exhorts us to love one another; he wants us to be concerned with them and look out for the welfare of the sick and the needy among us.

If we are pursuing a Christ-like character, these verses are very important to all believers in Jesus Christ because they tell us so much about God and our responsibilities. This verse explains to us that love is of God, that He is the source of love.

Apostle John explained that the true love of God normally becomes a part of man's nature. God is a living, dynamic, and powerful force in our lives. Every activity of God is love. Love can be seen in every activity of God. God creates the universe with love; God rules all the earth in love.

God judges all the nations of the earth in love. Everything that God does expresses His nature. God and His nature are manifested by everything that He does. By God's love, He was revealed and known. Love reveals God to man.

The existence of life in others besides Him is an act of love. God's love is revealed in His providence and care for His creations. God's love is the evidence of redemption and our hope for eternal life. God made us in His own image and likeness.

"But the hour cometh, and now is, when the true worshippers shall worship the Father in spirit and in truth: for the Father seeketh such to worship him. God is a Spirit: and they that worship Him must worship Him in spirit and in truth." John 4:23-24.

Our Lord teaches that true worship must come to God with complete sincerity and with a spirit that is directed by the life and activity of the Holy Spirit. Therefore, our worship must take place according to the truth of the Father that is revealed in the Son and received through the Spirit.

Jesus explained to the people of His days that those who worship and have set aside the truth of the doctrine of the Word of God have also set aside the only foundation for true worship. This means that we cannot express true love without the power of the Spirit of God that indwells all believers.

We cannot be what God wants us to be until we have the fruit of love that the Holy Spirit provides. All believers must love with the love of God in their lives. Jesus Christ teaches that, "God is a Spirit." "In Spirit" means the level at which true worship occurs.

Believers must come to God with complete sincerity and with a Spirit that is directed by the life and activities of the Holy Spirit. Truth is a characteristic of God incarnate in Christ, intrinsic to the Holy Spirit, and at the heart of the Gospel. Therefore, worship must take place in accordance with the truth of the Father that is revealed in the Son and received through the Holy Spirit.

Sacrifice is another vital part of God's love. God's love was manifest in His Son and is perfected in His people. God's love is perfected in the lives of all his children. We believers reproduce God's love among ourselves and the love of God flows through us to non-believers.

God is concerned about our blessing as well as about our perfection of his love in the lives of the saints of God. We can love according to God's love when we get closer to Him and do what is pleasing in His eyes. Believers must learn how to love God; we must follow his commandments, and maintain fellowship and an intimate relationship with him. God is love.

He forgives us for all of our trespasses and sin through His Son Jesus Christ, and He is the sustainer of the universe and everything that is in it. The Bible says, "Whosoever believeth that Jesus is the Christ is born of God; and everyone that loveth Him that begat loveth him also that is begotten of him.

"By this we know that we love the children of God, when we love God, and keep His commandments. For this is the love of God, that we keep his command-ments: and His commandments are not grievous." 1 John 5:1-3.

Genuine faith will express itself in gratitude to and for the love of the Father and Jesus Christ His Son.

Faith and love are inseparable, for when we are born of God, the Holy Spirit pours the love of God into our hearts. Love for others is the second greatest commandment for genuine Christians. Love is accompanied by love for God. Our Lord Jesus Christ stated that we should love the Lord our God and love our neighbor.

All believers must be obedient to Christ's commandments. The commandments of God are clean. The basic elements of love include what direction actions should take for us to show love. This means that obedience to God is the only means of proving our love to Him.

Obedience constitutes action submitting to God's commandments, principles revealed in His word, and examples of God or the godly. We must know that this is where godly love is in human beings. Obeying God's commands is love because God is love; His very nature is Love. It is impossible for Him not to love us.

He loved us before the foundation of the world. He gives us commandments in love, which will produce right and good results. Our Lord said, "If you love me, keep my commandments." John 14:15.

Keeping God's commandments is how we express our love for him. "If ye keep my commandments, ye shall abide in my love, even as I have kept my Father's commandments, and abide in His love." John 15:10.

Jesus Christ calls us to a life of holy intimacy and personal devotion to Him. This is possible because of

God's love for us, which He has poured into our hearts through the Holy Spirit. God the Father Almighty demonstrated His great love through Christ's death and resurrection, while we were still sinners.

We must remain in Jesus' love by pursuing spiritual intimacy and communion with Him, and by obeying His commandments just as He came to this world and obeyed His Father's commandments throughout His earthly ministry. By this we know that we know Him if we keep His commandments.

Love is the fruit, the product of the Spirit, which is now developing in our lives. The Holy Spirit guides believers and leads them to the truth. It is the responsibility of the believer to follow the Spirit's guidance and to obey the truths of God who created us in His own image.

Obedience to His commandments is godly love; the fruit of the Spirit empowers believers with the goodness of the Almighty Creator. Each aspect of the fruit listed here is simply a reflection of God's character, reproduced in us by His Spirit. "By this shall all men know that ye are my disciples, if ye have love for one another." John 13:35.

Christ is telling us that love must be the distinguishing mark of His disciples and of all believers—love that is self-giving and sacrificial, and that seeks good for others. This means that the relationship among all believers must be characterized by devotion and concern, sacrificially seeking the highest good of their brothers and sisters in Christ.

Christians must be sensitive to each other's feelings and reputation, and sometimes deny themselves in order to help other believers in Christ. The Holy Spirit has poured out God's love in our hearts. "And hope maketh not ashamed; because the love of God is shed abroad in our hearts by the Holy Ghost which is given unto us." Rom. 5:5.

"He that loveth not knoweth not God; for God is love." 1 John 4:8. Love is the foundation of His character. Apostle

Paul said, "Charity suffereth long, and is kind; charity envieth not; charity vaunteth not itself, is not puffed up, doth not behave itself unseemly, seeketh not her own, is not easily provoked, thinketh no evil." 1 Cor. 13:4-5.

This shows that every phase of the fruit of the Spirit is merely a specific expression of godly love. Love is an activity and manner, not just inner feelings or motivation. The various phases of love included here characterize God the Father, the Son and the Holy Spirit.

Every believer must seek to grow in this model of love. Jesus teaches us that we should not only love our friends and relatives, but we must also love our enemies. Our Lord again emphasizes our need for extra help from God the Holy Spirit. Our Lord said that we should not return evil for evil, but rather return evil with good.

Love expresses a desire that everyone in the universe holds. People sometimes think about love or see it as a sense of regard, a strong desire, to be satisfied by caring for one another. People of this earth express their love in so many ways that other people cannot imagine.

While a measure of caring for one another can be true love, caring by itself is not love. "And now abideth faith, hope, charity, these three; but the greatest of these is charity." 1 Cor. 13:13.

This verse reveals love's supreme value of love, faith, hope, prophecy, sacrifice, knowledge, and the gift of speaking in tongues. God gave believers all these gifts in order to serve Him in all areas of Church ministries.

Believers received the gifts of God with the Holy Spirit's power to enhance us in order to function in the Church's ministries and to be able to live fruitful lives as Christians. If any fruits of the Spirit are not use with love, this will not be what God wants for believers.

"Knowledge puffeth up, but charity edifieth means love builds up." Paul explained to believers that pride has the power to ruin the knowledge of a child of God. Our knowledge could be corrupted if the believer does not apply it with love. This is the main reason why Paul compares the gift of God with love to inform us of and to strongly emphasize the importance of love. Love is more important and is very valuable in the lives of the children of God.

If any believer does not have love, that person is not complete in Christ. The love of God always comes through the power of God in the Holy Spirit. Love is the fulfillment of the law.

Paul emphasizes love by telling us that we should submit to and honor government as God's chosen people managing human affairs. All Christians must follow government rules and regulations.

Love can motivate us to follow the law of the country we live in, which shows God's commandment that says if a believer exercises God's love in his or her life, he will also follow the ten commandments without breaking them.

Love motivates and its presence is needed in all we do in our daily lives, whether we are believers or non-believers. Another important aspect of love appears in our community and in our Church. The fruit of the Spirit should be known, revered, and manifested in the lives of all Christians.

This fruit characterizes all who truly walk in the Holy Spirit; these are the fruits that all Christians should produce in their new lives with Jesus Christ. Believers must be able to understand each of the fruits of the Spirit. "And we have known and believed the love that God hath to us. God is love; and he that dwelleth in love dwelleth in God, and God in him." 1 John 4:16.

God is love. Whoever lives in love lives in God and God in him, so we know and rely on the love God has for us. Love is through Jesus Christ. Our greatest goal is to live and do all things in love, to show love wherever we are, in whatever we are doing, and to do so with the love of God that he has shed in our hearts.

Love is the act of applying love everywhere, in every place, in everything, at all times, every hour, every minute and every moment. 1 Cor. 13:4-8. The fruit of the Spirit is very important for all Christians, whether infants in Christ or Christians with the solid food of the Word of God.

We are all in need of the fruit of the Spirit. Love is the first fruit of the Spirit, for a very good reason, because it was out of the love of God that man was created. God created human beings in His own image and He continually reaches out to human beings despite our behavior, as we are continuously running away from Him.

God's love for us made Him sacrifice His only begotten Son in order to save us from our Sin. Jesus Christ came to this world to save the sinners, the lost, the unbelievers, and the idol-worshipers. Christ preached the Gospel of God for good three years out of His love for us.

Christ shows His love to us when he was about to ascend to heaven, by giving a great commission to all of the apostles and believers after them, to "Go ye and preach, teach the Gospel in all the nations so that human beings will be saved from their past, present, and future sins."

This fruit of the Spirit's love comes in so many forms; the fruit of the Spirit's love is unconditional love. It is the love of a mother and child, where the mother has given her life in order to save the life of her baby. This is the reason it is listed first.

This is why Apostle Paul emphasizes that love is very important—it is the completeness, permanence, and supremacy over all mechanisms of the sustainer of human life. "I am the true vine, and my Father is the husbandman." John 15:1.

Here, Our Lord Jesus describes Himself as the true vine and His disciples and all believers as the branches. Our main goal is to remain attached to Him as the source of our life in order to produce fruit. God the Father is the gardener who takes care of the branches in order that they may bear fruit and more fruit.

God expects all believers to bear fruit. Our Lord Jesus stated, "Herein is my Father glorified, that ye bear much fruit; so shall ye be my disciples." John 15: 8. All Christians must exhibit the likeness of Christ to the world; we must let our light shine in order to glorify our Father in heaven. We imitate

Christ everywhere we are and prove that we are part of His body. He mentions fruit with regard to His commandments. "Ye have not chosen me. But I have chosen you and ordained you, that ye should go and bring forth fruit, and that your fruit should remain: that whatsoever ye shall ask of the Father in my name, He may give it you." John 15:16.

Christ made it clear that He was the one who chose every believer for salvation and eternal life. He chose us for discipleship and fruitfulness as missionaries and pastors, and for ordaining ministers and teachers of the Word of God. He chose for all Christians to go into the world to bear fruit.

To bear the fruits of Love, Joy, Peace, etc., and for doing our best to convert souls into His Holy hands. This instruction of our Lord shows clearly that a believer must live the life of a fruit-bearer.

Bearing fruit is generalized, clear, and precise; bearing fruit includes everything produced as a result of their labors of publicly preaching the Gospel, their service to the Church in pasturing, in all their ministry work, and their personal triumphs and growth in God's image.

The fruits of the Spirit are produced by the action of the Holy Spirit in us. "But if ye be led of the Spirit, ye are not under the law." Rom. 8:14. Not all believers in Jesus Christ are under the law because they are led by the Spirit of God.

To be led by the Spirit means to be lifted above the flesh and to be occupied with the Lord. When the Spirit of God fills us, we have no room to think of the law of the flesh. The Spirit of God will not lead believers in Christ to look at the law of the flesh; He will point believers to Christ as the only ground of acceptance before God.

Being led by the Spirit is a characteristic of all Christians. The Spirit of Christ indwelling us will resist the motion and any thought of evil in the heart of the believer. "Howbeit when he, the Spirit of truth, is come, he will guide you into all truth: for he shall not speak of himself; but whatsoever he shall hear, that shall he speak: and he will shew you things to come." John 16:13.

Our Lord says, however, when it, the Spirit of Truth, has come, It will guide you into all truth, for it will not speak on its own authority. Rather, whatever it hears, it will speak and it will tell you things to come.

The Holy Spirit allows us to choose voluntarily and consciously to submit to the Word of God. The power of God the Holy Spirit is described generally as the Power of God, which is correct, but power comes in a number of forms.

God loves us, Jesus Christ is the Word of God, and the Bible is the written revelation of God that was written because God is concerned about our minds and what we put in our minds, because whatever goes into our minds produces the fruit of our lives.

"And you hath he quickened, who were dead in trespasses and sins; Wherein time past ye walked according to the course of this world, according to the prince of the power of the air, the spirit that now worketh in the children of disobedience: Among whom also we all had our conversation in times past in the lusts of our flesh, fulfilling the desires of the flesh and of the mind; and were by nature the children of wrath, even as others." Eph. 2:1-3.

He made us alive. We were dead in our trespasses and sins, in which we walked according to the course of this world and according to the prince of the power of the air, the spirit who drives the sons and daughters to waywardness, where we once conducted ourselves in the lust of flesh, fulfilling the desires of the flesh and of the mind, doing things not approved of by God.

This is the reason that, after our conversion, God the Holy Spirit indwelled us and planted the fruit of the Spirit of God in us. "Now we have received, not the Spirit of the world, but the Spirit which is of God; that we might know the things that have been freely given to us by God." 1 Cor. 2:12.

Christ's blood enables us to have access to a new and infinitely larger and more beautiful life, beyond what we can imagine. We now possess good fruit in our minds and produce the fruit of the Spirit of God. We became a Spirit-filled believer.

"These things we also speak, not, in words which man's wisdom teaches but which the Holy Spirit teaches, comparing Spiritual things with spiritual but the natural man does not receive the things of the

Spirit of God, for they are foolishness to him; nor can he know them, because they are spiritually discerned." 1 Cor. 2: 13-14.

Love is one of the most important and fundamental concepts in the New Testament; love is a divine attribute. "For God so love the world." John 3:16. "We know love by this that He laid down His life for us." John 13:35.

This is best expressed by Christians' love within the body of Christ. The last aspect of God's love mentioned is a very important one of the Christian experience.

"Beloved, let us love one another, for love is from God; and everyone who loves is born of God and knows God. The one who does not love does not know God, for God is love." John 4:7-8.

Covenant love means the love of God that stands behind, stands in, and stands through His redemption, the redemptive work of Jesus Christ. It is a love that was born in the heart of God for lost humanity, and revealed to humanity in the redemptive work of Christ throughout the history of the universe.

It is God's love that sends Jesus into the world as an offering for our sins, a love incarnated in His Son Jesus Christ, and a love that is also incarnated in the lives of Christ's disciples and all believers in Christ until the end of ages.

All Christians are called to model and manifest Christ's love in their lives and to walk in love as he walked in their lives; believers must transfer the love of Christ in them to non- believers around them. Our Lord said, "Let your light so shine before men, that they may see your good works, and glorify your Father which is in heaven." Matt. 5:16.

Believers must love as Christ loves, they must be givers, giving to those who are in need and those who ask for help from them. "For God so loved the world that he gave his only begotten Son, that whosoever believeth in him should not perish, but have everlasting life." Rom. 8:16.

This verse reveals the heart and purpose of God. God's love is so big that it embraces all people on earth. God gave His son as an offering for sin on the cross. This atonement proceeds from the loving heart of God.

It was not something that anyone could force on anybody else. There are three aspects of believing in the Gospel of God. This includes the sure conviction that Jesus Christ is the Son of God and the only Savior for lost humanity.

Surrender to His lordship and fellowship with a heart obedient to Christ and with full assurance of trust in the Lord Jesus Christ. He is both able and willing to bring you to salvation and to fellowship with God the Father in heaven.

This love was manifested in Jesus when He gave, "And walk in love, as Christ also hath loved us, and hath given Himself for us, as an offering and a sacrifice to God a sweet smelling savor." Eph. 5:2.

This is the love of self-giving. It is a mysterious incarnation that affirms that God, who gave His Son, is also God who gave Himself. "To wit, that God was in Christ, reconciling the world unto himself, not imputing their trespasses unto them; and hath committed unto us the word of reconciliation." 2 Cor. 5:19.

Reconciliation is one important aspect of Christ's work of redemption the restoration of the sinner to fellowship with God the Father. Through Christ's atoning death, God has removed the barrier of sin and has opened a way for the sinner to return to fellowship with Him.

Reconciliation becomes effective for each believer through his or her personal confession of sins, repentance, and faith in Christ. Christ models the same self-given love through His crucifixion, His death on the cross.

Jesus Christ's sacrificial love was not only in the Old Testament as atonement, but in the sense of giving Himself for the life of people in the world. "Greater love hath no man than this that man lay down his life for his friends." John 15:13.

God's love is an intimate love; believers maintain personal and intimate love with God through the power of the indwelling of the Holy Spirit. Christ showed intimate love during His earthly ministry. He visits Mary and Martha and ministered to them in their home. Another aspect of the love of God is Jesus' unconditional love for believers all over the world. God's love stands steadfast, "We love Him because he love us first." John 4:19.

"But God commendeth His own love towards us, in that while we were yet sinners, Christ died for us." Rom. 5:8. This type of love involves complete acceptance of Christ. It also involves unlimited forgiveness, just as Christ forgave our sins. "Forbearing one another and forgiving one another, if any man has a quarrel against any: even as Christ forgave you, so also do ye." Col. 3:13.

The example of Christ's unlimited forgiveness was heard on the cross when He said, "Father, forgive them; for they know not what they do." Luke 23:34. Our Lord's first word on the cross was forgiving this shows His unlimited love for human beings and all His creations.

Believers must love as God loves, meaning loving vulnerably, unselfishly, and intimately, and having unconditional love for others. It poses the risk of being exploited, taking advantage of oneself, misunderstanding, and abuse.

It is a love that exposes the believer continuously to rejection, hurt, and persecution. Jesus Christ was rejected by people of His days, like the Pharisees, Sadducees, and all other people including some women when He was on the cross. "He came unto His own, and His own received Him not." John 1:11.

He was even misunderstood by his mother, brother, sister, and friends. The light of Christ shines in an evil and sinful world. The majority of the people in the world do not accept the life and light of Jesus.

Christ illuminates all who hear His Gospel by imparting a measure of grace and understanding, so that they may freely choose to accept or reject the Gospel, in order for them to be saved.

The people of the world means unbelievers who will never recognize Jesus they will remain as enemies of Christ and His gospel until the end of the age when Christ returns. Jesus Christ's love is enduring and everlasting.

God's love is steadfast and enduring for His children; God's love followed the Israelites from the Old Testament through the wilderness for forty years in the wilderness. "I have spread out my hands all the day unto a rebellious people, which walketh in a way that was not good, after their own thoughts." Isa. 65:2.

God responds to the prophet Isaiah's prayer by describing His continuous appeal to the rebellious nation to return to Him. God tells them to repent; otherwise, He will repay them with His judgment. God the Father transferred the same love to Jesus. Today, Jesus Christ's love continues in our lives and He continues to call us to repent and come back to the Father.

"Looking unto Jesus the author and finisher of our faith; who for the joy that was set before him endured the cross, despising the shame, and is set down at the right hand of the throne of God." Heb. 12:2.

The goal of believers' is faith; we should look to Jesus, focus all of our attention on Him, trust Him, and commit to His will for us. Believers will overcome temptation through prayer and by seeking the joy of completing the work that the Father calls us to do for His great glory.

Believers need to fix their eyes on Jesus at all times the author and finisher of our faith. The cross and life of Jesus were characteristic of humbleness and obedience to God the Father. Christ's obedience to the Father began at His incarnation.

He came to this world in our own form, "but made Himself of no reputation, and took upon him the form of a servant, and was made in the likeness of men. And being found in fashion as a man, he humbled himself, and became obedient unto death, even the death of the cross." Php. 2.7-8.

Christ voluntarily emptied Himself through love, His heavenly glory, His position, eternal riches, and the use of His divine powers. The main importance of His emptiness is the acceptance of human limitations, suffering, misunderstanding, ill treatment, hatred, and the curse of death on the cross.

Christ fully retained His divine nature; He also took on a fully human nature, with it temptations, humiliations, and weaknesses, yet without sin. "For consider Him that endured such contradiction of sinners against Himself, lest ye be wearied and faint in your minds." Heb. 12:3.

The love that sent Jesus Christ to the cross for us sinners is an enduring love. Let all believers, with their love for Christ, endure persecution in order to win souls for Christ. Love is the fruit of the Spirit; it is the result of sound soul fruit, and it is the fruit that the Holy Spirit produces for all the believers.

Every Believer must bear fruit in his or her own life, more and more fruit; so that he or she can clearly see God's sacrificial, self-giving love, which is incomprehensible, "And hope maketh not ashamed; because the love of God is shed abroad in our hearts by the Holy Ghost which is given unto us." Rom. 5:5.

God has poured out His love into the believer's entire heart. The love of God poured out in the believer's heart through the Holy Spirit is always greater than faith, hope, or anything in this world.

Christians experience the love of God in their hearts through the power of the Holy Spirit, especially in times of trouble. The Spirit of God continues to flood believers' hearts with love.

It is this ever-present experience of God's love that sustains believers in suffering and assures them that their hope for future glory is not misleading. Christ is coming back—this is very certain. Through the Spirit's life and power, we can possess and express a truly intimate, unconditional, and enduring love. God is always at work in us, "For it is God which worketh in you both to will and to do of His good pleasure." Php. 2:13.

God's grace works in His children to produce in them both the desire and power to do His will. God's work is not one of compulsion or irresistible grace. The work of grace within us is always dependent on our cooperation and response of faith in the Holy Spirit.

All believers in Jesus Christ must strive to bear the first fruit of the Spirit's love, which God himself demonstrated from the beginning of the creation of the world and in the lives of individuals through believers and non-believers. The Holy Spirit energizes the growth of the fruit of the spiritual lives of believers.

It is very important that Apostle Paul explained the difference between the works of the flesh and the fruit of the Spirit. The fruit is like a grown tree and the branches abiding in the vine. The Holy Spirit produces one kind of fruit, which is Christ's likeness.

All the fruit of the Spirit that was listed describes the characteristics of the children of God. Love is what God is, and that is what the entire body of Christ must be, while Joy is Christians' contentment and satisfaction with God and with His operations in believers' lives.

"Now these three remain: faith, hope and love, but the greatest of these is love."1 Cor. 13:13. Apostle Paul made it clear that God exalts Christ-like character more than ministerial work, faith, or the possession of spiritual gifts.

God values and emphasizes the character that acts in love, patience, kindness, unselfishness, honesty, endurance, and righteousness more than faith and great achievement in the ministerial work. The more important people in God's kingdom will be those who display genuine love for God and for people.

Love in Greek is called *"agape,"* which all Christians refer to and call unconditional love. Agape love means an undefeatable benevolence and unconquerable goodwill of believers in God that always seeks the highest in others, no matter what he or she does or is doing or is about to do.

It is the self-giving love that gives freely without asking anything in return, and does not consider the price of its object. Agape love is not a love by choice; it means love by chance, and it refers to the will rather than emotion. Agape-love explains the unconditional love of God for the universe; agape love is a sacrificial love, demonstrated by Jesus Christ on the cross at the Calvary.

"Love endures long and is patient and kind, love never is envious nor boils over with jealousy, is not boastful or vainglorious, does not display itself haughtily. It is not conceited, not arrogant and proud; it is not rude and does not act unbecomingly.

"Love does not insist on its own rights or its own way, for it is not self-seeking; it is not touchy or fretful or resentful; it takes no account of the evil done to it, it pays no attention to a suffered wrong.

"Love does not rejoice at injustice and unrighteousness, but rejoices when right and truth prevail.

"Love bears up under anything and every things that comes, is ever ready to believe the best of every person, its hopes are fadeless under circumstances, and it endures everything without weakening love never fades out or becomes obsolete or come to an end. Love never fails." 1 Cor. 13:4-8. (Taken from the *NIV New Believers' Bible Commentary*.)

The second demonstration of the Holy Spirit's power was the resurrection of Jesus, "when He raised him from the dead." Eph. 1:20. Jesus Christ was raised by the power of the Holy Spirit. Jesus was raised by the Father. The resurrection of Jesus Christ was attributed to God the Father. "Him hath God exalted with his right hand to be Prince and Saviour for to give repentance to Israel, and forgiveness of sins." Acts 5:31.

"And the angel answered and said unto her. The Holy Ghost shall come upon three, and the power of the Highest shall overshadow thee: therefore also that holy thing which shall be born of thee shall be called the Son of God." Luke 1:35.

"But if the Spirit of him that raised up Jesus from the dead dwell in you, he that raised up Jesus from the dead dwell in you, shall also quicken your mortal bodies by his Spirit that dwelleth in you." Rom. 8:11.

The resurrection of Jesus Christ was achieved by the power of the Holy Spirit. When they brought Christ down from the cross and His mother Mary held him on her legs and found out that He was completely dead, she lifted Him up.

His eyes were closed, His hands; she checked His side where the sword had pierced, the sword that the Roman solder struck on Him in order to be sure that He was dead. She saw the nails in his hands and legs, and found out that Christ was completely dead.

Everybody was surprised including Nicodemus, who was there to help Joseph, Arimathea, and all of the Apostles. He was put inside the grave and the stone was rolled to cover the grave. All life was gone on the third day He was raised up through the power of the Holy Spirit.

The illumination power of the Holy Spirit descend into the grave and came upon Jesus, shine upon His lifeless body, just as God spoke to prophet Ezekiel: "And he said unto me, son of man, can these bones live? And I answered, 'O Lord God, thou knowest.' And again he said unto me, 'Prophesy upon these bones, and say unto them, O ye dry bones, hear the word of the Lord.

Thus saith the Lord God unto these bones'; Behold, I will cause breath to enter into you, and ye shall live." Eze. 37:3-5.

Christ was made brand new; He arose. The angels rolled the stone away from the grave's entrance. When the Roman guards saw what happened and saw Jesus walking out of the tomb, they were terrified and ran away. Christ arose; death had no more dominion over Him. He conquered death forever and forever.

He arose, Halleluiah. Christ arose the blessed Ruler of the souls of all human lives forever more. "For Christ also hath once suffered for sins, the just for the unjust, that He might bring us to God, being put to death in the flesh, but quickened by the Spirit." 1 Pet. 3:18.

We see the power of the Holy Spirit in the work of grace; by His grace we are saved. "Not by works of righteousness which we have done, but according to his mercy he saved us, by washing of regeneration, and renewing of the Holy Ghost." Titus 3:5.

The power of the Spirit is the inner spiritual power of the Holy Spirit. The inner power of the Holy Spirit has power over men and women, including non-believers. The work and power of the Holy Spirit will continue until Christ's return onto this earth.

The Spirit of God holds this earth; He is the sustainer of this universe. If the Spirit of God should leave this earth today, this earth will perish. We thank

God for His unfailing love towards us in this universe; His Spirit will not leave until Christ returns to judge the quick and the dead, and all the eyes shall see Him.

8

The Fruit of the Spirit: JOY

It is very important to know that joy is produced by divine origin, which is God. This means that joy is not a human-based happiness that comes and goes; rather, joy came and originated from God.

It takes a whole heart given to God to totally and fully obey the commandments of God without the helper, the Holy Spirit, who proceeds from the Father and the Son. Whatever our position, hard times, and sorrow, we can still have joy, because He gave us His Spirit.

The fruit of the Spirit of God produces fruits in us every day that help us in any tribulations, afflictions persecutions, rejections and all the things that are happening in this world that we don't understand and that are very hard to bear and comprehend, unbearable situations.

"Behold, thou desire truth in the inward parts; and in the hidden part thou shall make one to know wisdom. Purge me with hyssop, and I shall be clean; wash me, and I shall be whiter than snow. Make me to hear joy and gladness; that the bones which thou has broken many rejoice. Hide thy face from my sins, and blot out all mine iniquities." Psl. 51:6-10.

"For his anger endureth but a moment; in his favor is life: weeping may endure for a night, but joy cometh in the morning." Psl. 30:5.

Another example of joy is that of Apostle Paul and Silas—both of them were thrown into prison and their feet fastened in the stocks. "Who, having received such a charge, thrust them into the inner prison, and made their feet fast in the stocks." Acts 16:24-25.

At midnight, the Spirit of God showered his blessings on them from above and they were full of joy that they had never experienced before in their lives; they began to pray and sing songs of praise to the Lord.

The prisoners heard them singing and they joined them in their singing. They sang songs of praise to the Lord because they were very happy in the middle of their circumstances. They trusted in the Lord, and they put their hope in him.

Their songs of praise reached heaven. The gate of the prison opened but they all stayed there; nobody ran away. This action of Paul and Silas made the Jailer ask them, "What do I need to do to be saved?" Acts 16:30.

The Apostles responded to him: believe in the Lord Jesus Christ. To believe in the Lord Jesus is to focus our faith and commitment on the person of Christ. He is our redeemer from sin, our Savior from damnation, and the Lord of our lives.

Believers must totally trust Him. He is the true Son of God sent by the Father and all authority has been given unto Him in heaven and on this earth. The jailer was saved together with his entire family.

Another example of joy is that of Job's sickness and afflictions on all his family, despite which, he never stopped trusting in the Lord. "And the Lord turned the captivity of Job, when he prayed for his friends: also the Lord gave Job twice as much as he had before." Job 42:10.

God gave His children many reasons to have joy in our lives, no matter what trials we are facing. Paul's thorn in the flesh did not stop his joy in the Lord: "My grace is sufficient for thee; for my strength is made perfect in weakness." 2 Cor. 12:9-10.

Paul replied and said, "Most gladly therefore, will I rather glory in my infirmities, that the power of Christ may rest upon me. Therefore I take pleasure in infirmities, in reproaches, in necessities, in persecutions, in distresses for Christ sake: For when I am weak, then am I strong." 2 Cor. 12:10.

We need the power and strength of God in our lives as believers in Jesus Christ. The grace of God abounds more and more everyday in our lives. Grace is the presence, favor, and power of God through the Holy Spirit. God's grace and power are most clearly seen and profoundly revealed in the midst of our human weaknesses.

The greater our weakness and trials for Christ, the more the grace of God will help us to accomplish His will. What God gives is always sufficient for us to live our daily lives, to work for him, and to endure our suffering.

As long as we draw near and get close to Jesus Christ, He will give us His heavenly strength and comfort. We will be able to see eternal values in our weaknesses, for it is Christ's power that rests upon us and lives within us as we walk through life towards our heavenly dwelling.

Paul and Job knew that God had a plan for their lives. Since they belonged to him, they were ready to suffer so that sinners could be saved. The birth of our Lord Jesus brought great joy to the world and the angel sang and said to them, "And the angel said unto them, fear not: for, behold, I bring you good tidings of great joy, which shall be to all the people. For unto you a child is born this day in the city of David a savior, which is Christ the Lord." Luke 2:10-11.

The life of Jesus on earth brings joy to those who believe in Him and followed Him during His earthly ministry. He healed the sick, preached, and taught the gospel of God. He performed many miracles: lame people walked, the blind received their sight, the dead were raised to life, the sick were completely made whole, the salvation of God was spread from Capernaum, Jericho, Bethlehem, Nazareth, Jerusalem, Galilee, and throughout the sea of Tiberea, Ganazarette and to the Garden of Gethsemane.

Our Lord brings joy to people wherever He goes: to the home of Matthew and Mary, to the home of Zaccheaus, to the home of Peter's mother- in-law, to the home of Matthew, to Mary-Magdalene, and to Matius, the son of Timeaus on the road to Jericho.

He brought joy to the man who was born blind, the man at the Bethsaida of thirty-eight years of infirmities, to the woman who was bent and could not walk right or see the sky, and to the man with the withered hand. He brought joy to five thousand men, not including women and children, by feeding them.

They were so full that the same joy extended and spread to the poor who did not have the means or opportunity to be there, but received the twelve baskets of leftovers. He also brought joy to four thousand people, with seven baskets of leftovers for the poor and needy.

Joy was brought to Malchus, one of the soldiers whose ear Peter cut on the night of Jesus' arrest; Jesus restored the man's ear back. Our Lord brought joy to the thief on His right hand by inviting him to meet

Him in paradise, on the night of His crucifixion. Jesus Christ brought great joy to the two people on Emmaus Road when He opened the Scripture for them; their hearts burned with joy as they ran back to the Apostles and told them that our risen Lord had spoken to them.

"And they said one to another, did not our heart burn within us, while he talked with us by the way, and while he opened to us the scriptures?" Luke 24:32.

He has risen indeed. Jesus brought great joy to the Jewish and the Gentiles because of His sacrifice on the cross in order to bring salvation to sinners and the lost, as well as unbelievers all over the world.

Jesus brought great joy to all who believed in Him and his gift of grace, eternal life, and everlasting life. "For God so love the world, that he gave his only begotten Son, that whosoever believeth in him should not perish, but has everlasting live." John 3:16.

Our Lord Jesus Christ continues to bring joy to all believers, all sinners, and all people of different world religions, because of his great commission for believers. "Go ye therefore, and teach all nations, baptizing them in the name of the Father and of the Son, and of the Holy Ghost: Teaching them to observe all things whatsoever I have commanded you: and, Lo, I am with you always, even to the end of the world." Matt. 28:19- 20.

Christ brings joy to all people in all nations because He does not want anyone to perish; He wants them to gain knowledge of repentance, pray for forgiveness of their sins, and be saved. Jesus Christ still gives us joy today through the power of the Holy Spirit. "I will not leave you comfortless, I will come to you." John 14:18.

"But the Comforter, which is the Holy Ghost, whom the Father will send in my name, he shall teach you all things, and bring all things to your remembrance, whatsoever I have said unto you." John 14:26.

Our Lord said that His Father would send the Holy Spirit, which will abide in the believer forever to teach them and tell them all the things that He wants them to know; he is the *Paraclete* heavenly guest. We believers have joy today because we know that Jesus loves us and that He is coming back to judge the quick and the dead, and all eyes shall see Him.

Therefore, we will continue to have joy no matter what we are going through, day by day; we can still be full of joy because of His love for us. Jesus Christ is the answer to all of the problems of this world.

The true fruit of the Spirit is joy. We must try to exercise joy every day. Many people have looked or are looking for the source of happiness in wrong places everyone on this earth, whether male or female, rich or poor, healthy or unhealthy, or middle class.

Researchers want to know what gives lasting happiness; some of them have thought that if they built the biggest or largest complex mansion, they would be happy, but the result does not last as long as anticipated.

Some people look for happiness in entertainment; they spend millions in entertainment that can sustain them during their mystery, but it is very hard for them to find happiness.

Some look for happiness in athletic hobbies, traveling around the world, dancing, fashion, alcohol, food, and any form of happy hour drugs. None of these forms of happiness enhancement helps them.

For example, King Solomon conducted many experiments with his great wisdom on how to be happy in this world or what can make people happy. King Solomon, at the end of his experimental research, said, "I said in my heart, Go to now, I will prove thee mirth, therefore, enjoy pleasure, and behold, this also is vanity. I said of laughter, it is mad: and of mirth, what does it accomplish?

"I sought in my heart to gratify my flesh with wine, while guiding my heart with wisdom, and how to lay hold on folly, till I might see what was good for the sons of men to do under the heaven all the days of their lives. I made me great work, I build me houses;

"I planted vineyards, gardens, orchards, and planted trees and all many kinds of fruits: King Solomon comes to the awareness and concluded; For God gives to a man that is good in his sight wisdom, and knowledge and joy:

"But to the sinner He gives travail, to gather and to heap up, that He may give to him that is good before

God; This also is vanity and vexation of spirit." Ecc. 2:1-11, 26.

King Solomon realized that only God can determine when He plants the fruit of the Spirit, joy, in our hearts, and whether we experience joy in our lives or not. Seeing people laughing does not mean they are full of joy.

The Bible tells us that everything has a time under the heaven. King Solomon stated that seeing people laugh does not mean they are joyful or experiencing joy. "Even in laughter the heart may ache, and joy may end in grief" Prov. 14:13.

This means that human wisdom is a poor basis for determining what is true or false, what is right or wrong, and what is worthy or unworthy. God's written word of revelation is the only true source for determining the right or wrong path for our lives.

Most of our ways in the system of life lead to death and destruction, but God's way leads to eternal life. King Solomon stated, after his extensive research, that all earthly pleasure, according to his research's findings, are meaningless money, wealth, kingdom of earth, pleasures on earth, cultural activities, delights, no long efforts to find meaningful fulfillment in a good life resulted into true happiness.

He found that he still felt emptiness and had no satisfaction in his life. He realized that we can only find lasting happiness, peace, fulfillment, and joy if we look for our happiness in God's will and in His provisions. King David said, "You will show me the path of life; in your presence is fullness of joy; at your right hand are pleasures forevermore." Psl. 16:11.

As long as we are close to God we will continuously receive incomparable joy that earthly problems cannot destroy. A personal relationship with God gives us confidence and, above all, intimate fellowship and an intimate personal relationship with the Lord's continual presence, bringing His guidance, protection, and joy, with the power of the resurrection and eternal life.

We have to see God's joy as a spring in the desert, flowing to all people—the just and unjust. Experiencing joy is when we get to the point that, through faith, we confidently feel the presence of God in our lives—past, present and future.

"Sing aloud unto God our strength: make a joyful noise unto the God of Jacob." Psl. 81:1. "He should have fed them also with the finest of the wheat: and with honey out of the rock should I have satisfied thee." Psl. 81:16.

When we follow God's orders, He will take total charge of our needs and feed us with the finest foods to eat, and we will experience the real joy and its satisfaction that God provides. God will remove all of our burdens so that we can rejoice in his love.

By then, it will come to us clearly that real joy is our relationship with Him; our relationship with God the Father, through our Lord Jesus Christ, makes this possible through the Lord's teaching of the beatitudes. Matt. 5:1-12.

We must live with joy in order to produce the qualities we need for the kingdom, and our work must produce joy in us as a part of the Holy Spirit's manifestation of God's workmanship through His Spirit.

Biblical joy is inseparable from and incomparable to our relationship with God, which springs down from our knowledge and understanding of the purpose of life and the hope of living with God for eternity when we will enjoy more joy.

If God is truly present in our lives, the joy that God's experience can begin in us will flow through us to other people, "Thou wilt show me the path of life: in thy presence is fullness of joy; at the right hand there are pleasures for evermore." Psl. 16:11.

With eternal pleasure at your right hand, when we experience joy in our lives, it is the sign that shows that our life has found its purpose, and its reason for being alive—it's a revelation of God. Jesus said, "No man can come to me, except the father who hath sent me draw him: and I will raise him up at the last day." John 6:44.

The Father is the one who draws people of all nations to Jesus through the Holy Spirit. God's work of drawing applies to all human souls on earth. This drawing can be rejected. Man himself is helpless; he does not have the strength to come to Jesus unless the Father first begins the work of regeneration in his heart and makes him alive.

Many people on earth do not realize that they are in need of Savior. Jesus' teaching made clear that God the Father is the one whose infinite love has acted in our lives, called us, and spoken to our heart.

For example, during our Lord's earthly ministry He felt sorrow for Jerusalem, "O Jerusalem, Jerusalem, which killest the prophets, and stonest them that are sent unto thee; how often would I have gathered thy children together, as a hen doth gathers her brood under her wings, and ye would not." Luke 13:34.

Our Lord shed tears over Jerusalem's unbelievers. He bore witness to the freedom of human freewill that resisted the grace God and the will of God. Our Lord condemns earthy pleasures. He warns that those who exalt themselves in this life will be put to damnation and shame in the kingdom of heaven.

It clearly shows that the joy of the children of God comes from sources that were not sought by the people of the world. Believers in Jesus Christ find joy through humbleness and joy, which is constantly supplied through the indwelling power of the Holy Spirit.

"Then he said unto them, Go your way, eat the fat, and drink the sweet, and send portions unto them for whom nothing is prepared: for this day is holy unto our Lord: neither be ye sorry; for the joy of the Lord is your strength." Neh. 8:10.

"The fear of the Lord is the beginning of wisdom: and the knowledge of the holy is understanding." Prov. 9:10. There is pleasure and joy in God as He works with His creations. God is a God of joy; it is in His joy that we find our strength. God is a joyful God; He always wanted to share His joy with us.

God is the source of real joy, just as He is the source of love, mercy, and truth. The joy of the Lord powerfully impacts lives. Jesus Christ came to reveal God the Father's joy to us; Jesus Christ is our joy.

"Behold my servant, whom I uphold; mine elect, in whom my soul delighteth; I have put my spirit upon him: he shall bring forth judgment to the Gentiles." Isa. 42:1.

The Messiah was to be one in whom the Father would delight; Jesus Christ was anointed with the oil of Joy. "Thy throne, O' God, is for ever and ever: the scepter of thy kingdom is a right scepter. Thou lovest righteousness, and hatest wickedness: therefore God, thy God, hath anointed thee with the oil of gladness above thy fellows." Psl. 45:6-7.

Our Lord said, "These things have I spoke unto you, that my joy might remain in you, and that your joy might be full." John 15:11. "And now come I to thee; and these things I speak in the world, that they might have my joy fulfilled in themselves." John 17:13.

The declaration of God's Word, accompanied by a sincere desire to follow its instruction, will result in true, heartfelt joy. This Joy of our Lord is based on reconciliation with God, in the presence of the Spirit in our lives. It is maintained by the assurance that we believers have been forgiven in Christ and that we have been restored to fellowship with God and now live in good harmony according to His will.

Joy acts as a fortress to guard us from the troubles and temptations of each day, as power and motivation to persevere in faith until the end of the world. When it comes to life through faith and walking with God, we might want to be in a hurry, but God is never in a hurry because God is never in a hurry.

We are going to try not to grow weary in our journey as He takes us along. We must learn how to appreciate God and how to press on, even when we are feeling tired or weak. God selected pastors, teachers, prophets, apostles, and evangelists to see who are among men and women, and He takes them from among men and women so that they can minister and witness to men and women.

He ministers to these men and women for the benefit of other men and women. We have to learn to differentiate between our happy feelings and cause joy to happen in the heart of God. The joy of the Lord is our strength, because there are going to be times when you are going to be working for God and when you are going to lose your strength. "Rejoice in the Lord always: and again I say, rejoices." Php. 4:4.

Believers must rejoice in order to gain strength by recalling all of the great things that the Lord has done for them and through them for other people around them. They must rejoice in the grace of God that abounds more and more in their lives, and also rejoice in the fulfillment of God's promises in their lives and the lives of their children, relatives, and friends.

Believers must always rejoice because joy is one of the important fruits of the Spirit. Joy is our daily bread. We cannot live on the joy we had yesterday; we must have daily joy. Joy gives us strength only when we possess it.

Believers must rejoice and gain strength by recalling the Lord's grace, His full presence in our lives, and His divine promises for us. Joy is an integral part of our salvation in Christ. It is an inner peace and delight in God the Father, the Lord Jesus Christ, and the Holy Spirit, and in the blessing that flows from our relationship with Him.

Joy is associated with the salvation God provides us in Christ and with God's Word. Joy flows from God as one aspect of the Spirit's fruit. It does not come automatically, but is experienced as we maintain an abiding relationship with Christ.

Our joy becomes greater when the Spirit mediates a deep sense of God's presence and nearness in our lives. Our Lord taught us that the fullness of joy is inseparable from and connected to our remaining in

His word, loving others, obeying His commands, and being separate from the world. Joy is delight in God's nearness and in His redemptive gifts.

It cannot be destroyed by pain, suffering, weakness, or difficult circumstances. God the Father made it clear to us that the true joy, the real joy from the heart, lies in the quality of our relationship with him through our Lord Jesus Christ.

Biblical joy is inseparable; our relationship with God, our knowledge, acknowledgement, and understanding of the purpose and hope of heaven with him should shed joy to our minds all the time.

Joy is the sign that our life has experienced God, that God is close to us, and that life has found its purpose for life, through His Spirit, and it also shows that the joy of the children of God is different from the joy of people in the world.

"And they, continuing daily with one accord in the temple, and breaking bread from house, to house, did eat their meat with gladness and singleness of heart." Acts 2:46. "And when he had brought them into his house, he set meat before them, and rejoiced, believing in God with his entire house." Acts 16:34.

The pouring out of the Holy Spirit by Jesus proves that He is the exalted Messiah, the true Son of God, now sitting at the right hand of God and interceding for His believers on earth. He continues to pour out the Spirit on those who believe in Him. The Spirit is Jesus Christ's presence for believers and the Spirit's empowering of believers will continue in their lives as long as they stay close to the Savior and read the Word of God daily.

Even today, when people are first converted they are always full of joy. "And you became followers of us and of the Lord, having received the word in much affliction with joy of the Holy Spirit." 1 Thes. 1:6.

The ultimate source of their joy begins at conversion when they completely give their life to Christ. They receive unspeakable joy. All the words in the chapters of the beatitudes characterize a believer's biblical joy.

In the book of Job, "Knowest thou not this of old, since man was placed upon earth. That the triumphing of the wicked is short, and the joy of the hypocrite but for a moment." Job 20:4-5.

"Folly is joy to him that is destitute of wisdom: but a man of understanding walketh uprightly." Prov. 15:21. When believers in the Lord are filled with the spirit of God, they will feel good about their lives and about who they are, value themselves, and accept themselves for who they are, what they're doing with their lives, where their lives are going, and what they have achieved because of their obedient walking with the Lord.

They will always feel joy and joy will always present in them. Others around them will also notice it.

God is our source of joy; therefore, our relationships with Him are the source and causes of any real, true joy believers might have. "Also that day they offered great sacrifices, and rejoiced, for God had made them rejoice with great joy: the wives also and the children also rejoiced: so that the joy of Jerusalem was heard even afar off." Neh. 12:43.

This was accomplished because they had a good relationship with God. Through the covenant, God himself is the cause and the source of their joy. This should be clear to every believer: that true joy is from God, who is the only producer of joy.

People of this earth can seek joy for their own pleasure but true joy must be sought God's way. True joy comes when people have yielded, surrendered their lives wholeheartedly to the will of God, who makes everything possible in our lives. Joy comes from the fruit of the Holy Spirit; it's rooted in the realization and awareness of God's transforming us into His own image.

Biblical joy arises when people hear the Gospel, review it, understand the grace of God, and believe in salvation with a repentant heart. Hearing and believing the word of the Gospel leads to repentance and a new life in Christ.

"And ye became followers of us, and of the Lord, having received the word in much affliction, with joy of the Holy Ghost." 1 Thes. 1:6.

The Thessalonian believers were going through great stress and confusion due to persecution; yet, in the middle of it, they continued to experience great joy, and their supernatural joy was due to the power of the Holy Spirit working in their lives.

Apostle Paul called it the 'Joy of the Holy Spirit.' Our joy must come from yielding to the fulfillment of God's great creative purpose, accomplished in the lives of all believers. "His Lord said unto him, well done, thou good and faithful servant: thou hast been faithful over a few things, I will make thee ruler over many things: enter thou into the joy of thy lord." Matt. 25:21.

With this word from our Lord, believers must know that their joy does not end here on earth it continues to eternity. "Looking unto Jesus the author and finisher of our faith; who for the joy that was set before him endured the cross, despising the shame, and is set down at the right hand of the throne of God." Heb. 12:2.

"But let those that put their trust in thee rejoice: let them ever shout for joy, because thou defendest them: let them also that love thy name be joyful in thee. For thou, Lord, wilt bless the righteous, with favour wilt thou compass him as with a shield." Psl. 5:11-12.

"For what is our hope, or joy, or crown of rejoicing? Are not even ye in the presence of our Lord Jesus Christ at his coming?" 1 Thes. 2:19.

We believers can always rejoice, knowing that God is always there to help individual believers, just as He continues to help all of the saints scattered around the world.

Apostle Peter, in his Epistle, offers words of encouragement to rejoice so that we can honor God by setting good examples when we are treated badly in the cause of God's services.

Even in times of pain or suffering, believers must continue to rejoice and be happy to participate in the sufferings of Christ our Lord and overjoyed when His glory is revealed.

"Beloved, think it not strange concerning the fiery trial which is to try you, as though some strange thing happened unto you: But rejoice, in as much as ye are partakers of Christ's sufferings; that, when His glory shall be revealed, ye may be glad also with exceeding joy." 1 Pet. 4:12-13.

God, in His plan of salvation, provides an opportunity for everyone living to understand the word of the Gospel, in his or her own language, and to repent and pray for forgiveness, which is only through Jesus Christ.

The Holy Spirit will strengthen us and make us strong, pouring out His patience on us and making us wait patiently with His power. Joy is different than happiness. Joy comes to the heart when a person becomes a believer in Jesus Christ.

The Spirit plants so much joy in the heart of that person that when the believer is going through persecution, affliction, rejection, and all forms of earthly problems and troubles, they will still feel the Holy Spirit's inner joy inside of them.

9

The Fruit of the Spirit: PEACE

We gain contentment through peace in the fruit of the Spirit. "Thou will keep him in a perfect peace, whose mind is stayed on thee because he trusted in thee." Isa. 26:3.

Perfect peace and inward peace lead to fullness of peace with God. Peace of conscience is knowing that one's sins are forgiven when they have asked for it; it is peace at all times and in all circumstances.

God's peace is different than the world's peace. God's peace comes from knowing Him and acknowledging His word; when we allow the Lord to be in control of our lives, our hope of going to heaven is best assured.

Peace does not come from changing circumstances; peace is the result of our personal relationship with the unchanging, all-knowing God of the earth.

The people of the world must first make peace with God almighty, before looking for peace in their lives. Believers will be able to see and know peace of God in all their difficulties and troubles in life.

We can also make peace with everyone around us. Peace of God is perfect contentment of being in the right relationship with God, with others, and with oneself. God is able to use all our difficulties, our circumstances, and our adversities in life for our good and for His glory.

God is the immortal, invisible, and all wise God; He knows what is best and He give the best to his children. He is loving and gracious and will not allow anything to harm us. He is omnipotent, which means there is nothing so great that He cannot solve.

The most important tool for believers is knowing that trusting God is very important in all circumstances of life. The ability to trust God should be demonstrated in the life of believers through willingness to obey God and to follow and do what is right at all times.

Believers must love God and keep His word, abide in Him and His word, and follow Him with peace that surpasses all understanding. The fruit of peace will grow and reach the above; is the peace of God that surpasses all understanding, for our perfect protection, which guards our hearts and minds, so that nothing can harm us beyond what He allows. It is peace beyond any expectation that we cannot imagine.

It is a perfect peace because we are totally connected with Him, to the point that we are at the center of Jesus Christ, the Prince of Peace. His peace fills us and overflows to other people around us. We begin to pour ourselves into other people and become problem-solvers or peacemakers.

Most importantly, we begin to multiply ourselves people learn from us and teach others. The peace follows as the river flows to so many areas of people's lives around us. Peace is the one of the fruits of righteousness.

Peace means an absence of civil disturbance or hostilities, or a personality free from internal and external strife. The biblical concept of peace is larger than anything we can imagine and rests heavily on the peace of God, which means to be complete, to sound good, to be completely whole, or to live well.

The covenant was always renewed or maintained with a peace offering such as prosperity, success, or fulfillment. The people of Israel used peace for greetings and farewells. It was meant to act as a blessing on the one to whom it was spoken.

Believers' lives must be filled with good health, prosperity, and victory. Peace must express completeness and safety. Peace is not a state of mind or a circumstance in nature it is a condition of the heart.

It is a fruit of the Spirit, a gift from God. People must know that true peace consists in the God of peace and in God's peace that sanctifies God's children. God alone is the source of peace, for He is "Yahweh Shalom." The Lord came to sinful humankind, historically, first to the Jews and then to the Gentiles desiring to enter into a relationship with Him.

He established with them a covenant of peace, which was sealed with his presence, "The Lord blesses thee, and keeps thee: The Lord make His face shine upon thee, and is gracious unto thee. The Lord lifts up His countenance upon thee, and gives thee peace." Num. 6:24-26.

The people and the participants were given perfect peace so long as they maintained a proper relationship with the Lord. "Thou wilt keep him in perfect peace, whose mind is stayed on thee: because he trusted in thee. "Isa. 26:3.

"Now the Lord of peace Himself gives you peace always by all means. The Lord be with you all." 2 Thes. 3:16. Throughout the Old Testament and the New Testament, it was anticipated and confirmed that God's peace would be mediated through the Messiah.

Peace with God came through the death and resurrection of Jesus Christ. Peter declared to Cornelius: "The word which God sent unto the children of Israel, preaching peace by Jesus Christ: He is the Lord of all." Acts 10:36.

The Scripture specifically states that there can be no peace for the wicked. Peace could be disturbed if one does not live before the Lord and with each other in righteousness.

"And the God of peace shall bruise Satan under your feet shortly. The grace of our Lord Jesus Christ be with you. Amen." Rom. 16:20. Our heavenly father is the God of peace; our Lord Jesus Christ is the Prince of Peace.

Peace is a condition of a positive nature in which there is active fellowship, harmony, and joy between individuals. Peace is a blessing that ought to be desired and engaged through the peace that God has provided, which allows access through the Spirit to the Father.

All believers belong to the family of God and peace allows us to reside in the temple of the Lord, a habitation of God in the Spirit. Peace comes when we are justified by the loving sacrifice of Jesus Christ's blood and continues to revive God's life.

Peace is with people around us. Peace comes from God and surpasses all understandings. Peace is produced when believers are one with Jesus Christ and blessed with the joy of justification, along with reconciliation, with both God and man.

Peace will come and be produced naturally. In order to maintain peace with God, we have to stay close to the Lord, focus on our Lord, love God's Word, keep His commandments, be diligent in prayer, fill our minds and souls with spiritual thoughts, and be of one mind of passion for one another.

When we have peace with God, we have peace within us whereby we are in a better position to make peace with others. Believers must pursue peace all of the time, have compassion for one another, love our neighbor, and be tenderhearted and courteous.

Believers should not return evil for evil, but rather, respond with a blessing. If we want to bear all fruits scripture says: "And the fruits of righteousness, is sown in peace of them that make peace." Jas. 3:18.

God wants all of us to enter into a true sanctification process with Him so that He can begin the process of molding, shaping, and transforming us into the image of his son Jesus Christ.

He wants to make us into better and holier people, filled with all the fruit of the Holy Spirit. He wants to transform us by renewing our minds. He wants to put correct thinking into our thought process.

Believers must be willing to cooperate with the Holy Spirit, by staying in the word in order to find out what God is going to change in their life, and what God wants to plant in them for them to fully belong to Him. The fruit of the Holy Spirit comes directly from God Himself.

All believers should do the best they can to cooperate and work with the Holy Spirit, allowing all of the fruits to work in our personality. All of these fruits can dramatically change the quality of life and the state of well-being of believers, if they allow the Holy Spirit to work these fruits into their personality. God's joy and God's goodness can become manifest.

Peace derives from remaining in a relationship with God. Peace is tranquility a state of rest that comes from seeking God. Peace is the opposite of violence and chaos. Peace is one of the most important fruits of the Holy Spirit that all the believers in Jesus Christ seek and find.

Peace is what the Spirit of God produces when He dwells in us. When a believer is filled with the peace of God, peace touches everyone around him or her.

The word, peace, expresses an idea of wholeness, completeness, and tranquility in the soul that is unaffected by outward circumstances or pressures. When a believer is dominated by peace, he has a unique character, calmness, and inner stability that results in the ability to conduct himself peacefully everywhere.

Even in the midst of any situation that could be traumatic or upsetting, without allowing the difficulties or pressures of life to break him. A believer who is possessed by peace is a stable person in all that he does.

Jesus Christ is the prophet and Prince of Peace on earth. He brought peace to the hearts of those who made Him the Lord of their lives. Christ said, "Peace I leave with you, my peace I give unto you: not as the world giveth, give I unto you, let not your heart be troubled, neither let it be afraid." John 14:27.

"Therefore being justified by faith, we have peace with God through our Lord Jesus Christ." Rom. 5:1.

"Now the God of hope fill you with all joy and peace in believing, that ye may abound in hope, through the power of the Holy Ghost." Rom. 15:13.

10

The Fruit of the Spirit: PATIENCE

Patience denotes mercy, forbearance, fortitude, patient endurance, and longsuffering. Patient believers have the ability to endure persecution and all sorts of ill treatment from those who hate God.

Patient believers have the power to exercise revenge but decide not to do so. Patience is also known as loyalty, perseverance continuance, bearing up, steadfastness, supportiveness, and hanging on to the promise of God.

Patient endurance means having unshaking faith and having the energy or courage to continue to bear under difficulties, situations, and circumstances, with hope that resists defeat. "For ye have need of patience, that, after ye have done the will of God, ye might receive the promise." Heb. 10:36.

"Strengthened with all might, according to His glorious power, unto all patience and longsuffering with joyfulness." Col. 1:11.

All of the fruits of the Holy Spirit are manifest in our lives; it is the sign that lets us know that we are fully with the Holy Spirit—when people see evidence of its fruit in us. Patience is one of the most important fruits of the Spirit that every believer of Christ must have in order to be able to receive His blessings.

Patience is a self-disciplinary behavior that does not retaliate against people's wrongs. When a believer possesses the fruit of patience, if someone does that believer wrong, he will respond with the Spirit of patience, which is the ability to accept delay or disappointment, take wrongs without getting angry or upset, to continue steadfast under any circumstances, and to continue waiting on the Lord.

Patience is calm endurance based on the certain knowledge that God is in control. Patience helps believers when they are hurting because of a situation over which they don't have control. With the help of the Lord, they may become a source of help, beauty, energy, and healing for those who are sick.

It is very difficult to be patient, because there are many circumstances that make patience contrary to human nature; but as we get close to the Lord, He produces the fruit of the Spirit—patience—in us.

Most people in the world are very impatient and, most of the time, very angry. They scream, yell at each other while driving, and when passing each other, most of the time, without knowing what they are yelling about.

Patience is difficult because of the cultural diversities of many people in our society or communities. Patience is contrary to some people's cultures, ethnicities, and lifestyles.

While people in developing, underdeveloped, and Third World countries live simply, in a relaxed and laid back way, people in developed countries are always in a hurry, rushing in and rushing out to things they don't even know and of which they have no knowledge.

They do not understand why people in other countries are so different from them. The Bible says: "He that is slow to wrath is of great understanding: but he that is hasty of spirit exalted folly." Prov. 14:29. "A wrathful man stirreth up strife: but he that is slow to anger appeaseth strife." Prov. 15:18.

We need to develop a character of patience in our lives. The only way that we can develop patience is to abide in Christ; the Holy Spirit will produce patience in us so that we will be able to help others.

As our Lord said in the book of John, we are the branches; if we abide in him, we will bear more and more fruits, and we will receive the best nourishment from Him.

After believers' conversions, they receive eternal life and the power to remain in Christ. With that power, believers must then accept that responsibility in salvation and remain in Christ.

The word, abide, means to live in Christ, just as the branch has life only as long as the life of the vine flows into it, so too believers have Christ's life only as long as Christ's life flows into them through their remaining in Christ.

The conditions by which we remain in Christ are: by keeping God's Word continually in our hearts, maintaining the habit of constant intimate communion with Christ in order to draw strength from Him, obeying His commands, remaining in His love and loving each other, keeping our lives clean and pure through the Word, resisting all sin, and yielding to the Spirit's direction.

We cannot and will not produce unless we abide in Christ; we must stay, read the Word of God daily, walk in His footsteps, pray without cease, spend time with Him in prayer and fellowship, and worship and reflect upon His holiness and what He is doing in our lives.

We need to patiently overlook the many things that bring frustration into our lives. "And Moses said unto the people, Fear ye not, stand still, and see the salvation of the Lord, which he will shew to you today: for the Egyptians whom ye have seen to day ye shall see them again no more forever." Exo. 14:13-14.

Therefore, we must be still and wait patiently on the Lord; our God has the power and energy to handle our problems. "The Lord is not slack concerning his promise, as some men count slackness; but is long-suffering to usward, not willing that any should perish, but that all should come to repentance." 2 Pet. 3:9.

God is patience and He wants everybody to gain knowledge of repentance and be saved; everyday, He is waiting for His creations to come to Him. Our Lord Jesus Christ opens the door of salvation because of His patience; the door to our Lord Jesus opens because the Lord is patient.

The opportunity to be saved from our past and future sins is still available because the Lord is patient; He does not want anyone to perish. Rom. 8:25. "But if we hope for that we see not, then do we with patience wait for it." Rom. 8:25.

"For they said unto me, make us gods, which shall go before us: for as for this Moses, the man that brought us up out of the land of Egypt, we wot not what is become of him." Exo. 32:23.

When the children of Israel were sitting at the bottom of Mount Sinai, waiting for Moses to come down from the mountain, several of them were so impatient that they went to Aaron to ask him for another god.

Moses was very angry at their impatience. Patience is one of the most difficult fruits of the Spirit to possess. It is a virtue that Christians, especially teens, wish to possess. God's timing is very important in the lives of believers because God might have other blessings for us, beyond those that we request.

No one can know God's way—we must trust him. If the promise is delayed, he knows the right time for everything in our life. Delayed promises always come with more blessings, and more rewards from the Lord. "The discretion of a man deferreth his anger; and it is his glory to pass over a transgression." Prov. 19:11.

Patience could be described as the willingness to endure disappointment, pain or suffering, without getting angry or giving up. Patience is also attributed to God's slow anger. God is slow to get angry with His people. He is patient with His people, despite the disappointment, pain, and suffering that we cause Him every day.

God is patient with us. God is the same yesterday, today, and forever. He is unchangeable, the God of heaven and earth; He continues to be slow to anger with us. He is full of steadfast love for us. We walk by the Spirit; we live, move, and exist through the Spirit.

We must be thankful to God for His patience, as we express our thankfulness to God, by being patient with our fellow citizens. Patience with one another is the true worship of God. Patience is the fruit of the Spirit; patience is the work of God, committed to building patience and perseverance in the lives of His people.

Patience reflects God in our characters; patience gets us through all circumstances in life and transforms our lives and the lives of the people around us. "Rest in the Lord, and wait patiently for him: fret not thyself because of him who prospereth in his way, because of the man who bringeth wicked devices to pass." Psl. 37:7.

"I waited patiently for the Lord; and he inclined unto me, and heard my cry." Psl. 40:1 "And therefore will the Lord wait, that he may be gracious unto you. And therefore will he be exalted, that he may have mercy upon you: for the Lord is a God of judgment blessed are all they that wait for him." Isa. 30:18.

Waiting patiently for God allows us to see His plan, to work, and to receive the blessings that He prepares for us; while waiting, we are able to be patient with other people around us. We indirectly help them to receive the grace of God in their lives.

Patience is one of the fruits of the Spirit with which everyone, all believers, struggle; it is hard because it takes time to listen, time for our situation to change, and time to wait on Almighty God to move in our lives.

God uses interruptions and trials and, quite often, the people in our lives to develop patience with us.

God stretches us and asks us to deny ourselves and consecrate ourselves to His will. This is the work of our Lord in our lives. He does all this with love and the goal of helping us to become like him so that His will may be fulfilled in our lives and that we may receive His blessings.

God works during the difficult circumstances in our lives in order to produce His character within us, "Knowing this, that the trying of your faith worketh patience. But let patience have her perfect work, that ye may be perfect and entire, wanting nothing." Jas. 1:3-4.

We exercise patience; God wants us to see Him in the middle of all circumstances, conversations, and relationships. "Be still, and know that I am God: I will be exalted among that heathen, I will be exalted in the earth." Psl. 46:10.

"Trust in the Lord with all thine heart, and lean not unto thine own understanding. In all thy ways acknowledge him, and he shall direct thy paths." Prov. 3:5-6.

In patience, we experience quietness and peace. We are able to trust God with what is before us. God is in control; his ways are beyond finding out. He knows what is best for our lives, and He is at work in us. He gave meaning and purpose to our wait.

God wants us to be patient in all circumstances, troubles, afflictions, and tribulations. Being patient is the result of our new life in Christ Jesus. Christ washes us clean from all our sins; Jesus calls us to experience His gift of grace and the newness of life in Him.

We are able to respond to life's circumstances with God's heart, new hearts, new eyes, and the enabling transforming power of the Spirit as part of our new life. "According as his divine power hath given unto us all things that pertain unto life and godliness, through the knowledge of him that hath called us to glory and virtue." 2 Pet 1:3.

"That ye put off concerning the former conversation the old man, which is corrupt according to the deceitful lust; And be renewed in the Spirit of your mind; and that ye put on the new man, which after God is created in righteousness and true holiness." Eph. 4:22-24.

"Therefore if any man be in Christ, he is a new creature: old things are passed away, behold, all things are become new." 2 Cor. 5:17. Believers must fix their eyes, hearts, and minds on Jesus, who gave us a patient hearts; we must trust and rest on His love for us through endurance, longsuffering, and being slow to anger or despair.

"With all lowliness and meekness, with longsuffering, forbearing one another in love; endeavoring to keep the unity of the Spirit in the bond of peace." Eph. 4:2-3.

"But thou hast fully known my doctrine, manner of life, purpose, faith, longsuffering, charity, patience." 2 Tim. 3:10. No human being can create the unity of the Spirit. It already exists for those who believe the truth and have received Christ, just as the apostle proclaimed to all people, not only believers, in Ephesus, that the Ephesians must maintain unity, not through any human efforts or organizations, but by living a life worthy of the calling they had received.

Spiritual unity is maintained by being loyal to the truth and by staying in step with the Spirit—it cannot be achieved by any human efforts. When everything is going our way, patience is easy to practice or demonstrate.

When people treat us unfairly, say bad things about us, or blackmail us, responding with impatience will bring about holy anger, while patience will reveal our faith in God's timing, omnipotence, and love. Most people consider patience to mean passive waiting or gentle tolerance.

Most people wait patiently for the promise of God to be fulfilled in their lives. All believers in Jesus Christ must seek more patience in all areas of life, every day, every moment; we don't want to wait for patience, we don't want to work for it, we want more and more patience to deal with everyday difficulties in life.

In times of war, we need patience to wait for our loved ones to come back from the battlefield.

Medical doctors and physicians need patience to perform surgery on sick people. Pastors and preachers of the Word of God missionary need patience to witness, pray, preach, and teach for years and yet see little positive response.

All believers need patience when we are at low points in our spiritual lives and do not feel that God is near. Patience is the tool with which Christians' faith holds to the promise of God, even though we may feel much more like the conqueror.

Patience comes from trusting the Lord. Believers exercise patience during the dark events or days in our life; patience helps Christians to not lose hope or control, but rather, to remain firm and steadfast in the conviction that obedience to God is required at all times and in all circumstances.

We must continue to trust when our trust seems to go nowhere, with all our hearts desire; continuing to trust helps us to wait patiently with obedience to our Lord and to continue to be patient. "And Lord passed I by before him, and proclaimed, the Lord, The Lord God, merciful and gracious, longsuffering and abundant in goodness and truth." Exo 34:6.

"The Lord is merciful and gracious, slow to anger, and plenteous in mercy." Psl. 103:8. "The Lord is gracious, and full of compassion, slow to anger, and great mercy." Psl. 145:8.

Our Lord is a God whose compassion, kindness, and forgiveness are united with truth, holiness and justice. The fact that God is gracious and compassionate shows us that He will not punish anyone unless and until His longsuffering love is rejected and despised. "But thou, O Lord, art a God full of compassion, and gracious, longsuffering, and plenteous in mercy and truth." Psl. 86:15.

You are a compassionate and gracious God, slow to anger, abounding in love and faithfulness. Lord, you are gracious and compassionate to all of your children. These repeated words in the Bible express God's delight in showing mercy, especially when He sees misery, which moves His heart to compassion.

He is also slow to become angry at our offenses and quickly shows love and mercy when forgiveness is requested. We must know that all who call on God in truth with sincere and upright hearts must be assured that He is near. He will hear their prayers, fulfill their desires for help, and work for their deliverance.

God's patience or slowness in unleashing His wrath, or anger, is not because of compassion or unwillingness to act; rather, His patient waiting is because he does not wish for anyone to perish, but for all to come to the savior with trust.

The Bible states that all believers must walk in the Spirit, bear one another in love, and show patience to those who are in the world to non-believers as well as the body of Christ. Jesus Christ's desire for the entire body of Christ, His Church, is for us to be joyfully strengthened by Him and to endure this life with patience.

Patience is also known as longsuffering. Longsuffering involves waiting and remaining patient with people who hurt us. We are expected to be patient and correct any wrongdoing and sins with Christ's love. Patience does not mean the same as tolerance.

Tolerance requires people to tolerate or put up with something to accept the issue or situation as agreeable and good even if the person clearly disagrees or if it is prohibited against God's law, or the Word of God. "For ye have need of patience, that after ye have done the will of God, ye might receive the promise." Heb. 10:36.

A patient person is mild, gentle, and constant in all circumstances, no matter what is going on in his or her life; the real test of patience is not in waiting, but in how we behave while waiting during trying circumstances in our lives.

We have a perfect example; the Scriptures tell us that we can be made into a perfect and complete person by having the patience that Jesus showed during his life on earth among us. He was very patient with the scribes and Pharisees.

"Blessed is the man that trusteth in the Lord, whose hope that Lord is. For he shall as a tree planted by the waters, and that spreadeth out her roots by the river, and shall not see when heat cometh, but her leaf shall be green; and shall not be careful in the year of drought, neither shall from yielding fruit." Jer. 17:7-8.

Believers are like a tree planted by water that sends out its roots near the stream. We should not fear when any earthly troubles come or worry about any adversities. We should know that our Lord and Savior is always there for us, to deliver us and sustain us throughout our trials and tribulations.

For example, the prophet Jeremiah was seen as a tree that is close to a stream, whose leaf is always green. We believers are like trees that must be close to a stream in order to bear fruits. Our Lord is the stream; He will provide for His people during hard times and under any circumstances.

We will be able to live for Him and bear more and more fruits to His kingdom. The tree bears the fruit of the Holy Spirit. Christians must produce the fruit of the Spirit, in order to grow and mature spiritually. Blessed are they who keep His words and seek Him with their whole hearts.

The Book of Psalms said, "With my whole heart have I bought have I sought thee, O let me not wonder from the commandments." Psl. 11:10. If we keep His word in our heart at all times, we will be able to understand and follow His commands with our whole heart, be obedient and pray effectively.

The fruits of our heart should be reciprocated with prayers of thankfulness. Our prayers will bring God down to earth and the gates of Heaven will open. Our prayers will flow to Heaven if we pray with our whole hearts and with patience.

11

The Fruit of the Spirit: KINDNESS

Kindness is the same as gentleness; it refers to kind behavior towards our neighbors and showing goodness and concern towards them. Sympathetic kindness can also mean showing mercy to others.

Kindness is a gift of the Holy Spirit to us. Kindness is one of the fruits of the Spirit of God that all the believers of Jesus Christ must possess. God wants us to use all of the fruits of the Spirit in our daily lives.

King Solomon, in the Book of Proverbs says, "The desire of a man is his kindness: and a poor man is better that a liar." Prov. 19:22. During his rule as the king of Israel, Solomon was looking for a kind person who had concern for others, who would put the needs of others above his own, who would put the needs of others first, before his own, and who would show kindness to himself and his neighbors. Jesus Christ God the Son is our model of kindness.

He emptied himself because of love when He left His Father's glory in heaven and came to earth. Christ died for our past, present, and future sins on the cross. "Or despisest thou the riches of his goodness and forbearance and longsuffering; not knowing that the goodness of God leadeth thee to repentance?" Rom. 2:4.

God the Father showed great mercy when He sent His one and only begotten Son on earth to redeem us from our sins. Reviewing Christ's kindness should turn you around from being a sinner to a converted Christian.

All believers have received the fruit of the Spirit so that they could exercise it towards their fellow citizens. "Grace be unto you, and peace, from God our Father, and from the Lord Jesus Christ." Php. 1:2.

May the loving kindness of God our Father and the Lord Jesus Christ bless you and give you peace. In summary, kindness is one of the important fruit of the Spirit, which is given to us for the ministerial work, in order to kindly or uniquely minister and witness to people.

When we show people the kindness through the power of the indwelling of the Holy Spirit, people gain tremendous benefits, and we can rejoice that we are using our gift of the Spirit, which is a direct reflection of how close we are and have been to the Spirit of God. If we truly have the gift of the Holy Spirit, we will produce good fruits. "Have mercy upon me, O God, according to thy loving-kindness: according unto the multitude of thy tender mercies blot out my transgression." Psl. 51:1.

King David is an example of kindness, "Wherefore I say unto thee, Her sins, which are many, are forgiven; for she loved much: but to whom little is forgiven, the same loved little." Luke 7:47.

Those who are deeply aware of their own past sinfulness understand how much they have been forgiven and, therefore, they love Jesus very much. Nevertheless, those who have a small understanding of their own sinfulness apart from Christ, will, correspondingly, love him less because they do not comprehend how much they have been forgiven.

Showing kindness is not always easy kindness is difficult. With a concerned, warm, and generous Spirit, however, our Lord Jesus Christ did what He requires. "Saying, Father, if thou be willing, remove this cup from me: nevertheless not my will, but thine, be done." Luke 22:42.

And David said, "Is there yet any that is left of the house of Saul, that I may shew him kindness for Jonathan's sake? and there was of the house of Saul a servant whose name was Ziba.

"And when they had called him unto David, the king said unto him, art thou Ziba? And he said, thy servant is he And the king said, it there not yet any of the house of Saul, that I may shew the kindness of God unto him? And Ziba said unto the king, Jonathan hath yet a son, which is lame on his feet. And the king said unto him, where is he?

"And Ziba said unto the King, behold, he is in the house of Machir, the son of ammiel in lodebar. Then King David sent, and fetched him out of the house of Machir, the son of ammiel, from lodebar. Now when Mehibosheth the son of Jonathan, the son of Saul, was come unto David, he fell on his face, and did reverence.

"And David said, Mephibosheth. And he answered, Behold thy servant. And David said unto him, fear not: for I will surely shew thee kindness for Jonathan thy father's sake, and will restore thee all the land of Saul thy father; and thou shalt eat bread at my table continually.

"And he bowed himself, and said, what is thy servant, that thou shouldest look upon such a dead dog as I am? Then the who is Lame in his feet" so the King said where is he? "Indeed he is in the house of Machir the son of Ammiel, in Lo Deba." Then the King Ziba, Saul's servant, and said unto him, I have given unto thy master's son all that pertained to Saul and to his entire house." 2 Sam. 9:1-13.

Mesphibosheth dwelt in Jerusalem; he ate continually at the king's table for he was lame at both feet. David kept his promise to his close friend Jonathan because he made a covenant with Jonathan before that he would show kindness to his family always. Mephibosheth was the son of Jonathan. David showed this remarkable kindness to him. God wants us to show kindness to others, including our enemies, at all times, in any situation, and in any circumstances.

King Solomon said, "The desire of a man is his kindness: and a poor man is better than a liar." Prov. 19:22. The wisdom of these two men concurs in that kindness is most evident when it is present and, when it is not, its absence is equally evident.

All of the fruits of the Holy Spirit are evident and based on love and kindness, which is the direct manifestation of love from the Holy Spirit. We are full of love because of the Holy Spirit's indwelling power in our hearts; we are full of joy because the Spirit of God will fill us with His joy.

Kindness is conditional behavior towards others; kindness is manifestation of other fruits of the Spirit in our lives, demonstrated by acts of love. Kindness is the work of God that demonstrates the love of God in all areas of our lives and in all instances.

It is very important for all people in this world to show kindness to the people around them. In the book of Second Peter, the Apostle urges us to show brotherly kindness to others. "For if these things be in you, and abound, they make you that ye shall neither be barren nor unfruitful in the knowledge of our Lord Jesus Christ." 2 Pet. 1:8.

Apostle Peter knew that, in order for all believers to grow in all of the fruits of the Spirit, true acknowledgment of brotherly kindness would be needed to seek the heavenly and divine nature, in the world of hatred and violence.

We must accept Jesus and allow His Spirit to live inside of us. In order to show kindness and love to others, we must accept Jesus and allow His divine nature to live through us. We must remember that there is always counterfeit and fake kindness around the world.

Lord Jesus, thank you for your kindness because, while we were yet sinners, you died for our sins. Help us to minister and show kindness as ambassadors, and representatives of your love and kindness on this earth. "Put on therefore, as the elect of God, holy and beloved, bowels of mercies, kindness, humbleness of mind, meekness, longsuffering." Col. 3:12-17.

"And he was withdrawn from them about a stone's cast, and kneels down, and prayed." Luke 22:41. "Wherefore seeing we also are compassed about with so great a cloud of witnesses, let us lay aside every weight, and the sin which doth so easily beset us, and let us run with patience the race that is set before us, Looking unto Jesus the author and finisher of our faith; who for the joy that was set before him endured the cross, despising the shame, and is set down at the right hand of the throne of God." Heb. 12:1-2.

Kindness is an attribute of God and a quality that is desirable but never consistently found in the lives of people in the world. "But love ye your enemies, and do good, and lend, hoping for nothing again; and your reward shall be great, and ye shall be the children of the Highest: for He is kind unto the unthankful and to the evil Be ye therefore merciful, as your Father also is merciful." Luke 6:35-36.

The reward will be great and you will be sons of the Most High, because He is kind to the ungrateful and wicked. The main problem is in understanding kindness and being able to distinguish kindness, mercy, and love. God's kindness is shown in all of his words, beginning in the Garden of Eden when God clothed Adam and Eve with animal skin. God's kindness is manifest in all of his creations.

"The Lord is good to all: and his tender mercies are over all His works." Psl. 145:9. The kindness of God is intended to cause repentance in our lives, not to rejection of Him. We believers in Jesus Christ appreciate God's kindness of forgiveness of our sins, with the blessing of salvation through our Lord Jesus Christ, eternal life, deliverance from fears, afflictions, and troubles.

"If so be ye have tasted that the Lord is gracious." 1 Pet. 2:3. Our salvation derives from the kindness of God. "Wherefore I was made a minister, according to the gift of grace of God given unto me by the effectual working of his power. Unto me, who am less than the least of all saints, is this grace given, that I should preach among the Gentiles the unsearchable riches of Christ." Eph. 3:7-8.

"In order that in the coming ages he might show the incomparable riches of his grace, expressed in his kindness." Eph. 2:7.

It is through of God's continuous kindness that we are saved. "Behold therefore the goodness and severity of God: on them which fell, severity, but toward thee, goodness, if thou continue in his goodness; otherwise thou also shalt be cut off." Rom. 11:22.

If any believer, or Churches of the Lord cut themselves off and followed the false prophets, Paul stated that they would be cut off. This is a serious warning to all people of God, regardless of their denomination, if they do not continue in His kindness, in the apostolic faith, and in the spirit of righteousness.

Kindness and meekness are the same; a kind or meek person is usually seen as a weak person, but a kind person is a very strong person who is the master of himself and a servant to other people.

A kind person will endure and pray instead of revenging wrongs that people do to them. A kind person is never proud; his strength is always under control. Our Lord Jesus Christ is the most kind and meek person on earth. He always exercises His strength under control. When all believers look at kindness, they see clearly that kindness is a condition of the heart and mind, while gentleness describes one's actions.

Kind strength comes from longsuffering and patience, which expresses every situation with love. Believers in the Spirit of kindness are mild, patient, and full of the Spirit of longsuffering. They do not have any Spirit of revenge or retaliation in them. Kind people possess the teachable Spirit and they are able to leave every problem and affliction in the hands of the Lord.

Kindness and meekness, being the fruits of the Spirit, are attributes of God the Father Almighty Himself and are very important to our existing in His image as true witnesses. These characteristics will determine how much peace and contentment are in our lives and how we will perform during our trials. Kindness and meekness are very important.

Our Lord Jesus Christ, in the beatitude, said, "Blessed are the meek" for they shall inherit the earth." Matt. 5:5. Meekness and kindness are active fruits. Both are internal and external in their operation in a believer's life.

When we come to God in deep penitence and with a clear mind of knowledge of ourselves and what God has done, who He is, and what He requires of his people, we will be able to serve God with the Spirit of humility that comes from the Spirit of God. The relationship between humility and kindness is that humility deals with a correct assessment and kindness covers a correct assessment of personal rights.

The example of a meek, kind person is that he or she changes from a selfish, ambitious, and self-willed person who cares about himself or herself alone and who is so proud about who he, to a new man or woman in Christ who has been crucified with Christ.

He or she changes to someone who sees things with the eyes of God or from God's perspective, seeking and focusing only on the Lord, how to serve him, and how to allow and fulfill his purpose in every situation in life. The example of Apostle Paul is that of someone who surrendered all to Jesus.

Paul saw the Father, the Son Jesus Christ, and the Gospel of the kingdom as His main focus; he wanted all the believers to focus their lives on Jesus. Paul told the Corinthian Church that they should imitate him as he imitates Christ. "And be ye kind one to one another, tenderhearted, forgiving one another, even as God for Christ's sake hath forgiven you." Eph. 4:32.

Kindness is the fruit of the Spirit that always acts for the good of other people, regardless of what they do, who they are, or what race or color they are. Kindness will also be seen as goodness and gentleness of heart in any situation with other people.

Kindness is being concerned and acting for the wellbeing of those around us. Kindness is the work of the Holy Spirit in the lives of the believers. Any believer that exercises this type of fruit or the fruit of kindness is considered to be compassionate. Such a person possesses a considerate attitude and is sympathetic to others' needs and problems, kind, gentle, and ready to help people.

The word, kindness, is characterized by interpersonal relationships, which conveys the idea of being an adaptable person to others, someone who can adapt to their problems, situations, and circumstances. A kind person will do good things for people without expecting anything in return.

Kindness is respect and helping others without waiting for someone to help you back. A believer with the fruit of kindness exercises kindness wherever he may be and in any situation. Apostle Paul said, "By pureness, by knowledge, by longsuffering, by kindness, by the Holy Ghost, by love unfeigned, by the word of truth, by the power of God, by the armor of righteousness on the right hand and on the left." 2 Cor. 6:6-7.

Kindness opens doors for serving the Lord. Barnabas, the son of encouragement, sold a field of land and gave the money for the relief of the saints. "Having land, sold it, and brought the money, and laid it at the apostles' feet." Acts 4:37.

Barnabas was very sensitive to hurting people in need of help. The Spirit later marked him as the first fruit. This act of kindness to support the poor was an important part of Barnabas's growth in service of the

Lord, which all the Christians should follow. Kindness softens the hard and angry heart of men. "A soft answer turneth away wrath: but grievous words stir up anger." Prov. 15:1.

Kindness shows Christ to the entire universe. It is with the power of the Holy Spirit that believers are able to produce genuine kindness, and it can only happen once we submit and obey the Holy Spirit, which means totally surrendering to the Holy Spirit's control.

The Spirit nurtures the positive character changes that are reflected in our relationship with the Lord. Through the love of God in our hearts, the Spirit of God is able to produce the fruit of kindness in our lives. Through the love of God, we found the sustaining power of the Holy Spirit, who turned us from unkind persons, to kind persons.

Our heavenly Father continuously pours His love upon all His children. The kingdom of God is righteousness, peace, and joy in the Holy Ghost, and righteousness is its first principle. Its peace-loving and selfless citizens are at war with unrighteousness in all forms.

It is the peace of mind and heart that the captive sinner experiences when He is reconciled with God. We must know that believers who produce the fruit of the Spirit do not come to terms with the unfruitful works of darkness. There is no other person in this world that is sinless like Jesus. He is the one that took away the sin of the whole world through His infinite love for mankind.

We are commissioned to go throughout the earth to tell, teach, and explain the good news of the Gospel, the work of redemption that was completed through Jesus Christ. Christ will return when our obedience with His great commission is fulfilled, so let us obey and go to the ends of the earth for Christ, who is our joy, our peace, and our righteousness.

12

The Fruit of the Spirit: GOODNESS

Goodness is the state or quality of being good, moral excellence, kind feelings, kindness, generosity, the best part of anything, and strength; it is a character recognized in the quality or conduct of a fully Spirit-filled believer.

"Wherefore also we pray always for you, that our God would count you worthy of this calling, and fulfill all the good pleasure of his goodness, and the work of faith with power." 2 Thes. 1:11. "For the fruit of the Spirit is in all goodness and righteousness and truth." Eph. 5:9.

Christians are exhorted to do good works, such as teaching and preaching the Word of God, encouraging, and serving in various ways within the fellowship of believers. "And let us not be weary in well doing: For in due season we shall reap, if we faint not. As we have therefore, opportunity, let us do good unto all men, especially unto them who are of the household of faith." Gal. 6:9-10.

Goodness is a quality that imitates God; when believers are filled with the Holy Spirit, they can exercise the goodness of God through a rich expression that will shows a Christian and Christ like character and a Christian personality.

Goodness and kindness are similar in their emphasis on moral values with a genuine excellence that is worthy of admiration. "A good man out of the good treasure of his heart bringeth forth that which is good: and an evil man out of the evil treasure of his heart bringeth forth that which is evil, for of the abundance of the heart his mouth speaketh." Luke 6:45.

Believers must imitate Christ's goodness to prove that the fruit of the Spirit called Goodness is in our lives; it must be seen in our thoughtfulness, truthfulness, sympathy, fairness, unselfishness, helpfulness, generosity, tolerance, and forgiveness.

If we exercise all these fruits, they will be manifest in our actions in life. God's Words are the source from which we are thoroughly furnished. In all good works, we are directed by the indwelling of the Holy Spirit. "Be not overcome of evil, but overcome evil with good." Rom. 12:21.

God's goodness is the truth of the Scripture. His goodness is praised in the Book of Psalms. Our Lord

Jesus Christ affirms the Father's goodness when speaking to the rich young ruler, "And He said unto him, why callest thou me good none good but one, that is, God: but if thou wilt enter into life, keep the commandments." Matt. 19:17.

"O taste and see that the Lord is good blessed is the man that trusted in Him." Psl. 34:8. God's goodness appears clearly in His dealing with all of His creations; God is not only good to all His created beings, but also to you and me. "Surely goodness and mercy shall follow me all the days of my life: and I will dwell in the house of the Lord forever."

Psl. 23:6. Believers' goodness is structured on divine goodness; goodness involves upright character, which expresses itself in kindness and other praiseworthy qualifications, including avoiding any evil thoughts that spring from the inner being. Goodness always involves particular way of behaving.

God is good. He is good to His people; when people are good they behave decently toward each other, based on God's goodness to them. The biblical words for goodness include the idea of upright behavior. Believers' goodness shows itself in various moral qualities.

Goodness involves not only correct behavior, but also avoiding its opposite, evil. The choice between good and evil has been laid before human beings since the garden of Eden, when Adam and Eve ate the fruit from the tree: "And out of the ground made the Lord God to grow every tree that is pleasant to the sight, and good for food, the tree of life also in the midst of the garden, and the tree of knowledge of good and evil." Gen. 2:9.

Believers who bear the fruit of goodness know that it has never been solely a matter of outward behavior it comes from within. A good person has good behavior, exhibits good behavior, and exhibits a good heart. Old Testament Scripture says that God's goodness to his people and their Goodness in response are based on the covenant between them. Goodness in the New Testament is the fruit of the Spirit.

The tree of the knowledge of good and evil was designed to test Adam's faith and obedience to God and His word. God created humans as moral beings with the ability to choose freely to love and obey their creator, or to disobey him and rebel against His will.

Goodness and love for the Lord will follow Christ's people all the days of their lives, and they surely will dwell in the house of the Lord from now to eternity. The Good Shepherd will accompany believers through life's pilgrimage; they will receive constant, abundant grace to help bring them kindness and support.

No matter what the circumstances are, they can trust the Good Shepherd to work, in all things, for their good. The goal of all believers following the

Good Shepherd and experiencing His goodness and love is that, one day, they will be with the Lord forever and serve him forever in His house.

We are commanded to overcome evil done to us by doing good in return. All Christians must know that it is their responsibility to yield to the Holy Spirit. It is very important that all Christians make the fruit of the Spirit part of their lives.

Yielding one's life to the direction of the Holy Spirit means involving oneself with the Word of God and being a doer of the Word of God not a hearer alone. Christian life is always a combination of the work of the Holy Spirit, God's originating fruit, and the cooperation of the will of God with individual believers of Christ.

Goodness builds up and promotes wholeness; when we focus on the goodness of the Lord, hope, encouragement, and faith are shown in us and we see the best in others and open up to them. We are willing to work together in order to achieve great victory in the goals we set for ourselves.

Believers remain focused on the goodness of God and His call to our lives. We find a deep sense of fulfillment, purpose, and satisfaction. This will change how we approach many things and the way we speak about them.

The Spirit of God will empower us, direct us, and help us to understand the reason why our enemies want to hurt us, by opening our heart to forgive them and showing goodness to those who hurt us. Those who manifest God's goodness think good thoughts, speak good words, and do good deeds.

Their words match what they do, and they maintain consistency of integrity in their lives. Goodness is the state or quality of being good, moral excellence, kind feelings, kindness, generosity, the best part of anything, and strength; it is a character recognized in the quality or conduct of a fully Spirit filled believer.

"Therefore also we pray always for you, that our God would count you worthy of his calling and fulfill all the good pleasure of his goodness, and the work of faith with power." 2 Thes. 1:11. "For the fruit of the Spirit is in all goodness and righteousness and truth." Eph. 5:9.

Christians are exhorted to do good works, such as teaching and preaching the Word of God, and encouraging and serving in various ways within the fellowship of believers. Believers should not be weary in doing good, because the reward will come from Him in due time; they shall reap if they do not lose hope.

Therefore, as we have the ability and the opportunity, let us do good to all, especially to those who are Christians to the entire household of faith. Goodness is a quality that imitates God. When believers are filled with the Holy Spirit, they can exercise the goodness of God through a rich expression that will shows a Christian and Christ like character and a Christian personality.

Goodness and kindness are similar in their emphasis on moral values with a genuine excellence that is worthy of admiration. All believers in Christ always bring out good treasure from their hearts in order to help others.

Believers must imitate Christ's goodness. In order to prove that the fruit of the Spirit, Goodness, is in our lives, it must also be seen in our thoughtfulness, truthfulness, sympathy, fairness, unselfishness, helpfulness, generosity, tolerance, and forgiveness.

If we exercise all of these fruits, they will be manifest in our actions in life. God's Words are the source from which we are thoroughly furnished. In all good works, we are directed by the indwelling of the Holy Spirit. "Be not overcome of evil, but overcome evil with good." Rom. 12:21

God's goodness is a truth of the Scripture. His goodness is praised in the Book of Psalms. Our Lord Jesus Christ affirms the Father's goodness when speaking to the rich young ruler. God's goodness appears clearly in his dealing with all of his creations.

God is not only good to all of His created beings but also to you and me. Believers' goodness is structured on divine goodness; goodness involves upright character, which expresses itself in kindness and other praiseworthy qualifications, including avoiding any evil thoughts that spring from the inner being. Goodness always involves a particular way of behaving.

God is good. He is good to His people; when people are good they behave decently toward each other, based on God's goodness to them. The biblical words for goodness include the idea of correct behavior. Believers' goodness shows itself in various moral qualities. Goodness involves not only correct behavior, but also avoiding its opposite, evil.

The choice between good and evil has been laid before human beings since the Garden of Eden, when Adam and Eve ate the fruit from the tree. Believers who bear the fruit of goodness know that it has never been solely a matter of outward behavior it comes from within.

A good person has good behavior, exhibits good behavior, and exhibits a good heart. Old Testament Scripture says that God's goodness to his people and their Goodness in response are based on the covenant between them. Goodness in the New Testament is the fruit of the Spirit.

The tree of the knowledge of good and evil was designed to test Adam's faith and obedience to God and His word. God created humans as moral beings with the ability to choose freely to love and obey their creator, or to disobey him and rebel against His will.

"Surely goodness and love will follow me all the days of my life, and I will dwell in the house of the

Lord forever." Psl. 23:6. The Good Shepherd will accompany believers through life's pilgrimage; they will receive constant, abundant grace to help bring them kindness and support.

No matter what the circumstances are, they can trust the Good Shepherd to work in all things for their good. The goal of all believers following the Good Shepherd and experiencing His goodness and love is that, one day, they will be with the Lord forever and serve him forever in His house.

We are commanded to overcome evil done to us by doing good in return. All Christians must know that it is their responsibility to yield to the Holy Spirit. It is very important that all Christians make the fruit of the Spirit part of their lives.

Yielding one's life to the direction of the Holy Spirit means involving oneself with the Word of God and being a doer of the Word of God not a hearer alone. Christian life is always a combination of the work of the Holy Spirit, God's originating fruit, and the cooperation of the will of God with individual believers of Christ.

Goodness builds up and promotes wholeness; when we focus on the goodness of the Lord, hope, encouragement, and faith are shown in us and we see the best in others and open up to them. We are willing to work together in order to achieve great victory in the goals we set for ourselves. Believers remain focused on the goodness of God and His call to our lives. We find a deep sense of fulfillment, purpose, and satisfaction. This will change how we approach many things and the way we speak about them.

The Spirit of God will empower us, direct us, and help us to understand the reason why our enemies want to hurt us, by opening our heart to forgive them and showing goodness to those who hurt us.

Those who manifest God's goodness think good thoughts, speak good words, and do good deeds. Their words match what they do, and they maintain consistency of integrity in their lives.

Summary

Complete, full knowledge and inspiration of the entire Bible is equally God-given from Genesis through Revelation. The Word of God, through Biblical inerrancy, points to the doctrinal position that the Bible is accurate and totally free of error, that Scripture in its original manuscripts does not affirm anything that is not true, or that is an error not only with regards to doctrine, but also with regards to history, science, chronology, and in all other areas of life.

The doctrine of Trinity is considered as being at the center of Christian doctrine. God reveals Himself to humanity through so many of the things that He has created, in such a way that all of His creations may find their meaning in relation to God.

The Spirit Power assists all Christians, including students and scholars of theology, who are interested in understanding their Christians life, in their hearts and minds. This book will be a great resource and a treasure. This book will help all Christians and theology students of all denominations, as well as all people of the other religions, to open up the Scripture for a greater spiritual understanding of the

Spirit Power and open them to the things of God, His power, and His will for all people on earth. The Power of the Holy Spirit in the lives of all believers in the body of Christ on this earth cannot be compared to any power.

It is incomparable, it is immeasurable beyond what anyone can think or imagine. Our Lord said, "But the hour cometh, and now is, when the true worshippers shall worship the Father in Spirit and in truth: for the Father seeketh such to worship Him." John 4:23.

Jesus Christ expounded upon this clearly to the Samaritan woman at the well. We must come to God with sincere hearts and with the Spirit of holiness, leading lives that are under the control of the Holy Spirit; we are created in the image of God.

Our new birth is different from our old birth, which was of the flesh. God's relationship with all of His children is based on the Spirit not on the flesh. It is like the relationship of a Father and His children it can never be erased. We are one in Him as He is one with the Father.

We must worship the Father according to the truth of the Father that was revealed by the Son and that the Holy Spirit controls and guides. The relationship that God requires of us must be a voluntary one that we enter into willingly and joyfully, surrendering our will to the will of God.

Our relationship must remain unconditional and be based on our faith in Christ, throughout our life on earth. Faith demonstrates and is characterized by sincere love and obedience to God. The only true worship is when we worship the Father through the Spirit of Holiness.

God gave us His Spirit and He continues to pour out His Spirit on all those who believe in Him, up until today. Every day, there is always a day of Pentecost in heaven, whereby the Spirit of God pours down into the hearts, minds, and souls of His converted sinners.

God gave us the power of the Spirit to dwell and perform His supernatural power through us, so that we may be able to live lives originating in the Lord here on earth. I urge all members of the body of Christ to use this power, claim this power, and use it in everywhere, in everything they do. He is waiting for you and me.

There is no power but the power of the Spirit of God in our lives, in the lives of our children, relatives and friends. Use the power of the Spirit of God in your office, neighborhood, community, city, state, and in the entire world with the unending love of the Spirit that dwells in you.

Exercise all the fruit of the Spirit wherever you go: love, joy, peace, goodness, kindness, and the other fruits of the Spirit. Allow the Spirit of God to continuously produce and pour out the fruits of His Spirit in our lives.

The Spirit of God the Father, the Spirit of God the Son, and the Spirit of God the Holy Spirit is one, and He made us one in Him. We should rejoice and continue in unending love and in the Spirit Power.

Jesus Christ is the truth; all believers must live in unity and speak the truth that Christ requires of us. Those who do not have the truth in them hide what is in their heart and they remain in darkness and automatically throw themselves outside the kingdom of heaven. Believers must speak the truth with the love of God.

Bibliography

Walter A. Walter Editor Evangelical Dictionary of Biblical Dictionary of Biblical Theology: Publisher Baker Book House, Grand Rapids, MI, USA.

William MacDonald, Edited by Art Farstad: Believer's Bible Commentary, Thomas Nelson Publisher, Nashville, TN, USA.

Thomas F. Torrance, Paul D. Molnar 1946. Ashgate publisher, Ltd: Distributed by Syndetic Solutions, Inc. Theologian of the Trinity. Christian Denominations Doctrine Theology the Bible. Farnham, England, Burlington, VT, USA.

Mathew Henry's Commentary in one Volume, Edited by Re. Leslie F. Church: Zondervan Publishing House, Grand Rapids, MI, USA.

D. Norman Geisler: Systematic Theology Volume Four, Church Last Thing, Bethany House Publishers, Bloomington, MN, USA.

Leadership Ministries Worldwide: Practical Word Studies in the New Testament Volume One and Volume Two from the Publishers of The Preacher's Outline and Sermon Bible: Zondervan Publishing House, Chattanooga, TN, USA.

James D. Smart: The Interpretation of Scripture, the Westminster Press, Philadelphia, PA, USA.

Biblical Index

Genesis: 1:2, 6:3, 41:38, 2:7, 2:9, 15:6, 2:16, 22, 1:19

Exodus: 31:3, 35:31, 14:22, 13:14, 32:23, 34:6

Leviticus: 19:2

Numbers: 12:3, 11-13, 11:17, 6:24-26, 14:18

Deuteronomy: 34:9, 6:4, 7:9

Joshua 1:9, 3:15-16

2 Samuel: 9:1-13

2 Kings: 2:2

2 Chronicles: 2:6

Nehemiah: 8:10, 12:43

Job: 33:4, 20:4-5

Psalms: 23:6, 57:11, 76:9, 149:4, 34:8, 104:30, 119:11, 139:7, 51:6-10, 3:5,16:11, 81:1,16, 16:11, 30:5, 5:11-12, 37:7, 140:1, 46:10, 103:8, 145:8-9, 86:15, 51:1, 34:8, 25:9

Proverbs: 14:13, 9:10, 45:6-7, 15:21, 14:29, 15:18, 19:11, 3:5-6, 19:22, 51:1, 11:17, 15:1, 28:20, 21:23, 15:2

Ecclesiastes: 2:1-11, 26

Isaiah: 4:4, 55:8-9, 65:3, 42:1, 26:3, 30:18, 25:1, 53:7-9

Jeremiah: 15:15, 29::11, 17:7-8

Ezekiel: 36:26-27, 37:3-5

Hosea: 10:12, 2:20

Joel: 2:13, 2:28-32

Zechariah: 4:6

Matthew: 28:19-20, 5:1-12, 25:21, 9:17, 19:17, 11:23-24, 6:4, 6, 11:29, 5:5-6, 9:3-6, 18:23-35, 8:4, 9:3-6, 18:23-35 8:4, 5:6, 6:33 11:11

Mark: 16:16

Luke: 23:34, 1:35, 2:10-11, 13:34, 6:35-36, 6:45, 11:13, 7:47, 22:4, 6:45, 16:10-12, 18:7, 9:48, 9:48, 3:8, 19:23

John: 4:24, 1:3, 1:1, 4:23-24, 14:7-9, 15:1-2, 14:16, 26, 16:8, 16:13, 16:7-8, 3:6, 6:63, 4:14, 7:37-38, 3:3-8, 86:16, 4:23-24, 15:10, 13:35, 4:7-8, 3:16, 15:13, 4:19, 1:11, 6:44, 17:13, 15:11, 14:27, 12:27, 16:13, 13:17, 1:7-9, 20:24-31, 3:3, 20:26, 16:22, 20:21, 16, 12-14, 20:21, 16:21, 4:23, 14:6, 16:13, 6:12, 2:25, 13:1

Acts: 11:16-17, 2:3-4, 2:38, 8:14-15, 3:31, 24:24-25, 9:17, 10:44, 1:8, 1:4, 5:31, 16:30, 12:46, 16:34,16:24-25, 10:36, 8:35-38

Romans: 8:16, 8:16-17, 6:3-4, 8:15-16, 8:27, 1:29-31, 13:13, 5:5, 8:14, 16:20, 8:25, 2:4, 11:22, 5:8, 8:11, 5:1, 15:13, 12:21, 10:17, 7:14-17, 8:3-4, 2:4, 9:22-24, 15:1-2, 10:10, 2:4, 3:25, 12:3

1 Corinthians: 10:31, 6:6-10, 13:1-13, 8:1, 13:4-8, 2:13-14, 13:13, 13:4-8, 1:1110:13, 9:27

2 Corinthians: 5:19, 5:17, 5:5, 3:18, 12:20, 12:9-10, 6:6-7, 1:18-19, 8:9, 10:1, 5:17, 12:7

Galatians: 5:22, 5:19-23, 5:18, 6:9-10, 5:23, 2:20, 6:1

Ephesians: 1:13-14, 1:13-14, 2:1-3, 5:2, 1:20, 4:22-24, 4:2-3, 2:7, 3:7-8, 4:32, 5:5-9, 3:16-17, 2:8, 4:2, 3:16, 5:17-25, 1:17

Philippians: 4:8, 2:7-8, 2:13, 4:4, 1:2, 3:9, 5:11, 2:5-8, 3:10

Colossians: 1:15-16, 3:12-17, 4:7, 1:7, 1:16, 15:1,8,16, 3:13, 3:12-15

1 Thessalonians: 1:6, 4:16-17, 3:16, 1:11, 2:23-26

2 Thessalonians: 1:6, 2:7-8, 1:6

2 Timothy: 3:10, 2:24, 2:25

Titus: 3:5, 3:2-3

Hebrews: 12:3, 12:2, 12:1-2, 11:6, 1:1-2, 12:2, 10:36, 11:6

James: 3:18, 1:3-4, 1:21, 1:5, 3:171

1 Peter: 5:7, 4:12-13, 2:3, 3:4, 3:18, 3:18-20, 3:15, 3:14 5:5-6

2 Peter: 3:9, 1:3, 1:5-11, 1:5-7, 3:9

1 John: 4:9, 4:4, 3:1, 4:7-12, 4:16, 2:3-6

Revelation: 21:3

Benediction

"The grace of our Lord Jesus Christ, the love of God, and the communion of the Holy Ghost, be with you all." Amen, amen, amen. 2 Cor. 13:14.

MAY GOD BE GLORIFIED FOR THE GREAT THINGS HE HAS DONE IN OUR WORLD.

Books previously
published by the author
Grace Dola Balogun by
Grace Religious Books Publishing
& Distributors, Inc.

**PRAYER THE SOURCE OF STRENGTH
FOR LIFE – English Edition**

Prayer the Source of Strength for Life is a powerful book that will energize your spirit to pray more and more until the prayer is part of your life and until the gate of heaven is opened and your prayer is answered. Your prayer life will change your life.

LA ORACION FUENTE DE FORTALEZA PARA LA VIDA – Spanish Edition.

Dios nos dio el poder de la oracion, quiere que lo usemos; debemos illamar, comunicarnos con el en todo lo que estemos pasando. El espera saber de nosotros.

Spirit Power Volume I and II both discuss the power of the Holy Spirit in the life of believers of Jesus Christ.

The Power of the Spirit of God begins from the creation of the world up until today. That power will also continue until Christ returns to reign. Hallelujah!

THE CROSS AND THE CRUCIFIXION

Our Lord Jesus Christ died on the Cross to bring forth love and compassion. Sin's impact on human life brings all other evil into our world, from one society to another society, from one culture to another.

But in Christ, we are clothed with His holiness. We have the gift of eternal life. The gate of heaven is open and we are eligible for our inheritance in heaven.

Hallelujah! Hosanna in the Highest. Jesus Christ paid it all, unto Him all we owe. The Cross of Christ is the Cross of joy, peace, and righteousness to all who believe in Him.

About the Author

Grace Dola Balogun graduated from Fordham University Graduate School of Religion and Religious Education in the year 2010 with an M.A. in Religion and Religious Education. She has been a prayer mentor and advisor for many Christians of all denominations since 1988.

Visit her online at:
gracereligiousbookspublishers.com
Prayerstrengthforlife.com
Spiritpower.info
salvationcompleted.com
Facebook
GSTwitter@prayersource

To Order This Book

To order additional copies of this book,
please E-mail:
info@gracereligiousbookspublishers.com

This book may also be ordered from 30,000
wholesalers, retailers, and booksellers in
the U. S., and in Canada and over
100 countries globally.

To contact Grace Dola Balogun for an
interview or a speaking engagement,
please E-mail:
info@gracereligiousbookspublishers.com

The Spirit and the bride say, "Come!"
And let the one who hears say, "Come!"
Let the one who is thirsty come;
and let the one who wishes take
the free gift of the water of life.

Revelation 22:17

MARANATHA!

COME, LORD JESUS!

For my grandchildren: Anna, Tommy, William, Jenni and
Sean

ACKNOWLEDGEMENTS:
A number of people helped me out with this novel by
critiquing it and advising me. Others read it and offered
more advice. Included in this group are Jan Clark, Mark
Henderson and Rebecca Stevenson. Without their help, this
novel would still be in the reworking stage. Diane Khoury
pointed out hundreds of typos in the book (It seems I'm
comma-challenged).

The cover artwork was done by Gary V. Tenuta.
He can be contacted through his website:
http://www.bookcoversandvideos.webs.com/

PROLOGUE

Sir John Falstaff and his page, Poulet, thundered through the city gates a few minutes ahead of the angry husband and his relatives, and seconds before the gates were locked. A partial moon gave them enough light to pick out the woodland road they traveled.

A few miles from the city of Cintri in southern Gundarland, Falstaff called out, "Slow down, Poulet. My horse is tiring."

"Next time, steal a horse, not a bag of bones." Poulet, bundled up in a brown cloak, rode a fine pony.

"Now you're a connoisseur of horse thievery? Is there no end to your learning?" Falstaff knew his hairy-toed half-pint page was right; the horse was an old nag, but under the circumstances, it was the best he could find.

"How can you expect a horse like that to carry all your excess weight?" Poulet called over his shoulder.

"Don't start in on my weight. The women like me the way I am." The fifty-year-old Falstaff wore an expensive dark blue doublet and matching hose. Both garments, a few years old and fitted to a much lighter man, threatened to burst at the seams with a wrong move. A scabbard with a jeweled hilt adorned his left hip.

"I'm gettin' tired of hustlin' outta town because some husband wants to kill you."

"Wooing noble women is the fastest and surest way to get money. The sweet thing I entertained this evening gave me a purse of coins to help me get away from her cretin husband. Besides, 'twas time to move on. I'm too well known now to get anyone to invest in a new scheme."

"It's good you gotta heavy purse, but we can't spend the coins in the towns around here. You'll get hung if we go near any of 'em."

"'Tis not my fault these small towns have silly rules about card sharping and wooing married women. Let's rest until dawn." Falstaff dismounted and his horse whinnied in relief. "With first light, we'll head north to Dun Hythe. I haven't been there in a number of years. Perhaps we'll find new faces and new opportunities." He stretched his muscles, cramped from riding, and slapped Poulet on the shoulder. "I have an itch in my palm and it bodes well for us."

PART ONE

CHAPTER ONE

Hamlet, Crown Prince of Denmarko, paced the castle battlements late on a clear, cool spring night. He walked with hands clasped behind his back and head down. He had a thin nose with brown hair and eyes. His scrawny build and clean-shaven face gave him the appearance of a starving waif.

He paused, gazed at the multitudinous stars, sighed and continued his pacing. A breeze brought the smells of the harbor: salt water and rotting fish guts. At last, he stopped, thrust one hand to the sky and declaimed, "To bee or not to bee?" He stroked his chin. "Whether 'tis nobler to buy honey from the peasant farmer in the market and thus provide him sustenance and income to support his brood of brats, possibly keeping him from rebelling over high taxes . . . or to grow my own honey thus gaining coins to assert my independence from my noble family and the sordid court? Hmm."

He paced some more, still troubled by his vexing question. Nothing less than his future depended upon the answer. Because his uncle, and now stepfather, Clodio, had usurped his right to rule the kingdom, he needed a profession and an income.

"Do you always talk to yourself?" a voice said from the shadows.

"Who . . . who goes there?" Hamlet's head snapped from one side to another while his hand grasped the hilt of his dagger.

"'Tis I, the ghost of your father. I bring a message for your ears alone."

Hamlet goggled at the specter who materialized in the shadows of a doorway. "You're not my father's ghost. My father was a dwarf and you're the ghost of an elf. You're an impostor and a dead one to boot."

"Hey, your father is busy and he asked me to fill in."

"Busy? In the underworld? What's he doing?" Hamlet clutched his red tunic and tugged downward as if to hide his shaking hands.

"He met a good-lookin' ghost of a female dwarf and he's wooin her."

"Dead not a month, and he forsakes his wife, my mother?

"You gotta understand. Life on this side — no pun intended — is pretty borin'. When you gotta a chance to do somethin' interestin', you gotta go with it."

Hamlet ran a hand over his face. Why me? he thought. "What's the message?"

"His death was no accident. It was murder most foul. Here is his exact message. 'But know, thou noble youth, the serpent that did sting thy Father's life, now wears his crown.'" The ghost paused then added, "Did your father always talk funny like that?"

"Murdered? By whom?"

"Didn't you listen? The message tells you who whacked him. Your father wants you to send this guy over here so he can talk to him. He doesn't wanna wait until the guy croaks from natural causes."

Hamlet watched in awe as the ghostly figure evaporated. A few seconds later, it popped back into sight. "Oh, I forgot to tell you. Your father says, 'Thy mother the queen is to know naught of this nocturnal visit.'" The ghost disappeared.

His father's murder shocked him. And the murderer had married his mother immediately afterward. Did the world have no morals?

He recalled his first thoughts when he'd heard of his father's death. How he admired the perseverance and tenacity his father must have had to commit suicide by suffocating himself with a pillow. Now all that admiration was wasted; the old dwarf had had help.

What to do? He needed to make decisions about bee farming and now he had to avenge his father. Was there no end to the demands on a prince's time? He said to the stars, "To bee-keep or to avenge? That is the question."

# # #

Othello, a dark elf, shouldered his way through the teeming streets of Dun Hythe.

Born in a forest in central Gundarland, he had rarely been in a town, let alone a large city like this. The sheer size of the population and the mix of races staggered him. He walked along the main street filled with the sounds of wagon traffic, cursing drivers, squeaky cart wheels. Together, the sounds produced a cacophony that assaulted his ears.

In the forest where he had grown up, the population consisted almost exclusively of dark elves, and anyone not a dark elf was viewed with suspicion. Dun Hythe had a population almost equally divided between large humans, criminally inclined elves, homicidal dwarfs and hairy-toed half-pints. The city also had a group of maniacal trolls.

Othello wondered why all these hordes of different races, packed together in tenements, didn't engage in racial warfare. Dun Hythe was beyond his experience and all the history of his tribe. He wondered if this strangeness would affect his ability to carry out his assignment as Minister of Homeland Security for the city.

His wife, born and raised in the city, had told him Dun Hythe had never been attacked. With a history like that, security shouldn't be much of a problem.

Othello marched up the steps of the city hall. He couldn't recall another day when he had felt so proud and so confident. He determined this time would be different; this time he wouldn't fail.

Two members of the Troll Patrol lounged by the door shooting dice. They ignored him. He hesitated a moment, undecided whether to chastise them for not recognizing and saluting their new commanding officer. In a gracious mood, he forgave them because Captain Iago might not have given them the word yet. Inside, he climbed the stairs to the second floor office of Mayoress Glyniss. An empty secretary's desk sat outside the office door.

He straightened his tan tunic and adjusted his matching tan kepi with a large gold C — for Colonel — on the front. He knocked on the door frame and smiled at the middle-aged woman sitting behind a large desk. Glyniss looked up at the sound.

"Come in, Colonel Othello." She stood and walked to a conference table near the door. "Let's get you sworn in, then we'll talk about your responsibilities." She gave him a frozen smile. "Raise your right hand and repeat this oath. 'I swear to protect the city of Dun Hythe and never betray the city's interests or to put my needs before the city's needs.'"

Othello swore the oath and sat down, careful not to wrinkle his tan pants. They were tucked into cavalry boots. He removed the kepi and placed it on the table.

"Nice uniform," Glyniss said.

"Thank you." Othello had designed it himself and added plenty of gold braid on it. He chose the tan color because it set off the dusky complexion typical of dark elves. Tall and lean, he had short, glossy, ebony hair and bronze-colored eyes. He also had a thin nose, broad lips, a pointed chin and large ears that stuck out from the head. "I'm anxious to get started."

"We — the Council and I — felt we had to establish this position because of the potential trouble caused by the outbreak of peace throughout Gundarland."

"I . . . I don't understand." Othello frowned. "I thought my position was to protect the city. How can peace threaten it?"

"Countrywide peace is an unknown factor. No one knows what will happen because of it. I used the public scryer network to contact every province in the country. All of them are at peace. I don't think it has ever happened before. You can see the most visible sign of peace everywhere in the city. It's the swarm of ex-warriors, almost all dwarfs, that came to the city looking for jobs. Most of them are unemployed and homeless and survive only by committing crimes. Since they are trained soldiers and came here with their weapons, they constitute a threat to law and order. They also present a threat of insurrection. Your most pressing assignment will be to get control of these soldiers and defuse their potential for causing trouble."

Othello squirmed in his chair. "Do you have any advice on how to do that?" He had thought of his responsibility only in terms of a threat from outside the city, not from inside.

"None at all." Glyniss stared at him. "I created this new position so I wouldn't have to solve problems like that." She pointed to a map of the city that covered most of one wall.

"I can tell you they tend to gather around the docks. They sometimes get day jobs loading or unloading ships."

"I won't disappoint you," Othello replied with more conviction than he felt. "I'll look into the situation immediately."

"Good. These demobilized soldiers present another threat to the city. They may join up with pirates and attack our shipping. If that occurs, merchants and traders will choose to avoid our port and go south to Cintri. That will mean a loss of customs revenue. The city has four patrol craft to dissuade piracy, but they may be overmatched if the soldiers get involved. You need to develop a plan and implement it to protect our revenue sources."

Othello recognized that his new job was more complex than he had imagined. Waving a sword around and shouting orders to his underlings wasn't going to do much to solve the problems.

"The next situation is just as vital. Dun Hythe is a free city. It has no overlord and that is unique. It is a free city because our trade benefits all the provinces. Every warlord and province chief has nightmares about one of their enemies seizing the city and using our revenues to build up an invincible army. The city never had to worry about that in the past because all the warlords were too busy defending their own lands or planning an invasion of their neighbors."

Othello had a bad feeling he would like his next task even less than the previous one.

"With peace, bands of ex-warriors now roam the countryside. Eventually, they will come together under a strong leader and attack the city. Unfortunately, the absence of a threat to the city for all those years meant the walls weren't maintained and now they are falling down. Our militia, who are supposed to defend the city, are in equal disrepair. They resemble a drinking club rather than an effective military deterrent."

"You want me to fix those problems as well?" Othello picked up his kepi and brushed imaginary dust from the brim. His breakfast lay like a lump in his stomach.

"Yes. I can't give you much money for the wall repairs, but it'll be enough to get you started on the worst sections. As for the militia, they need discipline and training. Here your military background should come into play and simplify the task."

Othello gave her a fleeting half-smile. "Can I use the Troll Patrol to work on any of these issues?"

"The Troll Patrol is under your command. Do what you think best." Glyniss stood up. "I'll let you get started with your work. Your office is on the first floor. I want frequent reports on your progress." She went to her desk, sat down and attacked a pile of scrolls.

He left Glyniss and found his office. A female troll sat outside it at a desk, filing her nails. "Are you my secretary?"

She was about five foot tall, yellow-skinned and wore a short, simple kirtle of rough cloth that displayed over-muscled arms and legs. "You Ofella?"

"Othello."

"Wot?"

"Othello. My name is Othello."

"Dat's wot I said."

Othello had a premonition that this secretary belonged on the long list of problems Glyniss had handed him.

"What's your name?"

"Emilia. Never saw a darkie before."

Othello ignored the racial slur. "Do I have any correspondence?"

"Don't know wot corr-is-pondts are."

"Letters, memos, notes?"

"Iffen I got any for someone named Ofella, I tossed 'em out."

"Do you know Captain Iago?"

"Married the bugger, didn't I?"

Othello blinked in surprise. After a moment's hesitation, he said, "Tell him I want to meet in my office."

"Okey dokey." Emilia stood up and yelled, "Iago! Get your stupid butt over here!"

Shaking his head, Othello went into the office and shut the door. He had a lot of thinking to do. His job involved many more issues than he had believed possible. Maybe he shouldn't have plumped his resume so much.

# # #

A short time later, Emilia opened the door, stuck her bald head into the office and said, "Got 'im." Her head disappeared and Captain Iago swaggered in.

Like all trolls, he had cruel, beady black eyes. He wore the Troll Patrol uniform of brown pants held up by a rope and nothing else — no shirt, no shoes. He did wear a blue sash draped over one shoulder depicting his rank as Troll Patrol Commander. From his walk and posture, arrogance dripped from him like water off someone fresh from a swim. Othello ignored the swagger. Here was his first chance to demonstrate his leadership qualities and solve one of the city's problems. He was sure Glyniss would be impressed by his creativity

"You must be de new guy," Iago said in a voice filled with sarcasm. "Yer in charge of Homeland Security and ya don't know jackshite about de town."

Othello started to react, but decided to ignore both the insult and the tone. "Yes, I'm Colonel Othello, your new superior officer." He pointed to a chair. "Mayor Glyniss gave me several projects to work on and I want to talk about a plan to solve one of them with the Troll Patrol."

Iago remained standing with his arms folded across his chest. "Da Patrol is mine."

"I know that. That's why we're meeting. Glyniss is concerned about the increasing crime rate in the city. She believes much of it is due to the influx of dwarf warriors. I want you to establish flying squads of trolls. They will show up unexpectedly in high crime areas and make arrests if they see any criminal activity. A few days of that will have the criminals thinking twice about breaking the law."

"Nope." Iago sneered at Othello.

Othello wrinkled his brow. "What does that mean?" His first solution seemed on the verge of evaporating.

"It means de Troll Patrol works traffic and guards dis buildin'. Dat's all we do and dat's all we gonna do. Ain't gonna arrest dwarf crooks."

"You are under my supervision," Othello growled. "That means you follow my orders. If I give you an order, you obey it. Is that clear?"

Iago's sneer turned into a smirk. "Da patrol ain't gonna arrest dwarf scum. Iffen ya make me order 'em to do dat, dey gonna go onna strike. Da Patrol loves to go onna strike. Iffen dey go onna strike, ya got no one to fix da traffic messes and guard da buildin'. Da mayor gonna wanna know why da Patrol is onna strike."

Othello glared at Iago while struggling not to shout at the troll.

"Ya need anudda plan," Iago said as he swaggered out of the office. He slammed the door to emphasize his departure.

Emilia stuck her head into the office again. "Nasty bugger, ain't he?" She giggled and shut the door.

Othello bit his lip and wondered how he would be able to handle his new job. Its complexities were far beyond his expectations.

# # #

The Troll Patrol was an institution unique to Dun Hythe. Long ago, the city leaders had recognized the need to control and direct the heavy wagon traffic that flowed to and from the port area. They organized a patrol of citizens for this purpose, and all went well for a while. No one recalls who allowed the first troll to join up, but word immediately spread throughout the troll community that one of their number had a paying job with unlimited donuts. Soon after that, every opening in the patrol attracted dozens of trolls who brazenly persuaded non-trolls to withdraw their applications. Within a few years, trolls had taken over the organization.

Trolls proved to be particularly inept at traffic control. A member of the Troll Patrol could station himself in the middle of a deserted intersection and within minutes he would create a traffic-snarling mess. To keep the enraged wagon drivers under control, the trolls relied upon truncheons. A whack or two in the head always knocked a driver groggy and made him a lot less noisy.

The Troll Patrol did prove effective in controlling the riots that resulted from their traffic mismanagement. Trolls had evolved from rocks and they had rock DNA in their systems. Hitting a troll in his head was a waste of energy. All it did was damage the weapon and focus the troll's attention on the head-hitter, much to the head-hitter's discomfort.

Trolls had a unique perspective on bribery. Often a visitor who had been apprehended by a troll on a charge — often a dubious one — would offer a sum of money to make the charge disappear. The troll always pocketed the money and then added bribery to the charge sheet. The bribed troll scrupulously shared the bribe money with the shift desk sergeant.

Early in the process of changing to the Troll Patrol, politicians discovered that it was impossible to fire a troll and remain alive. The fired troll took the firing personally and considered himself insulted. An insult to one troll insulted the troll's entire family, who then felt obligated to avenge their family honor by slaughtering the insulter.

#

Before Othello recovered from his disastrous meeting, he heard Emilia talking to someone. Her head popped into the office. "Ya gotta visitor." A troll with blue sergeant stripes tattooed on his biceps strolled into the office and nodded to him. "Name's Nark. Sergeant Nark. I'm yer new assistant."

"You are? How did you get that job? I didn't request an assistant." Nark had oversized shoulders, a huge head and a massive chest. He looked top-heavy.

"Iago sent me here."

"Iago? How odd. He didn't seem very friendly when we met. Perhaps I misread him."

"Naw. Iago da most unfriendly troll in da city. He wanted dis job. You got it so him very angry wid ya. Ain't gonna get any help from dat one. Dat no big deal 'cause him pretty stupid. See, him and me hate each other's guts and him wanna get rid of me for a while now. Dat's why I'm here and you gonna need me 'cause yer new in town. Now I got born here. I know all da streets and stuff. I know all da good taverns and da good bawdy houses, too. Iffen ya lookin' for a good time, I can tell ya where to go."

"I'm a married man, so I won't be needing your advice in that area. But you're right. I could use someone who knows the city and its streets." Othello's mood perked up now that he had a local expert to help him. "What can you tell me about the militia?"

"Dey not too good. Wanna go see 'em drill tomorrow?"

"Yes, I do. For now, can you show me around the city? I'd like to get more familiar with it."

"Sure."

Othello stood up and followed Nark out.

"See ya later, Sis," Nark said to Emilia.

"She's your sister?"

"Yeah. Iago and me are bruddas-in-law."

# # #

At the end of his first day in charge of Homeland Security, Othello walked into his home in the elf quarter. Exhausted and more than a little concerned about the scope of his responsibilities, the challenge nevertheless excited him. Dun Hythe was where he would make his mark and claim the fame and glory that had eluded him until now.

His bride, Desdemona, greeted him with two glasses of red wine. She kissed him and said, "Tell me all about your day."

"It was . . . different," Othello said as he took a glass.

Tall and lithe, Desdemona was a light elf with reddish-green hair and moss green eyes. They both sat down on the couch and sipped the wine. Besides the couch, the large room held a fireplace for cooking and a table with two chairs. A bedroom and an office — until it became a nursery — filled the rest of the apartment.

He told her about the problems he had uncovered. "The only good thing so far is Nark. He really does know the city. During our walking tour, we visited the port area. It's impossible to describe to folks who don't live here. So many ships, so many wagons, so many workers. Glyniss told me I have four small patrol boats to control piracy. Nark told me I only have three because one got rammed by a barge the other day and sank. How was your day? I know you're glad to be back where you grew up."

"My day was fine." Desdemona gave him a ravishing smile. "I went shopping, something you can't do very much of in Nexus." Othello was born and raised in the small town of Nexus, and the wedding took place there. "Oh, I received a note from my grandmother. She wants to meet you so she invited us to dinner in a few days."

"Ahh, I'll finally get to meet her. You said she raised you, so I was surprised she didn't come to the wedding."

"Grandmother never leaves Dun Hythe. She has too many responsibilities."

Othello paused in taking a sip. "What does she do?"

Desdemona chuckled. "You won't believe how many projects she has going at one time."

"Like what?" Othello tried to picture a wizened, old female elf engaged in multiple projects. It didn't make sense to him.

"Umm, I'm not going to tell you. You can find out for yourself when you meet her. I'll tell you this though. She's the most powerful individual in the city. She's much more powerful than you and the mayor combined."

Othello felt a surge of alarm flow through his body. His instincts told him the dinner meeting would be fraught with more danger to himself and his career.

CHAPTER TWO

Hamlet sat in his room reading a scroll on how to keep bees happy and productive, a situation that would prevent them from migrating elsewhere. Occasionally, he would stop reading and scribble a note on a scrap of paper.

His room occupied an entire upper floor in the keep. It held a table, a chair and a bed. Opposite the door, a large fireplace heated the room, chilly even in midsummer.

The door banged open and his mother yelled, "Hamlet!" He jumped out of the chair, dropping the scroll to the floor. When his heart stopped thumping, he made a face and said, "Ma! Stop doing that. Why can't you knock like visitors are supposed to do?" His mother, Gertie, wore a black velvet gown, her widow weeds even though she had remarried a week after her husband's death. She also wore a perpetual sneer. Her belly-button-long beard was woven into three braids, each decorated with ribbons and gold hair pins. She was much skinnier than the average female dwarf.

"I'm your mother. I don't have to knock. I came to tell you that the king grows suspicious of you. Clodio is concerned that you are plotting against him."

"Me? I don't really want to be king, so he did me a favor by usurping the throne."

"Nevertheless, you often disappear for an entire day, and he finds that suspicious. Where were you yesterday?"

"In the forest. I studied the bees in the wild. I learn a lot about them on these expeditions."

"Clodio wishes you would stay in the castle more often. He wants you to help him." She wagged a finger at him. "Ruling is a tough job, and he wants you to take on some of the chores instead of wasting your time on this bee nonsense."

"You mean he wants me to stay in the castle where he can watch me."

"Nonsense. He's just trying to be nice to you. I'll tell Clodio you're willing to help."

"I didn't say that."

"You would have said it if you weren't such a fool." She left, slamming the door behind her.

Hamlet grinned at his mother's back. He enjoyed thwarting her plans, especially the plans she thought up without consulting him. He pulled a face and sighed. He wouldn't be able to study anymore now that his mother had broken his concentration. He decided to go to the harbor and have an ale or two. He could go by way of the market and check out the honey competition.

# # #

Othello sat in his office taking advantage of Emilia's three-hour lunch break. He had learned to time his office work with her break periods. Nark strolled into his office and grimaced, an expression that passes for a smile in trolldom. "Quiet widout me sister, ain't it?"

"How did she ever get hired?"

"Da old mayor lost an election and Glyniss won. On his last day, dat guy fired his elf secretary and hired Emilia. So Glyniss got stuck wid her 'less she wants a troll vendetta on her hands. Den you showed up."

"Wonderful."

"Only way ya gonna get rid of her is to stick her on someone else like Glyniss did. Or kill her, but dat not smart."

"I guess I can grow accustomed to her."

"Hey, Boss, da militia gonna drill today. Wanna see?"

"Yes, I do." Othello stood up. "I have to see how well-trained they are or aren't."

"Dey ain't. But ya gotta see."

Five minutes later, they stood on the edge of the city's parade grounds where fifty of the militia lounged around on the grass. They sat in racial groups: the elven archers in one group, the pikemen in another, the half-pint slingers in a third and the dwarf axes in still another. They all smoked pipeweed and drank ale from a keg strategically placed in the middle of the groups. A half-pint in a military tunic with gold braid leaned against a tree looking disgusted.

"Dat's Cassio, the boss of da militia." Nark pointed to the tree-leaner.

Cassio saw them and hurried over. "Good afternoon sir. Captain Cassio at your service."

"Captain," Othello said and smiled to put the half-pint at ease. "I've come to observe the drill. What are they doing?"

"Finishing up lunch. I'll try to get them organized, but they're a bit sluggish after drinking a keg of ale."

"What is this, a militia drill or a bachelor party?" Othello chewed his lip. Glyniss' assessment was correct. How was he supposed to defend the city with this rabble? "Are you in charge or not?"

"Technically, I am. But I'm not a military type and the members know that, so they feel free to ignore me."

"What? How did you get the job?"

"No one else wanted it, so all the potential candidates' names were thrown into a bowl and my name got picked. I hate this job."

Othello put his hands on his hips and growled, "I'll get this rabble to shape up." He glared at the militia. "A week at hard labor repairing the walls will give them some discipline."

Nark caught Othello's arm and pulled him aside. "Dat's a good idea ya got, but it ain't gonna teach 'em to use da weapons. I gotta nudda idea, Boss."

"Let's hear it."

"Dey need a drill sergeant to help da captain. Wid all the warriors inna town, I should be able to find one quick."

"Do it. Meanwhile, I'll tell Cassio." Nark walked toward the port area.

"Captain, I think the answer to your problem is to hire a drill master. You will still be in command, but you turn over the drilling part to your new assistant."

"Thank you, Sir." Cassio looked relieved.

Othello controlled his anger and walked among the groups to introduce himself. The militia seemed unimpressed.

Nark returned fifteen minutes later with a grizzled, scarred dwarf whose lengthy beard was streaked with white. He carried a huge battle ax in one hand. "Dis is Sergeant Dunlap," Nark said. "He'll take de job for five silver pennies a month."

Othello shook hands with Dunlap and agreed to the wage demand.

"Get them up, if you please Captain," Othello said.

"On your feet and fall in," Cassio yelled in a high-pitched voice. The militia ignored the command.

"Can I sorta help out, Boss?" Nark said with a playful grimace.

"All right."

Nark walked up to the biggest pikeman. The bulky human watched Nark approach. "What's the militia comin' to, men? I think they let a troll join up."

"Da captain said 'stand up.'"

"Make me, troll."

Nark casually drew the truncheon tucked under his belt and clobbered the man in the head. He slumped, unconscious. "Next?" Nark looked around while slapping the truncheon against his open palm.

The militia plopped their iron helmets on their heads and buckled the chin straps before jumping up and pushing themselves into formation.

Once the shoving and shuffling ceased, Othello said, "With me is your new drill master, Sergeant Dunlap. He will report to your captain and will give me progress reports on your ability to defend the city."

Dunlap examined his new charges with eyes that gleamed with malevolence.

Othello turned to the half-pint. "Take over, Captain Cassio."

On their way back to the office, Othello considered his luck in getting Nark as an assistant. He was clearly smarter than the average troll and could think his way through a problem without hitting it with his cudgel, although he could do that if the situation called for it. With Nark's help, one of the problems may have been solved. If nothing else, the militia would become better than they were now.

# # #

Hamlet entered the dockside tavern known as the Sailor's Delight. It consisted of a long, dingy room smelling of pipe smoke, fried fish and spilt ale. Several drinkers saluted him by hoisting their mugs over their heads. Hamlet responded by patting their shoulders, calling their names and asking after their families. He was a popular figure in the tavern, the only noble the patrons would ever talk to. Hamlet liked the plain-spoken folks and enjoyed their gossip and gripes. Often, if he didn't have any coins, they bought him an ale or two.

"What'll you be drinkin', Prince?" The elderly elf bartender chortled. All he had to offer was ale.

"I have a thirst on, so I'll be wanting an ale today." Hamlet grinned.

The bartender grabbed a pewter mug, wiped it out with a dirty rag and filled it from a large barrel. Hamlet, as nobility, always got a clean mug unlike the other drinkers.

Hamlet took the mug and walked through a side door to the outdoor tables under an ancient oak tree. He sat down at one with three dock workers he had often talked to.

Annee, a rather pretty half-pint serving wench, smiled at him. "Prince Hammy. I wish you a good day."

"And the same to you, Annee."

"Prince Hammy, how are ya?" one of the workers asked. Everyone laughed at Hamlet's nickname. On his first visit several years ago, Hamlet had established that he was not to be treated as nobility as long as he was in the tavern.

"My bee project moves forward. I'm now ready to look for a beekeeper to hire."

"Never seen them two in here before," the second said, using his mug to point to a pair of burly men who just sat down at another table.

Hamlet looked at the table and recognized the two swells. They were knights from Clodio's court. They looked as out of place as a pair of sea gulls sitting at the table drinking ale. They noticed Hamlet looking at them and turned away.

"Excuse me, gents," Hamlet said to the dock workers and walked over to the other table. "Rosencrantz and

Guilderstern. I didn't think you frequented the docks. I thought you drank in the tavern on the other side of the market." Both men looked embarrassed.

"Just dropped in for a quick ale," Guilderstern said. He gulped his ale, stood up and left. Rosencrantz followed.

Hamlet stroked his chin. How strange. He had noticed them a few blocks away in the market when he had observed the honey vendor's stall. Did they follow him? Did they spy on him? Could they be acting on the orders of Clodio? Could he be after the secrets of beekeeping? Hamlet would have to be more careful in the future lest he let slip important information.

CHAPTER THREE

Hamlet, dressed in leather jerkin, pants, knee-high boots and a floppy hat — his beekeeping outfit — walked in a copse of oak and beech trees with a candidate for bee-chief. Low clouds threatened to drop rain at any time.

He turned and looked back toward the castle. Rosencrantz and Guilderstern were nowhere in sight. Hamlet grinned to himself. He had sneaked out of the castle so the two spies wouldn't see him and follow. He had learned about a secret door when he was ten. After that, he had used it a lot. He would roam the countryside on his own. He relished romping through the forest, but what he really loved to do was to sit quietly in a meadow and watch the bees collect pollen. He recalled the single time his father had taken him outside the castle by himself. They had sat in a meadow and watched bees buzzing around flowers. The old dwarf explained how bees used the pollen to produce honey. Ever since then, he dreamed about becoming King of the Bees.

The elderly man now with Hamlet walked with a limp, had stubble on his face and smelled of body odor and honey. He claimed to be expert on all aspects of bees and honey collection. "I've built hunnerts of hives," he said. "Sold thousands of jars of honey, I have."

"So, let's talk coins," Hamlet said as he stepped around a large tree. Meadows surrounded the copse and multicolored spring flowers undulated in a mild spring breeze. Hundreds of wild bees swarmed around the meadow. He was eager to get started on his beekeeping project before the bees set up new hives. He needed a bee-chief, but the ones he had interviewed seemed more interested in cheating him than in farming bees.

"Each new hive'll cost ya a silver penny."

"Others will charge me half that."

"Aye, but they build their hives the old way. Mine are built inna different manner. It's my secret. I can have a dozen set up inna week. Then ya need to pay me fifty coppers a hive for stuff I use to keep 'em healthy and livin' longer."

"Half a silver each? What is this?"

"More secret stuff. I mix it with bees' knees and whatnot and the bees love it."

"And the honey?"

"My jars have a way to keep the honey fresher. I'll sell 'em to ya for twenty-five coppers each. Also, I get half the crop to sell meself. That's me wages, so to speak."

"So to set up say, twenty hives, I'd have to pay you a total of thirty silver pennies. That's more than I'd make from selling the honey from those hives and you get half of the honey. See here, I plan to operate this as a business, and I can't make any profit with the prices you're charging."

"Aye, but only inna first season. After that, all ya need is the health stuff. Ya make yer profit next year and the years after that. One of my hives will last ten years at least. Oftentimes much longer. The other hives'll only last three years, maybe. Iffen ya want to run a business, ya gotta take the long look."

Hamlet sighed. Beekeeping was so much more difficult than it seemed. While this candidate talked a good game, he was also out to cheat him. Perhaps, he should do without hiring a bee-chief. Why couldn't he be his own bee-chief? If he bought the hives, he could set them up himself. Once established, the bees pretty much did everything themselves.

Empty jars for honey were easy to come by. Wild bees didn't use secret health treatments. It seemed everyone assumed they could cheat him out of vast sums of coins. Well, no more. He would start his bee empire by himself. He turned to the old man, who eyed him suspiciously. "I think you're a fraud. You're out to cheat your prince. Well, you'll not be my bee-chief, but I'll give you half a silver a hive, and I want twenty of them right away. Take it or leave it."

The old man hopped from foot to foot. "Half a silver? I'll lose money at that price and ya don't know wot yer doin'. Not hirin' me ain't smart."

"Well, do you want to sell me the hives or not? I've had other offers, you know."

"Yer cheatin' me," the old man growled. "Bad things happen to cheats. I'll sell ya the hives, but ya won't get a word of advice from me."

"Bring them here tomorrow. I'll bring your fee."

Hamlet watched him stomp out of the copse. He felt a satisfaction he had rarely experienced before, a sense of accomplishment. His mother, never in favor of his beekeeping plans, would be sore wroth when she heard of today's deeds.

Othello and Desdemona strolled arm in arm through the streets of the elf quarter on their way to dinner with her grandmother. He was curious to meet this female who Desdemona obviously admired. He also hoped to find out why she was so powerful.

The streets became dirtier and less inviting as they progressed deeper into the quarter and further away from the main streets. Gangs of young toughs roamed the quarter. He became aware that the inhabitants eyed him and his uniform with disdain or disrespect. He frequently touched the hilt of his sword to reassure himself. A burly elf followed their progress from the other side of the street. Desdemona gestured with her chin in the elf's direction. "My grandmother must have sent him to make sure we're safe." Twice, Othello noticed their escort wave at groups of low-lifers to keep from coming closer.

The tenement buildings shocked Othello. Born in a rural area where only the very rich had a home with two stories, he couldn't comprehend living in a four-story building, especially after his wife told him each floor was home to several families.

"I guess it's time to tell you," Desdemona said, "my grandmother is also my Godmother."

"How peculiar."

"It's different from you the way you're thinking. She's 'The Godmother' to hundreds of folks."

"Really?"

"Yes. All her godchildren are connected by oaths. That's what makes her so powerful. All her godchildren have sworn oaths to do her bidding."

"I don't understand that."

"Perhaps, she'll explain it to you. Whatever you do, show her great respect. The name you must use is Godmother, nothing else." Desdemona stopped in front of a house with gaudy red curtains in the windows and a gilt door. A sign hung outside proclaiming it the Wicked Bed.

"This is a brothel," Othello exclaimed. "Why are we stopping here?"

"Evenin', Desdemona," a heavily-armed elf said and opened the door. "The Godmother is expectin' you." He gestured for them to enter.

"This is the Godmother's home," Desdemona whispered, "and the center of her operations. From here, she runs all the brothels in the city."

They entered a large room where all the walls were covered with red velvet hangings. Light came from many candles with red glass chimneys.

An aged floozy in a revealing red gown smiled at them.

"Rosolia!" Desdemona beamed at the old elf. "How are you?"

"You look grand, Desdemona." The old elf fawned over Desdemona. "You look even more beautiful now that you're married."

Othello felt his face heat up when he noticed a dozen much younger females in diaphanous costumes lounging around. They all took their time inspecting him, much to his embarrassment. Led by the bodyguard, they passed through the brothel part of the building and entered the rear rooms. Another bodyguard held up a hand to stop Othello. "Your sword."

Othello bristled. Was his honor to be challenged? Did they dare think he would assault a female?

"Do it, dear," Desdemona said. "No one gets into her presence carrying weapons."

Othello handed over the sword while the other guard patted him down. He noticed both guards were missing two teeth on the top, one on each side. How could both of them be missing the same teeth? He then recalled the old floozy also had missing teeth.

Finally, they entered the inner room and Othello gasped. The walls were painted in garish colors of green, orange and yellow. Gold covered even the moldings. Silver and gold statues and artwork filled small tables scattered throughout the large room.

The Godmother sat on a throne-like padded chair wearing a tent-sized green silk robe. Her neck, ears, arms, fingers and toes carried enough jewelry and precious metals to ensure she wouldn't float if she fell into a lake. A thick pipeweed cigar hung precariously from her rouged mouth. Her dyed green hair had streaks of midnight blue and was arranged in tight curls that resembled an obscene halo. Turquoise makeup ringed her violet eyes, and her costly scent overwhelmed the odor of cigar smoke. Two voluptuous, scantily clad female elves stood behind the throne. Othello noticed the gaps in their smiles and that unsettled him. Why did everyone have missing teeth? And all of them missing the same two teeth?

"Desdemona! My grandchild! How happy I am to see you again! And this must be your husband, Ofella."

"It's Othello, Godmother."

"Come, let me hug you." She handed the cigar to one of the females.

Desdemona advanced close enough for the Godmother to wrap her massive arms around and squeeze.

Othello winced and hoped the old female hadn't broken any of his wife's bones.

After releasing Desdemona, the Godmother held out her right hand and said, "You may advance, kneel and kiss my ring."

Othello caught a look from Desdemona that told him he had better obey. He took a few steps, went to one knee and kissed the gold ring with a sapphire big enough to choke a mule. He felt humiliated.

"Now, let's eat." The Godmother snatched back her cigar and stood with a great effort. The two female aides each grabbed an arm and helped her walk to an enormous table set for three, where they eased her bulk into an oversized arm chair. One of them took up a flagon and poured wine. Othello took a sip and tried to hide his astonishment. It was the best wine he had ever tasted. The other aide clapped her hands and more servants rushed in with platters of food.

An hour later, after the best meal he had ever eaten, Othello sat back and groaned from the enormous amount of food he had tucked away.

The Godmother snapped her fingers, and a female handed her a fresh cigar while the other lit it. "Now to business. You two can go for now and shut the door on your way out."

Othello waited anxiously, knowing he was about to get the bill for the meal. He had never met a female with such enormous wealth and power before, and he wasn't sure he enjoyed the experience.

"It cost me a bundle of silver pennies — fifteen hundred of them — to get you put in charge of Homeland Secur —"

"What?"

The Godmother scowled at him. "Never interrupt me while I'm speaking."

Desdemona put a hand on his arm and squeezed gently.

"It cost that much because the city council is filled with greedy politicians, and that's what it cost me to get them to put your name in front of the mayor. I expect to earn that money back and to make a decent profit. How, you ask? It's simple. I want the contract to rebuild the city walls. When you're ready to seek bids, I'll let you know the name of the company I'm using. You will see to it that my company is awarded the contract. Is that clear?"

Othello bristled. "I'm sure that's not legal."

"It isn't and I know that for a fact. That's why I needed someone from my family to be in charge of Homeland Security."

"Godmother, I'm honor bound to uphold the law. If your company submits the winning bid, I'll grant you the work."

"Desdemona, why didn't you warn me you married an idiot?" She pointed a fat finger at Othello. "Listen up. My bid will be the most expensive one you get and you will still award the business to me. Otherwise, the council will find out about what you really did during the Battle of Twin Oaks."

Othello's eyes bulged and he gawked at the female.

She blew a smoke ring. "Far from being the hero who turned the tide of battle, you were a corporal in charge of five archers. Your unit was held in reserve and never even saw the battle line. So, your claim to be a hero in that battle is completely false."

"How . . . how did you find out?"

"It's easy to get such information if one is willing to spend money. Once the council finds out you falsified your resumé, you'll be out of that job. The reason Desdemona and a few others like yourself still have their teeth is because I don't want others to know you're part of my family. Once you lose the city job, I won't have that concern and you'll have two teeth pulled like almost everyone else in my family."

Othello tried to say something in his defense but couldn't think of anything. How did this monstrous female find old soldiers from the battle?

"And another thing," the Godmother said. "Do something about all these annoying dwarf immigrants and their unlicensed stealing. They're most vexing."

"Unlicensed stealing?" Othello's head spun from the implications of that statement.

"All stealing in Dun Hythe is done by the Thieves Guild, which I operate. Anyone who steals and isn't a dues-paying member is an illegal thief." She clapped her hands three times and two female servants reappeared. "You may leave," she said to Desdemona. "If I have anything to say to you," she pointed to Othello, "I'll send a note to your wife." The servants helped her stand and escorted her from the room.

Othello had never been so humbled in his life.

#

Desdemona left the brothel and glanced at Othello out of the corner of her eye. His forehead was wrinkled and he chewed on his upper lip. She knew he was thinking about the Godmother. Never had he met anyone like her. Not growing up in the forests, he didn't. Folks like the Godmother needed big cities to consolidate their power and to gain strength. Since Dun Hythe was the biggest city in the country, its Godmother would have the largest and strongest organization in the country.

Othello didn't realize it yet, but the Godmother affected everyone in the city and many in the surrounding areas. Powerful figures in government and business came swiftly whenever she beckoned and meekly agreed to whatever she demanded. Only Mayor Glyniss refused to come to the Wicked Bed. Glyniss and the Godmother hated each other as only two females could hate.

Desdemona had been surprised by the Godmother's deviousness. Her marriage to Othello had obviously been part of the plan. She was as stunned as he had been to learn that Othello didn't get his appointment on his own merits.

The wall rebuilding plan was the most devious part of the scheme; the Godmother must consider Othello to be spineless creature.

Desdemona foresaw a possible difficult situation arising. What if someday she had to choose between supporting Othello or the Godmother? She couldn't conceive of being in a worse position than that. She mumbled a silent prayer that it would never happen.

She was sure Othello had never met anyone with the power the Godmother wielded and he had no inkling of just how powerful she was. Even Desdemona wasn't sure how much power she really had, and Desdemona had grown up with the Godmother, in her house, and spent much time with her. She hoped Othello took the Godmother's wishes seriously, because the old elf had a bad temper when she didn't get what she wanted.

It was the Godmother's idea for her to wed out of the family. Once the Godmother had explained the need to bring fresh blood into the family, Desdemona immediately agreed to the plan. Much to her surprise, she acquired a husband that she liked and even grew to love. Othello was a good male and tried hard to please her. What more could a female ask for?

Walking arm-in-arm with Othello, she looked around the neighborhood and recalled many happy memories. Orphaned at three, her grandmother had moved her into the back of the brothel and raised her. Her father was Grandma's son, and her mother was the daughter of an underboss. She had heard rumors that her father had been killed in a fight over territorial rights. She knew her mother had disappeared shortly after that. Desdemona had never been able to find out what had happened to her mother, a subject Grandma refused to talk about.

CHAPTER FOUR

The next morning, the old man delivered ten hives with a promise of the other ten in a week. Hamlet spent all day in the fields, searching for the ideal locations and setting up the hives in likely spots. Every hour or so, either Rosencrantz or Guilderstern would call over to ask if he was almost done. The two groused all day about their lack of activity and lack of castle comforts.

Proud of the day's work and elated to finally get started in the business, Hamlet returned to the castle followed by the two knights.

In the corridor far from his room, he knew his mother awaited him. Her perfume saturated the hallway. Gertie didn't believe in bathing and compensated for it by using a quart of perfume a day. Once inside the room, he ignored her and opened a shutter so he wouldn't suffocate from the overwhelming stench of attar. To gain time to gather his thoughts, he listened to a dove cooing in a tree before turning back to Gertie. The top of her head with curly brown and gray hair only came up to Hamlet's shoulder. She had azure-colored eyes and a perpetual sneer brought on by a lifetime of being queen and therefore better than everyone else. "Clodio is very upset with you." She pointed a finger at him. "You haven't been very respectful to him, and he's your uncle, your stepfather and your king." Her voice had a petulant tone to it.

"Why should I be respectful to him? He took my throne. Not that I wanted it, but asking first would've been nice."

"Don't be absurd. Kings don't ask, they take. Clodio fears you plot against him."

"What? Why would I do that? I didn't want the job when father died, and I don't want it now." Mentioning his father's death brought back memories of the ghostly appearance and the demand to avenge his father's murder. He had to do something about that. Maybe after he set up the rest of the hives he'd have time.

"He wants to know where you were yesterday."

"Why doesn't he ask his two spies?"

"He did and they didn't know anything except they couldn't find you in the castle. The king was furious with them. So what were you doing?"

"Tending to my bee business."

She sighed and shook her head. "Clodio believes you are confusing Rosey and Guildy so you can meet with other plotters."

"The king is paranoid. I'm not a threat."

"And you're not a help either. Being king is a tough job, and he could use some help from his family. I want you to stop this bee nonsense and attend the court. Help your uncle. He has projects that would be perfect for you to work on."

"I'm not giving up my bees. In fact, my business has already started and I'll soon be rolling in honey."

"You fool!" Gertie stamped her foot. "You turn down the court preference I could have gotten for you. For what? A peasant's job. Well, I can't help someone who won't help himself."

"Stop treating me like I'm a dwarfling. I'm twenty-eight."

"Then stop acting like a dwarfling!" She spun around and marched out of the room. A second later, she stuck her head back in and snapped, "And grow a beard." Then she was gone. Hamlet smirked. He had shaved originally because of a rash, but once he discovered Gertie hated the look, he'd stayed clean-shaven.

In a somber mood, he pondered the situation. Could Clodio's suspicions be a threat? Was the king jealous of the beekeeping business? Did he want to be a silent partner? Perhaps he intended it as a sinecure for his two spies. Maybe he should begin a plan to avenge his father. It wouldn't do to get killed by Clodio. What would he say to his father in that case? He shook his head to clear it of all the unanswered questions he had.

Emilia arrived at her desk only thirty minutes late. She flapped a hand at Othello who ignored her. From somewhere in the building, Iago yelled at some poor troll who must have aggravated him. Iago had been in a bad mood ever since Othello had shown up.

Today was her first anniversary, and she thought back to her so-called wedding. It was the first time she had attended the Troll Patrol Benevolent Association weekend party. And she was still paying for it.

Back then, Emilia woke up in bed with a terrible headache. If she got out of bed, she was sure she would fall over or throw up. Maybe both. She flexed her hands and noticed the bruises and cracks. She knew she had a split lip, possibly a black eye and a sore ear, all sure signs of a fist fight. She wondered who she had fought with. It must have been a great party.

She tried to remember what had happened and drew a blank. All she could recall was having a few ales with her brother Nark on Friday night.

A noise grated on her ragged nerves. It slowly dawned on her ravaged synapses that the sound was snoring. She looked to the other side to the bed and gasped aloud. Iago lay sprawled across the bed. His pants and sash lay in a lump at the bottom of the bed along with her kirtle.

Emilia couldn't believe it. Iago was the last troll in the world she would sleep with. She despised his guts. She examined his inert form. Iago's knuckles also had deep cuts. He had two split lips and a swollen nose.

Suddenly, she was glad she couldn't recall the weekend. She wondered just what day it was. The trolls usually took several days — sometimes an entire week — to recover from the Association's parties.

Another thought made her shudder. Maybe her bruises weren't from a tavern brawl; trollish sex usually started with a viscous fist fight before ending up in bed or on the floor.

She decided to find out what happened and smacked Iago in his sore ear. He yelped, sat up, saw her and threw a punch at her head. Emilia blocked the feeble punch and bit his hand. Iago roared in pain, snatched back his hand and stashed it under his armpit. "What ya doin' in me bed, bitch?"

"Dis is yer bed? I bet I didn't come on my own. Ya hadda kidnap me to get me here."

"Me not kidnap an ugly troll like ya. Me not dat dumb."

Someone pounded on the door. Both Iago and Emilia groaned from the pain caused by the noise. "Go away!" he tried to yell. It came out as a loud squeak.

The door opened and Nark walked in.

"Git outta me house. Yer not welcome."

"Hello, Sis. How's married life?" Nark snorted and grinned at the two hungover trolls.

"Me gonna kill ya." Emilia shook a swollen fist at her kid brother. "Why did ya let me do dis?"

"Da two of ya looked like ya was havin' lots of fun. Dis one," he pointed at Iago, "even borrowed coins from da Association's Treasurer so's he could buy a coupla drinks for everyone in de bar." He chuckled. "Ya gotta big bill to pay off."

Iago groaned.

"Dis cheapskate bought drinks for everyone?" Emilia looked at Iago in awe.

"Yeah, dat's when ya fell in love wid him. Or somethin' like dat. Den da two of ya held hands and jumped over an ale keg to make it legal like. Course, ya both fell down after da jump and den me and some lads hadda pry ya apart cause ya was embarrasin' da families with young uns. After dat, both of ya disappeared. Guess ya went on yer honeymoon or somethin'."

Emilia glared at Iago and vowed to make his life miserable.

She sighed and went back to ignoring Othello who called for her to do something.

# # #

Falstaff and Poulet rode up to the rear of the Grubby Shoat. Falstaff dismounted from his black charger, the result of a midnight transaction while the charger's previous owner slept. Falstaff had left his nag as compensation for the farmer.

He shook ten days of road dust from his gray cloak and blue doublet and adjusted his mud-splattered blue hose. He hurt all over, his fifty-year-old body rebelling over sleeping most nights in the open. Poulet, half Falstaff's age, looked disheveled, but not tired.

Falstaff walked to the front of the tavern, which overlooked the port of Dun Hythe, the largest and busiest in all of Gundarland. Before entering, he ran his hands through his thick curly beard, black with white streaks, to search for evidence of his travels. He removed a twig and the remains of a few leaves. He took a deep breath to tamp down his excitement. He knew Dun Hythe would yield gold coins before long. All he had to do was identify the opportunity and seize it.

He pushed his way into the crowded room. Poulet followed in his wake. Inside, sailors and dockworkers stood three deep drinking their lunch. Falstaff inhaled the air filled with the foul odors of sweaty bodies, old ale and pipe smoke. "I love this place!" he exclaimed. "It's exactly as I remember it. Except for all the dwarfs with axes."

Curses, off-key singing, loud talking and shouted boasts assaulted his ears. The noise swelled and faded as if directed by a demented conductor.

Reputed to be hundreds of years old, the Grubby Shoat had no evidence to contradict the claim. Smoke had turned the rafters and plank walls black. The dirt floor held so many obnoxious stains that it appeared to be uniform in color. The table surfaces were thin from knife carvings and an annual cleaning. On his left stood a dilapidated bar heavily scarred from tavern brawls involving weapons with sharp edges. Despite the mild spring weather, a roaring fire spewed light, heat and smoke in the rear of the room.

Falstaff found a table with a bench and sat down. The bench creaked under his weight. "Fetch us pots of ale, Poulet. And be quick about it. I thirst."

"I don't suppose they have mead in here," Poulet said.

"Mead! How absurd. Get the ale."

Poulet wiggled his scrawny frame in between other patrons and arrived next to the bar. He stuck two fingers in his mouth and emitted a shrill whistle. The bartender, a filthy-looking, scar-faced man frowned at him, but filled his order. Poulet returned to the table with a mug in each hand. "Now what do we do?" he asked after sitting down. He examined his bare feet with his unkempt toe hair and shook his head. Half-pints never wore shoes in order to display their carefully preened toe hair. His parents had raised him to groom his toe hair like all reputable half-pints did — even the poor ones — but traveling had taken a toll and his toe hair was knotted and muddy.

"The first order of business is to find out what's happening in town. I recall all the shipping in the harbor, but these warriors are new and a mystery." Falstaff looked around and spotted a grizzled dwarf warrior with two pips on the sleeves of his leather jacket. He had an ax held in a leather harness on his back. The handle stuck up over his right shoulder. "Corporal," Falstaff called out. When the dwarf turned his head, Falstaff said, "A moment of your time."

The dwarf swaggered over to the table. "Yeah?"

To Falstaff's alarm, the dwarf looked familiar now that he was closer. Could the corporal be from the regiment that he had deserted so many years ago? It was too late to ignore the dwarf. He'd have to continue and bluff if necessary. "I just got into town after an absence of many years, and I'd like to catch up on the news. Poulet, stop admiring your confounded toe hair and get our guest a mug of ale. My name, by the way, is Sir John Falstaff."

Poulet gave Falstaff a dirty look and slipped through the crowd.

The soldier cocked his head to one side and studied Falstaff. "Ya know, I've seen you somewhere before. Ever inna army?"

"No, I've never been in the army. I've spent most of my life in the diplomatic corps for various dukes and princes. What's your name?

"Corporal Urquort. Whadda ya want to know?"

"For one thing, why are you and all these other warriors here? I don't recall a lot of axes when I was here before."

"Yeah, we're new. I took my squad and a bunch of others here after we was demobilized. It's that fricken peace that's goin' around. We was lookin' for work here, but there ain't any jobs. And no place to stay either. It's like livin' in the field and scroungin' what we can to survive." He shook his head. "We can barely get up the coins for an ale."

"Ahh, peace. I heard about that. Pity you got kicked out of the army. What is the constabulary doing about the presence of so many warriors? They must be concerned. You and your lads have to be a threat to law and order."

"They gotta new guy in charge. A dark elf named Ofella or somethin'. No, wait. Othello. His name's Colonel Othello. I heard a rumor he was a hero at the Battle of Twin Oaks. I was in that fight and I ain't never heard of this guy. Anyway, he's swearin' he's gonna cut down on crime by all us dwarf soldiers." He shook his head. "Don't know what he's doin' about it. All I hear is talk."

Poulet set a third mug on the table. Urquort drained it in one pull.

"Fetch another round, Poulet, while the good corporal tells me all about the battle."

Urquort spent the next five minutes talking about the battle while Falstaff's excitement mounted. When he finished, Falstaff said, "I'm seeking business opportunities in town, and I may have need of a few sturdy warriors. Can I call upon you to fill that need? There'll be compensation, of course."

"Aye, me and my mates are up for just about anythin'."

"I assume I can find you here?"

"Here or inna dock area." Urquort stood up. "Thanks for the ale. I hope to see ya again." He left to join a group of warriors.

Falstaff ignored his itching hand. "Poulet! I need writing materials, and I need them quick."

"Where am I supposed to find writin' materials inna seedy tavern like this?"

"'Tis not my job to tell you where to find them. I refuse to do your job and mine. My job is to write an important letter, and your job is to fetch the necessary materials."

"Who you writin' to?"

"Colonel Othello. I just discovered that I fought in the Battle of Twin Oaks. I want to offer my services to an old comrade. Afterwards, you must clean my clothes as best you can and give me a haircut."

# # #

Hamlet, wearing a cloak to ward off the chill night air, stood on the castle walls and examined the sky filled with a partial moon and a thousand pinpoints of light. He wanted to see if tomorrow's weather promised to be dry. If so, he planned to visit the new hives to see if any bee colonies had moved in. It was three days since he had installed the first ten, and he hoped at least some of them would be occupied. He tempered his enthusiasm so he wouldn't be too disappointed if the hives still were empty.

"Hey!" The voice came from the shadows.

Hamlet grasped the hilt of his dagger. "Who walks the battlements with me?"

"'Tis I, the shade of your father."

Hamlet peered into the shadows and sighed. "What is father doing that he must send you, an elf, in his stead?"

"He's chairin' a meetin' of the Former Monarchs Political Action Committee. They're workin' for better livin' — no pun intended — conditions for the dead."

"What message do you bear?"

"Same as the last one. Your old man wants to see Clodio over here and he wants to know why you haven't avenged his death."

"I'm in the middle of starting a beekeeping business. After I install the rest of the hives in a few days, I'll have time to ponder my filial duties."

"Your father says you're a fool to delay."

"Why do my parents keep calling me 'fool'?"

"You're givin' the king time to murder you as well. Your father says, 'make haste lest you suffer the same fate as he.'" The apparition disappeared.

Hamlet considered the ghost and the message.

"Oh, and watch out for your mother," the ghost added after popping back into view. "She's not to be trusted, your father says."

Hamlet shook his head. His mother urged him to go to court and join Clodio in ruling Denmarko. His father urged him to murder the king. Surely, he couldn't satisfy both parents. Did Clodio really mean to murder him also? Was the greedy king after the beekeeping business? If so, his life was safe until the business was fairly established. That meant he had a few months to come up with a plan, so he could concentrate on the bees for a while and then get rid of the king.

Now that he had figured things out, he felt better.

CHAPTER FIVE

Othello suffered from apprehension about meeting with Falstaff, whoever he was. Yesterday, he had received a letter from one Sir John Falstaff. The letter said the writer was in town and wanted to meet to reminisce about the good old days and the Battle of Twin Oaks. He also wanted to offer his services to an old comrade-in-arms. He wondered if this was a not-too-subtle way for the Godmother to apply pressure or something less sinister than that.

As reluctant as he was to discuss the battle with anyone, especially a stranger, he was eager to learn what help this Falstaff could provide, if any. Fates knew he was in over his head and it was only a matter of time before the mayor realized that and sacked him. Failure had been his routine for years: selling used freight wagons, warming up crowds at political rallies, reporting for a news-scroll, all failures. Then he had hit on the idea of plumping his resumé with deeds of valor at Twin Oaks. Suddenly, he received offers to speak at patriotic affairs. Politicians sought his advice on tricky issues. He had achieved a measure of success for the first time, even if it was built on a fabrication. He couldn't believe his luck when Desdemona's uncle had approached him with a marriage offer that included a sizable dowry. The uncle told him Desdemona's grandmother had heard of his battle exploits and, in the traditional elf custom of arranged marriages, suggested him as potential husband material. When they returned from the honeymoon, the offer from Glyniss awaited him.

Since then he had learned his real job was to be a front for the hideous old hag called the Godmother. Rebuilding the walls was the most serious problem he faced. If he gave her the contract to rebuild the walls without following proper procedures, he would violate his oath to the city. If he didn't, the Godmother would violate his mouth. Every time he thought of the evil bitch, his teeth started hurting.

He now knew that landing the job with Dun Hythe was an insidious plot. The marriage offer had been part of that plot and the chief inducement. Nevertheless, he believed Desdemona loved him as much as he loved her. She was the greatest thing that had ever happened to him.

Somehow, he had to save his marriage and his teeth.

# # #

Falstaff and Poulet dodged through a troll-made traffic jam and approached the entrance of the city hall building. Two trolls guarded the building by lounging on the steps. One of them snored while the other picked his nose. "Greetings, sir," Falstaff addressed the more alert of the two. "Where can I find the office of Colonel Othello?"

After a moment's thought, the troll said, "In dere," and jerked a thumb over his shoulder.

"Can you be more specific?"

The troll made a gruesome face and scratched his head. Finally, he replied, "Don't go up da stairs . . . me think."

Falstaff sighed. He'd ask inside and save himself some aggravation. "Poulet, why don't you entertain these fellows while I have my meeting."

Poulet reached into a purse at his waist and pulled out a well-used deck of cards. "Wake up your buddy and we'll play a game of chance."

Falstaff entered the building and obtained directions to Othello's office, where he found an ugly female troll reading a scroll. He stopped in front of her desk and, when she ignored him, cleared his throat loudly.

She looked up from her reading, scanned him toe to head and said, "Whadda ya want, Fatso?"

Falstaff bristled momentarily. "Announce to Colonel Othello that Sir John Falstaff is here to meet with him."

"Come back inna hour. I'm busy."

"Busy doing what?"

"Onna break. Announce yerself or come back inna hour."

Falstaff shook his head in amazement and knocked on the door to Othello's office.

# # #

Othello heard Emilia growling at someone. Falstaff must be here. He took a deep breath to settle his nerves and determined to take the visitor's measure. "Come," he said in response to a knock on the door.

A man threw the door opened, and advanced into the room. "Colonel Othello! How pleased I am to meet you. Sir John Falstaff. I apologize for the state of my clothing, but I have been traveling for some time now and haven't had a chance to buy new ones."

Othello winced at the visitor's booming voice. He hadn't expected anyone as huge as this man who stood in front of the desk. Falstaff was taller than he was and easily double his weight. Most of the visitor's bulk was concentrated in a large paunch that strained the buttons on his waistcoat. He had a pudgy face with small eyes surrounded by fatty flesh and curly hair. His broad nose ended in flaring nostrils. A neatly trimmed black and white beard hid the rest of the face.

The man stared at Othello and tilted his head from side to side as if to get a better view. "While there is a certain familiarity about you, I don't believe we met at Twin Oaks." He sat down in a chair facing the desk. The chair groaned.

"Where were you during the battle?" Othello held his breath.

"On my horse. My cavalry unit didn't take part in the battle itself, rather we were sent behind enemy lines to ensure that reinforcements didn't reach the front. Routed an infantry battalion, we did. Then the enemy line collapsed and we harried the retreating rabble. Hot work it was."

Othello relaxed. Falstaff wouldn't know about the reserve archers.

"But tell me, Colonel, what can I do for you? You must have problem areas with a position such as yours. Perhaps my wide range of expertise can be of service to you."

Othello decided to reveal a few problem areas to see if Falstaff could offer assistance. "I'm concerned with the number of unemployed dwarf warriors in town. Right now, they survive by committing petty crimes, but what will happen if they start rioting or threatening the government? Another concern is that they may join up with pirates and attack our trade routes."

Falstaff pulled a face and stared at the wall over Othello's head. He shifted his weight and Othello was sure the chair would collapse. Finally, he jumped up and paced the room, hands clasped behind his back. "I've seen the dwarfs milling about the streets and share your concern. They are potentially dangerous." He did a few more laps. "Certainly, if the warriors and pirates unite, they could become a major problem." He stopped in mid-stride. "Colonel, do you suffer from piracy now?"

"There are always pirates preying on our trade routes. We lose a ship or two periodically, I've been told."

Falstaff paced some more, then stopped and raised one sausage-like finger in the air. "What if . . . what if I used my shipping business to hire some of these idle dwarfs and go after the pirates?"

"You have a shipping business?"

"Not at the moment. I'm here in Dun Hythe to start one. I plan to initially use two cogs. Let's say instead of cargo, I put twenty-five warriors in each ship. I cruise around outside the harbor looking defenseless, and when the pirates attack me, I attack them in return."

"A splendid plan." Othello beamed at his newfound friend.

"Instead of getting profits from the shipping trade, I'll profit from the pirate loot and pay the warriors and crews from that same loot." He paced some more. "Yes, that will serve. I can do this."

"You have experience at sea, I presume?" Othello asked.

"I captained a ship for the navy down south in Cintri. My mission was chasing pirates." He paused as if the memory was painful, then he sat down.

Othello winced at the sounds coming from the tortured chair.

"A sword wound in my leg forced me onto the beach for a time. Before I recovered, my ship sank during a battle with pirates." He sighed. "All those splendid officers and crew." He shook his head.

"I am grateful for your assistance. I agree. Hiring fifty warriors will lessen the pressure from that concern."

"All my funds will be tied up in buying and equipping the two ships. I'll need additional cash to recruit the warriors. You see, a signing bonus is expected in these cases. I'm sure the city has funds that can be used for projects like this. Are you prepared to offer some monetary assistance so I can get this project out to sea?"

The demand for funds took Othello by surprise. After a second of thought, he saw the advantage of investing a bit of money to get rid of the warriors. "How much is a typical signing bonus?"

"Two silver pennies each will do it. Every warrior in town will want to sign up, and I can take my pick of the best ones."

Othello had a coughing fit. "A hundred silver? That's a small fortune."

"Think, my friend. I'll be able to hire the best of the lot. They're the ones who are the biggest threat to the peace. They're the ones who would lead during an insurrection. With those potential leaders employed elsewhere, the rest are rabble. You can easily handle them."

Falstaff's logic resonated with Othello, but the price was too high. "I can't do it. I don't have that kind of money available."

Falstaff jumped up from the chair and resumed pacing. "I can certainly help your piracy problem, but not without a contribution from the city that I'm helping. I can't be expected to shoulder the entire financial burden." After two circuits of the room, he paused and said, "I think I can still do the job with fifty silver. I'll just have to be a more persuasive recruiter."

Othello bit his lip. Paying out fifty silver would consume a major portion of his spare funding, but the money would buy a solution to one of his problems. What to do?

"I can't possibly do this for a copper penny less than fifty silver." Falstaff wiggled his eyebrows. "I have many other expenses, as you can imagine."

Othello pulled a face and made a decision. He'd just have to carefully watch the rest of his funds. "All right." He opened a locked desk drawer, took out a leather pouch and counted fifty silver coins. "I'll need a receipt."

"Of course. Shall I fetch your secretary?" He stepped toward the door.

"No! No, don't do that. If she agrees to write out a receipt —a dubious prospect — she'll spread the news all over the city. I'll write it out." Othello scribbled on a sheet of parchment and handed it to Falstaff, who signed his name with a flourish. He scooped up the coins and said, "I've taken up enough of your time, Colonel. I'm off to the port to put our plan into action. I'll send reports to let you know of my progress." He stood up, bowed and left.

Othello sat and reviewed the meeting. All in all, a piece of good work despite the cost, he concluded. A major problem had been resolved.

# # #

Desdemona sat on a park bench at midday and watched the young, slender elf maiden approach. The slight breeze blew Desdemona's reddish-green hair in front of her face, and she brushed it back with a hand.

"Hello, Sylvia," Desdemona said to one of the Godmother's personal attendants.

Sylvia grinned and handed Desdemona a cloth sack. "The Godmother's chef made us fish salad sandwiches."

Desdemona opened the sack and took out two bundles wrapped in white cloth napkins. She handed one to Sylvia after she sat down on the bench.

Both females ate in silence. They were the same age and had known each other since they were four years old. That was when Sylvia came to live at the Wicked Bed as the Godmother's foster child. They quickly became insuperable friends. Together, they played with dolls, invaded the rooms of the females working in the brothel and tried on their dresses and makeup. The brothel females treated the two of them as younger sisters and spoiled them terribly.

After patting her mouth with the napkin, Desdemona asked, "So, how is my Grandmother's health?"

"Not so good. She's fading. Slowly, mind you, but definitely fading."

"Tell me what's ailing her."

"Well, you know she's overweight. And she never goes more than five minutes without one of her pipeweed cigars. She even gets up during the night to smoke two or more of them."

"I didn't know she smoked so much. She didn't when I lived with her."

Sylvia made a face. "I think she smokes to diminish pains that she won't tell anyone about."

Desdemona expressed shock. "Really? Pain?"

"She doesn't talk about any pain, but we see her make faces as if she just had a bad pain somewhere. This happens quite a few times a day. Whenever it happens, she immediately calls for a cigar unless she already has one. Then she takes several big drags to ease whatever pain she's feeling. A lot of times, she has trouble catching her breath because she is filled up with congestion. She coughs and coughs and eventually gets a breath."

Desdemona sighed. "I fear for her, Sylvia. I think her time is running out."

"I believe you're right. You can be sure we'll do everything we can to make her comfortable."

"I know you will." Desdemona placed a hand on Sylvia's forearm. "I know you'll take care of her. I'll be grateful to both of you and I won't forget what you did for her."

Sylvia nodded. "Thank you."

# # #

An exhilarated Falstaff left the office and walked past the troll secretary.

"Have a bad day, Lard-butt," she called to his back.

Outside on the steps, Poulet and the two trolls played cards, and from the expressions on the guards' faces, the half-pint was winning and in imminent danger of getting pummeled.

"I hate to break this up," Falstaff said to the guards, "but my batman and I have important business to attend to."

Poulet scooped up the cards and a pile of coins, stuffed all into his purse and took leave of the trolls who appeared to be working themselves up to mayhem.

Off the grounds, Falstaff asked, "How much did you win?"

"About five silver pennies. A good morning's work."

"As your master, I'll accept half of your winnings."

"Since my master hasn't paid me in months, my master can get stuffed."

"I should turn you over to the guards and tell them you cheated."

"You're the one who taught me how to play cards. What's Othello like?"

"I'd say he's about thirty-five and thinks that he has talent." Falstaff whistled a few notes. "I believe I have met the perfect mark."

"Where are we goin'?"

"Back to the port," Falstaff said, "to find Corporal Urquort. We have business to discuss."

"What's goin' on?"

"I need him to recruit two full ship crews and a number of unemployed warriors. We're going to sea."

"In what? Last time I checked we didn't have any ships inna inventory."

"Fortune will provide, I'm sure. I'm destined to be an admiral with those ships."

Poulet sniggered. "You've never been on a ship before and suddenly you're an admiral?"

"By now, you should have learned I'm a man of many parts."

"An admiral should have a real sword, not just a scabbard and a hilt."

"Yes, I suppose it is time to invest in a new sword." He had sold the sword months ago to get money to invest in a "get-rich-quick" scheme that somehow didn't. The hilt had been once used as a stage prop, and he had stolen it from an actor in a traveling show.

He took a deep breath and considered his new project. On the one hand, it presented an opportunity to mint money. On the other hand, getting caught meant certain — and sudden — death. It was a gamble, a big one, but the rewards were worth the risks.

# # #

Poulet grinned; "a man of many parts" certainly described Falstaff. He ticked off some of the parts: con man, liar, storyteller, charmer, scoundrel and now, apparently, a sea dog.

Falstaff had been all those things at one time or another since Poulet had agreed to become his manservant or, more accurately, his half-pint servant.

Poulet had been born in Centi in southern Gundarland to poor, but mostly honest parents. He grew up on the streets in the slum area and learned how to survive and how to spot a mark and an opportunity. He also discovered that he was a fast learner and had a rare ability to analyze situations and see potential troubles in them.

Poulet had worked as a stable hand when Falstaff rode in on an exhausted horse. The horse recovered under Poulet's care, and Falstaff had made an offer that seemed too good to be true. Poulet's only career option at the time was mucking out the stable and caring for horses for the rest of his life. He opted to go with Falstaff, no matter if the opportunity was real or not. Getting away from horse manure was worth enduring almost anything else.

Falstaff had been true to his word that Poulet would see Gundarland. They had traveled into every corner of the country searching for opportunities and/or suckers. Poulet wondered where this new escapade would take him this time. Falstaff's gambits always involved a certain amount of danger and before long they would need to make a quick exit. He wondered how one made a fast escape at sea that didn't involve swimming.

Outside the Grubby Shoat, Falstaff stood looking at the harbor to determine what type of ships he wanted to use. He didn't have much choice. Almost all the ships were single-masted cogs. A few galleys with a large number of oars were the only other choices.

Inside, Falstaff found Corporal Urquort amid a crowd of soldiers and waved him to an empty table. He heaved his bulk down on a bench and turned to Poulet. "Fetch us ales," he shouted over the noise. "Use some of your winnings instead of hoarding them." His success with Othello and the heavy purse he carried convinced Falstaff his luck had changed for the better and he was headed toward riches and possibly even riches combined with power.

He turned to the dwarf warrior. "I have good news. I am now charged by the city to hunt pirates. I want you to recruit crews for two cogs. Captains, sailors and whoever else is needed."

"I'm a soldier. What do I know about ships' crews? And what's in it for me to do all this work?"

"Loot. Possibly lots of it. Find a beached captain and let him hire the crews. Tell him he'll get a bonus of two silver pennies for his efforts. I want you to round up twenty-five of your lads for each ship. Mind, I don't want any trench trash. I want top-notch warriors. You can attract the best by offering them a signing bonus of fifty coppers each. You get two silver like the captain."

"Fifty coppers? Half a silver? Each?" Urquort replied. "That'll get their attention. I can get the best for that much money plus a chance at loot."

Poulet returned with three leather mugs of ale. He saw Urquort's grin and said to him, "Been feedin' you a bunch of bull, has he?" He took a sip from his mug.

"Quiet, Poulet. You should know better than to speak when in the presence of your betters."

Poulet sprayed ale all over the table. "Please don't jest like that while I'm drinkin'."

Falstaff ignored his servant and asked Urquort, "When can you have the assignment done?"

"When you gonna come up wid the money?"

"For you and the captain, I'll pay now and I'll give you cash for the signing bonuses. Let's find a quiet and unobserved spot and I can count it out for you. Mind, if they take my coin, they better show up."

"Iffen you got the coins, I think I can have 'em all ready by tomorrow."

"Fine. We'll assemble tomorrow night. Say, an hour after the city gates close. We'll meet here in front of the Grubby Shoat."

CHAPTER SIX

After the city gates shut on the following night, Falstaff and Poulet found Corporal Urquort, the soldiers and the ship crews awaiting him on a moonlit beach. Urquort told Falstaff the dwarfs were all experienced and doughty warriors. Next, Urquort introduced him to the captains, one an old elf, the other a middle-aged man. "Where are we goin'?" the man asked.

"I can't disclose our plans until we are at sea," Falstaff replied.

"All right," the elf said. "Where's the ships?"

Falstaff waved a hand around the crowded harbor. "Some place in the harbor. We have to seize them, don't we? I expect you two captains to ensure we take good ones. I don't want a leaky old scow in my fleet."

"You expect us to steal ships?" The elf captain crossed his arms and glared at Falstaff.

"I've been appointed Admiral by the Minister of Homeland Security, given an assignment, and I need two ships to carry it out."

"You have a warrant I can see?" the other captain said. "One that lets you seize someone's property?"

"I don't carry secret government documents on my person. The warrant is locked up in my quarters."

"So, we just have your word?" The elf continued to glare at Falstaff.

Falstaff hadn't anticipated resistance from the captains. "Poulet! Did I not meet with Colonel Othello yesterday?"

"Yeah, you did."

"And, after the meeting, did I not tell you I'd been appointed Admiral?"

"Yup."

"There you have it."

Behind his back, Falstaff heard Urquort snap his fingers followed by the warriors shuffling their feet. Next came the creak of leather harnesses.

Falstaff noticed the captains' eyes open wide and pressed his advantage. With one hand on his sword hilt, he confronted the elf, "Anymore treacherous talk from you and I'll run you through like a dog and leave your body on the beach for the gulls. You took Dun Hythe's money and now you'll carry out your duties or die like a traitor. Which will it be?"

The elf took a step back and held up both hands in front of him.

Falstaff turned away from the captains. "Corporal Urquort. Appoint a steady hand to command one troop of soldiers. You'll command the other and sail with me."

"I gotta corporal that'll do," Urquort replied.

"Excellent. Have the troops fall in and let's get under way."

#

In late afternoon, Falstaff stood on the quarterdeck and watched the large, oceangoing ship close on them. Urquort stood nearby. It was the day after they left Dun Hythe harbor, and Poulet had spent all his time hanging over the rail making disgusting noises. His ship and the one that sailed behind were the largest cogs available in the harbor. Each had a single mast that carried a large sail.

"A merchant, without doubt," the captain said. "One of those new two-masted ones called a brig."

Falstaff examined the sleek lines of the ship and lusted to add it to his fleet. He had difficulty controlling his excitement. "It looks like a pirate or a smuggler to me," he said. "We'll sail up on our right side —"

"Starboard side," the captain said.

"What?"

"On a ship, that side is called the starboard, not the right side."

"I know that," Falstaff sneered. "I called it the right side for the benefit of the corporal who is a land-mucking soldier. As I was saying, we'll approach on our starboard side and tell her to stop so we can inspect her cargo."

"Drop sail, not stop."

Falstaff mumbled under his breath. The captain clearly did not see him as admiral material.

Thirty minutes later, Falstaff called to the merchant ship, "Dun Hythe Harbor Patrol. Drop your sails. We're coming aboard." His second ship approached from the opposite side.

Falstaff's captain expertly placed the ship alongside the merchant.

"Corporal. Have your men board and neutralize any resistance."

"You'll be leadin' us?"

"Don't be daft. I can't exercise command and control if I'm crossing swords with a sailor. No, I'll be behind you directing the troops if a battle ensues."

After Urquort boarded and ensured the ship was safe, Falstaff climbed a groaning rope ladder and found the angry captain, an old man, who wore a sword and looked like he wanted an excuse to use it. "We're looking for contraband or stolen goods," Falstaff said. "Be so good as to show me your manifests. Urquort! Search the ship. See if you can find anything unusual. I'll be in the captain's cabin."

In the cabin, Falstaff was leafing through a pile of scrolls when Urquort appeared without knocking. "Gotta couple bottles of strange lookin' wine. They look kinda foreign like."

"Excellent." Falstaff ran a finger down the manifest. "I see no imported wine on these documents, sir."

"The wine is my personal stock."

"A likely story. Your ship and cargo are confiscated. Corporal, disarm the captain. I'll take his sword."

Ten minutes later after destroying the cargo manifest and throwing his sword hilt out the cabin window, Falstaff addressed the assembled crew. "I'm a fair man, therefore you have a choice. I've confiscated your ship and I need a crew for it. You can join my fleet and earn a share in our enterprise." He paused and looked toward shore, shading his eyes with a hand. "Or you can swim for Dun Hythe. Looks to be about five miles. That's not too bad. You can make it before dawn tomorroS, I'm sure. What'll it be?"

The crew joined Falstaff's fleet, and the captain reluctantly went along with the decision.

"Urquort, detail six of your men to stay onboard and get seven more from the other ship. Appoint someone to take your place on that ship." He turned to the captain. "This is now the flagship of my fleet. Where is a snug harbor we can use to sell the cargo?"

The man sighed before responding, "I'm guessing you're not interested in docking in Dun Hythe, so the closest harbor is Denmarko."

"And where is that?"

"About twenty miles up the coast."

"Excellent. Denmarko it is." Falstaff sensed the reluctance of the three captains to go along with his piracy. He had a few words with Urquort about the captains. The dwarfs would ensure the ships didn't sail off during the dark hours, but he needed a long-term solution to bind the captains' loyalty.

He pondered his new problem as the soldiers adjusted their berths.

# # #

Falstaff, accompanied by Poulet and Urquort, walked down the pier in Denmarko and turned toward the harbor master's shed at the end of the dock. Squawking seagulls flew overhead and swooped to grab tidbits from the filthy harbor waters.

Before reaching the port, he had solved the loyalty problem with the captains, binding them with additional shares of loot. He had confidence that he was on the cusp of a lucrative project.

Falstaff wore a tan sea cloak taken from a terrified passenger. His two-masted flagship, now named Snatcher, lay against a pier where his crew unloaded the cargo. The ship's captain had explained what to expect from customs and Falstaff knew he could bluff his way through. Still, he faced a degree of danger. If the official was honest — a remote possibility — he could end up getting arrested. If he faced a dishonest and greedy official — a definite possibility — he could face an uncomfortable negotiating session. The official would have the threat of confiscation, prison and torture as his negotiating tactics.

While the other two remained outside, Falstaff took a deep breath and entered the harbor master's office. He nodded to the plump official sitting behind a desk. "Good day, sir. My name is Admiral Falstaff. I've been commissioned by Dun Hythe to eliminate pirate fleets from the sea. I captured one, and I'm unloading the cargo to sell here in Denmarko. What do you need from me?"

"A pirate hunter?" The official, a half-pint, raised an eyebrow. "I wish you good luck and much success. I'll need a list of goods you captured with the ship."

"Ahh. That list is a problem, you see. The pirate captain didn't make one for his stolen goods, and my lads can't read or write so they couldn't make a list of the cargo. Surely, you don't expect me, the captain, to make the list? Perhaps we can come to an arrangement that will satisfy all parties." He reached beneath his cloak and took out a cloth purse. He shook it so the official could hear the coins clinking. Falstaff dropped it on the desk and took out a second, much heavier bag. "The first is to compensate you for your time and effort. The second is to cover the custom duties. I've made a generous estimate of what they might be and paid in full." Falstaff gave the half-pint a quizzical look. "I expect to bring many more pirate ships back here in the future."

"I think this will be satisfactory." The official gave Falstaff a grin. "I'll make up a cargo manifest for you and file it in my office."

"Excellent. I look forward to many more pleasant visits with you. Mind, don't mix up the purses." Falstaff laughed out loud and left the office. "That went well," he said to Poulet and Urquort. "Let's avail ourselves of the port's hospitality in yonder tavern."

# # #

Poulet strolled along with Falstaff and Urquort to the Sailor's Delight, a tavern strategically located at the end of the dock where it would be hard for sailors to miss. Falstaff stopped and placed his hands on his hips while he examined the dark interior. He spotted a door leading to outdoor tables and walked toward it. Along the way, Poulet glanced at the serving maid, a female half-pint. He halted, his mouth fell open and Urquort bumped into his back knocking him forward a few paces. The maid tutted and delivered a round of ale mugs to a group of sailors. As she turned, Poulet said, "Hi. My name is Poulet. My ship just docked in port. What's your name?" He still gaped at her voluptuous figure on display in a tight kirtle, her pretty facial features, her brown eyes, her short brown hair and her groomed three-inch-long toe hair fastened with brooches holding bits of colored glass. She was the most gorgeous female he had ever seen.

She looked him up and down. When she came to his feet, covered with toe hair stubble and road dust, a look of disgust covered her face and she walked away without answering.

Poulet went outside and found the other two sitting at a table. While he sat down, Falstaff waved a hand to the maid. "Three ales," he said when she walked over. She avoided looking at Poulet.

"Do you have mead?" Poulet asked in a quavering voice.

"Ignore him," Falstaff said. "He doesn't have the coins for mead. When we want a refill, what shall I call you?"

"Annee." She walked into the tavern swishing her hips.

"Poulet! You should pay me a few silver pennies for the vital information I just obtained for you," Falstaff said.

Poulet made a face at Falstaff, then said, "I think I'm in love." After a big sigh, he added, "Did you notice her beautiful toe hair?"

"What's with you half-pints and the toe hair?" Urquort asked. "That's kinda weird, ya know, and how come you don't have long toe hair?"

"I used to wear it long, but I hardly ever got time to groom it. I cut it short onna ship 'cause the sea spray makes it all messy."

"I think this will end badly for you," Falstaff said and laughed.

# # #

Iago was already home when Emilia got there after work. He had been drinking, too. He did that a lot lately. She threw her lunch bag on a chair.

Nasty when sober, he had an annoying habit of getting even nastier when he drank. Emilia could look forward to an evening of arguing, shouting and possibly violence.

The wattle and mud house — a hut really — consisted of an eating area with a table and a fireplace, a bedroom and a pantry.

Emilia grimaced a greeting, and Iago replied with a burp.

"What's yer problem?" she asked. "Are ya still moanin' about Othella gettin' the job?"

"Yeah, I'm still pissed about it."

"Get over it," she said. "Dat happened a long time ago."

"I'm not gettin' over it. Iffen I can't have dat job, me gonna do somethin' else ta get noticed. Ya'll see. I ain't gonna stay wid da Troll Patrol. Me wastin' me time on the Patrol. Me got bedda things to do."

"Like wot?"

"None of ya business. Someday me gonna be a bigshot."

"Yeah, right." Emilia waved a hand dismissively.

"Don't talk to me dat way." Iago made a fist and shook it at her.

"Gonna stuff dat fist down yer throat if ya try anythin'." Emilia stomped off to the outhouse. She couldn't take much more of Iago's attitude. Iago's stupidity would surely bring disaster to whatever plans he had in mind. And that disaster could affect her and Nark. She would have to keep a close eye on Iago

PART TWO

3 Months Later

CHAPTER SEVEN

In the port of Denmarko, Falstaff climbed out of the cutter onto the dock wearing a hooded canvas cloak to ward off the rain. His flagship, Snatcher, rode at anchor in the harbor while the other two ships in his fleet remained at sea searching for more merchant ships to seize. His latest prize had docked at a wharf to unload. That ship's crew had been put ashore north of Dun Hythe while a prize crew sailed it to Denmarko.

Already, workers swarmed around the prize and the first of its cargo had come out of the hold and was stacked on the dock. His factotum in town, a half-pint skilled in selling and managing cargoes, oversaw the unloading. Later, the cargo would be sold in the market square. Merchants now made the trek from Dun Hythe to buy the goods in the market at bargain prices. Sometimes, they grumbled about buying the same goods for the second time.

Poulet climbed out of the cutter after Falstaff.

At the end of the dock, Falstaff met briefly with a ship broker who agreed to look over the 'smuggler's ship.' The broker would buy the captured ship for a small fortune to be added to the riches the cargo brought in. With the sales tax levied in the market place, the King of Denmarko was also making a fortune. Falstaff thought he should pay a visit to the King one of these days to see how grateful the royal wretch was.

Whistling a tune, he walked to the harbor master's office. Inside, he shook off the rainwater and greeted the customs official sitting behind a desk. The half-pint grinned at

Falstaff. "Cap't Falstaff! How good to see you again. Did you have a successful voyage?"

"Indeed. There is one less pirate trying to prey on Dun Hythe's shipping."

"Let me guess," the official said. "This latest pirate captain didn't itemize his loot. Am I correct?"

"What amazing foresight you have. Alas, I have no documents to present to you."

The official laughed. "This is the twelfth time you've shown up without the manifest. Oh, well. We always seem to work it out."

"Aye." Falstaff laughed and reached into his cloak pocket to pull out a cloth purse. "I hope this will compensate for the lack of documentation." He shook the purse. Coins rattled. He dropped the purse on the desk and took out a second, much heavier purse. "And this is my estimate of the duties I'd pay to the crown if I had a manifest." Falstaff winked at the official who slid the heavier purse into a desk drawer. The official took a sheet of parchment. "Sign the bottom of this and I'll fill in a list of goods for you."

Falstaff scrawled his signature and handed the parchment back.

"I wish you more good hunting." The half-pint gave Falstaff a warm smile

"I hope so too, my friend."

Outside the office, Falstaff said, "Back to the ship, Poulet. We're out to sea immediately."

"I thirst," Poulet said. "Let's head to the tavern for a quick one."

"You can try your luck with Annee next time." Falstaff patted Poulet on the head. "But I think you're wasting your time."

"No, I'm not." Poulet pouted. "I'll keep tryin' for as long as it takes."

Falstaff resumed whistling the tune. Never in his forty years had he been as rich as he was at this moment.

After deserting the army, he had bounced around the countryside trying his hand at various get-rich schemes. He usually ended up poorer than when he started. That often led to the need to resort to flat-out stealing. After a close call with army officials seeking deserters he changed his name from the common Jack Pennyworth to the more noble-sounding John Falstaff. Almost overnight, it seemed his schemes began to enjoy more success. People seemed to trust him more and money rolled in. Once he added "Sir" to the name, his financial prospects increased even more. Despite this success, he never managed to bank any money, and he lost it as fast as he took it in.

It was a pity he hadn't thought of piracy earlier in his career. If he had, he might be a duke by now. The only downside to his piracy was that by now Othello must have figured out what was going on, and the fool would have to respond.

Falstaff shrugged. He'd worry about Othello when the time came, not before.

# # #

Othello and Captain Cassio watched Sergeant Dunlap drill the militia. While the band of would-be warriors had improved over the last three months, they couldn't slow down a determined band of elderly grandmothers. Knowing the defense of the city could possibly rest on them was enough to make Othello shudder. If the city came under assault, could he order this group to the walls, knowing they would all be slaughtered?

Dunlap seemed frustrated. Sweating, he roared orders and insults. Cassio took the insults personally and flinched with every one that came from the crusty drill sergeant.

Today, the pikemen drilled. Once a week, each group of militia trained during the morning. Yesterday, the elfin archers had taken their turn, and tomorrow it would be the half-pint slingers. Othello had the City Council issue an edict giving employers the choice of paying the militia while they trained or paying higher taxes.

"Form up!" Dunlap roared.

The fifteen pikeman shoved their way into an almost straight line with the pikes pointing skyward.

"Ground weapons!"

The men placed their weapons on the ground.

Dunlap approached and saluted Cassio. "Sir. Do ya wish to order the final charge of the day?"

"I'd like that, Sergeant." Cassio marched over to the pikemen.

"Ya don't pay me enough to put up wid this nonsense, Colonel. I'm thinkin' of takin' me leave."

Othello clapped Dunlap on the shoulder. "Stick it out for another two months and there'll be a ten silver penny bonus in it for you."

"On one condition."

"What's that?"

"Ya pay the bonus to me widow iffen I take a knife and slash me own throat."

"Retrieve pikes," Cassio yelled in his high-pitched voice.

The men bent over, grabbed their weapons and struggled to get them standing vertical.

"Prepare to march!"

The men leaned the pikes against their right shoulders.
"March!"
The men moved forward. Most of them marched in step.
"Aim pikes!"
The men lowered their weapons until the pikes were
horizontal to the ground. More than a few pike points
wavered as they continued to move forward.
"Charge!"
The men changed to trot and struggled to maintain the
wall of steel. Two points fell to the ground and sent the pike
holders crashing into the men around them. The line
buckled in those places and several men fell down.
"Only two this time," Dunlap groused. "'Tis an
improvement. Last time they charged seven points hit the
ground." He walked over to the pikemen while cursing
loudly and creatively.
Othello sighed. Nothing seemed to go right for him.
Iago, the head of the Troll Patrol, refused to take orders from
him and openly sneered at him. Unemployed warriors still
plagued the citizenry, and the Godmother still wanted the
contract for rebuilding the city's walls. A pirate fleet
harassed the city's shipping and, from reports by the crews of
the pirated ships, the fleet was led by Falstaff. What really
galled Othello was that he had advanced fifty silver pennies
to the man to help him recruit the pirates. All in the name of
protecting Dun Hythe. He had no idea how to stop the
piracy, and the ship owners harassed Mayor Glyniss who
demanded action from him. He really was a rabbit chased
by a pack of hounds.
So far, his performance in Dun Hythe matched his
previous attempts to gain honor, fame and riches. He had
successfully accomplished only one thing in his life. He had
married a wonderful female, but the decision to do that had

been made by others. He had merely agreed to go along with the decision makers.

Nark strolled up and made a gesture that had a vague resemblance to a salute. "Got news, Boss."

Othello raised an eyebrow.

"Iago's spreadin' nasty rumors about ya."

"I'm learning to hate him. What's he saying?"

"Says dat ya belong to the Godmother's gang and yer followin' her orders. Says it must be so 'cause ya married the Godmother's grandkid. Did ya?"

Othello scowled. "Yes, I married the granddaughter of the old bat called the Godmother. But I'm not a member of her gang and neither is my wife."

He watched the pikemen some more while he pondered the city's defenses. "Sometimes, I think I should tell the Troll Patrol they'll fight on the walls if we're attacked, but their clubs would be useless."

Nark didn't respond right away. After a few seconds, he sniggered. "Wanna hear an idea, Boss?"

Othello brightened. He found Nark's ideas worth listening to. "Tell me."

"Why not get de trolls to come here and learn how to use dat long sticky thing." He pointed to the pikemen. "Trolls gonna love foolin' around wid dose things."

"Iago'll simply refuse to send them."

Nark made a gruesome face while he thought about Othello's concern. "Iffen dey don't show up, dey lose a day's pay and den get docked anudda day's pay as a penalty. Da Patrol don't care wot Iago says, not when it hurts da money."

"That may work." Othello rubbed a hand over his chin.

"Put da trolls and da pikes onna walls iffen the city gets attacked. Gonna be a big surprise to da guys attackin'."

"Brilliant, Nark. The Troll Patrol could make a big difference. Using the pikes would make them a formidable force." Othello stared at the militia for a few seconds. "Now, how do we break the news to Iago?"

"I'll do it. I love to jerk him around. He'll go crazy when he hears dis one."

"All right." Othello laughed for the first time in days. "I have to go back to the office. Emilia must be ready to leave on her lunch break so I can prepare for a meeting with the mayor tomorrow." He grinned at Nark. "I get so much more work done when she isn't around."

On the way back, Nark pointed to an elderly dwarf sitting under a wooden lean-to on a street corner. He had a sign that read "Medical deals this week." Surgery instruments lay nearby.

"Let's see what that's about," Othello said. "It looks suspicious."

When asked, the dwarf replied, "I've been inna army for thirty years as a barber-surgeon, and I suddenly got let go because there ain't no more wars and that meant no more wounded soldiers. Came here with some of my regiment and now I'm trying to make a living without stealing from folks."

"What's the deal?" Othello pointed to the sign.

"Free tooth extraction with any amputation."

Othello grimaced.

"After the amputation, they'll be in so much pain, they'll never feel the tooth getting pulled. I have to offer the deal because business is so bad in town. Have any problems I should look at? Aches? Stomach pains? Other complaints?"

"No, I'm fine."

"What this place needs is a good earthquake. Then I'll have so much business I'll have to turn patients away."

Othello made a sour face and left. He had to do something about getting jobs for the dwarf warriors before they took matters into their own hands. Despite all the troubles Falstaff caused, he did take some pressure off that problem by taking a gang of dwarf warriors with him when he sailed, apparently by stealing two docked ships.

# # #

Hamlet hoisted his mug of ale in greeting to a stevedore at a nearby table outside the harbor tavern. In the summer twilight, the stench from the rotting fish guts lessened as the breeze shifted away from land.

"Prince Hammy," an old elf codger said while approaching the table. "Marinny's cow is loose again. You might keep yer eye peeled on the way back to the castle. Mayhap, you'll spot the wanderer."

"I will do that. The cow likes her freedom, doesn't she?"

The elf pointed his mug at two swells lounging against the oak tree that shaded the tables. "Don't yer bodyguards ever smile?"

Rosey and Gildy looked bored. And thirsty.

"They're not exactly my bodyguards." He wondered how they would react if he was assaulted.

A dwarf farmer marched up to the table wagging a stubby finger. "I have a report to make, Prince. It's about that wayward Mistress Blanky. She's puttin' on airs again. Thinks she's better than the rest of us, she does. It's about time you had a word with her. There's a good fellow." He patted Hamlet's shoulder and went inside for a refill.

"And how are the bees, Prince Hammy?" This came from the half-pint serving female.

"They're thriving, Annee. I should be getting a honey harvest before long."

"Good. I'll buy me honey from you. That witch inna market's pretty uppity and charges far too much money. Besides, she's from out of town." She pointed to his mug. "Fancy a refill?"

Hamlet drained his mug and handed it to her. "I do indeed."

When she left, Hamlet recalled his visit to the hives early this morning. Every one swarmed with bees. The sight gave him a shiver of delight. He really was King of the Bees, with a harem of twenty queen bees. His success proved that he could complete a project on his own. He had no help from anyone in the castle, not that they cared what he did as long as he didn't sneak away from Clodio's two spies. Clodio's motives were still suspect. Did the king still lust after his honey farm? Possibly Clodio bided his time until the harvest was near.

Of course, if he followed the demand of the nagging ghost messenger and killed Clodio, the concern over the honey would disappear. But murder seemed so . . . final. So . . . bloody. A passing cloud darkened the setting sun and cast a shadow over the area. Hamlet shuddered. He had an ominous sense that matters would soon boil out of control, but he didn't know how to respond. He could only tend to his hives and hope Clodio plotted no additional evil.

CHAPTER EIGHT

Othello took a deep breath before he entered Glyniss' office in midmorning. Three strangers sat at the table with her.

From their garb, he knew they were sea captains, and from their body language, he knew the meeting would not be pleasant.

"Colonel," Glyniss said. "Please take a seat and I'll introduce you to my guests who represent the Seafarers Guild."

He sat down and gave everyone a false smile. After the introductions were made, she said, "Please tell my guests what progress you have made in your time as the Minister of Homeland Security."

Othello cleared his throat. "One of my major initiatives has been to increase the training of the militia." He paused to check for any reactions. There weren't any. The captains remained with their arms crossed and watched him with hard eyes. "I did this," he continued, "by hiring an experienced drill sergeant. Yesterday, I observed the pikemen drilling, and I can report their progress has been amazing. They will be a formidable defensive force if the city is attacked."

"But what are ya doin' about the pirates, we want to know?" an elf captain asked.

"Gathering facts." Othello stalled, knowing he had no plans to reveal. "We know the name of the pirate leader. His name is Falstaff. I believe he is the one responsible for stealing two ships from the harbor."

"So, yer not doin' a bloody thing to get rid of the pirates." The speaker was a human captain who looked like he was about to lose his temper.

"I have three small patrol boats." Othello tried to keep his frustration from showing. "They are too small to use against the pirate ships. I need bigger ships before I can come to grips with the pirate fleet."

"All right, I accept that," the third captain said. The dwarf pointed a thick, gnarled finger at Glyniss. "So what's the city doin'?"

"We have an anti-pirate treaty and alliance with Demarko. It was signed years ago, before I became mayor. The Colonel will be traveling there to get their assistance."

Othello gasped in surprise.

"Sorry, Colonel. I only found out this morning about the treaty, and didn't have time to tell you."

"Well, it's about time somethin' gets done," the elf captain replied.

"As for you ship captains," Glyniss said, "it's time to put up or shut up. When Colonel Othello returns, I want at least five ships put at his disposal to hunt down the pirate fleet. If you are not willing to donate ships temporarily for our use, then you can stop complaining about piracy and solve the problem yourselves." She paused and looked each captain in the eye. "What'll it be?"

The captains coughed into their fists, squirmed in the chairs and wouldn't return the mayor's look. Finally, the dwarf said, "I'm guessin' the mayor is right. The city ain't got the ships to go after the pirates. We gotta help to protect our own interests. My ship'll be available when the Colonel returns."

Othello's heart lurched. Glyniss had unexpectedly provided him with some much needed help.

"But ya gotta get soldiers onna ship." The dwarf looked at Othello. "My sailors ain't trained to fight. Besides, they can't sail and fight at the same time."

Everyone waited for Othello to reply. "Er. . . the militia! I'll use the militia to fight the pirates."

"Excellent," Glyniss clapped her hands. "That'll give them much needed battle experience." She stood up and faced the captains. "I thank you all for coming to the aid of the city." To Othello she added, "Stay a few moments."

Othello felt uneasy. He didn't think he'd like whatever she was about to tell him.

After the captains left she said, "This piracy has affected the city's revenues. Besides the loss of duties and cargoes from the pirated ships, the number of merchants entering our port has gone down. I'm sure the ships are sailing south and using the port in Cintri. That lowers our revenue even more. In other words, there are even less funds for rebuilding the walls than before. Yet it remains important. We can't defend the city with the walls in the present state." She shook her head. "If we get attacked by an army of demobilized warriors, we'll have to surrender without fighting." After making a face, she added, "Go to Denmarko and get their assistance. They have a new king up there, and he may not know about the treaty. I'll have a few copies made to show him. Leave as soon as the treaty can be copied. Meanwhile, I'll send a scryer message to Denmarko to tell them about your trip."

Othello left the office in a state of confusion. He was glad the mayor had come up with a plan, but was unhappy that he had to implement it. He ticked off his concerns. First, he had to get a king to agree to honor a treaty signed before that king had assumed the throne. Second, he didn't know how to negotiate with a king. He didn't even know how to act with a king. If the king refused to honor the treaty, what was he supposed to do? If he demanded the king honor it, his head may get lopped off. Third, there was the militia. They were now expected to board ships and fight a sea battle against battle-hardened dwarf warriors. Lastly, he had no idea how one went about finding another fleet on the high seas.

# # #

Long ago, the Wizards Guilds throughout Gundarland deployed a private scryer network. It connected all the guilds, chapter houses and magic schools. Using the network, wizards could swap jokes, rumors and plant false information to blacken the reputation of another wizard. One enterprising wizard found a novel use for the network. After developing a new spell, one that was potentially dangerous to the spell caster, he bragged about his spell, posted it on the scryer network and sat back to await news, either how grand the spell worked or the sudden, mysterious deaths of a few wizards who died while testing a new spell.

Another wizard, one with an unusual talent for business, organized a public scryer network. Scryer offices were established in every city, town and large village. For a few coins, a customer could give a message to a scryer operator who would load the message and forward it to another scryer office. At the receiving end, it would be unloaded, written down and given to a messenger who delivered it for a few more coins.

Half of the revenue from the network went to the Wizards Guilds which used it to fund Magic Night. On the longest day of the year, wizards put on magical fireworks displays to entertain the public. Occasionally, the displays went off without destroying any buildings, but that was rare. The scryer funds also paid for Wizards Night Out, another annual event, this one involving many barrels of ale.

To limit the local damage and carnage, towns prohibited both events from taking place within five miles of the city or town limits.

# # #

Hamlet, dressed in a white tunic and brown breeches, sat at a desk in his room working on a marketing plan for his honey. Steady rain prevented him from inspecting the hives, and he took advantage of the weather to prepare for selling his harvest. Should he sell it by the jar in the market square? Or in bulk to a vendor for resale? These and a dozen other questions concerned him. He hummed a ditty as he jotted notes.

Gertie burst into Hamlet's room. "I have news," she said.

A startled Hamlet scratched his ink-filled quill across the parchment sheet filled with figures and letters. He made a face at the black, diagonal line drawn across the parchment and snarled, "Why don't you knock?"

"Because I'm your mother, that's why." She wore her usual black velvet dress.

"Well, you're here, so tell me the news." He tried not to breathe through his nose so he wouldn't gag on the smell of her lavender perfume.

"I have almost persuaded the king to employ you at court. Soon, you'll have an important post, one that befits your royal status."

"If this is a plan to get me to give up my bees, it won't work." He crossed his arms and stared at her. Her belly length beard braids had been woven into a single intricate design that must have taken her females-in-waiting hours to make.

"You must take advantage of this opportunity and stop playing at little boys' games."

"Honey production is not a little boy's game. It is an activity that will help the economy of Denmarko."

"Economics is beyond me. All I know is that the son of a queen shouldn't be mucking about in the woods. You have Rosey and Guildy besides themselves. Clodio is at his wits' end listening to their tedious reports about you talking to the bees as if they're real folks." She walked to the window and peeked out. "I suspect Clodio will give you a position just so he won't have to listen to any more of their reports." On her way out the door, she stopped and turned. "Have your servants clean a good suit so you won't disgrace me when you present yourself at court."

Hamlet threw his quill down in disgust. It was a miracle he got any work done between his nagging mother, the obnoxious ghost and making sure Rosey and Guildy didn't get lost and in trouble with the king. Only with the bees did he have any peace of mind, or when he spent time in the port tavern. He glanced out the window at the rain. He smiled and decided to have an ale. It would annoy Rosey and Guildy no end to have to go out on a day like today. Their foppish wool cloaks stunk when wet and took days to dry out. He pictured them sitting at a table with their sodden, dripping wet cloaks. He laughed out loud.

CHAPTER NINE

Othello walked into his apartment at the end of a long day of preparing for his trip to Denmarko. He was sweaty from walking in the early evening heat and wanted a cool drink. Desdemona greeted him instead with bad news.

"We have to go to see the Godmother. I received a note from her and she's demanding a meeting with you right away."

Othello groaned. Much of his day had been spent avoiding Iago who stomped about the building with murder in his eyes because of the Troll Patrol's new training program. The only ones who could deal with him were Nark and his wife, Emilia. "There's a thuggish-looking elf downstairs," Othello said. "Is he the one who brought the message?"

"Yes, he'll escort us and protect us. He didn't say why she wants to see us."

"I bet she wants the contract to rebuild the walls."

The thug led the way through the elf quarter to the Wicked Bed. After a body search, they entered her office. She sat on her throne wearing a deep purple tent with orange hair streaked with indigo. A cigar stuck out of a red gash beneath her nose. "Ofella! It's about time you showed up." The two young female elves with breathtaking beauty stood behind her.

Othello had trouble understanding her because she spoke with the cigar still in her mouth. "Come, Desdemona. Give your grandmother a kiss."

Desdemona advanced and was enveloped in the purple tent. Released, she retreated. The Godmother scowled at

Othello and held her right hand with the enormous sapphire ring. Othello hesitated and his wife shoved him forward. The Godmother noticed his reluctance and her indigo rouge-ringed eyes flared with anger. After kissing the ring, he stepped back and waited. She took the cigar out of her mouth and gestured toward him with it. "When will you ask for bids on the walls?"

Othello took a deep breath before answering. "Probably never, Godmother."

"Why not?" She glared at Othello. "I want that business, Ofella, and I don't want to hear excuses."

"The city has no money for rebuilding the walls. The pirates have forced many merchants to sail south instead of docking here. The city's revenue stream has been reduced and, with it, any hope of rebuilding the walls."

Godmother stuffed the cigar back in her mouth and puffed furiously, sending up a cloud of bluish-white smoke while staring at Othello. After a few seconds, she removed the cigar and flipped it over her shoulder. One of the young females plucked it out of midair and put it into a small dish on a side table. "So, my investment in you was wasted. I'll never get my money back without the contract for the city walls." She held out her hand and the cigar reappeared in it. After more puffing, she said through clenched teeth, "Here is what you will do. Figure a way to get the mayor to fund the rebuilding. Terrorize her with stories of what happens when a city is sacked by soldiers. Tell her anything you can think of, but I want that contract and you will deliver it or else." She took a drag on the cigar and blew smoke at him. "And another thing. I want you to stop those dwarf immigrants from stealing. They're embarrassing the Thieves Guild. It's the least you can do to repay part of my investment." She waved a hand. "Go, before I think of yet another reason to punish you."

Othello hastened out of the bordello, pulling Desdemona in his hurry. The obese female terrified him and he never wanted to see her again. What had been a bad day before now had ended even worse. How was he supposed to persuade the mayor to spend enormous amounts of money on the walls? Just thinking about failure made his teeth hurt. He never should have exaggerated his accomplishments on his resumé.

And why was he supposed to protect the Thieves Guild?

# # #

The Thieves Guild was an ancient organization, possible the oldest one in the city, going all the way back to the time when Dun Hythe was a fortified village atop a palisade with fishing boats beached on the narrow strip of land at the base of the cliff. Back then, merchants came to purchase wagonloads of salted fish. Soon, a market area sprang up and other merchants came to sell various goods to the fish merchants and to each other. This concentration of wealth attracted traveling thieves who preyed on easy marks.

The local thieves objected to the visiting robbers; they believed merchants within the village walls belonged to them, not to outsiders. Another source of irritation was the visitors' belief that everyone was fair game, whereas the locals excluded some of the village inhabitants from thievery. Some were excluded because of family ties, others as necessary to dispose of loot. The locals organized patrols of off-duty thieves to protect the excluded. Naturally, this led to scrums between the home team thieves and the visiting players.

As the village grew into a small town and the fishing industry and the market expanded, it attracted more visiting cut-purses, leading to more patrolling. The constant need for patrolling cut into the working hours of the locals, reducing their incomes. Clearly something innovative had to be done. The working thieves couldn't earn an income and protect the excluded from the ever-expanding number of visitors; there weren't enough hours in the day.

Over time, in response to these pressures, a unique organization came into being, Gundarland's first Thieves Guild. The Guild grew powerful, and every thief in the country knew better than to try unlicensed thievery in Dun Hythe.

The genius of the Guild was that it offered an insurance policy to the shop owners and market vendors in Dun Hythe. For a weekly fee, the merchants received a guarantee they wouldn't be robbed. The fees provided compensation for the members when they pulled a stint of guard duty and patrolling. The merchants' protection policy didn't apply to the stores' customers, especially if the customers were from out-of-town. Any visitor to the city who bought jewelry or other expensive merchandise stood a good chance of getting robbed on the streets or having their rented rooms broken into. The Guild then gave the first right of refusal to the store owner. He could buy back his merchandise for fifty percent of whatever the customer paid for it.

The unemployed warrior dwarfs upset this delicate economic balance by robbing from everyone. If a fee-paying merchant found his shop broken into overnight, he filed a claim form with the Guild to get reimbursed for his loss. The unlicensed and unprincipled dwarfs drained the claim fund and forced the Guild to the verge of bankruptcy.

Since the Guild had wisely placed itself under the protection of the Godmother several generations back, it now demanded action from her to protect itself from the unscrupulous dwarf soldiers.

# # #

When Desdemona left the brothel, she felt like she had eaten a rock. It lay in her stomach, making it difficult to swallow and even breathe. Her Grandma was losing patience with Othello, and Othello couldn't do what she wanted. He couldn't do it himself, he needed the agreement of the politicians, the only ones who could allocate the funds for the wall project. He had told her about the financial problems Glyniss faced, but Grandma wouldn't accept that as an excuse. She wanted the rebuilding project and nothing less than that would satisfy her greed.

With a feeling of dread, she knew that she would soon have to choose between the only two she had ever loved. She didn't know how she could face that decision.

Grandma had always preached to her that what was good for the family was good for her. She wasn't sure it could be universally applied, but she never told Grandma about her doubts.

When she had reached ten, Grandma made her attend meetings on family business. Desdemona always sat in the rear of the room and never spoke to anyone. After the meeting, the old elf would question her on what she had seen and heard. From these meetings, Desdemona got an understanding of the workings of the business and met many of the sub-bosses.

At age fifteen, Grandma had moved her to a seat at the table and encouraged her to participate and offer opinions and observations. Soon, she became the principal advisor to the old elf and everyone at the meetings harkened to her advice.

At eighteen, Grandma explained the need to bring outside blood into the family and told her about a potential marriage match. Desdemona quickly agreed since she owed a huge debt to her grandmother and would never go against her wishes. Besides, the eligible males in the city were all distasteful to her. They were either bullies, stupid or thugs. An outsider would bring a fresh prospective with him, one that could better match her own views.

To her surprise, she fell in love with her new husband just as he had fallen in love with her. Her greatest hope now was to become pregnant and make Othello a father. If the baby was a daughter, she would be supremely happy. So would Grandma.

She glanced sideways at Othello and wondered if he would ever become accustomed to her grandmother and the family business. She hoped he would at least accept it for what it was — a lucrative business.

She sighed, squeezed his arm and received a small smile. She determined to make the most of the time remaining before she had to choose.

CHAPTER TEN

Three days after his meeting with the mayor, Othello set out for Denmarko with Nark at his side. Desdemona had given him advice on how to handle the negotiations. He wondered where and how she had learned to negotiate, but didn't ask lest he insult her. Despite Desdemona's help, he still felt uncomfortable dealing with a king. What if the king refused to honor the treaty? He had no idea how to respond in that case without aggravating the king, which could be fatal to his health.

It was midmorning when they left, and Othello set a brisk pace to reach Denmarko before dark. The road carried a considerable amount of wagon traffic. Othello noted the empty wagons going north and the full wagons coming south. The full wagons had attentive guards; elfin longbows stood in the back watching the woods, and swordsmen rode with the drivers. Those wagons traveled in convoys of up to twelve and had armed horsemen escorting them. In contrast, the northbound wagons moved singly with the archers and swordsmen playing cards or sleeping.

They came upon a wagon leisurely moving along in their direction. The driver, a man chewing on a twig, nodded to them. "Excuse me, sir," Othello said. "Can I ask you a question?"

"Sure thing."

"Why do the wagons have so many guards?"

"Dwarf bandits. The woods are filled with 'em. All of 'em ex-warriors."

"But why are your guards sleeping instead of standing watch?"

"The dwarfs may be bandits, but that don't mean they're stupid. Me wagon's empty. Ain't no profit in robbin' it." He took the twig out of his mouth and pointed at the southbound traffic. "Now them wagons over there are full. They's the ones the dwarfs are after." He shook his head. "Seems every time I travel to Denmarko the bandit gangs get bigger and tougher. I think they're joinin' together. Pretty soon, they'll be as big as armies."

A sudden idea popped into Othello's mind. Perhaps he had a solution to one of his problems. "There are plenty of unemployed dwarf warriors in the city. Why not hire some of them?"

"Why not just slit yer own throat and be done with it? Those buggers inna city probably know the buggers inna woods and may join 'em instead of fightin' 'em."

Othello's shoulders sagged. So much for his solution. The driver's information disturbed Othello. How could he defend the city with the current state of the walls if a bandit army attacked the city?

"Whatsa matter, Boss?" Nark said. "Ya look worried."

Othello told him about his concerns.

"Why can't ya just rebuild the walls?"

"The city doesn't have enough money. And the pirates are forcing merchant ships to sail to other ports so we lose those customs fees." He made a face. "I don't know what to do."

Nark pulled a face and stared ahead. Othello recognized the signs. Nark focused his trollish cunning on the wall problem, but Othello doubted if Nark could come up with a solution.

Late in the afternoon, a guard at the Denmarko town gates gave them directions to the palace, a series of buildings, all old and mostly made of wood. Only the keep was made of stone.

"We received a scryer message," a stuffy elf chamberlain said, "so we expected you." He glared at Nark, "But not the troll."

"He's my trusted assistant," Othello replied.

The chamberlain never took his eyes off Nark, as if he expected the troll to start looting the palace. "The king has graciously agreed to meet with you. He's prepared a reception to honor the representative from Dun Hythe. I'll show you to rooms where you can freshen up and rest until the reception takes place this evening." He stared at Nark. "Be warned. Everything in your room has been inventoried, and we will know immediately if you steal anything."

# # #

After being at sea for almost a week, Falstaff's fleet anchored in the Denmarko harbor while prize crews docked two more pirated ships at wharfs. A handful of sailors and warriors from each ship landed to spend some of their hard-earned loot in town before going back to their ship to be replaced on shore by shipmates. Falstaff had warned them to stay in the port area; he didn't want drunks tearing up the town and ruining his welcome.

Once on land, with Poulet and Urquort in tow, he settled matters with the customs official and talked with his factotum before heading to the market square. In the square, he wandered among the stalls. "Hah! Poulet. I love to see our cargoes getting snapped up and piled into wagons."

"Aye, more money for us," Poulet replied.

"Indeed, half the revenue from every sale flows into our coffers."

"'Lessen somebody's got sticky fingers and steals some of it," Urquort said. The dwarf was now a sergeant and had a new pip on his sleeve to join the two faded ones.

"I trust my factotum," Falstaff replied. "Nevertheless, I have eyes watching everything he does."

"Enough with the sightseein'," Poulet said. "Let's get a drink at the Sailor's Delight."

Urqourt and Falstaff both laughed.

"That servin' wench won't give ya the time of day, ya know," Urquort said.

"That's not true." Poulet's face belied his confident words. "Annee fancies me. I know she does."

"All right. I can use a drink." Falstaff pointed to the port area. "Away to the tavern. Urquort and I can amuse ourselves by watching you make a fool of yourself."

# # #

During the afternoon, Hamlet strolled through the bustling market square on his way to the tavern. Carts piled high with goods came from the harbor and returned empty. Merchants, many of them from other areas of Gundarland judging by their dress, wandered around touching, squeezing and arguing about prices. The presence of all the buyers boded well for his honey sales in the autumn.

Walking toward the harbor, he noticed a larger than usual number of ships, some at anchor in the harbor and others at wharfs. He entered the tavern and found sailors filling the bar and the outdoor tables. A number of dwarfs armed with battle axes sat at tables or lounged on the ground.

Annee saw him and chased a trio of sailors away from a table under the oak tree. "Here ya go, Prince Hammy. Set yerself down and I'll fetch ya a fine pint."

"Thank you, Annee." Hamlet sat down and looked around at the bustling tavern. Rosey and Guildy looked annoyed at being forced to lean against the tavern wall, the only available space.

When the ale came, Hamlet asked, "What's going on? Where did all these folks come from?"

"Oh, it's Falstaff. He's in port with two more ships. All these drunken sailors are from those ships."

"Who are the dwarf warriors? Where did they come from?"

"Falstaff's ships. They do his fightin'."

"What fighting?" Hamlet felt a touch of alarm. Foreign warriors in Demarko couldn't be a good thing. On the other hand, maybe they'd buy his honey.

"Falstaff's a pirate hunter. Or so he claims. And he brings captured cargoes here to sell in our market." She turned around at the sound of a booming voice greeting the bartender. "That's him now. Sir Falstaff."

Hamlet saw a tall man with a ponderous paunch plow through the mob. A half-pint and a dwarf warrior followed in his wake. The half-pint stared at Annee while Falstaff greeted others in the tavern.

"Pipe down, Falstaff." Annee yelled, stamped a foot and waved a hand at the newcomer. "Prince Hammy is here, so act like ya got some manners."

Falstaff stopped and his two followers bumped into him. He gave Annee a questioning look. She hooked a thumb over her shoulder toward Hamlet. Behind the big man, the half-pint smiled at Annee and waved to her. She ignored him.

Hamlet colored at the attention and focused on Falstaff. He wore hose, a bit ragged, and an enormous doublet that couldn't possible close over his stomach. Falstaff resumed his forward motion and steered toward Hamlet's table.

# # #

Falstaff considered Annee's words. A prince? His philosophy was to know as many powerful and well-connected folks as possible. A new prince would make a wonderful addition to his lists. The prince wore expensive-looking clothes and sat alone at a table in the crowded tavern, both indications of his rank. Falstaff tacked to the starboard and steered toward the prince. As he passed Annee, she snarled, "He's Prince Hamlet to you. He's not pirate scum like you lot."

Poulet smiled at her and waved shyly.

Annee continued to ignore him.

Falstaff reached out and grabbed her arm. "A round of your finest ale, my dear. Include a refill for the Prince."

"Let me help you?" Poulet asked.

Annee glanced down at his toe hairs, pulled a face, tutted and walked away without answering.

Falstaff marched up to the table and gave a slight bow. "Prince Hamlet! Finally, we meet. I've wanted the pleasure of meeting you for some time now." He sat down opposite Hamlet. "I am Admiral Sir John Falstaff." Poulet and Urquort hovered nearby. Falstaff waved a meaty hand in their direction. "May my short associates join us?" He studied Hamlet. Unlike most dwarfs, the prince was clean-shaven and rather scrawny, but had the usual brown hair and eyes. He noted the weak chin and decided he'd have to develop a scheme for Hamlet to participate in.

After Hamlet nodded, Poulet sat down alongside Falstaff while Urquort remained standing to keep an eye out for pickpockets and other mischief-makers.

"I hear you hunt pirates," Hamlet said. "Is that so?"

"'Tis so. My loyal crews and I scour the seas for those brigands who terrorize honest merchant ships."

Annee returned with a tray filled with leather mugs of ale. Poulet jumped up. "Let me help you with those."

She put the tray down and smacked his hand. "Leave off," she snarled, "before ya spill one onna Prince." She distributed the mugs and left.

"My friend Poulet here," Falstaff nodded to the half-pint, "is in love with Annee."

"Denmarko's finest serving wench." Hamlet grinned at Poulet. "Tell me, Admiral, how did you become a pirate hunter? Mayhap, there is a tale to tell."

"Not much of a tale. Poulet and I passed through Dun Hythe a while back and I heard Othello, an old comrade-in-arms, had been made Minister of Homeland Security. I visited him and, after we renewed our acquaintances, I offered my services. Colonel Othello commissioned me to eliminate his pirate problem, and that is what I do. Sergeant Urquort joined me to take charge of the soldiers I hired. When we take a prize, we sail it here to sell the cargo and the ship. I'm sure King Clodio is quite happy with his share of the customs duties and the taxes from the sale in the market square."

"Excellent!" Hamlet clapped his hands. "Then you'll be at the reception later on."

"Umm, what reception is that?"

"The one at the castle in honor of Colonel Othello. He's in town to discuss some dreary treaty with King Clodio."

Falstaff smiled to hide his concern. If Othello had traveled to Denmarko, it could only be to enlist allies against his pirate fleet. So the game became more dangerous. "Does Othello have troops with him?"

"Don't know." Hamlet shrugged. "I haven't met him yet."

He nudged Poulet with an elbow. "Drink up. You and Sergeant Urquort better start herding the crews back to the ship." To Hamlet he said, "Alas, as much as I would love to see the Colonel once again — we haven't talked in some time — I must be about the work he set me. We need to return to our ships shortly so we can sail with the evening tide." Falstaff stood, drained his ale and bowed to the Prince. "I sincerely hope we can meet again some day."

# # #

Hamlet, dressed in clean white shirt, blue breeches and white hose, entered the reception room with a brown cape draped over his shoulders. All his clothes had been laid out by his mother while he was in the tavern. Clodio and Gertie stood together drinking white wine. When they noticed him, his mother smiled and Clodio grimaced. "How nice you look, dear," she said.

"Why do I have to attend?" Hamlet wanted to stay in his room and read a new theory about increasing honey production.

"Because it's time you became involved in court affairs." Gertie wagged a motherly finger in his face.

Hamlet sighed and poured himself a mug of ale from a pitcher on a table. The king, wearing a black ermine-trimmed cloak over a purple shirt and breeches, said in a stage whisper, "As if he's capable of helping."

"But dear," Gertie replied, "Hamlet has his own way of thinking through problems and situations. His approach can give you a fresh perspective. The only advice you get now is to keep doing what you did in the past. That's all your stodgy advisors ever say."

A chamberlain opened a door and yelled, "Colonel Othello from Dun Hythe." After a brief pause, he added, with obvious distaste, "And troll."

Hamlet watched a dark elf enter the room. He appeared nervous and wore a tan uniform and a tan kepi with a large gold C on it. He wiped perspiration from his brow with a handkerchief and smiled at the room. A troll slouched in behind him wearing brown pants with a rope for a belt. The troll had blue sergeant stripes tattooed on both biceps, and the color of the stripes contrasted with his yellow skin. He carried a leather dispatch case.

With Othello and Nark out of town, Emilia left the office to go home to have lunch. She strolled through the humid streets to her hovel, no different from hundreds of other hovels in the outer fringes of Dun Hythe. When she neared her home, she heard the discordant sounds of several trolls coming from her house. One was Iago's, but she didn't recognize the others.

Inside the house, she found him and three others holding a conference. They all looked guilty when she burst through the door.

"Why dese bums inna house?" Emilia had seen the other three trolls before; all were thugs who hired out for strong-armed jobs.

"Dis my house," Iago snarled at her. "I brang dem here. We got bidsniss to talk about."

"Why ya got bidsniss wid low-lifers? Ya up to no good. I know it."

"Us bedda go," one of the trolls said. "Can't do nothin' now dat she's here." He stood up followed by the other two, and they all shuffled out the door.

"Why ya home? Why ya not on da job?" Iago asked.

"Got nothin to do inna office, so I came here for home-cooked meal. What ya plannin'? I wanna know."

"I ain't tell ya nothin'. Yet. I'll tell ya when it's over. Den ya gonna be proud of me."

"Hah! Proud of ya? Dat'll be da day." Emilia scoffed at Iago. "Hope yer plan makes me a widow. I give ya a good funeral."

"Bitch!" Iago threw a fist at her head and connected with her ear. She staggered backwards and bumped into the table. Iago yelled and charged after her. She sidestepped and punched the back of his head as he went past.

Iago landed on his stomach and slid on the dirt floor. Emilia jumped and landed with both feet on his back, knocking the wind out of him. She whooped in victory. He gasped for breath and pushed up on his hands and knees, throwing her off. Windmilling her arms, she stumbled into the bedroom and fell onto the straw-filled mattress. Iago, roaring a war cry, ran into the room and dove at her.

Emilia rolled away as Iago crashed into the bed. She sat up and threw a headlock on him. He grabbed her waist and both milled around the bed, heaving and struggling to maintain their grips.

Over the next few seconds, the fighting changed to tickling and stroking. The shouting and whooping died down while she drew her kirtle over her head and hurled it across the room. Iago threw his pants and sash on top of the kirtle.

# # #

Othello heard Nark shuffle into the room behind him. He licked his lips. Three people watched him enter. A female dwarf dressed in a white gown with purple trim could only be Queen Gertie. The aged, white-bearded dwarf must be King Clodio, and the young clean-shaven dwarf was an unknown, but had to be part of the royal family. He stopped in front of the king and gave a stiff, short bow. "Dun Hythe sends its greetings, Sire."

"Indeed," Clodio sniffed. "Let's get down to business so we can eat in peace. What's so important that Dun Hythe sent me a scryer message and then sent you up here? We like to be left alone, you know."

"Dun Hythe is plagued by a pirate fleet, and we call on our ally to lend us assistance in wiping them out."

"Pirates? We don't have a pirate problem. Why should we help?"

"Dun Hythe and your predecessor signed an anti-pirate treaty." He turned to Nark who opened the dispatch case and took out two scrolls. Othello took both and handed one to Clodio. "Here is a copy of the treaty."

Clodio took the scroll, broke the seal, opened it, shrugged and handed it to Gertie. The king sipped his wine and ignored Othello while Gertie read the treaty after turning it right side up.

The unknown dwarf approached him. "I'm Hamlet, the Queen's son. I never met a dark elf before. Or a troll. How exciting. Are either of you interested in bee farming? It's great stuff and I can give you a lot of information on it if you ever decide to go into the business."

"Stop boring the guests with your bee nonsense," Gertie snapped without looking up from the scroll. A minute later, she turned to the king. "It's true, dear. I remember my dead husband talking about this treaty. It says Denmarko and Dun Hythe each have to provide aid whenever the other party asks for it."

"Bah. Why should I honor a dead king's treaty?" He took the scroll and slapped it against his thigh. "What's in it for me?"

"Do you have any specifics about the pirates?" Gertie asked Othello.

"We know the pirate fleet has taken over a dozen merchant ships, and the captured ships sail north somewhere. The pirates are commanded by a man named Falstaff, a rogue if there ever was one."

"Falstaff?" Hamlet said. "Surely you're mistaken. I met him this afternoon, and he claims he is a pirate chaser working for Dun Hythe under your direction."

"Falstaff is here?" Othello gasped. "Where?"

"He bought me an ale at the tavern in the port area. He brings the captured pirate ships here, sells the cargo and the ship then sails back out to sea."

Othello tried to assimilate the news, but had trouble thinking. Dun Hythe's ally was in league with Falstaff? "Is he still here? Can we get some troops to capture him?"

"Alas, he sailed with the tide." Hamlet shook his head.

"A pirate is using my port?" Clodio looked astonished. "I never gave permission for that to happen."

"Falstaff told me you must be happy with all the revenue you get from the increased customs fees and sales taxes."

"Is that where it comes from?" Clodio's face softened. "Perhaps I should raise the customs fees and get even more money."

"Sire." Othello felt his mission's purpose sliding into yet another failure. He could never face Glyniss if he didn't succeed here. "Dun Hythe needs your assistance and requests you honor the treaty."

"Why? I see no reason to help you."

Gertie grabbed Clodio's arm and pulled on it. "Excuse us a minute, Colonel." She took the king into a far corner and jabbered in his ear. Othello watched and chewed his lip. Clodio's stern expression suddenly changed to one of surprise. He glanced at Hamlet and a slight smile graced his face. He patted Gertie's shoulder and left the corner. "The Queen has pointed out the benefits of ridding our seas of pirate fleets. We will, of course, honor the treaty. Do you have a plan in mind?"

"I do, sir." Othello tried not to let his immense relief show. "Our plan calls for a coordinated attack on the pirates from two directions, north and south. The pirates cruise around the Dun Hythe area, so we propose that you send a fleet of ships south in three days. I will lead a fleet out of Dun Hythe harbor on the same day. Between us, we will trap and crush this Falstaff and destroy his fleet."

Clodio puckered his lips and tapped the scroll on his chin.

Gertie beamed at Hamlet.

Othello took the queen's smile as a good omen and he relaxed slightly.

# # #

Bored by the talk, Hamlet let his mind wander. He made a mental list of beekeeping items to attend to. He suddenly focused his attention on his surroundings when he noticed his mother smiling at him. From long experience, he recognized an ominous sign. He heard Clodio announce, "I agree with your plan. I will hire three ships and send them south. They will sail under the command of my nephew, Hamlet."

Hamlet's face flushed and his heart hammered. How could he command a fleet and attend to his bees? He would have to explain to his mother that he couldn't sail until the fall when the bees' activities came to a halt.

"I know you're surprised, dear," Gertie said. "But it's for your own good. You need to broaden your experiences and get away from those wretched bees of yours. I'll have someone look after them while you're out destroying the pirates."

"Excellent!" Othello exclaimed. I'll leave in the morning to prepare my end of the trap." He strode over to Hamlet and grasped his hand. "I look forward to seeing you on the high seas."

Hamlet gawked in disbelief at Othello. "I can't possibly sail until the fall. I have too much to do."

Clodio pointed a finger at Hamlet. "You will sail with the fleet even if I have to tie you to the mainmast." He turned to Othello. "Now that the business is taken care of, let's eat." To Nark, he said, "Don't even think about stealing the cutlery. It's all been counted."

CHAPTER ELEVEN

Othello and Nark left Denmarko after breaking their fast with Hamlet and sending a scryer message to Mayor Glyniss. While they were eating, he had noticed that the prince still acted depressed by his promotion to fleet admiral and Othello harbored doubts about his suitability as a dependable ally. He couldn't be sure Hamlet would show up on time. He also wasn't convinced that Hamlet would be able to accomplish anything positive.

Later, on the road south, they passed a number of convoys loaded with pirated goods. The guards and escorts looked alert and fingered their weapons.

Halfway to Dun Hythe, they came across a convoy pulled to the side of the road. Several of the guards had wounds, two mules were dead in their traces and three barrels had arrows sticking in their sides. "What happened?" Othello asked of one of the drivers who sat on a wagon bandaging a blade cut on his arm.

"Bandits, curse them." He spit on the ground. "Fifteen of 'em. Maybe more. Biggest gang I ever saw. Even had a coupla archers with 'em. Got away with some of the stuff onna wagons."

Othello felt helpless because there was nothing he could do to help the crews or the guards. Still, he was reluctant to leave. Perhaps if he stayed, he could learn more about the bandit gangs.

"Gotta go," Nark said. "Gotta get ready to sail."

They left the convoy behind. A mile later, Othello sighed. "What am I supposed to do if these bandit gangs join together and decide to attack the city?" He pulled a face. "If

I could figure a way to do it, I'd use the trolls for something besides creating traffic jams." He sighed and flicked the horse's reins. "Iago threatens a troll strike every time I suggest a change."

"Hmm. Maybe ya got somethin' dere, Boss." Nark stared up the road.

After a few minutes, Nark said, "I gotta idea about how to fix da walls."

"Good, let's hear it." Othello fastened his attention on the troll. He needed every good idea he could find and Nark had already come up with several useful ones.

"Make da Troll Patrol da Wall Patrol. While dey guardin' da wall, dey also rebuild it 'cause trolls are strong and dey can lift da big stones."

"Iago will never agree with that."

"Hah! Him pretty stupid. Give him a promotion from lieutenant to captain and he gonna jump onna new job. Give de trolls a one penny raise."

Othello shook his head in disbelief. Nark had done it again! The troll's plan meant he didn't have to give the Godmother the contract that would bankrupt the city. But the old biddy would never believe that he hadn't come up with the arrangement to cheat her out of her money. He needed a way to protect himself from her wrath. Not to mention Iago's possible anger. He soon came up with a way. "I can't make this decision by myself. I have to get Glyniss and the city council to decide to do it. And to announce it. But how do we replace the Troll Patrol? Hire more trolls?"

"Naw. Hire a bunch of dem dwarf warriors dat're causin' all da trouble. Make dem da Dwarf Patrol. Or da Foot Patrol."

Othello bounced in his saddle and grinned. Hiring the dwarfs and making them responsible for both traffic control and preventing dwarf robberies would be a sop he could give the Godmother since the dwarfs would also be protecting the Thieves Guild. Overall, the city would spend more money because of the pay raise to the trolls and hiring the dwarfs, but the added expense would be small compared with the cost of hiring a contractor to rebuild the walls. While the increase in expenditures might be small, the city's defenses would be greatly strengthened.

"Could you recruit the dwarfs?"

"Nope. Gotta get Sergeant Dunlap to do dat."

Othello rubbed his chin. "Would the dwarfs obey a troll commander?"

"Dwarfs'll obey whoever pays dem."

Othello vowed to ensure that Nark got the new job as head of the dwarf contingent.

Several hours later, they were back in Dun Hythe. When they approached Othello's office, Emilia gave them an evil grin that sent a vibration of fear up Othello's spine.

"Iago mad dat ya din't tell him he's in charge while ya was gone." Her grin grew bigger. "Him get really pissed when me tell him dat ya put me in charge. Da bugger broke a lotta stuff when he hear dat."

Othello groaned, marched into his office and told Nark to shut the door. He didn't want Iago barging in right now. He had too much to do. "Your sister isn't nearly as smart as you are."

"Huh? She da smart one inna family."

Othello gave Nark a questioning look.

"Yup. She da smartest one by far." He held his hands three feet apart. "But she gotta really big mean streak."

Othello sighed. Maybe he could get Nark to figure out a way to get rid of her. He put that thought aside. "All right. Let's get busy. I'll go talk to the mayor about your idea to get the wall rebuilt. You find Captain Cassio and tell him the militia has to be called out and made ready to go after the pirates." He was sure the mayor would be pleased with his progress on the pirate issue and also with the solution to rebuilding the walls.

Othello left the office holding his breath and hoping he wouldn't run into Iago.

# # #

Hamlet strode into the port area. Despite his reservations about the pirate project, he was determined to do his best to support Othello. He felt self-conscious wearing the gold sash his mother had sewed up for him to denote his rank of fleet admiral. He knew it was his mother's idea for him to lead the fleet, and he knew she meant it to interfere with his beekeeping business. Nevertheless, he had a sense he was about to gain fame as a pirate hunter. Wouldn't it be fun to sit in the Sailor's Delight and tell of his adventure?

He passed the tavern. Annee waved to him and he waved back. "Prince Hammy," an old codger called out. "Come in and have an ale."

"Maybe later." Hamlet grinned. He may be looked down on in court, but at least in the port tavern he was a popular figure. At wharf number three, his fleet awaited his inspection. The closest ship was a small cog. The hull of the singled-masted ship once was black, but that paint had long since flaked off and could only be seen in a few patches. Hamlet examined the loose rigging, frayed in many places, and wondered if the ropes would last for one more voyage. He decided the captain must know what he was doing or the rigging would have been repaired. A few sailors in ragged clothes idled on deck and ignored his gold sash.

The second ship was a bigger cog. Every few seconds a jet of black, fetid water gushed from a pipe protruding from the hull, and Hamlet surmised a mechanical contraption must be responsible for it. It pleased him to see his ships so well equipped. A seaman leaned over a rail and watched him with a bored expression on his face. Hamlet wondered if he should muster all the crews onto the dock so he could introduce himself. He decided against it since he would only be admiral for a few days. Then he'd be back with his beloved bees.

He came to the third and largest ship in the fleet. It was an oceangoing cog, and he could smell it before he came close to it. The odor consisted of fish guts, feces, rotted material and unidentified smells. Hamlet wrinkled his nose and climbed the gangplank of his flagship. He examined the ship as he did so. The single mast had thick ropes wrapped around it in two places as if to keep it from breaking. In a number of places, the rigging had frayed apart and ropes dangled and swayed when the ship moved with the slight harbor waves.

"Who are ye?" a voice said.

Hamlet turned his head and saw an old elf. The oldster had a missing hand and eye on his right side. He had a wrinkled face, long filthy green hair and ragged, heavily patched clothes.

"I am Admiral Hamlet. I've come to inspect the fleet and ensure it is ready to sail in morning. And you are?"

"Me? Just call me Captain. We're ready. Or we will be when the impress crew rounds up a few up more lads."

"What's an impress crew?"

"Them's the ones who talk fine young lads inna takin' a sea voyage. Most of the lads will wake up before the ship leaves inna mornin'." He chuckled. "Wid a real bad headache."

"These ships seem rather old. I'm surprised King Clodio didn't insist on more modern vessels."

"Hah!" the captain cackled. "The Kingee went cheap. Ya can't get any ships cheaper than this lot. These scows are onna last legs. I'd bet one or more of 'em don't come back. They'll likely get swamped by a little bitty wave iffen the crew don't take care."

The hair on the back of Hamlet's neck rose. How were these old wrecks supposed to come to battle with pirates? "How many soldiers did the King provide?"

"He gave us a coupla archers for each ship. Most of 'em look too scrawny to shoot an arrow very far."

"We're supposed to fight a pirate fleet with a handful of archers?"

"That's not the way I heard the orders. We're supposed to chase the pirates south and let someone else fight 'em. After we chase 'em, we go back to port and get paid."

Hamlet realized that Clodio had upheld his end of the treaty in name only. He had no intention of sending a fleet to attack the pirates. He left that part to his allies. Hamlet was not going to get any fame from this voyage. He'd be lucky to return with his fleet intact even if they didn't see any pirates.

# # #

Falstaff stood on the quarterdeck of his flagship, Snatcher, as it sailed south of Dun Hythe. Poulet and Urquort leaned against a rail. The half-pint — after getting his sea legs — and the dwarf had become fast friends. Falstaff made a scan of the seas. Except for his other two ships, he looked upon an empty sea. "It seems we have driven all the shipping to other ports," he said to no one in particular. Since leaving Denmarko, the fleet had sailed south seeking prey.

"I'm guessin' most of them are headin' to Cintri." Poulet took a drag on his pipe and exhaled the smoke. The wind whipped it across the deck.

"Captain," Falstaff said. "Take us north. Mayhap, we'll find some entertainment there."

"Bugler," the elf captain called out. "Sound a starboard turn."

The half-pint bugler saluted and put a bugle to his lips. He blew three sharp blasts on it, the standard signal for a turn to the starboard. Within a minute, the other two ships repeated the signal to confirm they had received it.

At the captain's command, the helmsman spun the wheel and the ship heeled to the starboard. The sail flapped and cracked as it moved with the changing wind conditions. Sailors climbed the rigging to adjust the trim of the ship's sails.

Falstaff, with his hands behind his back, paced the deck and again considered Othello's possible motives for going to Denmarko. The only logical reason was to recruit an ally with the intention of crushing his fleet.

He always knew that piracy was a temporary career, and now the time to retire rapidly approached. Of all his career changes, this one had been the most lucrative. In his cabin, he had a small chest filled with jewelry and coins, both gold and silver pennies. He was rich for the first time. He reviewed his life and realized this was the fourth time he was rich. The three previous ones lasted a total of about twenty minutes, combined.

All his life he had searched for the main chance and now he had found it. Born to traveling merchants, he had spent his childhood in the back of a wagon. Early on, he realized that if he wanted something, he had to steal it. His father smiled on his early thefts as good training for a career in thievery. The old man emphasized if Falstaff got caught, he was on his own.

And caught he was, at age eleven. He sat in a jail and watched his parents wave cheerfully to him as they drove out of town. Given a choice of a flogging or joining the army, he enlisted. Big for his age, he trained with pike and sword, but he endeared himself to his mates with his ability to scrounge supplies. This ability came to the attention of officers, and he was transferred to a supply company. The craggy old supply sergeant took a liking to the young lad and taught him how to win at cards and dice. The sergeant also advised him not to cheat the other soldiers. He may need them someday during a battle, and he didn't want one of his mates to eliminate a debt by not coming to his aid and letting him get killed.

A few years after leaving the army, he played in a memorable card game with a bunch of drunken nobles and won his knighthood from a card player who put it into the pot. Not exactly a legal transfer, but it worked for Falstaff. Putting "Sir" in front of his name granted him instant respect, a useful device when running a scheme.

He shook his reminiscences from his mind and turned back to business. His safest course was to liquidate the operation now that an enemy fleet was likely searching for him. If Denmarko was still safe, that would be the best place to unload the business. Once he retired, he would cast about seeking investment opportunities. Perhaps it was time to develop a plan involving Hamlet.

He glanced overboard and noticed the ship's speed had decreased with the direction change. At this rate, it would take two or more days to reach port.

If Othello didn't butt in.

# # #

Poulet leaned over the side of the Snatcher and watched some large fish play in the ship's bow wave. He pondered his future. His share of the loot made him rich, and he had to do something with the money before Falstaff demanded it back to fund another scheme. He was also in love for the first time in his life. Unfortunately, Annee refused to have anything to do with a sailor. To woo Annee, he would have to leave Falstaff, and he was reluctant to do that. Life with the incorrigible man was filled with adventure and excitement, but that life prevented him from seeing Annee. Sooner or later, Falstaff would tire of being a pirate and the two of them would move of to some other part of Gundarland. That change would break his heart.

He had to decide between his current way of life with Falstaff and an unknown future trying to woo Annee.

CHAPTER TWELVE

Hamlet paced the ramparts late at night. The fleet would sail before dawn to catch the tide, and he couldn't sleep because of his excitement. He had only a small chance of gaining glory in the next few days with a decrepit fleet armed with a handful of archers. Clodio had betrayed his allies with his despicable actions. Hamlet's father would have sent better ships with more warriors. His father would have honored the treaty, not found a way to circumvent it. Clodio didn't deserve to be king.

"Your old man's disappointed in you." The voice came from the shadows near a doorway.

"Have you returned to nag me some more? I have responsibilities, you know. I'll take care of Clodio when I can fit him into my schedule." Hamlet paused and stared at the shadows. "Why are you here? Where is my father?"

"He's leadin' a demonstration of dead kings. They're marchin' onna temple of the Supreme Bein'. They want the Big Guy to share power with them."

"He's always too busy to talk to his only son?"

"Hey! He cares, but he's got duties. Anyway he sent me to tell you that Clodio has set a trap for you. If you don't whack the guy tonight, he's gonna arrange for you to have an accident onna voyage."

Hamlet couldn't believe his ears. Clodio planned to kill him? He wondered if his mother was part of the scheme. So many questions, so few answers.

"Iffen I was you and I didn't whack the king tonight, I wouldn't show up at the ships."

"That would be a coward's way out. Not only will I sail in a few hours, I will force the fleet to engage with the pirates. I will return victorious, or I shall die in battle."

"Dyin' is what you're gonna get. Your father's gonna be very disappointed to see you onna other side instead of Clodio."

"Begone, ghost. I must concentrate and prepare myself for battle."

# # #

Othello approached the clutch of five ship captains gathered in front of the Grubby Shoat. It lacked a few minutes to dawn and the horizon glowed reddish-gold.

His stomach muscles clenched into a ball and his mouth was dry. He had to command a fleet on a voyage that could end in a sea battle and he'd be expected to give orders and control the battle, yet he didn't know anything about organizing and directing a fleet. If it was a land battle, he had a chance to make correct orders, but not when at sea.

Nark shambled along behind him.

A group of Grubby Shoat patrons, leather ale mugs in hand despite the early hour, watched the proceedings and voiced opinions.

He nodded to the captains whom he had met at a second conference with the mayor yesterday. He turned to the militia grouped in companies a short distance away. They tried to look bored, but failed; their constant fidgeting gave them away. Captain Cassio and Sergeant Dunlap stood in front of the volunteers.

"We're all here," Othello said in a strained voice. "So let's get started. Where are the ships?"

"Over yonder," a captain replied. "What's with the half-pints? Are they slingers?"

"Yes, they're slingers. They're part of the militia."

"Can't use slingers onna ship," another said.

Othello noticed the half-pint contingent suddenly turned attentive. They exchanged glances and tilted their heads to hear better.

"Why not?" The captains' concern puzzled Othello.

"No room to use the sling. When they whirl it over their heads, it'll catch inna riggin' or brain my sailors. They gotta use swords or axes."

"But they're only trained to use slings." The unexpected objection annoyed him.

"Then we can't use 'em," a third captain said.

The ten slingers let out choruses of, "Aww" and "Darn" while their shoulders slouched in disappointment.

"Stop it, the lot of you," Othello growled. "I can't abide bad acting."

The slingers changed to cheers, hugs and handshakes. They crowded into the Grubby Shoat to celebrate their release from pirate hunting.

Captain Cassio looked expectantly at Othello.

Othello rubbed his hand over his chin. "Cassio, I want you to stay behind with the slingers. If an attack occurs, lead them and defend the city."

"Who's in charge of the defense? Me or Iago?"

Othello had no intention of getting involved in that decision. "You and Iago can settle that question if necessary."

"We must leave quickly," a captain said. "The tide is running in our favor."

"Sergeant Dunlap. Split the companies into five groups and assign each group to a ship. You will lead one of them and join me. Appoint temporary commanders for the other four."

"We'll use the standard bugle signals. Agreed?" one captain said. The other four agreed.

"What are these signals?" It never occurred to Othello that the ships would have a signal system. "I must know what they are."

"It's a simple system. One bugle blast is for locating ships at night or in poor visibility. Two blasts mean danger. Three means turn to starboard. Four means turn to port."

"Thank you." Othello had no idea what port and starboard meant, but he didn't think it smart to disclose that information. He was sure he'd learn soon enough by listening to the crew.

When Dunlap finished dividing up the warriors, each captain moved toward the wharfs where the ships were berthed. A contingent of eight or nine militia followed. Each contingent had a few elven longbows, dwarf ax warriors and pikemen.

Othello boarded a sturdy oceangoing cog. When the last militia came on board, the captain cast off the lines and got underway.

In the middle of the lake-like harbor, Othello got violently seasick.

# # #

Rosey and Guildy awaited Hamlet when he boarded his flagship in the morning. "Clodio ordered us to accompany you and protect you during the battle," Rosey said. Guildy smirked and added, "The king doesn't want anything to happen to you."

Hamlet scowled at the pair. They must be here to report back to Clodio about his command ability. Of perhaps his death. He would have to keep an eye on them. He tugged on the blue tunic his mother had found in an old castle wardrobe; it didn't fit very well. The tunic came with a gold braid, silver buttons and a few moth holes. She also made him wear a silly looking tricorne hat and a pair of breeches that hadn't been white for many years. A dagger in a scabbard hung from his hip. He straightened the gold admiral's sash to keep it from falling off his shoulder.

"Cast off the lines," the captain yelled. "Our fearless admiral has arrived." A few seconds later, he ordered, "Bosun, get the sail aloft."

The ship lurched forward as the wind caught the sail. Hamlet took a deep breath of sea air heavily tainted with dead fish and floating rubbish. His command was underway.

An hour later, they cleared the harbor and steered south. In the light of a brilliant dawn, Hamlet stood on the quarterdeck and watched the rest of his fleet sail in the wake of his flagship. Every few seconds, a gush of water came from one side of the second ship. The third cog seemed to have trouble with the almost nonexistent waves. It wallowed and the mast top swayed in alarming fashion. Hamlet wondered if anyone on it knew how to sail. He looked up at the sail on his ship. Most of the wind seemed to slip off the sides. "Captain, can you fix the sail so we can go faster? We have an appointment with destiny and I don't want to be late."

"We're goin' fast enough."

"As admiral of the fleet," Hamlet fingered his gold sash, "I order you to increase our speed."

"As captain of the ship," he paused to spit over the said, "I order you to bugger off. I ain't goin' faster 'cause the mast's old and rotten. It won't stand the pressure of a tighter sail."

Hamlet rocked under the direct disobedience of the old elf. He wondered if the elf lied or told the truth. At this pace, it would take them days to get close to Dun Hythe.

He looked forward and saw Rosey and Guildy sitting at the base of the mast. They grinned at him, and Hamlet felt a wave of fear climb his spine.

CHAPTER THIRTEEN

On the third day at sea, Hamlet stood on the quarterdeck and stared ahead past Rosey and Guildy, while wisps of fog drifted past his head. No matter how hard he tried, he couldn't ignore those two lounging near the mast. He inhaled deeply. He loved the fresh smell of sea air, so different from the harbor air with its stench of fish offal and floating garbage. The ship drifted on the tide and breeze after the captain had lowered the sail because of the dense bank of fog a quarter mile ahead. "We go in there," he had said, "we'll get lost. Can't tell what direction we're goin' in and can't see the other ships. We'll collide with 'em or strike a reef."

Frustrated, Hamlet cursed at Clodio who had given him the mission and then hired a fleet of ships that barely floated. His flagship didn't even have a simple compass. They had been at sea a long enough time to have reach Dun Hythe, but they were only at the halfway point of the voyage. So far, he had seen no evidence of betrayal. Disrespect, yes; treachery, no.

A bugle sounded from somewhere in the fog.

"Another ship!" Hamlet cried. "It has to be Colonel Othello. We must hasten to join him and find the pirates." The prospect of a battle looming in the fog gave him a chill of fear. Did the fog contain glory or death? Despite the cool air, his forehead beaded with perspiration.

"What are you babblin' about?" the captain asked.

"Didn't you hear a bugle?"

"I heard a seagull."

"There!" Hamlet cupped an ear toward the fog bank. "Listen to all the bugles." He frowned at the steady blast of bugles. There must be a dozen or more ships concealed in the fog. He hadn't anticipated so many ships coming together.

"Seagulls. I ain't takin' my ship inna the fog to chase birds."

# # #

Faced with the prospect of dissolving his fleet and retiring from piracy, Falstaff decided on one more patrol outside Dun Hythe's port. This morning he had awoken to find his ship in dense fog. He knew the sun shone somewhere, but on the quarterdeck it was twilight. He could see the foremast from his post on the quarterdeck, but nothing beyond that. The fog hid the bow of the ship.

They sailed south on a gentle breeze from the northwest. When they had left Dun Hythe harbor the first time, Falstaff had been amazed to learn that the wind didn't have to blow from the rear of the ship to make it move. Unless the wind came in off the bow, the captain simply slanted the tiller and adjusted the sails to catch the wind.

The captain paced with a worried look on his face. "I'm going to signal the other two ships to see where they are. I don't want us running into each other."

"All right," Falstaff said. "That's a good idea. We should know their location in case we find prey."

The half-pint bugler gave a single blast on his horn.

Seconds later, they heard a second bugle. Followed by a third, fourth and fifth blast.

"There's more ships out there!" Falstaff gasped.

A few more bugle signals came out of the fog.

"Does fog cause echoes?" Falstaff asked the captain who shrugged. The fog obscured the direction of the sounds so Falstaff couldn't tell if he was surrounded by ships or if they were all off to one side.

"Sound the danger signal," the captain ordered.

The bugler sounded two more notes.

A symphony of double horn blasts responded.

Falstaff felt the blood drain from his face. Some of the signals overlapped so he couldn't get a count on how many responded to the danger signal. He grasped the hilt of his sword. It had to be Othello. The dark elf must have gathered an entire fleet to come after him. "Urquort! Bring the troops to battle stations."

The dwarf knuckled his forehead and ran off the quarterdeck.

"I told you should have made for the harbor." Poulet glared at Falstaff.

Falstaff made a face and flapped a hand at his batman. "Forget about Annee for a while and help clear the ship for action."

# # #

Othello stood on the quarterdeck clutching a cloak closed with his hands. With the slight swells today, he had managed to keep from getting seasick, although he knew if the ship suddenly pitched or rolled, that could change. Never had he experienced a fog as thick as this one. The sailors around the mast looked like ghosts. As they went about their morning chores, tendrils of fog seem to cling to their bodies. He wondered where the other ships were. He hoped they weren't too close. With the poor visibility, a collision could easily happen.

With no visual reference points, he had no idea how far offshore they were. The captain, using a round device he kept in his pocket, insisted they still sailed north, but Othello didn't like the idea of trusting a device he had never heard of before.

The breeze off the port side freshened slightly and shredded the fog surrounding the ship. It was so gentle it hardly moved the ship.

A bugle blast startled him. He recalled a single note was used to locate other ships, so he must not be the only one concerned about a collision. The captain nodded to the bugler and the lad sounded a note in return. So did six other ships. Seconds later, a few more location notes were heard. "Nine or ten ships?" Othello gasped. "Whose are they?"

The captain looked puzzled. "Mayhap, a few ships gave the signal twice."

"I wish I knew where they all are."

"I wish I knew what their headings are." The captain turned to the bugler. "Sound the danger signal."

Before the bugler could follow the order, a double bugle blast came from somewhere else followed by a cacophony of sound. Othello's bugler joined the symphony. They heard still more danger signals.

The captain looked shocked. "I counted eighteen signals, at least."

"Maybe da fog makes echoes?" Nark asked.

"I never heard of it doing that." The captain peered into the fog. "Perhaps some ships sounded the signal twice because they thought another ship was too close to them." He looked at Othello. "But maybe there are a lot more ships than we expected."

Othello's stomach lurched, and it wasn't because of the ship's movement.

# # #

Emilia and three members of her knitting circle sat in her hovel. The knitted, sipped ale, swapped gossip and insults. Each tried to knit the most hideous towel possible. One depicted piles of horse dung, a second a flyblown dead dog. The third member refused to tell what hers was, but Emilia thought it looked like vomit. Her own towel showed the face of a yuk, the only race considered uglier than the trolls.

Oddly enough, the towels sold for many coins and were bought by rich folks who framed the towels and hung them on walls as artwork.

Iago burst through the door and glared at the females. He swayed and had trouble standing upright, so Emilia knew he was drunk, even if it was the middle of the day.

The other three knitters packed up and fled the hut.

Iago tried to focus his eyes on her. "Got da plan done," he managed to say. "Pretty soon, no more Othella."

"What are you talkin' about?" Emilia realized that she could pry the secrets out of Iago while he was drunk because he liked to brag. "What's dis plan yer so proud of? Tell me."

Iago put a finger across his lips. "Can't. Secret."

"What nonsense," Emilia tutted. "I'm yer wife. I oughta know. Maybe I can help."

Iago leaned back against the wall and closed his eyes. Emilia thought he had fallen sleep, but then he said, "Othella gonna be dead soon. Him gonna have big accident." He giggled and snorted.

"How ya gonna get away wid dat?" Emilia tried to hide her alarm. This was serious and must involve the thugs she saw him talking to. "Everyone know ya hate Othello. Dey gonna know ya did somethin' right away."

"Naw. Gonna make it so's the Godmother gets da blame. Everybody know he's married to someone inna family." He snorted again. "Good plan, ain't it?" He pushed away from the door, stumbled into the bedroom, fell across the bed and began snoring.

Emilia hugged herself in trepidation. Iago's plan was fraught with danger for him, her and Nark. If it succeeded, the Godmother would surely find out who blamed her. She had eyes and ears everywhere. Her vengeance would extend to Iago's wife and everyone related to him and that would include Nark. How was she supposed to protect herself and her brother?

# # #

Falstaff clenched and unclenched his fists as he pondered the situation. Somewhere in the fog was an unhealthy number of ships. Obviously, Othello had amassed a huge fleet. Denmarko might have contributed ships also. The most likely scenario he could come up with was that he had sailed into a trap. The fog saved his ships from getting annihilated for the moment by concealing his movements. Once the fog lifted, each of his three ships would be surrounded and overwhelmed. His warriors, lining the rails on both sides, would be massacred.

"Time to leave." He grabbed the captain's forearm. "Head north."

The captain ordered sailors into the rigging to adjust the sails. "Sound a turn to the port." He pointed to the bugler.

A few seconds after the bugler sounded the signal, sounds from other horns filled the air.

Falstaff held his hands over his ears as multitudinous bugles repeated the message. The Dun Hythe fleet chased his ships!

# # #

Othello pondered the situation. Obviously that rogue Falstaff had organized a trap. Dun Hythe's small fleet was outnumbered, and he had no idea where Hamlet was or even if he had sailed. Once again, he faced failure, but this time the penalty wasn't just disgrace; it could also include his death. If the ship was sunk, he could never swim far enough to reach shore. But before that happened, he would face death through combat with Falstaff's pirates, experienced warriors all. Falstaff's many ships would surround each of his ships and cut down the militia and crews. Still, he had to make an effort and hope for survival.

"Nark," he said. "See to the militia. Place the archers in the bow. Put the rest by the mast and have them prepared to defend either side of the ship."

The troll nodded approval with Othello's plan. "Dis gonna be fun." Nark had helped himself to a sword and a short pike from the ship's armory. He sauntered forward and disappeared below decks to fetch the militia.

To Othello's surprise, someone sounded a turn to port. The signal repeated for what seemed an eternity. The captain ordered the crew into the rigging and told the bugler to give the port turn signal.

"Why are we turning?" Othello asked. "It could be a trap set up by the pirates."

"It doesn't matter if it's a trap or not," the captain replied with a tinge of panic in his voice. "With all the other ships turning to port, we'll be sailing across their bows iffen we don't turn. It's only a matter of time until one of them comes out the fog and smashes into us. We have to turn with the others to protect ourselves."

Othello had a passing thought. He should have stayed on land and sent Iago out with the fleet.

# # #

Falstaff grabbed the quarterdeck's railing as the ship heeled over in the turn. Now heading due east, the sails picked up more of the breeze and the Snatcher increased its speed. While the bugle calls had ceased, voices came from the fog. At least one ship was close. Too damned close. He braced himself for a collision.

An apparition materialized from the fog on the port side. A large cog sailed less than ten feet from Snatcher, and it wasn't one of his ships. Falstaff saw archers in the bow and a group of warriors lining the starboard rail amidship. A harsh voice yelled "Fire" and three arrows flew into the Snatcher. Uquort, from somewhere near the bow, ordered the longbows to shoot back. Falstaff looked at the enemy quarterdeck and was amazed to see the fog-shrouded figure of Othello holding onto a backstay.

Othello saw him. A furious look appeared on his face and he shook a fist. More arrows flew in both directions.

The bugler, standing behind Falstaff, sounded another port turn. Falstaff jumped from the blasts so close to his ears, rounded on the half-pint and thumped him on the head.

A raucous chorus of bugles followed, and relief flooded over Falstaff when he saw the bow of Othello's ship turn away. After a few more arrows thudded into the deck and a mast, Snatcher was alone in a small universe of fog.

Falstaff shrugged. His pirate career had ended in an inglorious and profitless voyage. So be it. What should he do next? He needed an investment opportunity to grow his accumulated funds.

# # #

Othello grabbed a backstay while the ship executed a port turn and the bosun shouted commands to the sailors in the rigging. He wondered if the captain could hear his thudding heartbeat. At any moment, he expected a ship to charge out of the fog and crash into his ship. His adrenaline-fueled brain conjured up details of the ensuing carnage.

To his amazement, his expectations came to pass. A ship with two masts now sailed off the starboard side, and it wasn't one of his fleet. It couldn't be more than ten feet away. He exhaled in relief when he noticed the two ships sailed parallel to each other and weren't getting closer.

Nark yelled "Fire" from somewhere in the bow and a volley of arrows flew from his ship. Another voice sounded a command and arrows flew back from the enemy ship.

Shocked, Othello saw Falstaff standing on the quarterdeck of the other ship. He shook his fist at the scoundrel.

A port turn signal came from the other ship and Falstaff thumped the bugler on the top of his head. The signal was picked up by his bugler and the rest of the invisible ships.

More arrows flew back and forth as the ships turned away and became hidden in the obscurity of the fog.

His death grip on the backstay relaxed. His fleet headed back to Dun Hythe. Perhaps he had put a scare into Falstaff and he'd go bother some other port.

#

Desdemona sat at an outdoor table in a tea shop. Awnings protected the table from the hot sun. She needed information and hoped it wouldn't be all bad. When she saw Rosolia, the madam from the Wicked Bed, approach, she order tea and fruit slices. The old female elf greeted Desdemona with a hug and a kiss on the cheek.

"You look well," Desdemona said. "How are you keeping?"

"Old age isn't all it's cracked up to be. It's hard getting out of bed in the mornings because of the ache in my joints." Rosolia sighed. "And I tire so easily these days."

The tea and fruit arrived. After the waiter left, Desdemona filled the cups, then ate a slice of apple. Rosolia was one of Grandma's oldest friends and confidants. They had gone to school together, and Grandma ensured that her friend got an important job in the family. Rosolia was like a beloved aunt to Desdemona.

Rosolia sipped tea and watched her over the rim of the cup.

Desdemona interpreted the look as a premonition. "So, how does my Grandma fare?"

Rosolia made a face and shook her head.

"I know her health is failing, but what about the business? Is it thriving? Can she still handle it?"

Rosolia held out a hand and waggled it. "Sometimes she can't be bothered with the details."

"I don't understand." Desdemona pursed her lips.

"You remember how all the politicians and important merchants come every month to see the Godmother, make their donation and suck up to her?"

Desdemona nodded and ate more fruit.

"Well, more and more, she won't see them. She sends one of her attendants to collect the money and get any messages from the visitors. It's like she doesn't always care anymore."

Desdemona didn't like the sound of that last statement. Grandma was always a hands-on business elf. She never, ever delegated the important task of maintaining her influence among the city's elite and powerful. Until now.

"I'm afraid," Rosolia continued, "that she's suffering a lot more than she lets on. I think the reason she doesn't bother is because she's in too much pain." She gave Desdemona a look filled with anxiety. "I think her business decisions are being influenced by her pain rather than her mind."

"Don't worry." Desdemona reached out and patted her hand. "You'll be safe no matter what happens. You have my word on it."

"Thank you." Rosolia patted her lips with a napkin. "I better get back. Customers will start to arrive in little while."

# # #

A frustrated Hamlet ran to the bow to peer into the fog. A symphony of bugle calls reverberated in the mist. Some sounded close, others further away. With all the horns blowing it was sometimes difficult to tell what signal they gave. His ship still drifted with a lowered sail. At this rate, the battle would be over before Hamlet could reach it.

Hamlet determined to follow his orders from King Clodio. He ran back to the quarterdeck. "Captain, as Admiral of this fleet, I order you to hoist sail and join the battle."

Instead of replying, the captain signaled for Rosey and Guildy to join him on the quarterdeck. When they reached him, he said, "Our young Admiral claims he hears bugles inna fog. I say they're seagulls. What did you hear?"

"Gulls," Rosey replied.

"Birds, most definitely," Guildy added.

"Do either of ya see or hear any pirate activity inna area?" The captain grinned at the two knights.

"Nothing." Guildy shook his head.

"Nay." Rosey grinned back at the captain.

"Then we must have chased them south for the Dun Hythe fleet to take care of. Our mission is done. Bosun, hoist the sail." To the sailor standing at the tiller, "Head back to port."

"You can't do this!" An enraged Hamlet yelled and shook his fist at the old elf captain.

The captain ignored Hamlet's outburst and said to Rosey, "I think it's time you and your mate finish the business, don't you?"

"Aye, 'tis time, Captain. Come, Guildy." Rosey grabbed one of Hamlet's elbows while Guildy seized the other. "Can you swim, Prince Hammy?" Rosey's voice dripped with sarcasm.

"Unhand me!" Hamlet said.

Together, the two hustled Hamlet to the rail at the stern of the quarterdeck and threw him overboard.

When Hamlet's head broke the surface, he gasped for air and saw the three decrepit ships turn toward Denmarko. So, the ghost was right. He would meet his father again long before Clodio would. As for his bees, they would have to do without his supervision.

# # #

Falstaff's tension evaporated when his ship finally sailed out of the fog. Now he could determine if any of Othello's ships followed him, and he'd be able to make decisions instead of guesses. His other two ships sailed out of the mist like ghosts materializing from the underworld.

Now that his piracy career was almost over, sadness overcame him. It was most lucrative of all his shady enterprises and by far the most fun. While he was rich, now he didn't have any project to look forward to. Nothing to plan. Nothing to occupy his thoughts and his energies.

"Ahoy, the deck." The sailor atop the mainmast pointed toward Denmarko. "Three ships!"

Falstaff came alert. Should he commit one more act of piracy? Were the ships too close to Denmarko? He needed the port to safely disband the operation and sell off the ships.

"Ahoy, the deck!" Now the sailor pointed off the bow on the port side. "Someone's inna water!"

Falstaff frowned. What was a swimmer doing this far from shore? "Captain? Let's explore this mystery."

"Aye, sir. Three points to the port," he said to the sailor at the helm.

Five minutes later, Falstaff, holding a backstay and leaning over the rail, exclaimed, "'Tis Prince Hamlet, if you can credit it. I can't." He turned to the captain. "Fetch the Prince onboard." All ten of his fingers twitched

"Hah!" Poulet said. "You always told me good deeds were for the feeble-minded."

"This isn't a good deed." Falstaff grinned and rubbed top of the half-pint's head. "'Tis a golden opportunity." Once again, Fate smiled on him. "Both my palms are itchy.

PART THREE

CHAPTER FOURTEEN

Hamlet's hopes leaped upward when three ships sailed out of the fog. Exhausted from trying to stay afloat despite shedding his jacket, dagger and boots, he hoped the ships saw him splashing. Of his fleet, only the tips of the masts remained in sight. He still couldn't believe that two of Clodio's knights had thrown him overboard. The ghost had been correct. He had expected to fight a few pirates with his dagger and gain either a victory or a glorious death. Getting thrown overboard smacked of disrespect for his noble birth. Drowning was such a common death.

One ship veered toward him and he tried to yell encouragement, but swallowed a mouthful of water instead. After the ship loosened its sails and slowed down, a sailor threw him a line. He caught it and the sailor pulled him to the ship. He grabbed onto a rope ladder, but couldn't do more than hold on. Two sailors climbed down and clutched his arms. They pulled him out of the water, and he managed to get his feet on the bottom rung. They guided him to the deck where a large, fat man awaited him.

"Well met, Prince Hamlet. 'Tis I, Falstaff, at your service."

Hamlet gawked at the man who had introduced himself in the Sailor's Delight — the man Othello condemned as a pirate. Pirate or not, he owed Falstaff his life. He reached out and grasped Falstaff's hand. "Thank you. Thank you."

"'Tis nothing but my duty, my friend." He gestured to Hamlet's soggy clothes. "Remove them and we'll attach them to the rigging to dry out. I'll find a blanket to cover you with." He snapped a finger at Poulet who scampered off. "In the meantime, tell me happened. Why did you take a swim?"

While Hamlet stripped, he said, "I was thrown off my flagship, that's what happened."

"Where was the fleet going?"

"To drive you south. The king agreed to support Dun Hythe and ordered me to sea."

"Those three ships yonder." Falstaff pointed off the port bow. "Is that your fleet?"

Hamlet looked over the side. The entire masts could be seen from the deck. "Yes, that's them."

Poulet returned with a dirty wool blanket and draped it around Hamlet's shoulders.

"Anything worth looting on them?" Falstaff asked.

"Nothing. They're floating hulks crewed by miscreants."

"Urquort! Archers to the bow. With fire arrows. Set those three ships on fire." To Hamlet he said, "The crews will jump into the ships' boats and row ashore. My advice is that we don't let them see that you survived. I think we want them to assume you drowned."

Hamlet goggled at the man's self-confidence and air of command. "Are you really a pirate like Othello said? You told me in the tavern you were a pirate chaser."

To his surprise, Falstaff didn't answer, but paced the deck with his hands behind his back. After a short interval, he turned to face Hamlet. "I hunt pirates, like I said. Dun Hythe is a den of thieves. I suspect the pirates have the backing of powerful forces in the city. Forces who share in the loot the pirates capture. Further, I suspect these forces brought pressure on the city officials and Othello to put an end to my mission." He paced some more. "You and I must seek justice. We have both been wronged. An attempt has been made on your life, and an attempt has been made on my reputation. I propose, my Prince, that we make common cause to pursue justice."

Conflicting stories from Falstaff and Othello befuddled Hamlet, and contradictory questions swirled in his mind. It didn't seem likely that Othello journeyed from Dun Hythe to spread lies about Falstaff. So, did Othello or Falstaff tell the truth? Did it matter? Falstaff had rescued him from the sea. Perhaps that was all that mattered.

Falstaff held out his hand. "Shall we join forces?"

"We shall." Hamlet grasped the hand a second time and shook it. "We shall." He wondered what joining forces entailed.

# # #

"Take the Prince to my cabin," Falstaff told Poulet. To Hamlet, he said, "I'll join you after I dispatch these three ships." He pointed to the hulks making for Denmarko harbor. After Hamlet descended the steps from the quarterdeck, Falstaff grinned and danced a few steps of a jig. He couldn't believe the opportunity that confronted him . . . if he had the nerve to pursue it. He reviewed his conversation with Hamlet. Claiming he was betrayed by Othello and Dun Hythe was inspired. So was demanding justice and linking Hamlet's need for justice with his own. To make use of the opportunity, he had to make Hamlet the king. He sensed that Hamlet was scatteredbrained and indecisive. Once he became king, or kingee as the peasants would call him, Hamlet would need a strong mind standing behind the throne and whispering in his ear. Who better to fill that role than Sir John Falstaff?

He watched the archers set flaming arrows in their bows and launch them at the closest ship. One stuck in the sail and set it aflame. Three others struck the deck and mast. The crew hastened to pull them out and toss them overboard. While they went about that task, more fire arrows flew in. The sail, now a mass of flame, burned through its fastenings and fell to the deck. The crew stopped fighting the fires, launched the ship's boat and abandoned the blazing hulk. Falstaff turned his eyes to the other two ships. They soon burned merrily and the crews were in the process of panicky abandonment.

He took a deep breath, held it a few seconds, then exhaled noisily. "Right," he said aloud. "Time to achieve my destiny." He smirked. "And my justice."

#

Emilia, deep in thought, walked along the streets at midday.

Since Iago had disclosed his plans last night, she had pondered his stupidity and knew she had to do something about it, anything to protect herself and Nark from the Godmother's vengeance. All night she had searched for an idea, but came up blank. By herself, she couldn't think of anything to keep events from marching to their disastrous conclusions. Iago would kill Othello and blame the Godmother, who would then slaughter Iago, her, Nark and others. While Othello was away fooling around on some ships, she had decided to see his wife, Desdemona, and ask for help, or at least some advice. After all, she was rumored to be related to the Godmother. Perhaps she could help. Emilia had sent a messenger to Desdemona's house and received an invitation to lunch, much to her surprise; not many people allowed trolls into their homes.

She approached the house and stopped to calm her fluttering nerves. Would Desdemona help? Or would she throw Emilia out and call down the wrath of the Godmother on her even before Iago did anything? Even if it meant possible destruction, she had to try to protect her brother. After taking one more deep breath, she rapped on the door. Desdemona answered it. With a smile, she said, "You must be Emilia. I've often wondered when I would meet you because Othello frequently mentions you."

The warm greeting took Emilia by surprise; she had expected grudging admittance. Desdemona beckoned her in, and Emilia entered a large room with a fireplace, a table and chairs. Two places had been set. Also on the table was a loaf of bread and a bowl of food.

"I made shrimp salad for lunch," Desdemona said. "I hope you like it. Please sit down. We can chat to get acquainted while we eat and, afterward, you can tell me what your problem is."

While Emilia sat down, a bit dazzled by Desdemona's openness, Desdemona sliced off chunks of bread and placed two on Emilia's plate. Next she passed the salad bowl and said, "Help yourself." Emilia thought back to other homes she had been invited to — a rare event — and wondered if Desdemona had spent the morning counting the cutlery.

After eating, Desdemona removed the dishes and made tea. She sat down, picked up her cup and said, "Now, tell me what you wanted to talk about."

"It's me husband, Iago. He's up to no good."

Desdemona nodded. "Othello tells me Iago is tough to work with."

"Iago wanted da job Othella got. He's been inna bad mood ever since. But now he's gotta dumb plan dat's gonna cause a lotta trouble."

"What plan? Do you know what it is?"

"Yeah. He got drunk last night and I got it outta him. He's gotta bunch of thugs lined up and dey gonna kill Othella and make it look like da Godmother did it. Den Iago figures he gets Othella's job. I ain't gonna be his secretary, I tell ya dat right now."

"Why does he think the Godmother will get the blame?"

"Cause yer related to the Godmother and he's gonna spread rumors dat the Godmother don't like Othella."

"Oh, dear." Desdemona frowned and tapped her fingernails on the table. "This is troubling. I didn't know trolls could be so devious."

"Can ya help me? I don't want da Godmother thinkin' I gotta part inna plan. I don't want her thinkin' Nark's part of da plan."

"I can see why you're concerned. The Godmother does not like to be involved in other's schemes. I thank you for sharing this with me." She continued tapping her fingernails. Finally, she said, "I'll have someone give Iago a warning. One that tells him he better drop the plan. Will that help?" She stood and walked toward the door.

Emilia followed and said, "Yeah, as long as it gets Iago to stop da stupid plan."

"Thank you for coming." Desdemona opened the door. "I hope we meet again."

Emilia went outside but before Desdemona could close the door, she said, "Hey! Will dis warnin' make me a widow?"

"Of course not. I'm not going to have Iago killed."

"Dang." Emilia left to go back to her work.

After she closed the door, Desdemona smiled. She wrote a note to Rosolia and paid a young lad to deliver it.

She was sure the old madam could find someone to give Iago a warning in return for a free night in the Wicked Bed.

# # #

Othello exhaled aloud when his ship slid out of the fog, ending any possible danger of a collision or a surprise attack. The brilliant sunlight made his eyes tear. He squinted through wet eyes and scanned the sea looking for pirate ships. All he saw were two of his ships. In a few minutes, the other two emerged from the fog. He continued to look, half expecting Falstaff's fleet to sail out of the fog bank. When the pirates didn't show up after ten minutes, he relaxed. "Is there a signal to return to the harbor?" he asked the captain.

"No," he replied. "If any of them get within hailing range, I can give the order. Otherwise, the ships'll follow us."

Othello stared at the distant shore, now just a smudge, and wondered how the mayor would react when told about the voyage. He could honestly say he drove the pirates north. Would anyone believe his story that he had traded arrows with Falstaff's ship? Even though he had the arrows kept as proof and for souvenirs. For the first time in his life, he hadn't failed to complete a mission. He had actually accomplished something this time. While his success was modest, he vowed to build on it and achieve more so that, in time, his wife would have much to brag about.

# # #

Hamlet, still clutching the blanket around his shoulders, watched Falstaff enter the main cabin. The only light came from a small window. His huge frame filled the small doorway. He was glad the man was his friend and not his enemy. "I must thank you again for saving my life. I can't believe my luck. That you would show up just when I was about to abandon hope."

"I warrant it wasn't luck at all," Falstaff replied. "I'm convinced it was fate. Right now, your would-be assassins have abandoned their ships and row for port in small rowboats. We'll dock long before they reach land." Falstaff dropped into a chair, making it groan and squeak. "My Prince. We must discuss your situation."

"I will listen to any advice you may have for me. I'm without friends except for you."

"The king attempted to murder you. You have two choices and you must make a decision. Do you forego vengeance and leave for exile to live a life of fear, never knowing when the king's agents will strike again? Or," Falstaff jumped out of the chair, "do you take matters into your own hands and strike back?"

Hamlet chewed on a lip. He hadn't thought of his situation as stark as Falstaff put it. Clodio had attempted to murder him, but he didn't want to kill Clodio. Assassinating the king meant he would have to replace Clodio and he'd never have time to tend to his hives after that.

Falstaff interrupted Hamlet's musings by pointing a fat finger at him. "Know that I will be with you every step of the way if you choose to fight back. And remember, I command troops who will protect us. I'll have them off the ships in a trice."

"Wh . . . when would we strike back?"

"Tonight. We must do the deed before the word spreads that you are still alive. And word will spread. It will only take one sailor from my fleet to have a few drinks and try to impress a serving wench with the tale of your rescue. Therefore, we must strike tonight. If we do not, then by default, you choose exile and must leave."

"Tonight? I have barely recovered from my swim. Look." Hamlet shook his blanket. "My clothes aren't yet dry."

"My Prince, let me make it plain. You must overthrow Clodio this night or we must go our separate ways, each to seek justice without the aid of the other."

"You'll abandon me?"

"Nay. But if we fail to obtain justice for you tonight, then we waste the opportunity fate handed us."

Hamlet went to the small round window in the stern and looked at the sea. One hulk still burned, but the other two had disappeared beneath the sea. The water looked so peaceful in contrast to his churning mind. Of course, if he took the crown, the ghost would stop nagging him.

He turned back to Falstaff. "All right. We'll do it tonight. How?"

"You must know an unguarded entrance to the castle, do you not?"

Hamlet scratched his jaw. "Yes. There is one I know of. I used it when I was a child to sneak away from my nanny."

"Then, in the middle of the night, you, I, Poulet and Urquort will enter the castle and make you the new king."

CHAPTER FIFTEEN

Hamlet led Falstaff, Urquort and Poulet into the castle and up the stairs to the king's chambers. Widely separated sconces with torches provided a modicum of light. All the warriors had been disembarked from the ships and waited outside the secret castle entrance in case a hasty retreat became necessary. Hamlet carried a naked short sword taken from the ship's armory. His hands trembled making the point of his sword inscribe figure eights in the air. No matter how deeply he inhaled, he couldn't get enough air. At last, he stood outside the door. Urquort had disabled a pair of guards along the way, including one who had been sleeping at the head of the corridor. Poulet tied them up, gagged them and left them behind. Hamlet hesitated. Falstaff gripped his shoulder and squeezed. "Do it, laddie," he whispered. "You must have justice."

Hamlet pushed the door open and advanced into the room. In the light of a single candle, he saw Clodio lying in a tangle of blankets on a vast bed. A door led to his mother's chambers. A young page slept on the floor at the foot of the bed. Poulet went to him, placed a hand over his mouth and woke him up. He signed for the youth to remain silent.

Hamlet stood rooted to a spot near the bed. The old king looked pathetically feeble. The sword point continued to waver.

"Clodio!" Falstaff hissed.

Hamlet jumped at the sound of the voice.

"Awake to see your doom." Falstaff pulled down the blankets.

Clodio's eyes popped open in alarm. "Hamlet? Why are you here? Who are these ruffians? Why are they in my bedroom?"

Hamlet's brain finally started working. "I'm here to avenge my attempted murder. These 'ruffians' rescued me from the sea this morning."

Clodio grabbed the blankets and drew them up to his chin. "It was your mother's idea. She feared you were organizing a revolt." He gasped aloud as if in great pain.

"The woman has no idea who or what I am." Hamlet shook his head. "No idea at all."

"To business," Falstaff said in a gruff voice. "Stick to business. We're all in danger here."

Hamlet advanced closer to the bed. His sword point stuck into a clump of blanket.

Clodio groaned and lost his grip on the blanket. His eyes rolled back in his head and he slumped over.

Open-mouthed, Hamlet glanced at Falstaff who looked puzzled.

Clodio's face turned blue.

"Heart attack?" Falstaff said. He went to the bed and felt Clodio's neck for a pulse. "Nothing, he's dead." He turned to Hamlet. "The king is dead. Long live the king." He knelt in front of Hamlet. "My Lord. I swear allegiance to you." Poulet and Urquort knelt and likewise swore.

"What is the meaning of this?" A strident voice interrupted the ceremony.

Hamlet regarded his mother in her nightclothes and cap. "You are now the queen mother."

He could almost see his mother's mind working at feverish speed to assess the situation. Finally, she smiled at him. "Clodio was a weak king. He wouldn't follow my advice. You'll be a much better king than he was. I'll be at your side constantly to help you rule."

Hamlet hesitated. He hadn't considered that being king meant listening to his mother.

"We can do this," Gertie said soothingly. "You and I can rule Denmarko much better than Clodio did. You at least will listen to me, won't you, my darling?"

"I don't think you wanna have her around," Poulet whispered. "She's a threat to you, Prince. She wants to be the king. Keep her locked up inna room."

"Hush, Poulet," Falstaff said. "Mind your manners in the presence of your betters."

Hamlet started as the truth of Poulet's shrewd observation hit him. The half-pint had pegged his mother accurately. He made a face. It was bad enough he had to be king, but he wasn't going to let his mother order him around. "As queen mother, you will rule your chamber. You will be confined to it by guards. Your ladies can come and go, but you will remain shut up in the chamber."

She shrieked and sobbed. "You'll regret this. You'll be a failure without my help. You never listen to me." She retreated to the chamber while Urquort hastened her departure by waving his ax in a threatening manner.

"Now what happens?" Hamlet asked after the chamber door slammed shut.

"If you will permit me to act in your name, Sire? Poulet, can you find your way back to the outside?"

"I remember the way," Poulet replied.

"Then go and lead the warriors back here. We must secure the castle before the guards get organized. Urquort and I will defend the room if necessary until you return. Make haste."

Poulet slipped from the room.

Hamlet hugged himself. Clodio had been sent to meet with his father. That meant the nagging elf ghost would leave him alone. He wondered what a king was supposed to do.

# # #

Falstaff couldn't believe his luck. Hamlet had just become king and he didn't have a clue how to rule. He, Falstaff, was now the only friend and the principal advisor to the king. Power and riches waited to be clutched to his bosom. While Hamlet would be the ceremonial leader of Denmarko, he, Falstaff, would be the most powerful man in the kingdom. None could gainsay him. He had access to the treasury. He had access to the military. He controlled access to the king. All the threads of power were in his hands.

He had trouble organizing his thoughts. There were so many possibilities in front of him, he didn't know where to begin. Finally, reality set in. None of these possibilities were achievable until Hamlet became firmly ensconced on the throne. So, the first order of business was to inform the castle there had been a change during the night. "Sire?" he said.

"Umm." Hamlet looked intoxicated.

"I advise you to hold an audience immediately. Wake up everyone in the castle and have them come to wherever the throne is kept. When they show up, you will be sitting on the throne and you will inform all of them that you are now king. Wait, maybe we should stay here until Poulet gets back with the soldiers. Then we'll do it." Falstaff bowed to Hamlet. "Does that meet with your approval, Sire?"

"What?" Hamlet blinked a few times. "Oh, yes. Fine. Take care of it."

"Be assured that I will be by your side ready to defend you against anyone who doesn't accept you as the new king."

Hamlet nodded. "You're a good friend."

Falstaff smirked.

# # #

It was a few hours before dawn when the castle residents finally assembled in the throne room. Yawning and shivering, they regarded Hamlet. Most wore nightclothes with a cloak thrown around their shoulders. Torchlight reflected from the ax blades of Urquort's dwarf warriors who lined the walls while the longbows stood behind Hamlet.

Hamlet sat on the throne wearing a crown. He twisted the ring of kingship worn by Clodio until an hour ago. He tried to swallow, but his mouth was too dry. He had never address a crowd before, and fear of getting laughed at dominated his mind. He noticed the wary look on everyone's face. They're examining me like I'm a new type of bug, he thought. They're wondering if I'm harmless or dangerous.

"Hear the words of the king," Falstaff bellowed from behind the throne.

Hamlet stood up and coughed. "I apologize for waking you up, but I have an important announcement to make and it couldn't wait until morning. I'm the new king. Clodio died earlier in the night."

"From natural causes," Falstaff added.

Hamlet sat down and looked around at the crowd. Most appeared to be getting their heads around the royal change and how it affected them personally.

"Long live the king," the Treasurer called out. Hamlet noted the half-pint seemed to be the most quick-witted of the lot. "I always knew you'd be our king before long." He smiled, bowed and scampered about as if beside himself with happiness at Hamlet's ascension.

Hamlet's mouth dropped open. The half-pint had never said a kind word to him before. In fact, he often cursed at Hamlet in the past.

"Know, Oh Mighty Majesty, my troops pledge their lives to your safety." The head of the castle guard, a dwarf, smiled. Another resident who loathed Hamlet until tonight. Hamlet wondered why the guard hadn't been able to stop him and Falstaff from sneaking into the castle. Or hadn't noticed a war band of sixty axes and a dozen longbows stomping down a corridor near the king's chambers. Maybe the castle needed a new guard captain.

A fat elf pushed himself forward and bowed. Hamlet recognized him as Polonius, a banker often in conference with Clodio. He didn't know the banker had a room in the castle. Several times, he had brushed Hamlet aside without any greeting if they met in a corridor. "My best wishes, King Hamlet. I stand ready to serve you as I did your uncle and father before you." He made hand-washing movements. "I can offer the best interest rates in the kingdom. My unmarried daughter, Ophelia, has often admired you from afar. May I present her to you in the near future?"

Hamlet noticed many folks pushed and shoved trying to reach the foot of the throne. It looked a scrum was about to break out in several spots.

The castle chamberlain, a beefy human, reached the front of the crowd through judicious use of his fists and feet. The man had often squealed to his mother about Hamlet's conduct. "My Liege, I am prepared to give you excellent advice as your chief advisor, just as I advised Clodio and your father."

"Umm, Falstaff is my chief advisor." Hamlet almost laughed aloud as the man dropped his smile. His face now showed a look of cunning. He licked his lips and regarded Falstaff through hooded eyes. Hamlet said, "I don't see the knights Rosencrantz and Guilderstern in the room. I want them brought here immediately. See to it."

The man, now red-faced, bowed and strode away.

After Hamlet had received unctuous greetings from a dozen more residents, the chamberlain returned. "My Liege, those two fled the castle when they heard the rumor you were the new king."

"They are to be arrested on sight if found." Hamlet stood. "It has been a long day and night. This audience is over."

The dozen or more residents who hadn't had a chance to fawn over him, looked fearful.

Hamlet left the room followed by Falstaff.

"That went well, Sire," Falstaff said. "They accepted your kingship."

"Now what happens? After I wake up, I mean."

"The chamberlain probably has a schedule of events for Clodio. You should take care of that business to show the folks that nothing has changed. It will calm their fears."

Hamlet could think of nothing except sleep.

While Hamlet announced he was king and listened to the castle residents vying to see who could praise him the most, Falstaff checked out the potential threats to his new position. He also checked on possible allies.

The Treasurer was certainly one he had to befriend or cow into submission. The value of the cash and jewels in the treasury was vital information and he — and Hamlet, of course — needed that information. Once he knew how much cash he had to work with, he could figure out how to spend it.

As to the captain of the guard, that dwarf seemed barely competent. Right now, Falstaff wanted to know how many guards he commanded and how well-trained they were. Possibly, the guards were trained but poorly led. In either case, he had to figure out if the captain would enter into his future plans or not.

Polonius, the banker, presented interesting possibilities. Easy access to large amounts of cash loans that others would have to pay back sounded like he had died and gone to a happy place. The elf had actually had the nerve to offer his daughter as Hamlet's mistress. That gave Falstaff another interesting action item. What if someone rich or powerful offered a candidate to be queen? How would he respond? He must be prepared for that possibility.

The chamberlain was the most dangerous of the residents. He, Falstaff, had to control access to the king, not the chamberlain. Whatever it took, the chamberlain had to be neutralized. Judicious murder might be the answer to that conundrum.

Falstaff wondered why a general hadn't announced himself. Denmarko surely had an army and an army implied there had to be a general. So where was he? Why hadn't he attended the audience? What was he doing? He had to find out how strong the army was before he could begin planning how to use it or how to stop a possible rebellion.

Falstaff let Hamlet sleep for a few hours. While the king ate breakfast, he said, "I'm surprised that the general in charge of the army didn't acknowledge you as king. That could be a serious challenge to you. Do you know who he is and where he is?"

"As far as I know, there is no general because we don't have an army," Hamlet replied. "All we have is the captain of the guard. Armies cost a lot of money. Even I know that."

"But without an army your kingdom is at risk of being conquered by anyone. Even a gang of bandits could plunder the city."

"I hadn't thought about that. I know Clodio was cheap. Maybe that's why we don't have an army."

Falstaff started. An unforeseen opportunity for more power had popped up. He had to seize it before it disappeared. "Besides the army issue, Sire, the guard captain doesn't seem to be competent."

"I thought the same thing." Hamlet scratched his stubble. "If he was competent, I might not be king right now."

"Exactly. We have a big problem here, Sire. It is a danger to your rule. Denmarko needs much better security."

"Umm, do whatever you think is best."

"I'll need more authority than I have now. Why don't you appoint me General of the Army? With that rank and power, I'll be able to address the problem and develop a solution."

"Done. Have an announcement written up and I'll sign it." Hamlet pulled a face. "I think that is the way things are done."

"It'll do fine. I'll have the announcement ready within the hour." Behind Hamlet's back, Falstaff smiled and hugged himself. His wildest fantasies were about to come true.

CHAPTER SIXTEEN

On the morning after the battle, Othello stepped onto the wharf. His legs almost buckled under him when he tried to walk, and Nark caught his elbow to steady him. The ship's captain followed the two. From the ship came sounds of Dunlap roaring orders as he organized the militia to leave the ship. The other captains awaited him at the end of the wharf, and even from a distance, Othello could see they weren't happy. With newfound confidence, he smiled and said, "Congratulations on our successful mission."

One captain rolled his eyes, another spit over the side of the wharf and a third snorted. "What success?" the fourth sneered. "We never even saw the pirates. All we did was hear a bunch of ships inna fog. Could have been anyone."

"Nonsense," Othello replied. "We saw the pirate flagship and traded arrows with it."

The four captains looked skeptical.

"Aye, we did," Othello's captain said. "Then he turned and disappeared."

"So nothing really happened except we lost time and money. Falstaff'll keep on takin' ships and we'll keep on losin' money."

"Not so," Othello said with an air of bravado. "We sent the rogue packing. He'll think twice before coming around here again. Why, I'll bet he sails off to bother some other harbor."

A short while later, he entered the city hall and found Emilia guarding his office door. "Ya made it back? Me hadda bet wid anudda worker dat de ship sink. Me lose ten coppers. Ya gonna repay me?"

"No, I'm not." Othello shook his head. "Anything happen while I was gone?"

"Yep. Iago and Cassio got inna shouting' match about who was in charge. Dey both got really pissed when me tell 'em ya put me in charge again and dey betta get outta me face. I tried to get dem to fight a duel, but it didn't work out."

Othello tried not to groan. "Go ask the mayor if I can meet with her to give a report."

"Can't." Emilia pulled a canvas sack out of her desk and opened it. "Onna break now."

Othello entered his office and slammed the door.

# # #

After breakfast on the second day of his reign, Hamlet sat on his throne awaiting the start of his first judgment audience. His job, as explained by the chamberlain, was to decide the disputes that came before him. Mangy-looking, foul-smelling peasants filled the room. Most of them looked like they came straight from the fields. Falstaff stood by his right shoulder and the chamberlain on his left. The two had scuffled a bit before assuming their positions. Hamlet assumed the chamberlain was accustomed to standing on the right of the throne and resented Falstaff's presence. He beckoned the chamberlain closer and whispered to him, "Aren't there local courts and judges to hear the peasants' cases?"

"Yes, Sire, there are, but when word got out that there was a new king, they exercised their right to be heard by you. I guess they think they'll get a better deal from you than from the judges. Leastwise, that is what they're hoping will happen."

The chamberlain read the particulars of the first case. Hamlet promptly forgot the names and details as two angry litigants — both peasants to judge by their looks and smell — stepped forward and gave a cursory bow to Hamlet. The chamberlain pointed to one and said, "Proceed."

"This un's dog got loose and killed five of me chickens. And he won't pay me fer the chickens. I want me money, Kingee."

"Is this true?" Hamlet asked. "Did your dog kill his chickens?"

"Aye, but it weren't me dog's fault. His chickens was runnin' about loose. Iffen he wanted to keep his bloody birds alive, he shoulda had 'em in a chicken coop. Then they wouldn'ta gotten kilt."

"So, you're saying the chicken owner is to blame for the deaths of his birds?" Hamlet struggled to keep a straight face. He hoped all the cases would be as easy as this one. He didn't even have to think about the decision in this one.

"Aye, that's a fact, Kingee."

"That's ridiculous. How much are the chickens worth?"

"Three coppers each."

"I rule in favor of the chicken owner. You are to pay him fifteen coppers for the damage your dog did to his property. And both of you will pay another fifteen coppers to the court for wasting its time. You should have settled this dispute without bothering the authorities."

The dog owner gasped and the chicken owner made a face at Hamlet.

In unison, the rest of peasants in the room cried out in alarm. A general rush for the exits followed the decree. Within minutes, the room was emptied of litigants.

"Well done, Majesty," said the chamberlain. "Well done, indeed."

CHAPTER SEVENTEEN

Two days later, Othello joined Glyniss in her office for a meeting with the City Council. He hoped to hear a decision on the wall rebuilding plan that he had explained to her before sailing. Everyone in the room sweltered in the midsummer heat. The open windows did nothing except let in more heat.

She opened the meeting by addressing him. "While you were at sea, we discussed changing the Troll Patrol to the Wall Patrol and recruiting a new force to control traffic and crime in the city. Today, after pondering the decision for a few days, we will vote on the idea."

Othello tried to hide his excitement, but had difficulty not bouncing in his chair. If approved, the change would eliminate the need for him to ask for bids to rebuild the wall. That would save him from awarding the contract to the Godmother or risking his life by awarding it to someone else. And, since the decision came from the Council, he would be protected from the wrath of the hag.

"Does anyone have anything to add or say before we vote?" Glyniss looked at the six Council members, elderly males and females representing the city's diversity. Everyone shook their heads. "Then all in favor of approving the plan, raise your hand."

Othello squirmed in his chair and tried not to look at the members as they voted. Sweat dripped down his forehead. Lastly, Glyniss raised her hand. "It's unanimous. Seven votes for and none against." She looked at Othello. "Thank you for bringing this plan to my attention. It goes a long way to solving the defensive needs of the city without bankrupting the treasury."

Othello beamed at the mayor and stammered, "Thank you."

"How do you want to proceed?"

He had thought about this possibility and had an answer prepared. "Since it is the Council's decision to give Iago a new responsibility, I'd like the Council to tell him it was their idea. After that, I'll explain the details of his new job to him."

"All right." Glyniss stood up and walked to the door. To her new secretary, she said, "Please find Iago and have him come to my office immediately."

Othello had told Emilia to have Iago stay in the building this morning for just such an event. The Council discussed other business for a few minutes before Iago entered the room. Always suspicious and angry, he glowered at Othello, then gave the mayor and each member of the Council a hooded, crafty look.

"Lieutenant Iago." Glyniss gave the troll a beatific smile. "The Council has just voted to undertake an important change that will considerably improve the defensive capability of the city. Minister of Homeland Security Othello has recommended to us that you are the best candidate to lead this project. To demonstrate the importance of the post, it will be headed by a captain. So, if you accept, you will be promoted. Naturally, a raise in pay goes with the position."

Iago frowned and looked around the room one more time. "Me ain't gettin' fired?"

"Is that why you thought we called you here?" Glyniss looked amused.

"Yeah." Still bewildered, he gave Othello a wary look out of the corner of his eye. "Guess me take de job."

"In that case," Glyniss said, "you are now Captain of the Wall Patrol. The staff of the Troll Patrol are also transferred to your new command and each one gets a small raise. The raise is to compensate them for the added responsibilities they now have."

"Wot new respona . . . bilties?" Iago frowned at the mayor.

Glyniss looked to Othello.

"The Wall Patrol will have two primary duties," Othello said. "The first is to defend the walls in case of an attack."

"Wid our clubs?"

"No, the trolls will be issued short pikes. Most of them have now trained with the militia and can use them effectively. The rest of them will be trained immediately. The second duty will be to rebuild the walls."

"How we gonna do dat?"

"Trolls are very strong. I think two or three can easily lift the stone blocks back onto the wall. They will have to be cemented into place, of course, but we can find a mason to teach you how to make cement and offer advice on where the blocks should go."

Iago gave Othello a look of pure hatred. "Dat hard work."

"And of course, since this is a new position," Othello pointed to the troll's blue sash, "you decide what color your sash of office will be."

Iago blinked in surprise.

"And you can decide how wide and long it should be."

Iago grinned and fingered his sash. "Who gonna handle da traffic?"

"I will recruit a new force to control traffic. They will also be responsible for patrolling the city and controlling crime. They'll be called the Foot Patrol."

Iago continued to grin.

"If you don't have any questions, Captain," Glyniss said, "we will let you get on with your new duties. You can work out the details with Othello who will remain your commanding officer."

Iago sneered at Othello, turned and sauntered out the door. He stopped and asked, "Hey! Who gonna be in charge of de new guys?"

"Nark." Othello held his breath, expecting an explosion of trollish curses. Instead, Iago sneered again and said, "Him too stupid to do dat job," and slammed the door.

Othello exhaled. "Thank you all," he said to the Council and Glyniss. "I'll tell Nark about his promotion to lieutenant and get him started on his new job."

As he left the office, he wondered what Nark would do about the sergeant stripes tattooed on his biceps. He also wondered if he would have the nerve to explain the changes to the Godmother.

# # #

A despondent Hamlet showed Falstaff the woods where his hives were located. Bees flew to and from the surrounding meadows. Poulet showed interest in the project while Urquort leaned against the trunk of a tree and looked bored. It was midmorning on a hot summer day.

"See how the bees thrive," Hamlet said. "This is my work, not listening to peasants complain about their neighbors and certainly not listening to ministers whine about how hard they work. Yesterday, I wasted the entire afternoon listening to the ministers' drivel." He wagged a finger at Falstaff. "Why, not one of them ever worked a day in their lives."

"I can understand your frustration, Sire," Falstaff replied. "But it's your royal duties."

"My real duty is here among the bees. My plans were to add a dozen or more hives next spring. And the same every spring after that. Within a few years, I could be the biggest producer of honey in the land. I'll export the stuff to Dun Hythe and even Cintri." Hamlet made a face as he wandered among the trees. "But that will never happen now that I'm king. I must waste my time in foolish court affairs instead of doing real work."

"I'm impressed," Poulet said waving a hand around the copse.

"You're interested in bees?" Hamlet replied.

"Not so much, but I love mead and you need honey to make mead."

"Poulet has rich tastes and an empty purse." Falstaff chuckled and rubbed the half-pint's head. "I made the big mistake by buying him a cup of mead one day."

"Someday I'd like to brew my own mead." He dodged away from Falstaff's hand.

"Still," Hamlet said, "I'm glad someone has an interest in bees besides myself."

Falstaff, with a bemused expression on his face, said, "Sire, I have a suggestion for you."

"Let's hear it then."

"Friends help friends out. Since we're friends, I'm willing to take on the chores you find so burdensome. This will free up more of your time to tend to the bees."

"You would do that for me?" Hamlet's depressed spirits soared like an eagle flying from its nest.

"We are friends, M'Lord."

"Even so, already you're in charge of the army and now you want to take on even more of my chores. You really are a good friend. I accept your offer." He grasped Falstaff's hand and shook it.

"You'll still have ceremonial duties, Sire, and you'll have to sign documents and read announcements. There may even be a parade or two you'll have to lead."

"Yes, I'm sure you're right. There is no escaping one's destiny entirely. I suppose it's the least I can do as king. Thank you, my friend." Hamlet took a deep breath and examined the area to find suitable sites for expansion.

# # #

Falstaff fanned himself as he followed Hamlet around as the king inspected the grove. He couldn't believe Hamlet had just handed him the keys to the kingdom. Now he had to figure how to maximize his profits. During his investigations, he had seen the barren treasury. Whatever tax revenue the kingdom collected barely covered the bills; there was no tax surplus to store in the treasury and the crown jewels were shoddy. Mold covered some of them, and others were made from gold-covered lead with some of the gold worn off. It didn't have enough cash for him to live an extravagant life as the king's favorite. Already he tired of the frugal meals everyone ate in the castle, washed down with vinegary wine. In effect, Hamlet had handed over what must be the poorest kingdom in Gundarland. He could raise taxes, of course, but it would take years to build up the treasury to the point it would be worth stealing. As for the armory, it held nothing but a few rusty spear points and some dented armor.

No, he had to use his power to snatch wealth someplace else. First things first. He was now a general, not a pirate. Time to get rid of the ships. They should fetch a pile of silver pennies that could be used as seed money. But for what? He needed a project to occupy his energy, a lucrative project worthy of his talent and new powers.

If the money he craved wasn't in Denmarko, where could he find it? After a few moments of thought, he decided it was in Dun Hythe. It was the richest city in Gundarland and just a short march down the coast road. There, he could renew his acquaintanceship with Othello. Another thought jostled its way into his mind. While Dun Hythe was rich, attacking it would be a big gamble, perhaps the biggest gamble of his life. He pondered the alternatives. If he didn't gamble, he'd never acquire the riches he deserved. Even if he lost the gamble, it would be exciting. He looked around. "Poulet! I have a mission for you."

The half-pint meandered over to Falstaff. "What is it, Boss?"

"Go to each ship and tell the captain I will meet with all of them tomorrow morning in the tavern."

"Right. And after I tell them, I'll go there myself to ensure we have the best table in the place."

Falstaff sighed. "Tell Annee I said 'hello.'"

CHAPTER EIGHTEEN

Late at night, Hamlet strolled the parapet and hummed a tune the court musician had played earlier at dinner. His life had changed for the better and his outlook had improved now that Falstaff had taken over much of the burdensome chores of a working king. In addition, his mother no longer bothered or nagged him. He also could now enjoy a nighttime stroll without getting startled by the ghost.

"Hey!" a voice called out from the deep shadows.

Hamlet gave a small yelp and his heart thudded in his chest.

"Your old man sent me to say 'Thank you' for doin' in Clodio."

"Will you stop sneaking up on me?"

The ghost looked perplexed. "I don't think ghosts can appear any other way. I'm pretty sure it says so inna Handbook of Ghostin'."

"Where is my father this time?"

"He's negotiatin' with the Archangelic Board of Directors about a power sharin' arrangement."

"And Clodio? What happened to him?"

"Your old man pulled some strings and Clodio is now in the palace dungeons charged with gettin' rid of the rat ghosts. Hah! That'll take him all eternity. Those little buggers breed like vermin."

The ghost disappeared and Hamlet resumed his stroll.

"Oops! I forgot to tell you somethin'."

The startled Hamlet jumped and yelped again. "What?" he snarled.

"Your old man says to tell you, 'Somethin' is rotten in the state of Denmarko.'"

"What is that supposed to mean?"

"I'm not sure. It might be somethin' about you pickin' bad advisors. I heard him mumble somethin' like that." The ghost popped out of existence.

Hamlet held his breath for a few heart beats in case the ghost returned a third time. When he didn't, Hamlet went back to walking and pondered the warning. Did his father refer to Falstaff? If so, why was Falstaff a bad advisor? Perhaps he should ask someone for advice, but the only one he could think of asking was his mother, and he was far from being that desperate.

# # #

Late at night, Emilia prepared her lunch for the following day at the office. She sautéed a batch of breaded rodent fillets and buttered two chunks of bread.

The door crashed open and Iago staggered in holding a rag over his bloody right shoulder.

Emilia's heart leaped into her throat at the sight of blood dripping from her husband's hand. "Wot happened?"

"Got stabbed." Iago looked at the wound. "By someone dressed in black. Me and da others couldn't get ahold of him and he got away. But he didn't get anudda stab wid his knife."

"Why would someone attack ya?" She got her knitting equipment from the bedroom.

"Don't know." He eyed Emilie who was threading a hooked needle. "Whatcha doin'?"

"Gotta stitch up da hole inna shoulder." She grinned evilly at him.

"Dis gonna hurt?"

"As much as I can make it hurt. Gonna be fun. For me anyways." She pointed to a chair. "Sit."

Reluctantly, Iago sat.

Emilia put the needle on the table and fetched a bottle of rotgut whiskey. "Take away da rag." She gripped his other shoulder. When Iago removed the rag to expose a large, deep stab wound, she poured the whiskey into the hole. Iago gasped and squirmed under her ministrations. She took a gulp of whiskey and handed the bottle to Iago. He drained the rest of the bottle.

"Now hold still." Emilia took the needle and started to sew up the wound. She cackled at Iago's groaning. When she was done she rinsed out the bloody rag, placed it over the wound and tied it down with string. "Gotta hold yer arm still 'til the wound heals."

"How me gonna lead trolls wid only one arm?"

Emilia shrugged. "Not me problem. Who ya think did dis?"

Now Iago shrugged. "Don't know."

"Dumb troll. I know who did it."

"Who?"

"Da Godmother. Dat's who. She knows about yer plans."

"How she know dat?" Iago grimaced.

"Da Godmother got spies everywhere. She found out about ya plannin' to kill Othella and then blame her and she don't like dat idea so she sent da assassin after ya."

"Hah. She need new assassin. Dat one not too good."

"Yer extra stupid even for a troll. Dat assassin gave ya a warnin'. Iffen da Godmother wanted ya dead, ya'd be lyin' inna street, not sittin' here."

Iago screwed up his face and digested Emila's words. After a minute, he asked, "Wot me gotta do now?"

"Iffen I was ya, I'd keep on wid da plan. Try to knock off Othella anyways."

He frowned. "Why keep tryin'?"

"'Cause da next time da Godmother sends an assassin, me gonna be a widow."

Iago cursed, stood up and bunched his left hand into fist.

Emilia also stood, blocked his punch and smacked the back of her other hand into the wound.

Iago screeched in pain.

"Every time ya say or do somethin' nasty, me gonna smack yer wound." Emilia grinned at her husband, anticipating a pleasant few weeks of living with Iago.

# # #

Othello and Nark strolled down the main street toward the city walls. Nark had solved the problem of his tattooed sergeant stripes by fashioning blue armbands to cover the stripes. He used the armbands in place of the customary sash of office and rank. Already, his command consisted of twenty-five dwarfs and he had a candidate list of over a hundred names for the remaining openings. The Foot Patrol directed traffic and patrolled a few prime robbery areas at night. The after-dark patrols would expand as the force grew.

"Did ya see Iago's shoulder?" Nark asked.

"He has a rag covering some sort of wound, but he wouldn't tell me what happened," Othello replied. "And Emilia got all giggly when I asked her."

"Somebody stabbed him," Nark said. "Dumb troll probably doin' somethin' stupid."

They came to a major intersection where port traffic and local wagons came together to pass through the gates. Two dwarfs, battle axes on their backs, handled the traffic. Unlike the Troll Patrol, the Foot Patrol had the traffic under control and flowing freely. Both dwarfs alternately cursed, glared and grinned at the drivers. This close to the wall, Othello could hear the trolls struggling with the blocks as they heaved them back into place.

"I know dat guy." Nark pointed to a human dressed in leather pants and shirt. "He's a merchant. Let's see if he's got any good stuff to tell us."

Othello believed that Nark knew everyone in town.

The man waved to Nark. They shook hands and Nark introduced Othello. "Any news?" the troll asked.

"Yeah. Just got back from Denmarko. Big doings up there."

"Like what?" Othello asked.

"Gotta new king. Young guy he is."

"Hamlet?" Othello guessed.

"Yeah, that's him."

"What happened to the old king, Clodio?"

"Nobody knows. Some say the old guy was murdered in his bed. Others say he fled with a few retainers. Doesn't really matter. The new guy is king, and some fat guy tells him what to do and when to do it."

Othello gasped in shock. Could the advisor be Falstaff? Hamlet had admitted that he knew the rogue. "W . . . what's the advisor's name? Do you know?"

The man scratched his head and looked thoughtful. "Falsip? No, that ain't it, but it's close."

"Falstaff?" Othello hoped the man answered negatively.

"That's it. Falstaff. Seems to be a nasty piece of work.
Always got a half-pint with him and a dwarf soldier. Gotta
go. My wagon should be ready to go north again."

"When you get back, come and see me in the city hall.
I'd like to learn more about what's going on in Denmarko."

"Sure thing. I'll be back in four days."

Othello thanked him. He wondered why he had a
sinking feeling that he'd soon meet Falstaff again.

# # #

Falstaff left the castle with Poulet and Urquort to meet
the captains. Along the way, he asked Poulet, "How's
Annee?"

"She's worried about her job. The owner's old and sick.
Iffen he dies, she could lose her job."

"Making any progress?"

"She still won't talk much to me. Says she ain't gettin'
involved with a sailor 'cause they're away too much. But I'm
not givin' up."

"Typical female," Falstaff replied.

"You like gettin' turned down, don't you?" Urquort
teased the half-pint.

Poulet didn't reply and pouted the rest of the way.

In the Sailor's Delight, the three captains sat in the shade
at an outdoor table enjoying the pleasant morning
temperatures. Falstaff sat down with them while Poulet
looked for Annee.

"The crews wanna get back to sea," the elf captain said
to start the meeting.

"Yeah," the older man added. "They've spent all their
loot, so they can't go ashore and get drunk. It's borin' layin'
at anchor for days at a time."

"The situation has changed," Falstaff replied. "I now have other responsibilities and can't go pirating any more."

The three captains looked surprised and glanced at each other. Finally, the younger man said, "I reckon we can do without you once we get the soldiers back on board."

"Urquort and the soldiers stay with me." Falstaff folded his arms.

"Then what are we supposed to do?"

"I'll tell you what I have in mind," Falstaff replied. "I'll sell each of you the ship you command. At a reasonable price. Then you can go pirating on your own. Or you can paint the hull and trim, rename the ship and go back to being an honest merchant."

"How much?" the old captain had a wary look.

"Two hundred silver pennies each for the cogs and three hundred for the brig. These are bargain prices and you all know it. Don't tell me you don't have the cash. I know how much loot you each earned with the extra shares I gave you. You all have more than enough to buy the ships."

"I'm not paying." The elf pounded his fist on the table.

"If you don't buy the ship from me, I'll have Urquort burn it to the waterline."

The captains looked shocked at Falstaff's statement.

"Well, you have to choose how you plan to leave the harbor. You can walk or you can sail. What'll it be?"

"I'll buy the ship," the elderly captain said. "It's a sturdy one and worth the coins."

"I'll pay too," the younger man said.

"All right," said the elf. "I'll buy my ship."

"Excellent! I'll wait here while you fetch the coins from the ships."

Once the captains left, Poulet asked, "What are we doin' without the ships?" He beamed and bounced on his toes while talking to Falstaff.

"As the general of the Denmarko army, I have no time for sailing all over the coastline."

"You mean we're stayin' here in town?"

"In so many words, yes."

"I have to tell Annee." Poulet ran into the tavern.

"Urquort," Falstaff said, "I have a mission for you. After the captains pay for their ships, I want you to take half of the coins and recruit more soldiers. We need a lot of them. The rest of the money will be used on supplies for them."

"What are they for?"

"'Tis a state secret at this time. Get me some more troops and you won't regret it." Falstaff grinned. His newly hatched scheme was moving forward.

# # #

Inside the tavern, with a lunch crowd gathering, Annee served mugs of ale to a group of workers at a table. "Watch it, you clod," she yelled at one of them. "Iffen you step on my toe hairs, I'll dump a mug of ale over your head."

Poulet ran up to her with his heart in his throat. He wondered how Annee would react? "Annee, I have news. Can we talk?"

"Come back later. I'm busy." She slammed a mug on the table and shoved a wisp of hair away from her forehead.

"This is important news. We have to talk."

She pulled a face, but didn't say no. She finished with the table and walked to the bar followed by an anxious Poulet. She turned, leaned against the bar and said, "Well? What is it?"

"Falstaff just sold his ships." He grinned at her.

"So what? Why are you tellin' me that? Why would I care if he sells 'em or keeps 'em?"

"Don't you see? It means I'm not gonna be sailin' anymore. Falstaff now works for Hamlet."

"Falstaff works for the kingee? King Hammy?"

"Aye. We got rooms inna castle. He's Hamlet's advisor and general of the army."

"Army? What army? We gotta army? Never seen any of 'em in here."

"Falstaff's startin' one."

"What for?"

"If he's a general, he's gotta have an army, don't he?" He gave here a tender look. "And that means no more sea voyages. I ain't a sailor any more."

Annee stared over Poulet's head for a few seconds while he held his breath. Finally, she gave a flicker of a smile. "Well, it's a start, I guess."

"And I'm lettin' my toe hair grow."

She looked down at his stubble-covered toes. "You gotta long way to go before you can do anythin' with that mess." Her own toe hair looked squeaky clean, was curled and had bows made from colored yarn. She gave him a wan smile. "Maybe there's hope for you yet."

"Will you help me groom my toe hairs?" Poulet voice squeaked from excitement. "After they grow long enough?"

Annee smirked at him. "Maybe."

Poulet's heart gave a lurch.

CHAPTER NINETEEN

Three days later, the Godmother granted Othello his request for a meeting. Accompanied by Desdemona, he approached the Wicked Bed in a state of agitation. He was certain the old harpy wouldn't be happy with his news.

After the usual body search, they entered her office. It reeked with perfume and pipeweed smoke. She overflowed her throne and wore an ash-stained cream-colored gown with purple cuffs. Her hair, piled on top of her head, had been dyed lime green. The usual cigar jutted from orange lips. As on the previous visits, the two young female elves standing behind the Godmother took his breath away with their beauty and their skimpy outfits.

"Ofella! You better have good news for me." She took the cigar out of her mouth, gave it to one of the attendants and said, "Desdemona, come and give your grandmother a kiss."

Desdemona advanced and was enveloped by the cream gown. Once Desdemona retreated, the Godmother held her right hand with the enormous sapphire ring and gave Othello a questioning look. After kissing the ring, he stepped back. She snapped her fingers and took the cigar back, then gestured toward him with it. "Are you asking for bids on the wall soon?"

"That's what I wanted to talk to you about. There will be no bids."

Godmother scowled and bit her cigar in half. The lit portion fell into her lap and she spit the other part across the room. One of her attendants jumped forward and snatched up the lit end. The second one produced a fresh cigar from a box on a table, lit it and offered it to the old hag. She puffed furiously, producing a bluish cloud of smoke that partially hid her head.

Othello shifted his weight from foot to foot while the Godmother recovered from a coughing fit.

"Speak. Be careful. My love of Desdemona can only protect you so far."

Othello sucked in a big gulp of air and said, "The Mayor and the Council decided to use the Troll Patrol to rebuild the walls. It's the only way to do it because the city doesn't have the money to issue bids for a contractor."

"Whose idea was this?" Her voice had a dangerous undertone to it.

"I assure you it was not mine." Othello spoke with an air of false confidence. At least this utterance was true.

"Why didn't you stop them?"

"They discussed it while I was at sea chasing pirates. By the time I got back, it was decided and approved. I wasn't part of the discussion or the voting."

"So, I ask you for a simple favor to repay me for getting you this post and you fail me. What good are you? Desdemona, I apologize for marrying you to this abject loser."

"Grandma, he isn't a loser. He successfully chased a pirate fleet away and I love him."

The Godmother puffed on her cigar and stared over their heads.

Othello tried to placate the old elf. "I started a Foot Patrol to replace the Troll Patrol, and they have cut down on thievery, like you requested."

"Leave! Both of you. Desdemona, you are welcome to visit me, but I never want to see Ofella again. And don't mention your husband's name in my presence."

Othello grabbed Desdemona's arm and walked out with as much dignity as he could muster. His wife's arm steadied him and concealed his quaking hands. The dryness in his mouth made it difficult to swallow. Outside, he said, "Th . . . that went well."

"You're still alive and that's all that matters to me." Desdemona squeezed his arm. "I think Grandma will get over her anger after a while."

# # #

Outside the brothel, Desdemona struggled to get enough air. Her worst nightmare had been realized. She knew Othello didn't understand the Godmother's rage. Desdemona had seen the old elf go into rages before, and things always ended badly for the cause of the rage. Usually, the character responsible was never seen again. She didn't want to see her husband harmed because of this episode over which he had little or no control.

She knew there was no hope of trying to talk rationally to her Grandmother. Not for several days or even a few weeks. Eventually, she would calm down and listen to her granddaughter. Until then, Desdemona had to figure a way to protect Othello. She also knew he would be mortified if he realized she was doing anything to save him from the Godmother's wrath. He would also be shocked to learn how vindictive the Godmother was.

She had to act surreptitiously, but quickly. With luck, Grandma would never know about her involvement. When it came to the dreaded decision, she had chosen Othello over her Grandma. The surprising thing was how effortlessly she made that decision.

To lighten her mood, she looked around at the tenements and recalled which ones her playmates used to live in. It suddenly dawned on her that the Godmother must own all the buildings on the block because every tenant belonged to her family. She wondered how many buildings she owned altogether? Desdemona shook her head. Even after living with her so many years, even after being her chief advisor, the Godmother still kept secrets from her.

# # #

Othello sat in his office reviewing the diplomatic reports Glyniss had sent him. Emilia guarded the office door like a gorgon. No one showed up for a casual visit unless she was on her three-hour lunch period or one of her extended breaks. Only the most determined visitors braved her insults and challenges. Even the wounded Iago acted timid in her presence.

"Wot do ya want?" he heard her say. "And wot are dese filthy guys doin' in me office?"

"Sis! Ya look even uglier den usual." Nark apparently was the only one Emilia couldn't intimidate. "Is dat a new burlap dress ya got on? Who'd ya steal it from?"

Nark strolled into the office followed by four sturdy dwarf warriors. "Dese guys," Nark swept a hand toward the dwarfs, "are ya bodyguards. Dey'll be wid ya whenever ya go onna street."

Emilia stood in the doorway, arms crossed, watching and scowling.

"Bodyguards?" Othello responded. "Where did you get the idea I need them?" From experience, he knew Nark had a great amount of common sense and an unbelievable number of contacts that fed him vast stores of information.

He knew more about what went on in the city than anyone else, possibly including the Godmother.

"Yer in charge of defendin' da city. If someone gonna attack da city, da first thing dey oughta do is pop ya. Dat's why I think ya need dese guys. I gotta anudda four gonna watch yer house at night."

"That's an awful lot of Foot Patrol resources. I think you're overreacting." Othello tamped down his concern. If Nark thought he needed all these warriors to protect him, the troll must have heard alarming news. "Are you going to tell me the real reason why you're doing this?"

"Get dese guys outta here," Emilia said, "so I can go back to work."

Othello smiled at her contention that she did actual work. "Well?" he asked Nark.

"Only reason I got is yer a bigshot and ya oughta be guarded." He addressed the dwarf in charge of the detail. "Ya wait outside de office. When dis guy leaves, ya leave wid him. And don't pay any attention to her. She don't give ya orders and ya don't listen to her."

"I gonna get ya for dis, big brother." Emilia looked offended.

Othello shrugged. Clearly, he wasn't going to win this dispute with Nark. Listening to Emilia and the dwarfs insult each other might be amusing.

# # #

"Good morning, Sire." Falstaff greeted Hamlet while trying to gauge his mood. Over the last few days, he had drawn up plans and now he needed Hamlet to approve them or at least not forbid them. Without Hamlet's tacit or implied support, his plans for power and wealth would fail.

"Morning, Falstaff. Do you have any news?" Hamlet sat at a table eating his breakfast, oatmeal swimming in ale. Only the very poor drank water in Denmarko.

Falstaff deemed the king to be in a malleable mood and replied, "Nothing to note locally, but my spies send me disturbing news from Dun Hythe." He held his breath.

"You have spies in Dun Hythe? Why? . . . Never mind. I suppose it's the stuff advisors have to do."

"Of course I have spies." Falstaff felt his tension evaporate; he was sure Hamlet would go for the plan. "I've had spies in the city ever since I sensed Othello would betray me. I never trusted that dark elf. The spies tell me the city is gathering an army."

Hamlet raised an eyebrow and slurped a spoonful of oatmeal.

"I asked myself, Sire, why would an open city, not in danger of attack by any province, need an army? I've thought long and hard on the matter and my conclusions are not good news."

"I suppose I have to listen since I'm the king." Hamlet attacked a piece of toast. "Can't even have breakfast in peace these days. Did you hear my mother yelling last night? Demanding that I let her out and make her the regent. What nonsense."

"A born troublemaker she is."

"So what's this bad news?"

"Dun Hythe is preparing to attack and annex Denmarko. They want to expand their territory and power." Falstaff paced the room. "What knaves they are." He smashed a fist into the other palm.

Hamlet threw down the toast in disgust.

"Our only hope is to attack them first."

"With what? All we have are the castle guards and your soldiers."

"The captain of the guard tells me Denmarko has a militia. They can be a vital element in our plans. You must raise the militia when we are ready to strike. Urquort is recruiting more soldiers and has signed up over fifty so far."

An ashen Hamlet gulped. "Are you sure we have to do this?"

"It comes down to this. Whoever strikes first will win."

"When would we attack?"

"Soon. You, of course, will lead the army to victory."

"Why me? I made you the general."

"I will issue the orders in your name, but the king must lead the army. It's a time-honored tradition. I don't suppose you have a suit of armor somewhere? A king in armor sitting on a warhorse always looks brave and inspires the troops."

"I'm a dwarf. I won't fit on a warhorse. And no, I don't have armor."

"Hmm. Perhaps we can find a war swine for you to ride."

"I don't like this, Falstaff. How do you know your spy is correct?"

"I have similar reports from three different spies. And a traveler from Dun Hythe confirmed the recruiting effort. Othello is hiring unemployed dwarf warriors using a cover that they are needed for traffic control. To do nothing is to yield to the miscreants without striking a blow to defend ourselves. And then there is the matter of my justice for Othello's unprincipled attack on my ships."

"There is that matter, isn't there?"

"I helped you attain justice, and an attack on Dun Hythe will achieve two goals at once. First and most important, it will keep Denmarko free, and second, I can rest easy after I gain justice by hanging Othello."

"Oh, dear. That's a bit extreme, isn't it?"

"He deserves nothing less."

"Oh, all right. We must do it fast so the militia can be back in time for the harvest."

"We will. Dun Hythe's walls are in terrible shape. They've fallen down in many places. The city will never be able to withstand our attack." Falstaff could hardly contain his excitement until he left the room. Once Dun Hythe was conquered, he'd convince Hamlet to let him govern it in his name. It shouldn't be too hard to become the king of Dun Hythe before long. Wealth and power would be his. And Dun Hythe had women, unlike Denmarko. Wouldn't his father be surprised if he was still alive? "I'll have everything organized and ready to go in a week. That's when we'll march."

# # #

Nark strolled into Othello's office without any interference from Emilia, who was on her morning break and ignored everything around her while she ate a bacon and egg sandwich.

"Dat guy is back from Denmarko. Da one ya wanted to tell ya wot was goin' on up dere. Remember?"

"Yes, I do remember," Othello replied. "Where is he?"

"Inna cafe a block from here, eatin' breakfast. Wanna go meet him?"

"All right." Othello stood up and followed Nark out the door.

As they passed, Emilia said, "I take good care of de office. I gonna fire a coupla dumb workers."

"Don't do anything," Othello ordered her. "Just stay on your break until I get back." His four bodyguards jumped up, stood at attention and fell in behind the pair.

"Someday ya gonna forget to tell me dat." Emilia chuckled. "Den me gonna have fun."

Outside the building, two guard dwarfs from the Foot Patrol stood at attention and saluted smartly as Nark and Othello went past them. Othello couldn't help but recall the casual attitude of the troll guards.

On the way to the cafe, his bodyguards spread out: one in front and one in back and the other two on either side of Othello. "This is ridiculous," he said to Nark. "No one is going to assassinate me during the day on the main street."

"Gotta be careful. Don't look good for me if da boss get kilt."

Othello heard swishing noises behind him and turned to see a dwarf swinging his ax while glaring at a slim figure dressed in black who darted away.

"What happened?" Othello asked.

The dwarf looked sheepish and replied, "My shoulder is gettin' tight so I swung my ax a few times to loosen it up."

"Who is that guy in black?"

The dwarf shrugged. "Don't know."

Nark pointed to an outdoor cafe and the merchant sitting at a table. The man grinned and nodded to Othello.

Othello sat down at the table after shaking hands with the merchant. Nark sat down at an empty table. The guards leaned against the side of the building and ogled passing females.

"What is the situation in Denmarko?" Othello asked.

"Strange. The new king is never around. Apparently, he does something with bees, if you can believe it. His advisor Falstaff runs the place. He calls himself General Falstaff now. And he's recruiting troops. Don't know why. Who would threaten a backwoods little kingdom like Denmarko?"

After chatting for a few minutes more, Othello thanked the man and left. On the way back to his office, he pondered the news. Falstaff calling himself a general could only mean he intended to command soldiers. For what purpose? From his little experience with Falstaff, the man plotted evil for someone. After a moment's reflection, he decided Falstaff must have Dun Hythe in his plans. There was no other place in the area that an army could attack. If he still had his pirate ships, the attack would be by land and sea.

The possibility of an attack sent a shock wave through his body. Falstaff had been in Dun Hythe and had seen the rundown condition of the walls. Had he also seen the militia attempting to drill? Both factors could lead a schemer like Falstaff to conclude the city was ripe for harvesting by an army of mercenaries.

Ignoring Falstaff would be a fatal mistake. He had better see to the city's defenses. Just in case.

PART FOUR

1 Month Later

CHAPTER TWENTY

Hamlet strolled through the copse of oak and beech trees. Bees swarmed around the area on flights to and from the hives. The sight of the activity gladdened his heart and, for a few minutes, took his mind off the invasion of Dun Hythe. Falstaff's determination to conquer the city still puzzled Hamlet. While he understood that Othello had betrayed Falstaff — according to Falstaff — sacking a city to avenge the elf's deed was a bit extreme. Poulet had suggested that Falstaff use the scryer network to send a challenge to Othello. Hamlet thought it was a sensible idea, but Falstaff sneered and gave Poulet a head thump. Falstaff sneered at everything these days. Whatever Hamlet said bought a sneer from his advisor. It was as if Falstaff no longer had any respect for him or for his crown. Perhaps his father and the ghostly elf had it correct: Falstaff wasn't the best choice as an advisor. Poulet gave much better advice whenever Falstaff let the half-pint make a comment.

The militia and their role in the attack presented another problem, a serious one. The start date for the invasion was now running weeks late, and Hamlet's suggestion that the militia should stay behind in Denmarko to work the harvest was met with a towering rage. The only ones in the court who showed him any respect were Poulet and the court chamberlain who, for unknown reasons, had become Falstaff's archenemy.

Whenever Hamlet tried to reason with Falstaff, the man brought up the rescue at sea and claimed Hamlet was ungrateful. Not for the first time, Hamlet wondered if Falstaff would have plucked him from the sea if he hadn't been a prince. He knew the answer and he didn't like what he knew; it implied Falstaff had only rescued him to manipulate him. Hamlet had to admit Falstaff did in fact manipulate him. In retrospect, Hamlet knew he had made a mistake by allowing Falstaff to accumulate too much royal power. He made a mental note to take back much of that power. It wouldn't be easy. To be honest, Falstaff scared him with his size, brashness and loudness. When angry, Falstaff was like a violent thunderstorm, charging around the room, bellowing and throwing stuff at servants. Perhaps all this was an act to cow folks into agreeing with his position. If so, it worked.

Hamlet cleared his mind and watched his bees go about their duties. If only his subjects would act like the bees, life would be so much easier.

# # #

Othello and Nark inspected the walls where they met the steep palisade that ended in the port area a hundred feet below. This section of the wall hadn't been repaired yet. Most of the stones had fallen down and now lay in heaps at the base. Further away, they could hear a group of troll workers heaving stones back into place accompanied by curses, snarls and insults.

"I shudder to think about the wall if the Council hadn't taken up your idea about rewarding the trolls," Othello said.

Nark shrugged. "Gotta know how da trolls think. Gotta make it so dey wanna do da work."

The newly commissioned Wall Patrol had reacted in anger to the demand that they repair the walls. The Council, following Nark's advice, announced that for each large stone put back in place, ten copper pennies would be donated to the Wall Patrol Benevolent Association, formerly the Troll Patrol Benevolent Association. The Association hosted a weekend party every year, and it took most of the trolls an entire week to recover from the effects.

"If Denmarko is serious about attacking us, they could walk over this part of the wall, even if our entire defensive force was concentrated here." Othello felt a pang of despair. His reputation was threatened by Falstaff and whatever the cretin had planned for Dun Hythe. If he couldn't defend the city, he would add another failure to his resumé. He would also betray Desdemona's faith in him.

"We gotta coupla days more to work onna walls." Nark scratched his new tattoos. These showed twin yellow bars and were placed above his sergeant stripes, which now had a broad red diagonal slash added over them.

"How do you know that?"

"Gotta a coupla half-pints inna Foot Patrol. Use dem as messengers and stuff. Dey now onna road to Demarko watchin' for the bad guys. When dey see dem, one of da half-pints gonna run back and tell us. De other one'll keep watch on the buggers."

Othello could only shake his head at the incredible piece of luck he'd had when Nark was assigned to help him. Without the cleverness and contacts of the troll, he, Othello, would have accomplished nothing.

# # #

Falstaff raged and roared in his quarters in the castle. His plans to attack Dun Hythe were far behind schedule and Poulet was nowhere to be found. Again. It had to be that damned Annee; Poulet was infatuated with the serving wench and he hadn't slept in the castle in over a week.

Falstaff ticked off his current problems on his fingers as he paced around the suite of rooms. Item: the food stocks for the soldiers still had to be assembled. Item: his ax warriors were getting fidgety and bored. They would start to desert before long. Item: They didn't have enough oxen to pull the supply wagons. Item: his chain mail hauberk didn't fit and had to have additional links added to the sides before it would slide over his paunch and wouldn't be ready until tomorrow. He had spent half of his piracy loot on the hauberk and a war charger. If nothing else, he would cut a magnificent figure in front of Dun Hythe's walls. Item: Hamlet was getting to be a pain in the ass. The king had started to think for himself and questioned Falstaff's motives, a dangerous development. He had to remind the king every other day that he, Falstaff, had saved his, Hamlet's, life. Item: Urquort, now promoted to a lieutenant, wanted to be a captain, not a lieutenant, and constantly nagged about it. Urquort claimed a lieutenant was the lowest rank of officer and the only difference between a lieutenant and a private was the pay.

Falstaff gave up on the problems and turned his mind to more pleasant thoughts: ruling Dun Hythe. With the customs duties flowing into the city, he would have access to a limitless supply of coins. As king, he would have plenty of women, power and money.

What more could a rogue ask for?

CHAPTER TWENTY-ONE

Poulet entered the room and caught Falstaff whirling in front of a mirror. The effort of moving while wearing the hauberk left the heavy man huffing. The half-pint had to admit it fit perfectly. Falstaff looked like a silver statue. His size and armor should be enough to have any defenders in Dun Hythe quaking at the sight. Now that he had the hauberk, Falstaff would issue the order for the troops to march south.

Falstaff noticed the yawning Poulet and his toe hairs. While still rather short, they had been groomed and slicked back.

"It's about time you showed up, you wretch. Pack your things. I hope you gave Annee a goodbye kiss. We march within the hour."

"I'm not goin'," Poulet replied, "and I'm leavin' your service."

"What are you babbling about? Fetch your stuff and join Urquort."

"I bought the Sailor's Delight and Annee and me are gonna run it together. You need a new batman."

"You ungrateful scoundrel! After all I've done for you! After all I taught you, you desert me when I'm about to gain fame and fortune. You could be the batman for a king, and you intend to throw that away?"

"Let's see." Poulet extended his fingers and turned them down one at a time. "You taught me how to cheat at cards and dice. You showed me how to escape over city walls inna middle of the night. You taught me how to starve most of the time. You taught me how to sleep onna ground durin' rain storms. I guess I've learned everythin' you know. But I've learned somethin' you didn't teach me."

"What nonsense. What could you possibly have learned that I didn't teach you?"

"I've learned what it is to be loved by a great female. And that is somethin' you know nothin' about." Poulet turned to leave. "Even if I hadn't met Annee, I wasn't goin' with you. We've done a lotta bad things together, but mostly we hurt stupid or greedy folks and many of 'em deserved what they got. But attackin' Dun Hythe is wrong and I ain't gonna have anythin' to do with it."

Falstaff grabbed a wine cup and threw it at Poulet who ducked. The cup clanged against a wall near the door.

# # #

Falstaff sat astride his war charger and fumed and sweated in the hot afternoon sun. He had just discovered that the supply wagons still didn't have all the teams of oxen hitched up. Drovers tried to back the stubborn creatures into the last remaining wagon traces. The dwarf ax-warriors had gotten kegs of ale from somewhere, and many of them were now staggering around the assembly point. The militia lounged about like they were on a picnic. Even worse, his nemesis, the court chamberlain, watched from the castle battlements and laughed at him. And still Hamlet hadn't shown up.

In disgust, he dismounted and walked to the shade of an oak tree, once again surprised by the weight of his hauberk and by how difficult it was to move while wearing it. The chain mail was also hot, especially when the sun beat down on the metal links. Under the armor, he was soaked from sweat. He leaned against the tree and appreciated the coolness of the shade. With a sneer, he watched a group of dwarfs holding each other up and singing bawdy verses.

A half-hearted cheer from the militia caught his attention, and he saw Hamlet ride through the gates in the city walls. He wore a white tunic and black pants under a dented breastplate. He also wore a pair of greaves, obviously made from copper since they were a dull, greenish color. Like all Urquort's warriors, he carried an ax on his back in a shoulder holster. The king sat on a white war swine that headed for Falstaff's tree, no doubt hoping to find acorns on the ground.

"Greetings, Sire. Are you ready to go to war?" Falstaff saluted as Hamlet rode up. The swine sniffed his feet.

"I still think we should talk with Dun Hythe before we attack."

"We've been over this, Majesty." Falstaff's voice dripped with sarcasm. He was sick of Hamlet and his repeated demands to defer or abandon the plan to attack. "We attack first and talk later."

"What are the latest reports from your spies?" Hamlet gave him a studied look.

"All is well. For us that is, not them." Falstaff snapped his fingers and a groom walked over with his black charger. "Now that you're here, we can begin the march. The wagons without oxen yet will have to follow and catch up." He looked around the assembly area. "Urquort! Get this rabble to fall in on the road and we'll begin."

"Where is Poulet?" Hamlet asked looking around.

"The stupid fool bought the Sailor's Delight and abandoned my service."

Hamlet raised his eyebrows then said, "With all the delays, we have only a few days before the militia must return for the harvest."

"Not to worry. There is plenty of food in Dun Hythe. The wagons can deliver it to your city."

"The militia is needed to bring in the harvest. And they will leave to return here by the weekend. Since that is the case, this conquest better be as easy as you claim it will be."

"The city folk can't defend walls that have fallen down. We'll be in the city an hour after we begin the attack." Falstaff mounted his horse with his back to Hamlet so his anger wouldn't show. Hamlet was getting out of control. After he conquered Dun Hythe, Falstaff would spend some time deciding if Hamlet had a place in his future plans.

# # #

Othello sat in his office the afternoon after inspecting the walls. Outside, Emilia sang a plaintive trollish love song. Othello thought it sounded like nails scratching on a marble surface. The song stopped mid-note. "Hey, who are you?" she demanded of someone he couldn't see. "Da guy inside da office is important. He don't see everybody wot show up, ya know."

Othello got up and went to the door. The merchant who traveled back and forth to Denmarko stood by Emilia's desk looking confused. "Come in," Othello said and waved his hand to enter the office. Emilia gave them both furious looks.

"Have you been north lately?" Othello asked.

"Aye. Left there this mornin' and came here as soon as I got back."

Othello had a sinking feeling he was about to hear bad news. "What did you find out?" He held his breath.

"When I left, there was a lot of dwarf warriors lined up near the road. So was the militia. They was all standin' around while a bunch of oxen were gettin' hitched to supply wagons. The big guy I told ya about — Falstuff? — was wearing armor. I know one of the militia officers and I asked him what was goin' on. He said they was gettin' ready to march here and attack the city."

Othello exhaled. Now what was he supposed to do? "When will they get here? How much time do we have to get ready?"

"Gonna be a couple of days, I think?"

"Why so long? Denmarko isn't that far away. You made it in less than a day."

"Yeah, but I rode a horse and went ahead of my wagon and the convoy it's in. Those oxen in Denmarko ain't gonna move very fast, and the soldiers can't go faster than the wagons. And the dwarfs were drinkin' while they hung around waitin'." He made a face while thinking. "I reckon it'll take 'em two or three days to get here."

"How many soldiers do they have?"

"I'm guessing they got maybe two hundred dwarfs and another seventy-five to a hundred militia."

"Thank you for telling me." Othello gripped the man's forearm and squeezed.

"I'm not stickin' around. I'm gettin' some trade goods and heading south." The man left while edging away from Emilia's desk.

"You ain't gonna stick around and fight?" she said. "Stinkin' coward."

Othello wished she wouldn't eavesdrop on him. Before long everyone, or at least all the trolls, would know about the imminent attack.

He sat down at his desk and rubbed his face. He had to prepare the city for an attack, but he didn't know how to organize the defenses. Besides, his contingent of defenders were outnumbered by Falstaff's army.

# # #

Hamlet's thighs hurt from riding the war swine so he had started walking, but now his feet hurt from the combat boots he wore. He couldn't think of a time he'd been as miserable as he was now. The further south he went — either walking or riding — the more convinced he became that this invasion was madness.

He didn't think the folks in Dun Hythe would have much trouble defeating the rabble that marched with him. The ax warriors were undisciplined and mostly drunk. After the march began, Hamlet noticed they had barrels of ale stashed in the wagons — many barrels covered with straw and canvas tarps. From the look of things, Urquort couldn't or wouldn't control them and often drank a mug of ale with a group of soldiers.

His militia, while not drunk, were no better disciplined. Many dragged their weapons in the dirt, stopped for a break whenever they felt like it, often without telling him, their commander. An unknown number had decided to return to their families or their businesses. The further south they went the smaller his militia contingent became.

Falstaff rarely said anything on the march. He rode his gigantic charger wearing his expensive armor and ignored the deteriorating condition of his army. Hamlet analyzed the situation and determined the main problem was that the army didn't have anyone acting as a chief-of-staff to organize things. Neither Urquort nor Falstaff had any interest in doing that job. He suspected neither one of them had any inkling about what had to be done. Urquort had been a corporal and wouldn't have had any contact with a chief-of-staff or any knowledge of how a campaign got planned and implemented. Falstaff didn't care and seemed to believe the planning and implementation happened simply because he wished it to happen.

Hamlet now believed he never should have agreed to be a part of this folly.

Yesterday afternoon, they had made three miles before pitching camp in a farmer's wheat field. The enraged half-pint farmer had nearly gotten himself killed before Hamlet gave him a signed scrap of parchment to bring to the castle to get reimbursed. The farmer's disrespectful attitude embarrassed Hamlet, and he ordered Falstaff to leave farms alone in the future. The entire army had only one tent. It belonged to Falstaff and only Poulet knew how to assemble it, so a furious Falstaff slept on the ground like the rest of his army.

Today they weren't making much better progress. He figured they would reach Dun Hythe by tomorrow afternoon, probably too late to do anything. So the attack wouldn't take place until the following morning. That left very little time before the militia would have to go back to take care of the harvest.

# # #

At the end of another day, Othello still struggled with the questions of how to defend Dun Hythe. He wondered where the Denmarko army was and when would they would get here? Nark had placed the Foot Patrol on alert and cancelled all leaves. The Wall Patrol had also been alerted. Mayor Glyniss had become wroth over Denmarko's betrayal and promised vengeance on the northerners after Othello defeated their army.

Weary, Othello walked to his home surrounded by his four bodyguards. In a gloomy mood, he decided he never should have plumped up his resumé He never should have spread rumors that he was a hero at the Battle of Twin Oaks. If he hadn't, the Godmother never would have heard of him.

The bodyguard on his right whipped out his ax and stuck the blade to his front. An arrow thwacked into it and dropped to the ground. "Wh . . . where did that come from?" Othello asked. The arrow would have hit him if it hadn't been blocked.

The dwarf made a face and replied, "Someone must be practicin' with a longbow and sort of lost control of the arrow. Happens sometimes."

Othello returned to his musings. He had been sure Dun Hythe was where he would finally win fame. Most likely, his only fame now would come from dying heroically on the walls while defending the city. That would be a fitting end to his false and useless life.

He reached his home and watched the bodyguard hand over the responsibility of keeping him alive to the four house guards. All eight dwarfs exchanged complicated and secret handshakes to establish their authenticity. That done to everyone's satisfaction, they saluted each other, then turned to him and gave him a mass salute to end the handover ceremony.

He trudged through the door to find a grinning Desdemona wearing a long, gold undergarment that showed because of the short sleeves and short hemline of her expensive blue kirtle. Her reddish-green hair had been worked into a thick braid that hung down her back. All this meant she wanted to go out. He stifled a groan and instead gave her a smile and a hug. She responded to his perfunctory hug with one of great enthusiasm. He pulled back in her arms and gave her a questioning look.

Desdemona beamed at him for a few seconds and finally said, "I'm pregnant! We're going to have a baby!" After she jumped up and down a few times, she gave him another hug, then grabbed his hand, sat down on a couch and pulled him down besides her. "We have so much to do! We need names. We need furniture. We have to move your office stuff out of the nursery. Oh! This is so exciting! Let's celebrate by going out to eat."

Othello gawked at her. The news foretold of serious changes in the future. The last thing he needed now was another problem to worry about. He couldn't handle the ones he already had, and now he had to learn to deal with a pregnant wife and, after that, he had to figure out how to be a father. He cleared his mind and forced himself to think only of Desdemona's joy and excitement. He gave her a smile and said, "One thing at a time, dear. I still have to get used to the idea of being a father. I need a cup of wine. Let me relax for a time and adjust to parenthood. Then we'll go out for dinner."

"All right. I'll get you your wine."

When she returned with his wine, he took a sip and reviewed his new situation and his additional responsibilities. With parenthood looming in his future, he could no longer hope for a heroic death on the walls. He had to survive the fighting. Even if the enemy broke through, he had to live to protect Desdemona and her unborn baby from the carnage that would follow.

Already, the baby was forcing changes in his life.

# # #

During the middle of the night, Othello and Desdemona woke from a deep sleep when they heard a strange noise on the roof.

"Go back to sleep, dear," she said. "It's probably only a cat."

Sounds of a quick struggle were followed by a muffled gasp and the thump of something heavy hitting the ground. "That's not a cat," he said.

"Then it's probably a burglar and the bodyguards have everything under control. Go back to sleep."

Othello pulled the blankets up to his shoulders. He had enough problems to worry about without members of the Thieves Guild stealing stuff. His last thought before falling asleep was that he didn't have anything worth stealing.

While Othello slept, Desdemona planned her visit to her Grandma. She had asked Rosolia to set up a meeting by telling her that she, Desdemona, had important news to impart. Rosolia reported back that Grandma had agreed, but seemed torn as if Desdemona had been tainted by being married to Othello.

Desdemona knew Grandma would be ecstatic over the news of the pregnancy, and both of them would hope for a daughter. Female children had much better chances for advancement within the family where all the top positions were filled by females.

Once the godmother digested the news, Desdemona would have to work on getting Othello accepted again. That would require a great deal of tact and, possibly, even cunning.

CHAPTER TWENTY-TWO

Othello, despite the approaching military crisis, sat in his office doing paperwork to keep himself busy so his thoughts wouldn't turn too depressing. If only he could come up with a way to increase the defensive strength of the city, he would rest easier. Somehow, word had spread that danger approached and a number of folks had fled the city. He was surprised that many of them were the unemployed dwarf warriors. Once he saw them leaving, it occurred to him — belatedly — that he could have hired them to bolster the defenses. He had instructed Nark to try to hire some of the remaining dwarf axes, but they had all refused, saying they had other plans.

Outside the office, Emilia sang baby songs. She had started singing right after Othello had told her about his wife's condition. Her sole remark had been, "I hope da kid ain't dark and ugly like you."

He heard a commotion outside the office and saw Nark and Dunlap hurrying toward the door. With a feeling that the situation was about to get worse, he waited.

Emilia stopped singing. "Here now," she snarled. "Ya can't go inna office wid an ax. Take it off and leave it wid me."

Dunlap put his hands on her desk, leaned closer and replied, "Make me."

Emilia's head snapped back at the implied threat.

"Has the enemy shown up?" Othello asked.

Dunlap and Nark entered his office. "Ya gotta hear dis one, boss," Nark said as he waved a hand at the dwarf sergeant.

"Me and my lads are leavin' Dun Hythe. I appreciate you givin' us jobs for a while, but somethin' big has come up and we gotta leave to make sure we get in on it.

Othello gasped. "You can't," he managed to croak. "An enemy army marches on the city." Of all the possible news, nothing could be worse than this. He counted on the Foot Patrol dwarfs and their axes to form the backbone of the wall defenses since the trolls were lazy and unreliable and the militia untested.

"Yeah, I know. You've had us on alert for the last few days. The trolls and the militia will have to stop 'em. I can't stay. Got somethin' important to do."

"What's that?" Othello asked.

"Count Eustace's hirin' warriors. So's his neighbors. Gonna be a big war over that way pretty soon. We gotta get on the road so we can be included inna muster. Besides, this Foot Patrol stuff is kind of borin'. And so's siege warfare. It's much more fun to be the attackers than bein' inside the city. "

"You're running out on us in our hour of need?" Othello couldn't believe his bad luck. How was he supposed to protect his wife and unborn child now?

"The bachelor warriors already left. They're gonna reserve spots for the rest of us. Only the married ones like me stayed behind. We're gonna escort our families. All our wives and dwarflings are packin' up. We'll all be leavin' inna mornin'."

"Hey. Nobody gets inna office wid muddy feet." Emilia roared just as a half-pint in a forest green outfit ran in and threw a sloppy salute at Nark.

"Dis is one on my scouts. Where's da bad guys?"

"Two miles outta town. They stopped inna forest. I bet they attack tomorrow at dawn."

Othello's shoulders slumped. He felt the end approaching. He sensed another failure looming in the morning.

Dunlap started. "How many soldiers?"

"I saw about a hundred-fifty dwarfs, maybe two hundred. And maybe a hundred militia."

"So they got around three hundred." Dunlap rubbed his chin. "Any cavalry?" He stared at the wall over Othello's head.

"Didn't see any. Only some fat guy onna big horse."

"Widout da Foot Patrol, us got fifty trolls and anudda fifty militia. Dis gonna get nasty."

"Dang," Dunlap said and pulled a face. "Our families won't be able to get outta town before that army gets here at dawn, and we can't risk tryin' to get 'em through a besiegin' army. If the town gets sacked, our families'll still be inside." He scrunched up his face and slammed a fist on Othello's desk. "We can't risk that. We gotta protect our families." He grinned at Othello. "I guess we're stayin' for your party."

With Dunlap changing his mind, Othello's tension evaporated for a brief instant. It returned with a thud. He still didn't have a clue how to organize the city to beat off the attack. And he had only a few hours to do it. He put his hands in his lap so the others wouldn't see them shaking. "H . . . how many warriors will you have?"

"Over a hundred including the Foot Patrol," Dunlap replied. "Well, let's get to it." Dunlap pulled a face and stared at the floor for a time. "Who's givin' the orders? Do you have siege experience?" he asked Othello.

"Er, no I don't."

"I do. Put me in charge and I'll get things squared away."

"Yes, good. You're in charge." Othello's hands stopped quaking. "You will act with my authority." Maybe Dunlap could save the city.

"Those troublemakers are in for a big surprise. Now then, call out the militia and get them to the walls with their weapons. I'll get the Foot Patrol to do the same thing. No one goes home tonight. Everybody sleeps at the walls with their weapons. You," he pointed to Othello. "Organize a way to get food and drink sent to the wall. And send someone to muster the trolls. I want all of 'em at the walls 'cause I don't want any of them wanderin' off and not bein' in on the fun in the mornin'."

"I'll tell da trolls," Nark said with a big grin. "I love givin' Iago orders."

"After everyone assembles at the wall, I'll assign defensive positions."

"Wot about me?" Emilia said. "I wanna have some fun."

"You need a weapon," Dunlap replied. "Somethin' besides your mouth."

Despite the pressure, Othello had to smile. Finally, someone stood up to his secretary.

"A weapon I got. And I'll bring me knittin' circle gals. Dey's always up for a bit of fun."

#

Falstaff called a halt two miles short of Dun Hythe since it was too late in the day to attack. They camped in a forest clearing and he ordered no fires lit, lest the city be warned of their approach. Now, with the sun setting, he heard two wolves howling in the distant. Much closer, an owl hooted.

In a better mood now despite the hardships of the march and the desertion by Poulet, he sensed the fateful day tomorrow would be filled with surprises — pleasant ones, he hoped. He gulped chunks of cheese and bread from his saddle bags. He did it behind his horse so the troops wouldn't see that he hoarded food while they starved. The saddle bags also contained the rest of his pirate loot; he had no intention of returning to Denmarko, not when he would have Dun Hythe as his new playground.

On the eve of battle, Falstaff decided to address the troops and he ordered them to assemble. In the semidarkness, he stood on a wagon, long emptied of the small amount of food brought along for the trip. He gazed out on the army and frowned. Surely, the militia was much bigger when it assembled before the beginning of the march. Where were the rest of them? They must be in the forest hunting for food. The hungover dwarfs slouched around in a sullen mood because they had run out of ale.

"Soldiers!" Falstaff began. "Victory is within our grasp. It will be ours in the morning. I know you are hungry. So am I. But I hunger for glory, not food. Tomorrow, our army will earn eternal honor and glory through the conquest of Dun Hythe. The rewards of victory will be more food and drink than you ever imagined. All free, whenever you want it. So we have to go hungry for one more night. But think what the result of our shared sacrifice will bring us. Riches! Honor! Glory! Food! Drink!

"Here is my plan. Before dawn tomorrow, we will assemble in front of the walls of the city so that when dawn breaks, the town can look out on our vast numbers and behold their doom. If they surrender without a fight, I wouldn't be surprised, but I'll be disappointed. I want to storm the walls and take the city by force. I know you all want the same thing.

"Thank you for your attention. Now get some rest. Tomorrow will be a busy and long day. It'll take us some time to uncover the loot and share it."

By now it was full dark and as he climbed down from the wagon, he noticed only Urquort still stood where the army had been.

"Good speech, General," Urquort said.

"Where is the army? Didn't they hear me?"

"They started driftin' away as soon as it was dark enough so you couldn't see 'em."

Falstaff wondered about the discipline in his army and whether it was strong enough to see him through the battle.

CHAPTER TWENTY-THREE

Hamlet stood alongside his war swine holding the reins. His position was to the left of the main road leading to the city's gates. He shivered in the cool, dark air before dawn.

Behind him, the remnants of his militia force stood leaning on their weapons. He had learned the ones who hadn't deserted were the dregs of Denmarko, ones without a family, without a job and some even without a home. All of them showed respect for Hamlet if only in an informal way. They all hoped to get rich the easy way, without working for it. He wondered how many of them would actually attack the city if they faced a force of defenders.

Falstaff had positioned himself on the road directly in front of the city's gates and vowed to be the first one into the city. Hamlet could make him out only because the metal links in his hauberk reflected a bit of starlight.

A breeze blowing in from the sea brought a smell of salt air and middens.

The darkness faded from black to dark gray, and Hamlet heard muttering from his troops. He peered straight ahead and saw the outline of a solid, regular line of stone, not the ruined walls Falstaff had claimed. How could that be? Falstaff had been in Dun Hythe a few months ago and said the walls were a wreck. With a shock, Hamlet realized that Falstaff didn't have spies in the city and the man had lied to a king. He tried to remember if lying to a king was treason or some other crime. He knew it was punishable.

He heard sounds of movement from the area of the walls just as the first rays of sun flashed over the rooftops and reflected off the tips of pikes held by trolls.

He joined his militia in a collective gasp of alarm.

# # #

Falstaff sat on his charger and stared at the dark mass of Dun Hythe. He and his troops waited in the clearing between the city and the forest. The citizens used the hundred yards of cleared ground for picnics and sports. Beyond the city, the sky held a hint of light, a different shade of black. A myriad of stars filled the moonless sky.

Falstaff could hardly contain his emotions. He willed the sun to rise faster so he could taste military victory as soon as possible. Around him his army stood in what Urquort called a battle formation, but, from what he could see, resembled more of a chow line. His horse snorted and pranced a few steps. He patted the animal's neck and made soothing sounds. He heard a few coughs in the distant blackness. It must be tradesmen waking up for the day's work. He smiled to himself. Those workers were in for a big surprise as was everyone else in the city.

He passed the time until the start of attack by ruminating on how to rule the city. One of his first acts would be to find an artist and have him make a portrait of Dun Hythe's new ruler wearing armor and sitting on his horse.

The area around him grew lighter and he could see faces of the troops closest to him. A few minutes later, he could see his three-deep battle line, and he was shocked by how small it looked. Hamlet commanded the militia on the left flank, a hundred feet away. In the gloom, the king appeared to have only a few dozen troops. Suddenly worried about the small numbers, Falstaff dismissed the negative thought; the size of the army wouldn't matter with the rundown condition of the walls. He stood in his stirrups to try to get a better view of the walls. He frowned at the details revealed by the growing light. Why did the walls look so even? Surely, the broken-down walls should show jagged lines, not smooth ones? He heard muttering from the troops. Some of them must have noticed the same thing.

In a few minutes, he could make out more details and he had a moment of panic. The walls had been repaired! More muttering came from the soldiers. "Silence!" Urquort whispered in a hoarse voice.

Falstaff heard a rush of footfalls behind the walls and suddenly pike-armed trolls stood on the walls facing outward.

Falstaff stifled a sob of panic.

# # #

Before dawn, Othello peeked through a spy hole in the city's main gate. As dawn progressed, he saw more details of the army standing astride the main road. "Ah, there's Falstaff. He's got a war horse and armor. Makes him look even fatter than he is."

Nark and Dunlap stood by him using their own spy holes.

"He does look impressive," Dunlap agreed, "but it's all show. He'll never get over the walls. He's too fat and the armor must weigh a ton."

"If we can see them, they can see the walls," Othello said. "Shouldn't we put some troops on top of it?"

"You're right, Colonel." Dunlap turned and snapped a finger to Iago and pointed to the steps leading to the parapet.

Iago, his shoulder still bandaged, glared at the dwarf for a few seconds before obeying the command.

Not for the first time, Othello thanked the stars that he had Dunlap to direct the city's defenses and Nark who came up with the idea on how to rebuild the walls. Without the two of them, the city would be defenseless and his pregnant wife in danger.

Dunlap took another glance through the spy hole and muttered, "Rabble. I can see 'em pretty clear now, and that army don't have a chance of takin' the city. Iffen they had four times as many troops, we'd work up a sweat defendin' the walls, but they still wouldn't get through. As it is, they ain't got enough troops to do more than annoy us." He turned to Cassio who stood nearby. "Might as well get your militia into position. Make sure the slingers and longbows can be seen."

"Right." Cassio mounted the walls, then gave two short whistles. Ten half-pint slingers and a dozen elfin archers stood up. They had spent the night on the roofs of houses and shops just inside the walls. From their elevated position, they could fire on the enemy over the heads of the wall defenders. The attackers would have to cross the open field, exposing themselves to the arrows and the bullets from the slingshots. If the attackers reached the walls, the slingers and archers would hurry down and join the others on the walls.

"Now what?" Othello asked Dunlap. He felt light-headed from the imminent prospect of combat.

"We wait. Until Falstaff either gets up the nerve to attack or figures out he ain't gotta chance of winnin' and leaves."

"Do you think he'll actually leave?" Othello stomach lurched over that possibility.

"Iffen he got enough brains to blow his nose, that's what he'll do."

\# \# \#

Falstaff, still astride his charger, chewed on his lip as he tried to come up with a way to salvage his plan to sack the city and become its king. The repaired walls made the assault much more difficult, and the trolls made it much more dangerous. His dwarf warriors muttered and made noises disrespectful of their general. Urquort was among the noisiest of them. He knew the dwarf was trying to figure a way to get out of the battle without getting tagged as a coward. Falstaff knew that because he was doing the same thing and, in many respects, the two were kindred souls.

Hamlet rode over and interrupted Falstaff's desperate thinking. "You said the walls had fallen down," the king said in a panicky voice. "You said we could walk over them."

"The walls were fallen down when I was here a few months ago." From his horse, Falstaff had to look down to address the king. "I don't understand how they could be repaired this quickly."

"What I don't understand," Hamlet said, "is why your spies didn't report the change in the walls."

Falstaff coughed, but didn't reply.

"Unless you didn't really have spies in Dun Hythe and you lied to me."

Falstaff made growling noises in his throat.

"Lying to the king is treason in Denmarko. Did you know that?"

"What are you gonna do?" Urquort asked. He had moved to Falstaff's other side. "My warriors are on the verge of desertin'. They ain't happy about attackin' the walls. Not when the walls have trolls with pikes onna top."

Falstaff ignored Urquort as he absorbed the new information. Hamlet sounded like he had grown a backbone. That meant his ability to tell the king what to do or not to do was doomed. Urquort no longer spoke with respect, another sign that this adventure verged on falling apart. If the dwarf warriors deserted, there was no telling what that cretin Othello would do. He might even have the city's defenders issue out and attack. The militia would never stand for a battle. That meant there would be no troops to keep him from getting captured. Or even killed.

This was the worst jam he had ever been in, and he couldn't see a way out.

# # #

Othello stood on the parapet of the wall and watched the enemy army. Even though it was light enough to attack, they milled about and looked undecided. Hamlet and Falstaff conferred and appeared to be having harsh words. It occurred to Othello that the enemy was confused by the strength of the walls. Obviously, they hadn't expected that. Maybe Dunlap had it right — there wouldn't be an attack. If they didn't attack, what would the enemy do? March away like nothing had happened? If they didn't attack the walls and started to leave, was he supposed to attack them? How would he do that? If he didn't attack them, the enemy army would be intact and could come back and try again in the future. He groaned from the many unanswered questions he had along with the questions he didn't know enough to ask.

"Hello! What's this, then?" Dunlap said. "Colonel, I know that dwarf standin' alongside the fat guy. I don't believe it, it's my old buddy."

"That's nice, but now isn't the time to renew friendships."

"Oh, but it is. I can befuddle the dwarfs and maybe get 'em to desert."

"What?" Othello looked down on the dwarf sergeant.

"Watch this." Dunlap climbed on a water butt so he could be seen, cupped his hands around his mouth and bellowed, "Hey! Corporal Urquort? Is that you out there?"

"Hey, Lard Butt," another voice made Othello jump. "Get over here. I gotta present for ya."

Othello turned and saw Emilia waving a huge war hammer over her head. She saw him looking and said, "It's been inna family a long time. Grandda stole it." Alongside Emilia, a dozen other female trolls waved a variety of weapons at the enemy. Each one had a pair of knitting needles tucked into her kirtle.

"Sergeant Dunlap? It's me, Urquort. But now it's Lieutenant Urquort."

"You're an officer when ya was barely competent as a corporal? Doesn't say much for whoever is leadin' yer army."

"Hah! That from the worst sergeant in the regiment? What are ya doin' onna walls? Ya must be pretty desperate for work."

"I trained the city's militia. I wanna see what they can do in battle, so get the attack goin'. I ain't got all day to stand around waitin'." When Urquort didn't respond, Dunlap added, "Have ya heard the news? Count Eustace is hirin'. Seems the peace is about to end. Most of the lads in the city left over the last few days."

"Where'd you hear that?" Urquort advanced a few yards toward the walls. He waved a derisive hand at something Falstaff said.

"A recruiter came to the city. Hey, what do ya say we combine our forces and march to join Eustace? Why bother screwing around with attacking the walls or even with a siege? We can have some real fun with Eustace and his mob."

Urquort's dwarfs buzzed with excitement. They broke formation and gathered in small groups talking excitedly and gesturing with their hands.

"All right," Urquort said. "How do we gonna do this?"

"I gotta escort the families in town and their wagons to Eustace's when we're done here. Why don't you go down to Milestone One onna Trade Road? I'll gather up the families and meet ya there inna couple hours. Then we can both protect the wagons on the way to Eustace's territory."

"Done!" Urquort turned to the dwarf warriors. "Form up inna marchin' order and let's get outta here."

Falstaff said something that couldn't be heard from the walls, and Urquort made an obscene gesture and grabbed his ax handle. Falstaff backed up his charger a few paces and shrugged.

Othello couldn't believe what he had just seen. Dunlap had defused the entire situation. Already the dwarfs marched south toward the Trade Road. Now what happens? he thought. Hamlet is still in the field with a small group of soldiers. Should he have Dunlap launch a sortie through the gates and attack Hamlet?

"Well, Colonel, I'll be on my way." Dunlap gave him a salute. "Gotta lot to do to get the wagons onna road."

"Wait! You can't leave. Falstaff's still out there, and what about the other soldiers?"

"That rabble ain't a threat. They'll melt away. One minute they'll be standin' there and the next they'll all be inna forest. Thanks for the job." He winked at Othello. "Iffen peace ever breaks out again, I'll stop by to see iffen ya need any help."

"Hey, Fatty!" Emilia yelled. "Get over here. Don't make me come and get ya."

Othello made a face. Without the experience and decisiveness of Dunlap, he felt naked. He had to make a decision. While he pondered what to do, he saw Hamlet exchange heated words with Falstaff, who suddenly lashed his horse and sprinted toward the trees. Hamlet rode closer to the walls.

# # #

Hamlet couldn't believe what he saw and heard. A dwarf on the city's walls had just persuaded Urquort to desert Falstaff and join another army someplace else. The entire military expedition had collapsed under Falstaff's incompetent leadership. Denmarko's field army now consisted of a few dozen ill-armed militia. Meanwhile, Falstaff sent curses at Urquort's back while Hamlet's troops broke ranks to discuss this latest development. From the tones of the voices, they weren't too happy with the dwarfs leaving.

What was he to do? Dun Hythe certainly would declare Denmarko an enemy and possibly launch a counter-invasion. An idea popped into his mind. Perhaps Dun Hythe would consider peace if he turned over the culprit and explained how he happened to have brought an army outside their city walls.

"Falstaff!" Hamlet cried out.

Falstaff turned his horse and looked at Hamlet. "Why are you bothering me? Are you going to run back home and desert me like Urquort?"

"I'm not going to desert you. I'm going to arrest you for treason and turn you over to Othello. Soldiers! Arrest this man."

The militia broke up their discussion groups and looked confused by the order. Falstaff sitting on his charger towered over them all.

"Arrest me, will you? You ungrateful wretch, I'll have your head as a souvenir." Falstaff drew his sword.

"He's after the kingee," one militia screamed.

"We gotta protect the kingee," another shouted.

The militia moved between Hamlet and Falstaff.

"Whack the horse's legs," a sergeant called out. "Let's see how big he is off the horse."

Falstaff hesitated now that he faced a determined mob of armed soldiers. "Bah! You ungrateful wretch. After I saved your life, you turn on me."

"You only saved me to use me." Hamlet shook a fist at Falstaff. "If I wasn't a prince, you'd have let me drown."

"Did ya hear?" a soldier shouted. "He tried to drown the kingee."

"Get him," another yelled.

"Vengeance for the kingee!"

"Let's give him a rope necktie."

"Are ya crazy? Where we gonna get a rope strong enough to hang him?"

Falstaff yanked the horse's reins and turned it around. He dug his spurs in and rode the horse from the field, but in a different direction than the one Urquort had taken.

"Thank you, lads," Hamlet said to the militia. "I do believe you have saved my life. I'll reward you when we get home." Now all he had to do was figure a way to get home without having an army follow him there.

He drew his ax, dropped it on the ground and rode his war swine closer to the wall where he called out, "Othello? Are you there?"

# # #

A few minutes later, Hamlet fidgeted in his saddle and watched Othello leave the city through a postern gate in the walls. Othello spread his arms to show he didn't carry a weapon and walked closer to the war swine. Hamlet dismounted and waited for Othello to get close. The sun now stood higher than the walls and reflected off his breastplate. He tried to get some moisture into his sand-dry mouth before speaking. "Greetings. I want to explain how I allowed an army to invade the city's territory."

"I suspect it had something to do with that Falstaff rogue." Othello gave Hamlet a faint smile.

The smile made Hamlet a bit less nervous. "Indeed. When I became king, he offered to be my advisor and I agreed."

"What? You allowed a pirate admiral to advise you?"

"While I led the fleet against him, my uncle's minions tried to kill me and Falstaff saved my life. And he maintained you had betrayed him."

"Hmm. It seems Falstaff always has his own interpretation of events."

"He told me he had spies within the city and that you were gathering an army to invade and conquer Denmarko. Falstaff said we had to attack the city before you attack us."

"And you believed him?"

"Yes."

"He is a convincing liar. I know that from personal experience with him."

"I tried to arrest him and turn him over to you just now. As a way of making amends. Alas, he escaped."

"I watched that from the walls. There is a considerable height difference between the two of you on your mounts. It was very brave of you to take on that criminal."

Hamlet took a deep breath and said, "Well, the attack was all a mistake and I'm to blame for it. So, how do we make things right again?"

Othello scratched his chin and made a face. "I'm not sure I'm allowed to negotiate peace treaties." He folded his arms and stared at the tree line. "On the other hand, I'm the only one out here. So, how about this? We both swear the attack was all Falstaff's fault and we both put out warrants for his arrest on piracy charges —"

"And treason."

"Piracy and treason charges. We agree on a mutual defense pact and use the scryer network to keep in touch so there are no more misunderstandings. At least once a month, we should exchange messages and news. How does that sound?"

"I agree with it all. Here's my hand on it." Hamlet stuck out his hand. Both shook hands.

Hamlet's militia gave a weak cheer.

"There ain't gonna be any fun, then?" Emilia yelled from the wall. "Dang!"

CHAPTER TWENTY-FOUR

An enraged Falstaff spurred his horse along a dirt road that led west from Dun Hythe. Oak trees formed walls on both sides of the road. All his plans had been upset by perfidious folks he had trusted. The very people he had raised up had betrayed him starting with Poulet, the ungrateful wretch. Doomed to a life of hard work and early death as a stable hand, Falstaff had taken him on as a companion and showed him the entire country, had taught him how to survive, how to live by his wits. How did the half-pint repay him? By deserting him for a serving wench! And spending his hard-earned loot on a business! A wife and a business meant Poulet would spend the rest of his life slaving for a living when he could have been traveling without a care in the world. How could he have foreseen that Poulet would throw it all away for that git, Annee?

He didn't want to contemplate how Urquort had repaid his trust and preferment. A lowly corporal, Falstaff had raised him to officer rank, placed him in charge of hundreds of troops and gave him a chance to sack the greatest city in the land. Instead of availing himself of the opportunities opened up by Falstaff, the dunderhead had marched off to join another army destined to fight battles and besiege castles. Urquort now had a splendid chance to end up dead in a short time or, even worse, not dead but old, crippled and poor. Falstaff didn't begrudge Urquort those futures. In fact, he hoped the dwarf ended up old, poor and disabled. A long, lingering death was what he deserved.

As for Hamlet, the most ungrateful of the three, Falstaff had saved his life, helped him gain revenge on his uncle and relieved him of the tedium of ruling Denmarko so he could tend to his silly bees. Then Hamlet had turned on him just when he needed the help of friends. With Poulet and Urquort gone, Hamlet was the only one left that Falstaff could rely upon, and the royal bastard betrayed him in his hour of greatest need. With the militia still in the field, Falstaff was sure he could have bluffed Othello into making a deal to save the city from fighting a battle. Did Hamlet let him explain the new plan? Of course not. He had ordered the militia to arrest him as if he was a common thief.

He dismissed thoughts of the past and concentrated on the future. He had his hauberk and charger, both worth plenty of money and easily sold. His saddle bags held a fortune in jewels and coins. He had the wherewithal to fund new enterprises; all he had to do was find promising opportunities and nurture them into producing more cash.

Getting tied down in a city, even if he ruled it, probably wasn't a good match for his temperament. He needed fresh challenges and changes in scenery.

Maybe getting betrayed was a good thing. It freed him from responsibilities.

#

In the evening on the day after the battle, Othello trudged home, exhausted from dealing with the aftermath of the attack. He had spent most of the day with Glyniss and the Council. Furious because he had negotiated a treaty with Hamlet and ecstatic because he had defended the city, the Council spent hours trying to decide whether to punish him or reward him. Finally, they ordered a silver commemorative medal to be struck in his honor and issued a stern warning to stay out of treaty negotiations.

Iago had presented a different problem. He wanted his job back as head of the Troll Patrol, but the mayor refused to let trolls ever again misdirect traffic and Iago's trolls remained the Wall Patrol. Nark received instructions to recruit a force of citizens for traffic and crime control.

During the deadly boring debate by the Council, Othello had figured out why he had succeeded in this job despite his usual bumbling and indecisiveness. He had succeeded because of Nark and Dunlap. The lesson he had absorbed was to hire competent assistants and let them figure out how to solve the problems. In other words, his job as Minister of Homeland Security was to find and hire talented individuals. No wonder he had failed so often in the past. He had worked on everything by himself.

Now he no longer felt like a rabbit getting chased by a pack of hounds; now he was the watchdog protecting the city. What a change!

He left the town hall and walked the streets feeling somewhat lonely without his squad of dwarf bodyguards, now on their way to join Count Eustace in central Gundarland. Over the last few weeks, he had gotten to know them and chatted with the four as they walked the city's streets. He reached his house and noted the absence of the household guards. He made a mental note to ask Nark why he had needed guards before and not now.

Inside the house, a beaming Desdemona greeted him with a hug and a long, lingering kiss. She followed that up with a glass of red wine. Still grinning, she led him to the couch and they both sat down. She said, "Guess what? I visited my grandma today to tell her about the baby."

"How did the old bat respond?"

"She became more excited than I've seen her before."

Othello raised an eyebrow. He'd have thought the baby would be cursed by the Godmother because of the child's father.

"This will be her first great-grandchild, and she actually bounced up and down on her throne."

"Tell me it broke. Please?" He sipped his wine.

"No, silly. I told her the baby needed its father, and she agreed after thinking about it for a few seconds."

"Huh? What does that mean?"

"It means," Desdemona placed her hand on his forearm, "that she called off the contract on you."

"What contract?" Othello furrowed his brow trying to understand what his wife was talking about.

"After you told her she wouldn't be hired to repair the walls, she took out a contract to pay a hundred silver coins to whoever assassinated you. But now she's called it in, so you're safe and you can be the baby's father."

Othello's mouth dropped open. Assassination? Was there no end to the fat elf's perversion? A new thought staggered him. The murder contract was the reason why Nark gave him bodyguards. How did Nark know about the contract? He asked Desdemona.

"Didn't you tell me Nark knew everything that went on in the city?" she replied. "He found out about it and assigned the guards even before I asked him to do that."

"You knew about it?"

"I have my own sources of information within the family. Several spies actually."

Othello slumped on the couch and relaxed. Life was good and would be even better if he could just get rid of Emilia.

"After all," Desdemona continued, "I'll be the next Godmother."

Othello groaned aloud.

"And if we have a daughter, she'll be Godmother after me."

Othello spilled his wine all over his lap.

# # #

In late afternoon two days after returning from the battle, Hamlet strolled into the Sailor's Delight in a reflective mood. He had business to conduct and he couldn't predict how it would turn out.

"It's the kingee," an old codger yelled.

"Have an ale wid us, King Hammy," another called out. This one sat at a table with four others and an empty seat.

"Perhaps later, lads," Hamlet replied with a big grin. "I have to talk to Poulet."

Annee walked over to him, smiled and dropped a curtsey. "What can I do for the kingee?"

"Please fetch your husband and both of you sit with me for a few minutes."

"Will you be wanting an ale while we talk?"

"Indeed. That's a good idea." Hamlet walked outside, found an empty table under a tree and sat down.

Annee came out a few minutes later carrying a tray with three mugs of ale. Poulet followed her. Hamlet noted his luxurious growth of groomed toe hair and that Poulet and Annee had matching brooches on all four feet. Poulet bowed to Hamlet and sat down.

After talking a swallow of ale, Hamlet said, "So, Poulet, you really are a tavern keeper. And married, to boot."

"Aye, I am." Poulet beamed at Annee and squeezed her forearm.

"Recently, I have come to value folks who give good advice and you always seemed to be a few steps ahead of Falstaff and always told it true. I have hopes of persuading you to become my advisor."

"I'll always tell you what I think iffen ya ask me about a problem, but I don't wanna live inna palace. Not anymore, leastwise."

Hamlet drained his mug and made a face. "I need advice from someone who isn't trying to advance his own career. Will you two come to the palace once a week and have dinner with me?"

Before Poulet could respond, Annee said, "Absolutely not!"

Hamlet's mouth dropped open at the answer and Annee's stern tone of voice.

"We'll eat in the palace one week and you'll eat here the next week." Annee smiled and winked at Poulet.

Hamlet laughed. "Done." He remained silent for a few seconds and added, "It's a good idea for me to get out of the palace occasionally. The atmosphere in there is rank with ambition and greed."

"How's yer honey comin' along?" Poulet asked.

"It's almost ready to harvest, but I can't make up my mind whether I want to sell it by the jar or in bulk. By the jar is messy, but I don't know anyone who will buy it in bulk."

"Yeah, ya do," Poulet said. "I'll buy every bit of honey ya have and I'll give ya a fair price."

"You? Are you planning to sell honey in the tavern?"

"Naw. I wanna make my own mead and to do that I need honey."

Hamlet tapped his empty mug on the table. "With the coins I get for the honey, I'll buy more hives and install them in another copse of trees. Next year I'll have twice as much honey. Will you still be interested in buying it all?"

"I'll take all yer honey for as long as ya produce it." Poulet held out his hand and both shook to seal the honey deal.

"Excellent. Then it's settled." Hamlet stood up. "Thank you for the offer. I'll expect you tomorrow night and a week after that, I'll come here."

Hamlet left the tavern and walked back to the palace in a good frame of mind. He really was king of the bees and of Denmarko for good measure.

# # #

After they went to bed, Desdemona couldn't sleep. Her mind was awhirl. Grandma's health had deteriorated and Desdemona knew the old elf would never see the baby. Rosolia predicted the end would come within a month.

Instead of sleeping, Desdemona made lists of what she would have to do. Rosolia would get a large cash bonus and a retirement offer. Sylvia would become the new manager of the Wicked Bed. And then there was Iago. Desdemona was intrigued by the opportunity the Wall Patrol presented. All she had to do was tell Iago what she knew about his attempt to kill Othello and blame the Godmother, and he would do whatever she wanted him to do.

Iago and the trolls would be a new source of cash for the family business.

EPILOGUE

Falstaff strode into the tavern and sat down at a table. He waved to a serving wench and yelled, "Ale." When the female dwarf returned with the mug, he said, "I just rode into town. What's its name?"

"Ashton, sir. Will there be anything else?"

"Yes, have the owner attend me."

Falstaff gulped most of his ale. Starting a new project always gave him butterflies. He fidgeted with the ale cup while he awaited the tavern owner.

A few minutes later, a middle-aged elf approached and said, "Ya wanted to talk to me?"

"Yes." Falstaff jumped up and shook the elf's hand. "My name is General Falstaff and I recently retired from commanding an army."

The elf looked impressed with the title.

"Please sit down and have an ale with me," Falstaff continued. "I'm new in town and tavern owners always know the most about a town and the locals. I want to open a business, and my extensive research tells me that Ashton is the ideal place to do that. It'll mean new jobs and new business for your fine tavern."

"Wot do ya need to know?" the elf asked.

"After years of service in the army, it is my observation that weaponry hasn't advanced in generations. Soldiers today still use the same weapons to stick holes in the enemy that their great-grandfathers used. My business will design and build modern weapons. Generals and other commanders will flock to Ashton to see them and buy them." Falstaff drained his mug of ale and waved the mug over his head. The elf stared at him in openmouthed fascination.

"I need a large, sturdy building that is suitable to be a factory and I don't want to waste time constructing one. Do you know of such a building that is available?"

"Aye. There is such a place on the other edge of town." The elf pointed to his right.

"Excellent. Building weapons is an expensive undertaking, especially when new designs are involved. Perhaps you also know of some investors who seek low-risk, high-reward investments."

The elf nodded, slightly bug-eyed. "I might be interested. And I can gather some others who might have money for this stuff."

"Fine," Falstaff said. "Can you arrange a meeting, say tonight, where I can share my plans and discuss financing?"

The elf nodded. "I'll send a messenger to fetch them here tonight. I've got a room inna back that will serve."

"That will do nicely. I won't take any more of your valuable time. Until tonight then."

The elf left, but glanced over his shoulder a few times to ensure that Falstaff wasn't an apparition.

Falstaff took a deep breath to tamp his excitement. Commanding a fleet and an army weren't bad diversions, but his real love in life was pulling off a scam. Like claiming to build a weapons factory.

Life was good and about to get better.

ABOUT THE AUTHOR

And now, a few words about the guy who makes these things up, Hank Quense.

If you enjoyed these tales, you'll enjoy reading more of his books. You can chose from:
<u>Tales From Gundarland</u>
<u>Zaftan Entrepreneurs</u>
<u>Zaftan Miscreants</u>
<u>10 Great Fantasy Short Stories</u>

Better yet, why bother choosing? Get a copy of all of them and lay in a supply of laughter.

Hank is currently working on Zaftan Combatants: Book 3 of the Zaftan Trilogy along with several novels set in Gundarland and two more collections of short stories. The next one will be called "10 Great Scif Short Stories" and that will be followed by "10 More Great Fantasy Short Stories".
Who knows what will come after that.

Links? You want links? Here you go:
My website: <u>http://strangeworldsonline.com</u>
My blog pages: <u>http://hank-quense.com/wp</u>
My Facebook fan pages:
<u>https://www.facebook.com/StrangeWorldsOnline</u>
Twitter: <u>http://twitter.com/#!/hanque99</u>